When a princess on the run wakes up a cursed ancient king, she could never imagine the trouble she's about to get herself into.

Altara needs to leave her tomb of a palace home, but when she arrives to the topical island paradise that her mother once called home, she realises that not everything is as it seems.

When a beast of myth, a cursed ancient prince and his three bloodthirsty warrior brothers unexpectedly wake up after two hundred years in slumber, they set a path that will change everything for both our princess and the entire island kingdom of Ellythia.
They're going to take their kingdom back and they won't let anyone, let alone a rival princess, stop them.

This is a 18+ New Adult Fantasy Romance and is recommended for mature readers. Each book has a cliffhanger ending but the trilogy will finish with a HEA.

Tropes: Fated mates, hidden identity, break a curse, enemies to lovers, villain gets the girl, healing magic.

I0593282

THE ARCHER PRINCESS

EBP

HOUSE OF ROMANTASY

E. P. Bali's
House of Romantasy

The Archer Princess is a work of fiction. Names, characters, places, incidents and locations are the product of the author's imagination or are used fictitiously. Any resemblance to actual events, locations or persons, living or dead is entirely coincidental.

This first edition published in 2022 by
Blue Moon Rising Publishing
www.ektaabali.com

ISBN ebook: 978-0-6454650-9-9
Paperback: 978-0-6455686-3-9
Hardcover: 978-0-6455686-4-6
Paperback (Pastel Edition): 978-0-6455686-5-3
Hardcover (Pastel Edition): 978-0-6455686-6-0

Illustrated Cover design by Carly Diep
Naked Hardcover by Etheric Designs
Map artwork by Najlakay
Chapter Header by Etheric Designs
Book Formatting by E.P. Bali with Vellum

The author acknowledges the Traditional Custodians of the land where this book was written. We acknowledge their connections to land, sea and community. We pay our respects to their Elders past and present and extend that respect to all Aboriginal and Torres Strait Islander Peoples today.

A NOTE ON THE CONTENT

I care about the mental health of my readers.
This book contains some themes you might want to know
about before you read.
They are listed at www.ektaabali.com/themes

E.P. BALI

THE
ARCHER
PRINCESS

THE ELLYTHIAN ISLES

THE GREAT
WESTERN OCEAN

LOTA CITY

LOTA ISLAND

TIGER ISLAND

LEVU VILLAGE

GULAB VILLAGE

JUNGLE
SCHOOL

TARAKA TOWN

THE LOTUS

SEA

BONEWEAVER ISLAND

PRONOUNCINATION GUIDE

Altara: Al Taa ruh
Atax: Ay tacks
Cheshni: Chesh nee
Daanav: Daah nuv
Ellythia: Ill ith ee uh
Geravie: Jer ah vi
Gulaab: Gul aahb
Harranpul: Har ann pull
Jessine: Jess eene
Kai: K eye
Keshmi: K air sh mee
Levu: Lair voo
Lobrathia: Lo brath ee uh
Malika: Maah lick uh
Pia: Pee uh
Reshmi: Resh mee
Rani: Raah ni
Raen: Ray en
Saraya: Sar eye uh
Trisane: Tris ayne
Vayashi: Vay ah shee
Yasani: Yuss ah nee
Zale: Zay-l (rhymes with gale)

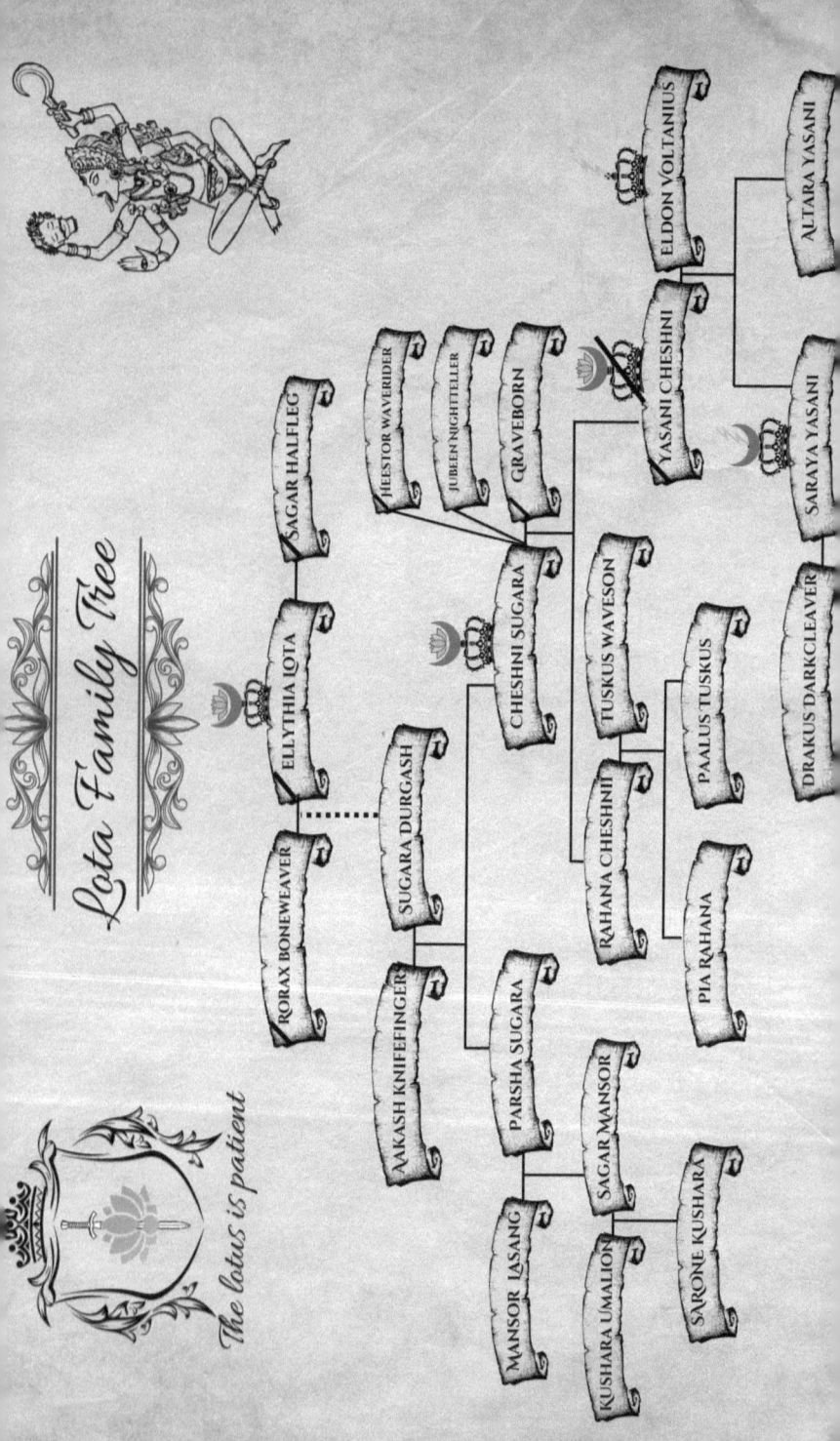

Lota Family Tree

The lotus is patient

Bonewearer Family Tree

The jungle always wins

ASHBOARAX — TIGERA

ASHGNAX BONEWEAVER

SAFFRON IVORY — ASHZALE

URAXA

YETI BONESONG

KAISEN

KISANA

IAXAN — REEFA SEADAUGHTER

RAEN

TORUS BONEMASTER — SYREN

ATAX

This one is for all the girls with a little darkness tucked away in a far flung corner of their hearts. One day, when you show it the beauty of the stars, it will weep with joy.

1
ALTARA

The princess was caught in a compromising position with the blacksmith's son.

It was this thought that made me hastily push Sam's head out from between my thighs. If my stepmother's spies found us, I'd be as good as dead. Sam, the strapping son of the best blacksmith in Quartz city, looked up at me, his sweet face confused, the evidence of said "compromising position" all over his mouth and chin. I sighed and unhooked my leg from his shoulder, where he'd had me pressed up against my old nursemaid's bedchamber wall.

He'd followed me and my sister here, my designated escape route out of the palace. Once she'd hugged me and left, Sam had fervently rushed toward me and...well, I'd always had a soft spot for him.

"I must go Sam," I said quickly, picking up my undergarments and sliding them back on. "This was a lapse in judgment on my part. I cannot delay, not today."

Sam picked his clothes off the floor as I straightened my

1

skirts—we were old hats at this point, as Sam and I had been sneaking about for the past four years.

"If we're caught before I leave," I began as Sam stood with his handsome, sullen face, "Geravie will spank me. Even at my ripe old age."

I was eighteen, and a year away from being considered a full-grown adult, according to Lobrathian law set by the ancient Lightning Kings, but it hardly mattered to *me* or to my elderly nursemaid.

"I'm not going to see you again, am I?" His deep voice was grave and no matter how manly he looked now at twenty-two, he would always be that gangly boy who'd stammered and fumbled his way through my ballroom gown that first night many years ago.

"You must not tell anyone that I'm leaving, Sam. You understand me?" I poked his expansive chest for emphasis. "If you do I'll come back here and slit your throat myself."

"Yes, Your Highness." He obediently nodded at the floor and looked so sad that I pulled him down by the collar and gave him a kiss on the lips. His face brightened. "I got you a gift."

From inside his cloak he brought out a roll of leather.

"Made them myself," he said softly, his big fingers deft as he undid the ties. "You might want to use them…wherever you're going."

Two beautiful daggers, the hilts made of golden butterflies inlaid with pink quartz for their wings. They were delicate and flat, made for concealing under a sleeve or stocking—just the way I liked them. "They're almost too beautiful to use," I said, stroking them reverently. "You made them out of your wage didn't you? Naughty boy. Take this, and that's a royal order." I took out six gold coins from my belt purse and pressed them into his reluctant hand.

"I will miss you," he whispered. "*Will* I ever see you again?"

"I'll miss you too." We kissed again, and I didn't answer his question because I had no idea. I couldn't bear it any longer. The risk was too great, the stakes too high and I'd already delayed too long. I turned, unlocked the main door and pushed Sam through it. Rushing to the back of the bedchamber, I yanked open the servant's door and hurried down the steps at full pelt.

The day my mother died was the day the palace ceased to be my home. Now my sister was being taken away by the fae, this quartz-studded building became no more than a tomb.

When I first came to learn that my father had made an unbreakable marriage contract with the dark fae, I had thought it all very exciting. But seeing my sister actually leave with the fae, get engaged into that strange, beautiful family we'd known for decades as monsters, I knew what was about to happen was no joke at all.

But my sister was a different breed of person. We both were. We'd been trained by our mother.

Perhaps as much as that training had helped Saraya, it would help me on my gaol-break too.

Nodding to myself, I secured my cloak around my neck. The backs of my eyes burned but I forced my feet to move. If all went well, I would not be noticed, and no one would search for me until we were at sea.

This thought sent my magic tumbling out of me, enveloping me in its soft caress and I took on the appearance of my surroundings. It wasn't *quite* invisibility, but it served me and my exploits just as well.

I ran down the servant's corridor and yanked open a large door, heading down wide, stone steps that would lead to the delivery passage under the palace. I came across no one on my way as the entire palace had turned out in the entrance hall to wave the eldest princess away. No such fanfare for me. Oh no, my way was hidden and secret.

And I didn't mind that at all.

Warm air brushed my skin as I reached the giant archway that marked my exit. I squinted through the beams of sunlight as the waiting carriage came into view, already loaded with my mother's trunk packed with my things. Waiting before it was my former, elderly nursemaid, Geravie, hunched in her black travelling cloak, silver hair neatly braided, wringing her hands in uncharacteristic nervousness.

She couldn't see me, but she could hear my boots against the stone. Relief smoothed her brown face and she stepped backward, allowing me to charge right into the carriage. It shook a little as I sat and the driver gave a shout.

Geravie shouted at back him for good measure and stomped into the carriage, yanking the door shut.

The driver, who no doubt had his instructions well in advance from a stern Geravie, immediately set the horses charging off.

Geravie peered in my general direction. "Did anyone see you, little star?" she asked in Ellythian—the tongue we were now to speak.

I grinned and then remembered she couldn't see me. "No, Geravie," I replied in the same language smoothly back.

I would need to practice my mother's native tongue as much as possible before we got to the Ellythian Isles if anyone was going to believe I was native. Any suspicion on the

Ellythians' part could mean an alert sent back here, to my stepmother.

As the carriage turned westward down the harbour road, hooves rapidly clacking, I turned eastward, only to see a line of black carriages trundling off in the distance. Fae carriages —one of them carrying my sister. Not only were we both leaving Lobrathia, but also my father, lost to the abyss of his diseased mind.

I missed him—the old version of him. But I'd been missing him for the past four years. I felt the black snake of guilt, wrapping around my heart at the thought of leaving him here with *her*. But he had never protected Saraya or I from her either, and as much as I loved him, a deep-rooted part of me had been so ruined, my very marrow was now marked with darkness. And I could never forgive him for that.

Women were not permitted to take the throne in Lobrathia, so once my father died, I expected Uncle Ansel would be called back from his travels to finally take back up his responsibility here.

No, this was for the best. Saraya would go her way to the Fae Realm, and I would go mine, over the sea, where both of us would be safe from the depraved hag of a woman our people called Queen.

For me at least, it might even be a fun reprieve from my troubles—a grand, secret holiday in a mysterious tropical paradise. Compared to getting married to a haughty prince, I was *definitely* getting the better end of the bargain.

2

ALTARA

Being an invisible princess was so much fun.

The ship docked half a mile from the powdery-white sanded shore, and despite the stifling tropical heat, I tugged the hood of my pink cloak down a little more.

None of the sailors bustling about noticed the small ripple in the air that was me as I walked onto the deck of *The Silken Lady*—nor did they suspect that she held a stowaway.

But I, naturally, knew *all* about the crew after a week of snooping around the deck and cabins, eavesdropping on their conversations and watching them work. I knew that cheery Rana had two wives, one on each of the two northern islands of Ellythia. Farshan, the silent one, preferred men and wept every night over a picture of his lover. Jakor, the captain, was ambidextrous and could not be bested at throwing daggers. Now, *that* had caught my attention because I was always up for a challenge. I'd been itching to grab one of the six hidden daggers I always kept on my

6

person, but of course, down in the den of the ship where they kept their thick wooden practice board, I couldn't risk adding my knife to the mix. I had come to learn that Ellythian sailors might be relaxed in demeanour, but decades trading with us Lobrathians had made them as sharp as any knife they threw.

But the game wasn't done, and right now, I wouldn't dare think about my old home lest any sadness befuddled my senses. As the midday sun beat down upon the deck, I only had eyes for the island lying lush and alive before us.

The Ellythians spoke about the islands as if they were real living, breathing things, and in particular, the southernmost Ellythian island was known to be more predator than paradise.

And I was positively bursting at the seams to step ashore.

Coconut trees stood tall in the warm breeze, their splayed leaves drifting as if they could brush the clouds. The jungle was dense, wild, and teeming with secrets in the most alluring way. The humid air was sticky-sweet mixed with the smell of salt from the sea.

This was my mother's home, and now it was to be mine.

Her gold lotus chain sat heavy on my ankle as I blinked away the burn from my eyes, then darted around Geravie to avoid a passing sailor. My magic allowed me to take on my surroundings—that included passing people and the wider environment. I wasn't perfectly invisible and sudden movements on my part were a bad idea.

Loud voices burst out on deck as Geravie and Captain Jakor took up an argument they'd been having the entire week of the voyage. The weathered captain was heavily averse to dropping anchor near the southern, Boneweaver Island, saying it was infested with "bad luck" and far too dangerous. He was insisting he take us north, to the capital, where it was safer and more "civilised."

But I was the spitting image of my mother, and we couldn't risk going north as I'd be recognised instantly by my emerald-eyed Lota side of the family. No, we needed to go to the Jungle School on *this* island and keep my presence a secret for as long as possible.

Geravie won the argument, it seemed, because I watched two men help my poor nursemaid down a thick rope ladder and into the waiting boat. She cast her eyes nervously downward at the swelling, crystal-blue ocean as they manhandled her. She swatted their hands away, grumping at them in Ellythian, and they put their hands up in submission, still keeping close as she climbed down as slowly as a newborn sloth.

Though the voyage had been easy, I'd have to be careful about how I made my exit.

Geravie made a show of descending the ladder, cussing like a low-born lady that made me grin despite myself. But it made for a good distraction for the men as I darted to the ladder and carefully descended while she did. The two dark-skinned Ellythian sailors in the boat, Jetta and Rana, muscled with years of hard labour, hid their smiles at Geravie's dirty mouth.

But one of them blocked my way into the boat as Geravie took her seat. Panicking, I made a jump for it. The boat—no more than a dinghy really, rocked violently as I landed. Geravie gave a shout as Rana grabbed her by the arms, seafoam splattering our faces.

They righted the boat, and I almost sighed in relief as the confused men cast their eyes around for the source of the disruption and smoothly passed over me now sitting primly behind Geravie.

For good measure I tugged my cloak back around to cover my legs. Geravie had helped me make it along with the purple one that I'd given my sister for her nineteenth birthday—a matching set. It made me feel close to her, just as the gold lotus chain around my ankle made me feel closer to my mother. I'd never travelled without my family, and I felt their steady absence like a lump of black quartz in my chest. But I was eighteen and practically a woman grown. I could do this, and damn it, I would have fun while I was here.

Goosebumps erupted all over me, and I clutched onto the edge of the boat as the men began to ease the dinghy away from the ship and row towards the shore, the tiny boat rising and falling in the unsettled water. My magic pulsed a little inside of me, as I knew it would. It wanted to help the bulky rower, Jetta, who had a mildly leaky mitral valve, and Rana, who had a urinary tract infection. I hadn't been forced to sit in close proximity to them before this, and it was triggering my magic.

I sighed and gave in, letting my power reach out like it wanted to. As eager as an over-enthusiastic puppy, it rushed for Jetta's heart, sought out the ailment in his mitral valve and sucked it up like a fish sucking back water. My heart gave a little uncomfortable stutter as it took on the malfunctioning valve, leaving the Jetta with a perfect one. It took me only a little focus to fix the cardiac fibres of my own heart, tightening the valve and making it function normally. A minor issue. All in a day's work.

My magic didn't work like my sister's. Of course *I* had to get the sorry-end of the bargain. Where Saraya could go inside a woman's body and fix their reproductive issues, I couldn't work directly like that. *My* magic instead took on the issues of others and *then* healed it. Worse, my magic was always *looking* for problems. Like a pup she wanted to play, seek out and bound back to me. Unless I kept a tight leash on her, she ran rampant, bringing me back gifts of disease and illness.

It was why my training had been a little more...vigorous than my sister's. Where Saraya had spent her time apprenticing with the city's head midwife, I was practising in the Quartz military infirmary—and less often with the city's public healers. I pretended to cut and roll bandages, all the while studying the injuries of the patients and secretly fixing them.

Our boat reached the jetty, and the sailors hurried to secure the ropes before helping a scowling Geravie onto land. I slinked past Jetta, stopping my magic from sliding into Rana and his urinary tract. I avoided manhood problems as a general rule—not because they were gross but because I didn't really know what would happen if I tried to transfer a penis issue onto my own body. It was a risk I really didn't want to take and my mother had generally warned me away from it.

I would also have to remember that, unlike Lobrathia, where magical ability had dried up a hundred years ago in the Ellythian Isles—where the people kept themselves apart from the rest of the world as if their lives depended on it—magic ran rampant.

We arrived at a small wooden jetty and I followed Geravie up a second ladder. A little too quickly for my liking, the two sailors hauled our luggage onto the jetty, scurried back into their boat and paddled away as if the devil himself was at their heels. Shaking my head at their folly, I turned and gave a military salute to both men, neither of whom would ever know I existed.

Secret was the way we had kept it since I was a child. *No one can ever know about your magic,* my mother drilled into me. So, me and my sister had kept it that way—for me, at least. *Her* little secret had gotten out, though thankfully, the women of the city kept tight-lipped about who fixed their pregnancy and birth issues out of gratitude for her.

I'd been successful at hiding my powers until my stepmother arrived.

"Alright there, Altara?" Geravie said out of the corner of her mouth.

"Yes, Geravie," I murmured, "we made it."

"The journey isn't done," she grumbled, looking up at the jungle path waiting before us. Up close, the jungle, with its closely packed palms and heady atmosphere looked even more mysterious than before and I was eager to see what lurked within it.

We walked down the short jetty with me hoisting both trunks, though I hoped no one was watching because two trunks floating in mid-air would certainly be cause for question.

I'd just made it into the sandy beach when the ground trembled beneath us. I dropped the trunks and lurched forwards, gripping onto Geravie with alarm, not wanting her to fall over. The very planet groaned beneath us but the crazy old woman was cackling as if she were enjoying it. I stumbled around, staring at her aghast.

The ground steadied, and I swore out loud. "Dear Goddess, what was that!"

"I miss a good-old earthquake!" Geravie panted, patting

me on the arm. "They happen every so often around here, what with the few volcanoes we have nearby."

Volcanoes. Noted. I'd have to ask more about that later.

"Well, now what?" I frowned, looking up and down the pristine white beach. The sand was so soft and white it could have been baking flour, and the dancing ocean water was a turquoise so vibrant it hurt my eyes.

"They were supposed to meet us here," Geravie said with her hands on her hips. "I wonder what happened? Oh! That must be it."

Sure enough, the sound of a carriage jostling on the dirt path came towards us, and cool relief sighed through me.

Indeed. We'd only just begun in our new world. Well, new for me. Geravie had grown up in Ellythia before she'd chosen to leave with my mother when she left to marry my father for political stability.

The *heat*, for one, pressed on my skin like a dense blanket, making me very happy that I'd changed into a loose cotton summer dress this morning. The cloak itself protected my skin from the harsh overhead sun and also helped my mission to stay hidden. I'd sewn the lining myself, infusing each stitch with as much of my magic as was possible. A painstaking task, but it had been well worth it—I don't think anyone would see me at all while I was wrapped in it.

But we were still by the sea, and we were supposed to head into the heart of the jungle where this blasted ladies' finishing school was supposed to be. No doubt the heat would get worse, plus there would be mosquitoes, terribly large hairy spiders and those muscular snakes that could eat grown men for breakfast. *Thank* the Goddess for my magic, or I wouldn't be able to have any proper fun around here.

As we waited for the carriage, I thought about the days

when I'd been free to roam the palace grounds, shirk my tutors and spend days picnicking with my mother and Saraya on the back lawn of the palace. But those days were long gone, and reminiscing would not serve me at all.

The carriage trundled into view, and Geravie pursed her lips when she saw it. It was a crumbling wooden thing, ancient and squeaking, with rickety wooden wheels that had half their spokes missing.

Due to Geravie's slow elderly hobbling—because of worn cartilage in her hip, which she refused to let me fix—we slowly made our way to it. We couldn't see the driver, and he didn't hop down to greet us either. I knew he'd be in for a tongue lashing.

"Now you listen here, young man," Geravie said loudly in that authoritative way of elderly women from wealthy families.

But as we rounded the carriage, there *was* no driver or any horse. My stomach did a little jump as I looked wildly around the wooden structure. But magic oozed from every grain, and I exchanged a look with Geravie.

"Interesting," she said, shrugging. "I didn't think Boneweaver Island would have one of these."

I looked at her in alarm as she spoke loudly once again. "You there! Carriage! Drive reasonably. I am old but not stupid. Get us to the school in a prompt manner, or there'll be consequences. I was born and bred on this great island kingdom and know the Old Way—I'm not some Lobrathian noble, understand?" She tugged on a necklace from under the collar of her dress, holding it out for the carriage to see.

I squinted at the golden pendant, and abruptly, the carriage gave a little twitch like it had understood. "Dear Goddess, help me," I murmured.

"Good girl," Geravie said in approval as she hoisted up her travelling trunk. "Pray to all the Gods. You'll need as much help as you can get."

Grimacing, I hurried to pick up my trunk and loaded it into the back of the carriage, and by the time I was done, sweat was dripping down my back. We sat ourselves onto worn and mildewed wooden seats and shut the door. The carriage lurched forward, and we were off, deep into the wild of the jungle. There was no glass on the windows on the doors, but somehow the carriage was cool inside. Geravie gestured to tiny green quartz crystals embedded into the ceiling as if she'd been wondering about the same thing. Lobrathia was a wealthy kingdom because of our Quartz Quarry, and I knew it was the only reason the Ellythians traded with us in the first place. In Lobrathia the sole purpose of quartz crystals was for light, but here they clearly used it for some type of magic. This was magnificent news for me, because one of the reasons I was excited to come here was to learn more about magic and how the Ellythians used it day to day.

We were not five minutes into the trip when the carriage gave a sudden jarring bump as it bounced over a large stone on the road.

"He wants to kill us, does he?" Geravie said loudly, thumping on the panel behind her. "What kind of fool drives over a boulder?"

I grinned, hoping the rest of the island was like this, old magic seeped into every corner, just a part of their daily lives. What a joy to live here!

Geravie turned back to me in a business-like manner. "Now, Altara. We need to choose what name and backstory you're going to give. The Headmistress will no doubt be very curious as to why she hasn't heard of you before now."

Saraya had been quite explicit that I leave my name and face behind during my stay at the *school*. Otherwise, it was a sure way my stepmother would track me here. My face twisted in disgust as I thought about the concept of a place where teachers held supreme authority. As a princess I'd never had to attend such a thing, as our lecturers and tutors travelled to us, and because Saraya and I were less than a year apart in age, we had our private lessons together. In between classes on history, mathematics, economics, agriculture and elocution, my mother had taught us about our magic, and we were taught weapons use by our palace Armsmaster.

But the idea of creating a new identity was what gave me a sort of thrill. A place where I was not the half-breed Ellythian-Lobrathian princess and could be free to do as I pleased? All I could see was an opportunity.

"Hmmm," I said, tapping my chin and looking at the passing jungle. Goosebumps puckered all over my skin again, and I frowned, rubbing at my arms. There was more magic in this place than in Lobrathia; no doubt my body was responding to that unfamiliar volume. I'd have to get used to that. Even so, the sailors spoke about the place with a reverence, mixed with wariness. Almost the same sort you'd give to a lion or a tiger, and I could see what they meant now. You wanted to know what it was thinking, wanted to stare at it and know its secrets, but you could never venture too close for fear of it consuming you. As much as there was bright light and gentle breeze, there were also shadows and ancient trees. And it was daytime right now. I couldn't imagine what this place was like at *night*.

"What about Zara?" I asked. "That's close enough to my real name."

Geravie nodded in the direction of my voice. "Excellent. And you will be from my own Harranpul House. If anyone asks, you are my granddaughter who was too ill to attend the school before now."

I chuckled. "That fits. It's not even a lie, really." I had my fair share of illnesses, after all. It's just none of them had been my own.

Geravie smiled fondly in my direction as she clutched her gold family pendant in one hand. Harranpul was an old house, as old as my mother's house, Lota, the house of the Ellythian royal family who still held the throne under my grandmother Queen Cheshni. She was probably really old now, but my mother had never really spoken about her and, I think, had forbidden Geravie to speak on it as well. Something had gone amiss between mother and daughter before she'd been shipped off to Ellythia to marry my father, the Voltanius Lightning King.

But my mother was dead, and my father was still a mess after five years grieving her—his mind barely functioning properly anymore. The only family I had was Saraya and Geravie. The last time I saw Uncle Ansel was mother's funeral and even then he'd left the next day.

Geravie had been one of the few people that had come with my mother from Ellythia, and then the only one to stay once my mother died and my father's advisors sent the few Ellythians back, so I knew she was keen to get back to her real home after two whole decades away.

The backs of my eyes burned again, only this time I didn't have the heart to stop the hot tears from spilling. I'd left a note for my father, keeping things vague, telling them not to start a continental search for me. That I was safe and fine.

But a tiny, dark part of me wondered—after the fuss of the dark fae royalty arriving to take Saraya back to their realm—how long would it take them to notice that I was missing?

3
ALTARA

We arrived in Taraka town—more of a village in my eyes—three hours later. Since Ellythia was a secretive, isolated kingdom, I actually had very little clue about it other than what I'd gleaned on the voyage over. There were many tiny islands scattered about, but there were three main, larger islands, all of which were much larger than us mainlanders had been led to believe. Lobrathian maps drew Ellythia as three minuscule islands, but in reality, Boneweaver Island was at least four times the size I'd expected. I suspected this had less to do with mainland cartographers guessing land mass and more to do with some power play. Making our neighbours seem smaller made everyone a lot more comfortable from a military point of view, especially given the fact most of the population had some form of magic and the Ellythians trained both their men *and* women in fighting arts.

It was one of the things my mother had brought with her to Lobrathia. Both my sister and I had been trained with weapons from a young age—and in my case, the palace Armsmaster had determined that throwing daggers and archery were my speciality. Anything that you had to aim and shoot from a distance, I had a great talent for.

I hadn't been able to bring a bow with me, which made me itch uncomfortably as I'd never been travelling anywhere without it and a quiver of arrows. So I'd compensated by strapping extra throwing daggers to my person. Their weight against my skin made me substantially more relaxed. If there were, say, a tiger coming for us, I'd be able to dagger it in the eye no trouble and be worried about it afterwards. I had two on each thigh, two on each ankle and one on each forearm—thank the Goddess for loose sleeves. Along with Sam's pretty ones, I had more packed in my trunk since I didn't know what the weapons situation would be at the School.

My throwing daggers had been the only way I had felt safe waltzing about the grounds surrounding the palace on my own at any time of the day or night as well. All the guards had been so caught up with ensuring Saraya's safety when she'd sneak out of the palace to attend to her labouring women, that they all assumed I was tucked away safe in my room, being a good girl.

Little did they know about Sam, who I'd visited almost daily since I was fourteen—or nightly when our schedules lined up. He was a simple and kindly boy, but I never needed him for his brain—or his kindness, for that matter. My backup companion was Alistair, the palace fletcher's apprentice, with deft fingers and strong wrists that I took advantage of whenever Sam was busy.

Both would drop their tools happily for me at a moment's notice—and their pants while they were at it—but I couldn't bear the thought of them missing their work, or of me getting caught with my skirts above my waist if their fathers came to look for them—so we met discreetly at predetermined locations.

I smiled at the memory of my boys, who were no doubt pining for me after a week, wondering where I'd ended up. I wondered if the fletcher in the Taraka Town had a handsome son. I'd have to make sure I noted the various tradesmen and labouring men right away. They always had sons a little older than me.

After what felt like hours, our self-driving carriage trundled into the village with Geravie fanning herself with a sheaf of parchment and me looking out the window, trying to make out what type of place I was going to have to live in for an indefinite period of time.

The town began as a line of large wooden, weather-worn houses built to withstand the tropical heat and humidity. They stood high on stilts and were thatched with dried palm fronds. Children ran about, kicking a leather ball, pieces of mango in their hands, and it made me smile. It seemed like a nice place to grow up.

As we got into the main part of the town, the road became paved, mismatched stone set neatly together, and the buildings also made of stone. People walked barefoot or in light sandals, the women in colourful, light cotton sarees, holding babies or baskets on their hips. The men wore breezy trousers and loose shirts, their dark skin gleaming in the sun. The people stopped to stare at us—or Geravie, rather—and a woman even dropped her basket when she noticed the carriage, her mouth hanging open.

I supposed they didn't get visitors often.

Geravie must have also been eyeing the darker-skinned Ellythians and murmured to me, "At least our story of you being ill and indoors all the time will explain your lighter skin."

I pressed my lips together, wondering if anyone would actually believe that. My skin was a light brown, borne of my dark-skinned mother and pasty-skinned Lobrathian father. Pairings like that were uncommon due to the Ellythians rarely leaving their island. Here, I would stand out without even trying. Perhaps I needed to spend more time in the sun, so I went darker and blended in more. It was imperative that I didn't look different if I was going to successfully hide from my stepmother. My Lota House green eyes would make it hard enough to hide as it was—but *that* one, I had a trick for.

I mentally catalogued what I saw, noting that even my clothes would stand out here as I didn't have any sarees at all, only Lobrathian long sleeved dresses. I'd need to arrange for a local seamstress to cut all my sleeves short because according to. Geravie, Ellythia was practically summer all year 'round.

We passed the town rounding a corner, and I saw the place where I'd be living. On the far edge of the town, bordered by jungle on all sides, a gigantic stone castle came into view, haloed by faraway mountains, and a flag—a blue field with an open shark's mouth flying atop it. I frowned at that because the Lota Flag was a sword and lotus, their house colours pink and black. Perhaps it was the town flag? The castle was small, as expected—a place that could house around fifty people. Geravie seemed to think we had a cousin at this school. Perhaps I would have someone to confide in while I was here.

I blew out a slow breath as Geravie banged on the carriage door and called for it to be still. We trundled to a stop outside a stilted house with a thatched roof and wraparound veranda.

I watched as the door slammed open, and out rushed two elderly women, their faces struck with such fear that I made to warn Geravie. But my old nursemaid let out a cackle and was already climbing out of the carriage.

But the two elderly women, similar enough to be twins—tiny and plump with silver hair and loose flowery dresses—ambled down the steps of their house, their faces wide with shock.

"Geravie?" The first breathed, a hand over her mouth.

"Yes it's me!" Geravie called, stretching her arms out, a happy grin on her face.

"Geravie Harranpul, what are you doing here?" The second cried, rushing over to pull Geravie into a tight embrace.

They hugged but Geravie was quickly let go.

"Holy Mother! Get into the house quickly!" the first twin hissed, yanking Geravie by the arm while the second cast her eye about the jungle as if concerned something would jump out at us.

Both twins, to my surprise, had black crescent moons marked on their foreheads, and their hands bore fading, decades old tattoos inked in strange blue symbols.

I frowned as I watched the women rush Geravie inside. This had not been the reception I'd expected.

Geravie hastily turned back to look for me, her face a mirror of my own confusion. She gave a jerk of her head towards the house—a silent command to shut up and follow.

I glanced around us, and while we were surrounded by jungle on all sides, I didn't want to do any magic and emerge out in the open. The goosebumps returned anew, and I squinted into the dense green foliage in front of the house.

There was magic everywhere here, and it was prickling the back of my neck like it was watching me.

The twins grabbed our trunks and dragged them into house. Wide-eyed, Geravie and I followed them inside.

My second pang of homesickness caught me off guard as I strode up the steps into the house and through the door Geravie was holding open for me. I dabbed at my eyes. We had been a week at sea, certainly not enough to warrant tears, but we were finally here and it felt both comforting and alarming at the same time.

The house was surprisingly cool, likely by some method of magic I couldn't see, with smooth wooden floorboards, chairs woven out of an unusual material that looked natural —some type of plant, and they'd thrown hand knitted rugs over it. There was a tiny kitchen in which the white insides of a coconut were being magically ground against a blade, a small lounge and against the back door, sat a weathered bow and quiver. It felt like a place of comfort and safety, but as soon as the door was shut behind me, the first twin rounded on Geravie.

"Geravie, you should not have come."

"This is a disaster!" the second one huffed, putting my trunk down. "An absolute disaster. Reshmi, what do we do?" She turned back to Geravie. "How did you even get onto the island?"

Geravie shook her head in confusion. "What is wrong? You knew I was coming. I sent the missive and assumed—"

"You assumed wrong, cousin!" shrieked the one called Reshmi. "Sister, we must have her leave before sundown."

"It's too late," Keshmi sighed, pinching her nose. "I don't know how she got in, but there's no way out." She ended in a string of swear words that had me raising my brows.

23

Geravie had been strangely tight-lipped about who her "contacts" were, and I was right in assuming they were distant relatives. But now we were here, my usually stoic nursemaid looked nervous and worried.

"Tell me what is wrong!" Geravie demanded. "We arrived here with no difficulty though the ship's captain did not want to set anchor. As soon as we came to land, that carriage came to meet us. I assumed you sent the rickety old thing."

Reshmi sighed and sat down on the couch, putting her head in her hands, and then her head snapped back up, her face ashen. "We? Please don't tell me you brought your princess too?"

Geravie was silent for a moment before saying quietly, "She is here."

The twins exchanged a dark look before casting their eyes around the house, squinting. "Where?"

"Show yourself, girl," Geravie said darkly, hefting herself onto the couch opposite Reshmi. "So that my cousins may lose their wits completely."

I did so, letting my magic fall away and sucking it back inside of me.

The two women covered their mouths as I appeared, and I bobbed a swift curtsey.

"Pleased to make your acquaintance," I said politely. "Though, I'm afraid the Lady Geravie has not disclosed whose esteemed presence I am in."

They stared at me, and for a long moment, only the rustle of the breeze through the jungle sounded around us. Finally, the old women introduced themselves as Reshmi and Keshmi Harranpul.

"Twins," Reshmi said, shrugging in the manner of those who've been explaining their similar name for decades.

"She looks like Yasani," Keshmi breathed, coming to stand before me. "I'm sorry, princess," she said. "It is not safe here. Geravie should not have brought you."

"Bring me water, you awful woman," Geravie shot in annoyance. "Is this how you treat your guests? It might have been twenty years, but we are still family!"

Keshmi gave her sister a look of great alarm and hurried into the kitchen. When she returned, I took the offered glass, appreciating its chill against my sweaty hands.

"I'm sure you know, princess," Reshmi said as Geravie gulped down her water, "that we do not speak of Ellythian matters outside of the islands."

"And that's what led us to this mess," Keshmi grumbled. "Dear, Goddess."

"For the love of said Goddess, now that we are here, tell us what the problem is!" Geravie cried.

"Now you are here," Reshmi said seriously. "Neither of you will be permitted to leave." A chill ran down my spine as she continued. "There is a barrier around this island, and there has been for three years. Daanav Kingdom finally won, sister."

Geravie dropped her empty glass, and it landed on the carpet with a *thump*.

4
ALTARA

I hadn't heard of the Daanav Kingdom before and was trying to rummage through my brain to figure out who it could be.

"Surely not," Geravie said in such a dark voice that I couldn't help but stare at her.

"I'm afraid so," said Reshmi. "After nightfall they come out. I think it will be a good idea if the princess goes to the School immediately. There are certain agreements that have been made, and it will be safer for her with the other girls than with us, out here."

"It'll be sundown soon," Keshmi said, hauling herself off the couch. "I'll get the carriage. The girls there have been unharmed for the past few years. You should be alright until we can figure out a way to get you out of here."

"Okay," I said slowly. "But who is—"

"And what is your name?" asked Geravie sternly, seemingly recovered from her stupor.

I opened my mouth and closed it abruptly. Grinning, I

swept another curtsey. "Why, I am the Lady Zara of the noble House Harranpul, of course."

"Good girl," Geravie said, but she did not smile. This whole thing was bound to be interesting now with these apparent political changes. Geravie grabbed the hands of the twins in a vice-like grip. "I need to show Altara the temple before she goes. Goddess, *I* need to see it again, and I won't hear any arguments."

The twins reluctantly smiled as some sort of shared understanding passed between them all.

"Temple?" I asked tentatively.

"We are priestesses of the temple in Taraka town," Reshmi said proudly.

So that explained the black crescent moons on their foreheads. "We only have temples of the triple goddess in Lobrathia," I admitted as Geravie and I followed the twins through the house and out a back door. "My mother always insisted it was an insult to only have the three."

As we walked down a set of long stairs, the twins murmured in sadness: "We lost a great deal the day Yasani left," Keshmi said. My stomach flopped in a sort of guilt. But the elderly lady cast me a smile over her shoulder. "But because of her leaving, we are blessed to have you two princesses."

I blinked at her response. She hardly knew me. Or my sister. I didn't understand why she looked like she meant it, but I took it as a compliment anyway.

The jungle behind the house had been cleared to make a wide path, paved with old stones greyed with time. Something rustled in the foliage, and I gave a violent twitch. My daggers were in my hands just as I saw a long furry creature leaping away.

"Mongoose," Reshmi chuckled. "They're everywhere."

Geravie gave me a sharp look, and I hastily sheathed my weapons.

Old palms towered over us as we walked down the path, and in the distance came the crash of waves and the saline smell of the sea.

"The coastline sweeps toward us here," Keshmi explained to me, "and our temples are always built where they can see the moon over the ocean. Its twin, the Temari temple, was built by the ancients exactly at this position but across the sea."

"Oh, right," I nodded in recognition. "The Lobrathians kept the Ellythian name. They're ruins now though, in the Temari forest."

The twins made sad tutting sounds in disapproval at the downfall of the temple, but there had been no Ellythians there to maintain it, I supposed. And in Lobrathia each town and village had a Temple of the Goddess and Temple of the God. Saraya and I had visited our own Quartz Goddess Temple to make offerings before the fae arrived. I was glad we'd had time to do it because it might very well have been the last time we got to do anything together for *years*. My heart gave a little shudder at the loss I felt, but I shoved it away as quickly as it came. This was a new world for me, the place of our mother, surely I'd gotten the better end of the bargain than being married to an unknown man?

As we rounded a corner, the jungle suddenly opened up, and I gasped. The long rays of the setting sun haloed an intricately carved structure, twice the size of the twin's house. It was a burnished stone of some kind, perfectly golden in the sunset with images of the seven Goddesses carved into its front and sides with such detail it took my breath away.

Before the entrance was a magnificent arched gateway, the sides of which were made out of two naked women standing guard, their strong arms holding up the top of the arches. In their spare hands, one held a bow and arrow and the other an axe.

Every inch of it was ancient, stunning and my insides tingled at the raw potential magic of the place.

The name of the temple was inscribed into the smooth stone of that entrance arch. And as we passed beneath it, I let out a choked sob and fell to my knees in shock. Geravie rushed over to me, but I couldn't hear her soft words of comfort as I stared. And *stared*.

Yasani Temple

The twin priestesses stood at the temple entrance, their eyes glistening as they looked at us. Geravie took my hand and kissed it as I tried and failed to control myself. She patted my face with her handkerchief, and I let her, simply staring at my mother's name.

"'Yasani' is an ancient word," Reshmi said softly, a hand pressed over her heart. "It is the root of female power. Here." Her hand moved to her lower belly, right above the apex of her thighs, and I raised my brows. The three old women chuckled at my expression.

"Wait until you see inside," Geravie murmured. She took my hand in hers, and together, we followed the twins.

"Come come!" Reshmi said, ducking inside the temple. "Look here."

She swept her arms around to indicate the insides of the magnificent building, and I was quite quickly taken in by the sheer ancient beauty of the place.

It was wide and circular in design with seven-foot-tall carved quartz statues of the seven goddesses standing strong in a semicircle. I'd *never* seen quartz sculptures that huge and that detailed in my entire life. They sparkled by the natural beams of sunlight that shone through the circular opening in the domed roof.

But the sunlight also lit up what lay directly beneath it on the floor. Right in the centre of the temple was a ceramic structure that made pure delight flood my being.

"No," I whispered in disbelief, stepping up to it.

Spanning six feet long were folds in the shape of a petal. There were two outside folds, two inner folds, a small bulb joining them at their apex.

It was biologically accurate, and it merely sitting here so unassuming took my breath away.

"You meant 'root of female' power literally," I said in disbelief to Reshmi. Both twins chuckled at my reaction.

"This is Agnolthi's abode," Geravie explained quietly, nodding to the quartz statue that stood at the head position, directly opposite the entrance. "Do you remember the names of the seven?"

I nodded slowly, walking up to the first statue to recite their names.

A rose quartz statue of a cherub-faced, dimpled girl holding a harp. "This is Cherimani, the sweet maiden."

I walked to the next—a yellow quartz statue of a woman with a veil over her head, coins pouring out of a benevolent palm. I said quietly, "This is Lasanthi, the All-Mother."

The next statue was a deep red, depicting a woman with her gown falling off her shoulders, a substantial bosom and wide hips to rival my own, poised as if she were about to saunter off her podium and right up to me. I grinned and said, "Luana, the seductress."

On the other side of the temple was a pure-white quartz statue of a hunched elderly woman with a cane and a skull. "Cholnayak, the widow," I murmured.

Next to her was a blue quartz, fierce woman with a curved sword in one hand and a mace in the other. She wore battle armour and a helmet. "Xalya, the warrior."

Next to her, in a quartz that was such a deep blue it was almost black, was a frightening goddess, her fangs bared in a snarl, naked but for a garland of skulls and long hair covering her breasts, a sword in one hand and the severed head of a demon in the other. I shivered, "Umali, the raging goddess."

Finally, I strode to the guardian of the temple, standing proud at the helm and made out of purple quartz. She sat on the back of a tiger, her robe flaring around her. In one hand she held an arrow and in the other, the handle of a cauldron. On her forehead was carved a black crescent moon struck through with an arrow. Somehow, she sparkled, giving her eyes a glittering, magical sheen.

"Agnolthi, the witch." I brushed my fingers across the tiger's feet in wonder then looked to the twins, the same moon marking on their foreheads. "Your temple is beautiful."

I wished we could have stayed there much longer, even just to stare at the masterful, intricate workmanship of the quartz statues, but the twins insisted I be inside the school before the sun disappeared. As we left, I noticed the temple path continued around the back of the building. Curiously, I peered into the dense jungle as this path was not as well kept as the path leading up to the temple. "What's back there?" I asked.

I didn't miss the way both twins' eyes slid past me in a

mildly uncomfortable manner. Geravie also stilled. I looked behind me once again, immediately deciding I wanted to see what they were being secretive about. I took a step on the next paving stone and a tingling sensation grew in my chest. Excitement bubbled in my stomach. *Magic* was down there, and a lot of it. I took another step, fully intending to stride into the wilderness, but Keshmi's sharp voice halted me.

"It is a cemetery of sorts, my sweet. Full of old people, long gone. That is all." I turned to look at her and though she smiled, a shadow had drawn over her eyes. "Tigers still roam about here. We do not venture back there anymore. Come along."

Geravie fanned herself and gave me a look that told me to behave myself. "I'm dying in this heat. Let us go, *Zara*."

My feet dragging like a sullen child, I gave in and followed the elderly ladies back down the path. There was definitely condensed magic of some sort down there—and in a cemetery? Goddess, it was drawing me in like honey to a bee. I needed to take a look whenever I came back here.

INSIDE THE COOL OF THE HOUSE WITH FRESH FRUIT JUICE IN HAND, we plotted and schemed. Well, we settled into practical matters, and our twin priestesses quickly told me what I needed to know.

They gave us an update of the current living members of House Harranpul so I would be able to answer questions about my family if asked, as well as the estate and the lands it was on up north on Lota Island. They told me not to answer any questions about how I got here, except to say that I arrived by commissioned ship with no trouble. They told me to keep my head down and my mouth shut—and not to look surprised if anything...unexpected happened. If I stayed within the school, I would be safe from the invading kingdom. But they gave Geravie a dark look as they spoke about it, and I got the feeling they weren't telling me the full story. It was likely they thought I'd be scared. But they didn't know me, did they? I'd have to prise it out of Geravie later.

Harranpul estate was on the northernmost Lotus Island. Which was also where the bigger cosmopolitan capital of Lota City was located, including the royal palace where my mother's relatives were. The south island, which we were currently on, was looked down upon by northerners, and land on the middle island—Tiger island—was the source of many a feud between the two groups for centuries. My grandmother, Queen Cheshni, was feared and revered amongst the northerners but there was resentment there from the southerners.

I tried to cram all this information in, thoroughly annoyed that I'd never been taught any of it before.

The history of it was mind boggling, and I think Geravie knew my concentration was waning because she clapped her hands. "I'm rather excited to be staying here with my cousins after so long being away." She put her arms around the two women sitting either side of her and gave them a squeezed. The twins returned her conflicted expressions.

"You're staying here?" I asked.

"I can't very well attend a school for young ladies, can I?" she waved her finger at me, and I supposed I agreed. I had thought I'd have some sort of backing from her in the unknown school but, whatever happened at this place, I was sure I could manage it.

"Here we go, then!" I said, and I couldn't help the grin that overcame my features. This school had no idea who they were taking in, and neither would the other girls. I'd have no chance to use my status to get my way with anything. I didn't need any *schooling*, as it were. I was just here to hide out, and I'd be damned if I wasn't going to find some entertainment while I was at it.

Geravie was giving me a warning stare, and I smiled leisurely back.

She knew me too well.

5

ALTARA

The carriage was waiting as we hurried out of the twins' house just as the sun began to disappear behind the jungle canopy. Geravie handed me the letter I was to give the headmistress and palmed me a few more gold coins for Ellythian good luck. I had my own purse on me, plus more in my trunk, which I'd taken from the palace coffers on the pretext of studying Ellythian currency. The coin masters of Quartz had only allowed me half the amount I'd wanted, so I'd snuck back down to the treasury, invisible, and taken some more. The last thing I wanted was to be caught penniless in an unfamiliar land. I might not be a princess in title here, but surely I could still spend coin like one?

I climbed into the carriage and Geravie banged on the front of it with her closed fist, yelling at it to hurry me to the school or she was going to take an axe to it.

The carriage jerked forward like it believed her and my stomach did a little flip of excitement. I gave the three ladies a cheery wave, and standing arm in arm, they forced the worry off their faces with smiles.

Still. This was the first time in my entire damned existence that I was travelling alone, and it made my stomach twist just a little, especially given recent political turmoil with this Daanav Kingdom. I needlessly adjusted the straps of my forearm sheaths. It's not like I thought I'd get attacked at the school, but the surrounding jungle, thick with chirruping cicadas was making me tingle in a way that was making me a hairs breadth away from nervous.

I didn't like nervous.

It made me want to jump into the forest and find out exactly what was making me uneasy. I just needed a machete to hack my way through the undergrowth. Surely, there was one around here somewhere. I fully intended to explore this place completely at the first chance. It was hard finding private, secluded spots where you wouldn't get discovered by strangers with a young man between your legs.

Bar one tiny instance with Geravie, it hadn't happened to me yet, and I intended to keep my winning streak.

Riding up the path to the castle, I tried to be observant, looking for any clues as to what my time here would have in store for me.

I had no plan for how long I'd be here, and I think neither did Geravie. Honestly, I was hoping that Saraya would whisk me away to the Fae Realm once she was settled there and find me a pretty fae to live with. He didn't even have to be a noble. From what I'd seen of the fae when they'd arrived, even their soldiers, were supernaturally, ridiculously, tall and handsome. They hadn't looked particularly *nice*, on the other hand, but I knew Saraya could hold her own. Raised in the way that we were, I don't think either of us would have an issue dealing with arrogant royals, even preternatural ones.

But the grey stone castle now looming over me like a stern taskmaster was no fae royal palace.

It was a full and proper—urgh—school. Were they strict tutors? Was there a curfew? And what type of guards did they have here? Casting my eye about the trimmed green lawn before the castle, I saw no one. No students or any guards at all.

My heart leapt. If they had no guards on watch, that meant I had even more free rein to roam than I originally imagined. For a place full of young, noble, very eligible women, that also meant that the school and this area was ridiculously safe, proving our priestess twins correct. Clearly this Daanav Kingdom weren't the trouble making sort. I fingered the flat handle of one of the knives on my thigh, marvelling at the thought of wanton freedom.

The carriage stopped right outside the front doors, and I promptly climbed out. But importantly, I used my touch on the wood of the carriage and pulled its colour into me—to take on the appearance of brown irises. It was going to be a difficult thing, hiding my telling emerald green eyes by taking on the colour of whatever brown thing was closest. I would have to pay constant attention all day. My power did not work at a distance.

I swept forward in a lady-like manner as one of the double wooden front doors opened. Smiling broadly at the severe, proud-looking woman who awaited me, I breezed up the steps. She looked down at me and I knew her right away to be the head housekeeper as she had that icy, no-nonsense sort of look. Not one of the hairs in her greying bun was out of place and her long slate coloured saree had been ironed by a firm hand.

"I am here to see the headmistress," I said imperiously, handing her Geravie's letter. The woman took one look at the Harranpul sugar cane and sword crest on the wax seal, and her eyes widened. Her head snapped up and she graced me with a quick curtsey. I inclined my head regally in return.

"This way, my lady." Her voice was sort of nasally, I noted, as she turned and led me inside. Sinus problems were likely—a lack of adequate drainage. My magic made an attempt to go to her, but I squeezed it down more quickly than a virgin clamping her legs. I needed to be vigilant if I was going to keep my magic a secret and couldn't let it run rampant here. Noble girls were more likely to have powerful magic, and they would know at once if I was using it.

I was right about the housekeeper being severe. The entrance hall was spotless, and two maids were dusting a vase, their gazes cast down as we passed.

We didn't see any students as the housekeeper led me up a winding staircase and down a series of corridors, but they were bound to be here somewhere. Perhaps they were at lessons, given the time of day.

She sat me down in an airy room and snapped her fingers. Out of nowhere, a maid rushed forward, carrying a tray with a glass of clear juice.

I took it, smiling at the young girl who glanced at me curiously before averting her gaze as if she were frightened of me. That made me sad. My own maid, Lucy, had become a good friend of mine, and I didn't like the idea of fearful servants. My mother had taught me to be kind from the cradle—that station didn't matter. I almost snorted as I realised that was probably why I was so comfortable cavorting with the local boys of the city. My mother's teachings had backfired on that account.

I sipped the cold juice, marvelling at the taste. I knew it at once to be coconut water, and finding it delicious, I gulped down only a quarter of it so the housekeeper knew I was a proper lady.

Said housekeeper returned and stood before me, unsmiling, with her hands clasped before her. "The headmistress Jessine will see you now, my lady."

I smiled and stood in the most graceful fashion I was capable of. Mistress Housekeeper needed a kindly man—*that* would get her smiling once again, no doubt about it. I would have to keep that at the back of my mind so I could scout for men of an eligible age. She looked about fifty; I'm sure there was a groundskeeper or smith around here somewhere of the right age. Or perhaps someone younger might do to keep her on her toes?

I followed the woman into a large square office that reminded me a little of my father's in the way the massive wooden desk was set up facing the door.

A scary room to discipline naughty noble girls like me. I vaguely wondered if they used a cane here. More than one of my tutors back at home had wanted to use one on me—I knew that much from the red-blotched cheeks and the huffing and puffing.

None of them dared, though. They all knew I was a perfect shot with any sharp instrument. And a quill made for an excellent weapon in the right hands.

The headmistress stood from her wing-backed chair, holding Geravie's letter. She was a plain woman of fifty-something, her face lined from what I guessed was the excessive stress of running a school like this. She was straight backed and lean under her sharp blue saree—as if she still trained regularly—and her narrow waist cinched in with a lovely jewelled belt. My respect for her went up considerably.

I hastily changed my irises to the colour of the wooden door behind me and gave a polite curtsey. Even though my supposed family ranked higher than her, she was still the head of this school, and that meant I had to treat her as if she were the Lady of the House.

"Pleased to meet you, Headmistress," I said softly as the housekeeper left and shut the door.

"The pleasure is mine, Lady Zara," she said, gazing at me curiously. "This your first time out of Harranpul estate?" Under her gaze I felt like an army of ants were crawling all over my skin.

I nodded demurely and made my voice whisper soft, placing a hand over my heart for good measure. "It is. I'm afraid I find all of this *very* overwhelming." In another life I could have been made a wonderful player in the theatre.

But the headmistress made a sound of interest in her throat and was looking at me up and down as if assessing me for my height, weight and shoe size. "And you made it onto the island with no trouble?"

I stared at my feet, the picture of a naive girl. "Yes, my lady."

"Is Harranpul House sympathising with the Daanavs now?" she asked curiously.

"Oh, I am not well versed on political matters," I piped quickly over a nervous laugh. "I stay away from it at all costs."

She suddenly stood straighter as if deciding something. "Well, you won't know anything of the ways of the Southerners, nor the dangers of the jungle." She beckoned to me like a child, and I shuffled obediently forward to peer out the window where she was pointing. "Look out at the jungle there. See how wild it is? Well, it spans weeks and weeks. Get lost in there, and no one can bring you back. There are untold beasts, and Goddess knows what else lurking about—as well as Daanav warriors and that's without falling down a trap into the Forests of Eternity. If you want to be frightened, simply ask a local for a bedtime story." She held up a finger. "I do *not* want my ladies wandering around without reason." She stood a little straighter. "My ladies are from dignified houses and behave as such."

Nodding, as if I agreed most vehemently, I made my eyes wide. "Of course, Headmistress."

"Good girl."

I beamed as if I was glad for her approval, and it was then I noticed the black quartz pendant she wore so tightly around her neck that it sat right in the hollow of her narrow throat. It glimmered in a sluggish, sinister fashion, and it was with great alarm that I felt a darkness oozing from it. Quartz did not naturally come in solid black, and I knew right away that its colouring was due to some type of foul magic. I took a step away from her, suppressing a shiver, but she didn't notice, because she was staring at my waist as if she could assess my diet by looking at it.

"Very unfortunate you have no magic," she murmured, casting her eye over the letter again as if she didn't quite believe it. "From such a powerful family, I would have hoped there would be some power in you."

The pendant blinked at me as if it were sensing it was being watched and I tore my eyes off the awful thing.

"I was always ill," I sniffed mournfully as if it was all very painful. "The Goddess gifts as she desires."

She looked up at me, her eyes softening. "So she does.

41

Despite that I can see you are of good breeding. Finding a husband should not be difficult for you. We will have many suitors approaching us, I am sure."

I almost choked. "Approaching us?"

She frowned at me in disapproval. "I know it can be frightening to have men knocking on your door, dear, but you must remember your ancestry! Harranpul House has always bred the strongest warriors. You must do your family proud and hold your head high when the suitors arrive for the scheduled meetings."

I felt the blood drain from my face. This is what I had been running *from*. "Meetings?" I'd not yet been called 'stupid', but that's how I sounded now.

The headmistress spread out her hands. "Yes? This is why your family sent you here, is it not?"

It took me half a breath to register what she was saying. The school had transformed from finishing school to a bride factory. Looked like things had changed in the twenty years Geravie had been in Lobrathia.

It didn't matter when I could mysteriously disappear at a moment's notice. I knew I could wheedle my way out of this.

She looked me up and down. "We haven't had anyone wear a white sash over the uniform in quite some time."

"There's a *uniform*?"

She sniffed. "You can wear your own dresses in the evenings and on weekends, otherwise you must wear our prescribed clothing. Here on Boneweaver Island, we value tradition, Lady Zara."

I crossed my arms but bit my tongue as I followed her out the office. I had promised Geravie I would try to blend in, and I knew my Lobrathian clothes were bound to stand out a little anyway.

She led me down the corridor and into a large room where three maids worked, sewing clothes by hand. They all jumped to their feet as we arrived, curtseying deeply.

"Girls, this is our newest guest, Lady Zara of Harranpul House." I beamed at them all. I had always made better friends with low-born women than the noble kind. Perhaps my new friends would be in this very room. "Bring out a set of suitable day clothes and a white sash."

A round-faced girl bobbed another curtsey and dashed into an adjoining room. She returned within seconds, handing the headmistress a pile of pink clothes. She showed me a length of white silk embroidered with white lotus leaves.

"The sash marks what manner of power you have. Those with no magic wear the white." I accepted the bundle with both hands.

"Thank you, Headmistress Jessine."

"You are fortunate to have arrived on a Friday. I will take you to your room, and then you may settle in to get ready for the weekend. Ladies are expected for the evening meal just after sunset."

I noted the sun's position. I would have to wait until after everyone went to sleep to take a look around the castle and figure out where everything of note was. I strode after her eagerly, through to the other side of the castle where the sleeping chambers were.

Up a set of stairs, the headmistress knocked on a mahogany door and strode in.

There were four beds. I exhaled slowly in despair as I'd stupidly imagined a private room. No sneaking boys into my bed then; all activities would have to be external to the school.

"Ah, Lady Pia. This is Lady Zara Harranpul."

A low, feminine voice came from behind me: "I've never seen you before."

I turned around. Oh, *Goddess* those emerald eyes—it was just like looking into a mirror.

So this was my cousin.

6
ALTARA

Pia, princess of the mighty and ancient royal House of Lota, was one of the most beautiful young ladies I'd ever seen.

She was the first blood relation I'd met on my mother's side, and the resemblance was obvious. Her skin was a rich brown, which made her bright emerald eyes, framed in thick black lashes, all the more noticeable. She had full lips, curly black hair that had been tamed into a long, thick braid down her back with loose strands curling about her face. The school uniform, which I could see now was both lovely and practical, was a pink half gown—half in that it was long at the back and sides but only up to the waist in the front, leaving her free to move in brown lace-up pants. The sleeves of the dress were short, cutting off at the bicep, showing arms toned with heavy weapons use, and the sash around her waist was the same green as her eyes.

She was second in line to the throne of Ellythia, after her mother, Crown Princess Rahana, and I would need to find out why she was so far from home.

Her eyes flicked down my body—and to the white sash that sat on top of my new bundle of clothes. Our mothers had been raised together, which likely meant that Pia had been trained to control her no doubt powerful magic. It also meant that I would have to be extremely careful around her.

"An honour to meet you, Princess," I said, smiling and keeping a strong hold over my the brown irises I'd taken on from the dormitory door. "I've been unwell most of my life. This is first time I've been well enough to leave my home."

She looked upon me, her face showing no emotion, and I took in every tiny movement of hers. I needed to know exactly how different the Ellythian royal family were from us Lobrathians.

She crossed her arms and finally said, "Interesting."

The headmistress shifted uncomfortably, and I swore in my head. She was suspicious of me already. I'd have to prove I meant no harm to her as soon as possible. I couldn't very well have one-day Queen of Ellythia looking into me.

Unless...

If I confided in her, perhaps this whole thing would go easier for me. But I had to see what type of royal Pia was. If she was ill-tempered or the jealous sort, that would spell real trouble. She could very well see me as a threat. Being a matriarchal society, I was technically fourth in line for the Ellythian throne if they still considered us a part of the family. Their opinion of us, though, was something I would have to find out. No, it was better that who I was remained a secret until I figured out what she thought about us.

Were they the type to assassinate their competition?

I suppressed a shiver, the weight of my throwing daggers comforting once again.

"I suppose you don't know how to fight then?" Pia asked suddenly.

I swore internally again as I hadn't even thought about the implications of me being supposedly "unwell" all of my life. I sighed and softened my features. "Unfortunately not, Your Highness. I was bedridden as a girl."

"Hmm," she said, narrowing her eyes upon my frame. Though I was well endowed with breasts and wide hips, I had been training to fight since I was toddler, making my waist narrow, my legs and arms well-muscled. I curled my hands shut in case she looked down and saw my bow-calloused palms and fingers.

The headmistress sighed. "Let us have the Armsmistress assess Zara, and we will go from there, hm?" I beamed and nodded eagerly. "Well, I leave you to get settled. Follow Her Highness and do as the others do. The dressing rooms are through there, and the bathroom there. Ring this bell for your maid." She pointed to two adjoining rooms, then a tiny pink quartz bell on a side table, and I bounced a curtsey back to her. She smiled in approval and swept out the door. I suppressed the urge to look surprised at the bell. It was glowing with magic that I was discovering was the norm here. Like with the magic carriage, we had nothing of the sort in Lobrathia.

As soon as the headmistress was gone, Pia shot forward and gripped my arm with surprising force. When I looked into her eyes, I found them wide with urgency.

"Why are you here?" she hissed. "How did you get here? Do you have a way you can leave?"

I stared at her, clutching my new clothes to my chest. "Uh, no, Your Highness, I don't know… I came here by boat, and the boat left?" Why I was stuttering like a child was beyond me, but I had not expected this. She let go of my hand.

"*Never* let yourself be alone with that woman," Pia said firmly. "Do you understand me?"

"Yes," I said slowly, putting down the clothes at the end of the bed where my trunk had mysteriously appeared. This must have something to do with that black quartz around her neck.

"You look quite well," Pia said, sitting stiffly on her bed. "Is Harranpaul House plotting against the queen?"

Fuck. A loaded question and straight to the point. So I shook my head vigorously. "I don't know, Your Highness. They just sent me here. Honestly, I don't understand the politics."

"Pia."

"I beg your pardon?"

"Call me Pia; it's easier."

I gave her a genuine smile. "Thank you, Pia."

She pinched the end of her nose and sighed. "I was hoping to get girls *out* of here, not bring more in. How did you get past the Daanav shield?"

I assumed she meant a magical shield, but hadn't even seen or felt a anything like that when we came in. "I don't know. We just did."

"Really?" Her eyes searched my face as if she didn't believe me. "My grandmother....well...there's nothing I can do." She frowned at me again. "Your parents really didn't tell you anything about Boneweaver Island? What did you do wrong to get sent here?"

"What did I do wrong?" I repeated lamely, and then her words registered and I looked wildly around. "Is this a place of punishment?"

Pia sighed. "Dear Goddess, you poor girl."

She was looking at me as if she were trying to see under my skin to my organs. I suddenly wondered what type of magic she had and quickly checked my mental defences. They were near-perfect, though, as it was the one thing that had been drilled into me since infancy.

"As it stands," she continued, raising her chin, "Once the Boneweavers died out, Ellythian nobles have long sent their wayward daughters here to teach them a lesson."

"And to find husbands?" I said dryly. I didn't know who the Boneweavers were either.

She grimaced. "*Indeed.*" But it was more of curse. "So we have someone to keep an eye on us."

"What should I know about this place?" I asked quickly. Whatever punishments were given to us, I was sure I could manage. I'd just hide back at the twins' house whenever I could. "Can we go into the town whenever we like?"

"Not anymore."

That didn't matter. I could sneak off unseen anyway, so I just nodded as if I accepted it.

She said darkly, "Just...just keep quiet, is my advice. Don't stand out. Being magic-less they'll probably leave you alone."

Why was everyone intent on me not standing out? I was honestly hoping to be as invisible as possible—well, visible to right people at least. "So, these Daanav Kingdom invaders don't cause trouble?"

She was about to reply when female voices sounded in the distance, and she instead nodded her head towards the closed door. "That'll be the others finished for the day. We have two more girls in this room, and then there's two other rooms, and that makes all of us in our age group."

"What happens now?" I looked around the room uncertainly, never having been in a group situation before. My maid in Lobrathia, Lucy, always just went along with the schedule my father's councillors had planned, and failing that, whatever I wanted to do.

Pia sat down on her bed and began to unlace her leather boots. "We bathe and get ready for dinner."

The door banged open and through it came two grumbling girls in the same pink and brown uniform. They saw me and stopped at the door, their eyes widening in surprise. One had the type of curved body that men lusted after, not dissimilar to mine—full hips, generous breasts, but she was long limbed, whereas I was a little shorter, and her sash was red. The second girl was lean like a beanpole, lanky with a long, messy braid and frizzy hair sticking out at all angles. Her sash was orange.

It was she who spoke first. "Oh! Hello there, friend!"

"Hello," I said smiling again. At this rate my cheeks would be more muscular than any other part of my body.

Pia saved me with an introduction. "This is Zara of Harranpul House." She plopped back on her elbows and said dryly, "She's just arrived." The two girls stared at me with raised brows as Pia continued. "Don't question it, girls. Zara, that's Rani with the wild hair and Malika who looks like she's eaten a slug."

They both gave me tentative smiles. Malika seemed rather pleased by the insult and Rani gave me a cheerful wave. "Wild hair indeed," she said, striding towards her own bed and unlacing her boots. "Has someone rung the bell? I need to fix it before the Baboon corners me again."

I quickly reached for the bell on the table next to me as Malika sauntered towards her own bed on the other side of the room, hips swaying. "If you'd only let me try my magic on it, I'll have it sorted, and the *headmistress* won't bother you. I've been saying—"

"I saw what you did you Farrah's hair the other day!" Rani scoffed. "Not in the name of any Goddess, I tell you, my mother would have a fit if I went around with red hair!"

I rang the quartz bell, and instead of making the high-pitched noise I expected, it just vibrated in my hand. I quickly put it down, rubbing my wrist.

Malika scoffed as Rani continued. "Well, I'm glad you're here, Zara. We've been simply dying for a fourth room member. Now we won't be uneven in sparring class."

Pia made a sound of uncertainty, glancing at me.

There was a polite knock at the door, and it opened to reveal four serious maids carrying fresh towels and wash-cloths. They bobbed curtsies and hurried into one of our adjoining rooms.

I looked at my trunk that someone had put by the spare bed. I would need a change of clothing and underclothes, but I'd never actually unpacked my bags myself before. Lucy had packed them for me back in Lobrathia, and Geravie had sorted our clothes on the ship. That fact made me feel a little foolish now, but one of the maids hurried out and curtseyed again. She was young, possibly only thirteen or fourteen, with a sweet round face.

"My lady," she said so softly I had to lean in to hear her. "My name is Gally, and I will be your maid."

I almost sagged in relief. "Oh, thank the Goddess, Gally! I thought I'd have to unpack this blasted trunk by myself."

Gally looked up at me in alarm, no doubt at the casual manner of speaking I'd obtained from years spending too much time listening to wounded soldiers. I grinned at her, rolling my eyes, and she bit back a smile.

"Can you help me, please?" I gestured to my trunk.

She nodded, and I liked her immediately. Together, we stowed my clothes in one of the wardrobes set against the walls opposite each bed.

Watching her from the side of my eye, I knew the exact moment she became flustered with confusion. She leafed through my Lobrathian dresses over and over again but said nothing to me.

I followed her into the bathing room and peered around. I had been worried we'd be bathing together in a large pool or something similar, but thankfully, they had four tubs, each separated by a pink curtain.

ONCE WE'D BATHED, WE HAD TO GET DRESSED INTO OUR DINNER clothes. The girls were helped by their maids, wearing the Ellythian traditional saree—long lengths of colourful silk or cotton that could be wrapped in a multitude of ways around the breasts and hips to form a gown. Gally, in her blessed astuteness, had obtained a simple one from somewhere in the castle. It was yellow with little pink flowers, and I loved it.

"I spent most of my time indoors," I explained sombrely, by way of explaining my dresses. "And I was always terribly cold. It feels warmer here in the south, though. Perhaps the seamstress can alter my current dresses too." I had seen some of the women in the village dress simply in Lobrathian-style dresses, with modified shorter sleeves, which had no doubt that had come from our long relationship in trade.

Gally nodded and looked upon my lighter skin with sorrowful eyes.

I noticed the other girls in the dressing room had quietened as they observed me. I'd been the last to get ready, and now I hastened to run the brush through my hair.

"Oh, don't worry!' Rani piped up, wearing a saree of green and yellow. "And my!" I set down my brush, and she came to loop her limber arm around mine. "What straight hair you have. You must tell me all your secrets."

The smile I gave her was genuine as I eyed her long, wild tresses, which had been braided as neatly as her maid could manage. "Oh, I don't know—I quite like your hair. It reminds me of—"

I almost clamped a hand over my own Goddess-damned mouth. I had just about to say that it reminded me of my sister's more curly hair. The three girls were staring at me as the maids tidied up the dressing room. I gave them an apologetic look and said softly. "It reminds me of my mother's hair."

Rani brightened, "Oh, high praise I'm sure, Zara! Your mother must be most beautiful." She led me out the door after the others.

Pia cast a curious look at my shoulder, and I realised my face had fallen. I took a deep breath. "Was," I corrected. "She *was* very beautiful."

Rani gasped and covered her mouth as Pia and Malika stopped to turn and look at me.

"I'm so sorry, Zara!" Rani exclaimed. "I'm just a silly old mongoose. That's what my father always says. You mustn't take anything I say seriously at all, really—"

"Zara," Pia interrupted softly, and Rani immediately shut

her mouth. Malika looked haughtily over me as if this was a mild inconvenience for her.

The lump that had formed in my throat was very real as I looked at Pia's bright-green eyes, which were now cast in sympathy. "I am sorry for your loss. What was her name?"

Five years since I'd lost her and still the pain lurked within me like a venomous snake sinking its fangs into my very spine. At the same time, Pia's voice held an undercurrent of something more than mere curiosity—she was still suspicious of me, I realised. Smart girl. But I still had my wits about me and remembered all the names Geravie had made me repeat over and over again.

I gave her the name the twins advised me to use in place of my mother's, but my mind chased its way to the ancient temple behind the twins' house and the name carved into the stone archway. The grief must have been quite plain on my face because Pia softened. "But please, I do not want to make us late." I gestured towards the corridor.

Rani gave me an apologetic pat on my shoulder, her arm still looped around mine, and together, we trooped to the evening meal.

7

ALTARA

We were the last to arrive at our assigned dining room. The long table was split into age groups, and we were in the eldest section, all of us almost legal adults. Eight other girls were standing around a long varnished, mahogany table with bunches of white frangipani and hibiscus flowers in pink, orange and red set beautifully in the middle.

As if we were sitting for a grand seven-course banquet, each place setting had a full set of goldware, a ceramic dinner plate, bread plate, soup bowl and wine glass.

I refrained from raising my brows as Pia took the seat to the left of the head of the table while Malika sat next to her. Rani disentangled herself from my arm, and I followed her to the spot she indicated to me.

"Newest students take this spot for the first dinner," she whispered as I stood opposite Pia. "After tonight you'll sit on my other side." She nodded to the seat next to her, and I suppressed an eye-roll. Status be damned, I was no longer a princess after all, and couldn't care less about where we sat. But what were we all waiting for?

I got my answer when another side door opened, and a beaming young woman, no older than thirty, swept in, green palm leaf–patterned saree whispering.

"Good evening, ladies!" she chimed.

We returned the greeting in unison, and the girls ended it with "Lady Trisana." She was an elegant woman who clearly placed high importance on the way she looked. Her curly hair was cleverly braided back from her face in a complex style that I'm sure took at least half an hour, her lips and cheeks tinted with a rose pink that brought out her high cheekbones and downplayed a large nose. Her saree was a bold forest green trimmed with yellow and finely embroidered with tropical flora.

She was breathtaking, and when she cast her dark eyes upon me, I smiled without thinking.

"Lady Zara, what a pleasure for us to be acquainted. Isn't that right, ladies?"

I looked around at them all, and they curiously looked me up and down, murmuring in what was likely to be feigned agreement.

I bopped a curtsey. "Thank you for having me, my lady. I am quite excited to be here."

She beamed. "Then let us sit. We have much to catch you up on."

Maids hurried in with dishes, followed by the hawk-eyed lady housekeeper. Trisana leaned conspiratorially towards me as they served us tiny parcels of savoury pastry. "The maids come here to train under the vigorous Housekeeper Yona so that they may one day work in a prosperous house and bring an income for their families."

"How ingenious," I said genuinely impressed. It was something my mother would have loved. Perhaps this was the Ellythian way because in Lobrathia, my mother had instated all sorts of programs to help the poorer citizens of Quartz, sending the children to school and providing contraceptive potions. My father's councillors had looked down upon it, and once she'd died, I'd been ashamed to see the programs revoked. Saraya and I had done our best to provide for the common folk, but there was only so much we could do without full access to the treasury and permission to act.

We ate the entree silently, although I noticed Lady Trisana and Housekeeper Yona watching me closely to, I was sure, assess my eating skills. Unfortunately for them, I had been trained by my mother and an etiquette mistress from childhood. I knew my manner was perfect, as appearing perfect was the only way I ever got to have any fun afterwards.

When they trusted you, they stopped watching you as much.

Once the entree was finished and the main meal was brought forward, a plate portioned into many sections that I would have to carefully poke my way through.

Lady Trisana spoke to the entire table: "Are our sarees all complete for tomorrow's meeting with the gentlemen?"

My heart leapt into my throat, and I looked up at Trisana with wide eyes. She had expected my inquiry because she immediately said, "We meet with the gentlemen every two weeks, so we can get to know them. Our latest project is hand stitching our own sarees to make for a talking point at the meeting."

"It's tomorrow?" I asked, trying to contain my excitement.

"Don't be nervous," she said, and oddly, she grimaced. "The gentlemen are...polite. I'm sure you will have something suitable to wear in any case, we can commence your saree at our next class."

Malika was grumbling into her flatbread, clearly annoyed about something. But next to her, Pia stared blankly at her curry, and next to me, Rani shifted uncomfortably. Perhaps they wanted to get married as much as I did, which was to say, not at all.

During dinner I was briefly introduced to the rest of the girls, all of whom were high-born. And I'm assuming because this was a supposed place of punishment, they all beheld me with mixtures of curiosity and suspicion but otherwise didn't seem like they would cause me trouble.

Which was good because as soon as I could manage, I was going to do something a little risky.

AFTER THE MAIDS HELPED US UNPIN OUR SAREES AND GET READY for bed, they turned all our quartz-lights off and left us to sleep. I waited, lying on my back in bed, listening to the sounds of the other girls breathing. They hadn't been particularly chatty after dinner, and if anything, they were rather tense. Rani sighed dramatically, Pia had a constant frown and Malika twitched every so often. I think it had more than to do with the gentlemen coming tomorrow, but *that* I would have to ponder in the morning. I, for one, was excited because I wanted to see what type of men Ellythian noblemen were.

It took all of an hour for the girls to get to a deep enough sleep that I could sneak out the door.

Once I was sure that Rani, who was on the bed next to me,

was breathing in the rhythmic manner of solid sleep, I allowed my magic to cloak myself, and fled the room as silently as I could. I took the opportunity to take note of the way the castle was active at night, and it looked like everyone else was still up. The maids were out, dusting, sweeping and chatting quietly, but like the girls in my room, they were nervous, stiff in their movements and low in their voices.

I noted their anxiety and moved on down a series of long corridors that led to a set of stairs into the entrance hall—

Where I stopped dead in my tracks before shifting back into the shadows.

Striding into the hall towards the gathered Headmistress Jessine and other teachers was a group of cloaked and hooded men. There were exactly ten of them, stalking into the hall as if they owned the castle, arrogance dripping from every step, every one of them with a muscled warrior's posture. Large hands, large feet...with the backs of their hands tattooed in symbols I recognised right away.

My breath seized in my throat.

Struck by a fear that had not come over me in four years, my magic surged. I scrambled to rein it in, violently forcing my power back under my skin, where it hovered ready for attack as I tried to calm myself.

Because these were not Ellythian men. These were not humans at all.

Symbols that had been carved upon my own skin against my will, and I would never, not in all of my days, forget every heinous curve of those *demonic symbols*.

Ten demons stood in the school entrance hall, and I knew it because my stepmother had taken me to one, in the dark of the night, as punishment for my rebellion after she'd arrived. She had called him *The Butcher*, and I had only been fourteen.

Bile rose up my throat, and my magic surged again, wanting to protect me, wanting me to fade into nothing so no demon could ever hurt me again. But I could not show my power here, not at all, so I clenched my teeth until they creaked.

I roped in my magic, tying it around my body, calming myself down loop by loop.

By all the Goddesses in the realm, what the fuck were demon males doing here?

They wore light plate armour under cloaks and were marked with a white shark's head. They were armed to the teeth, and the threat they created was obvious.

Blue skin that was slightly scaled, long black hair and bright yellow eyes. Fangs for teeth and a still, silent way about them. Their forms promised danger and lethal efficiency. These creatures had been created to kill.

Lady Trisana stood to the side, wringing her hands, and a woman I guessed was the Armsmistress, judging by the sword at her waist, stood protectively over her. Housekeeper Yona shuffled up to the headmistress, who to her credit, showed fear only in the slight trembling of her hands.

In those hands she held a lump of glowing clear quartz and presented it to the frontmost demon with a tiny bow. "This week's tithe, captain," she said so quietly I almost missed it.

Tithe.

The demon held out his massive hand and leaned forward to see him greedily take the glowing quartz and hand it to the demon behind him. The second demon put it inside a black cloth sack, and without a word, the group of demons turned and strode back out the door.

The teachers sagged with relief as the tension in the room

dissipated. It was only then that I uncurled my fingers, one at a time, from where they were clenched into fists.

Something wild and dark inside of me urged my legs to move.

That familiar over-muscled body, those giant, long-nailed, powerful hands and a memory in the back of my mind drew me in like a moth to flame. And because I am an incredibly stupid girl, I found my feet moving across the flagstones and right through the entrance doors after the demons.

If the headmistress and the four other women standing there noticed the patter of boots and a wind passing them, they did not show it.

As my boots crunched on the gravel behind the demons—who were making enough noise of their own to mask mine—my brain uncurled itself from its cold alarm and began to think. Pain had always made me think.

"*Tithe*," the headmistress had said. "*Daanav Kingdom*," everybody kept saying. Had I not heard of Daanav Kingdom because it was a demon kingdom? Perhaps that was why they demanded magic stored in quartz as a payment. It also had to do with Jessine's black quartz pendant—I just knew it. I shivered as I jogged into the night and down the main road after the demons.

They set a good pace, thundering down the dirt towards the town, and here in the dark jungle, it was a warm and humid night. Cicadas chirped loudly in the undergrowth, birds rustled above, and I grit my teeth against my fear. This is what I had wanted to see after all—the real Ellythia, what went on behind closed doors.

And apparently, they were dealing with demons.

It was an odd thing because in Lobrathia, these creatures

were relegated to myth and legend. They had not been seen above their subterranean realm for a century.

Except that one time my stepmother had shown me three of them.

I began to sweat, but thanks to a disciplined training by my own palace Armsmaster, I kept up easily, keeping a wise distance from them.

They slowed down when they reached the twins' house, and my heart thudded in a mad, haphazard beat as I crouched behind a palm tree.

Yellow quartz-lights glowed through the windows of the verandah as the demons trudged towards the Priestesses' house.

Just when I wondered if I could somehow warn them—warn Geravie that assailants were about to enter—green light shot upwards right where the demon captain had placed his foot. He jumped back, barking a curse. Magic tickled my nose and skin, and I gaped at the now visible green dome-shield around the twins' property.

I grinned in triumph, happy to see magical defences being used against the demons. The twins obviously knew how to keep safe in their house on the outskirts of the town—the shield probably protected them from animals and human men too.

The front door rattled as the demons angrily prowled about the shield, grumbling in low, gravelly voices.

Both twins appeared—Geravie had clearly been told to stay out of sight—and they stomped down the wooden stairs, each holding a glowing quartz in their hands.

"Pay the tithe!" one of the demons barked.

"We know!" one of the twins called, an edge to her voice.

"We've been paying it every Friday for the past two decades. *We know.*"

The demon gruffed, and I watched as the twins threw the glowing quartz crystals in a wide arc through the air, aiming for the demons. Two of them caught the crystals, and they shoved them into their collection bag.

Without a word the twins trudged back inside the house and slammed the door shut.

I let out a slow, relieved breath. I had imagined the demons storming into the house, breaking and hurting the three elderly ladies. But this....*transaction* held the energy of habit.

One of the twins had said *twenty years*. They'd been doing this every Friday.

When the demons took up their jog down the dirt road towards the town, I did not follow. I simply watched the dark shadow of them grow smaller and smaller.

I suddenly realised that with the leaving of the demons, I was now surrounded by a dense cloak of silence. Even the cicadas had stopped chirping.

Thunder boomed above me, and I threw myself to the ground, knife in hand, frowning up at the stars twinkling in a cloudless sky. The ground trembled and I gripped onto the palm tree behind me for dear life, squeezing my eyes shut as the entire world seemed to shake on its foundation.

The tremble receded and I shook my head in dismay as I hastily got to my feet, heart pounding in my ears. If these fell earthquakes were going to be a regular thing, I don't know if I could ever get used to it. But this odd-silence of the jungle had me shaky with what my Armsmaster called a 'warrior's twitch'.

I glanced back at the twins' house before turning on my

heel and running back the way I came in a solid and desperate sprint, still gripping my knife tightly.

I had to move. I had to shake the oozing, shifting sludge that had suddenly come over me.

In twenty years things had changed for the worse here and one thing stuck me like a castle-sized gong—the one significant thing that had happened twenty years ago was that my mother had left for Lobrathia.

8

ZALE

I heard the world first.

And it was hundreds of years older than when I'd heard it last. Palm trees shifted on the sea breeze, gulls squawked, and the song of the great Boneweaver Island chimed in my bones once again. My body rattled as my tomb shook on its foundation, the rumble vibrating through my body and waking up every muscle.

I opened my eyes. Hanging on the wall, I could see that directly opposite me, the stone door of my tomb had been opened, letting the cool night air brush my bare skin. Without warning, the spikes that had been hammered into my arms and legs retracted of their own accord.

I fell to the stone floor with a thud that should have been painful. Easing myself up, bones and muscles creaking from however long being held in one position, the wounds left by my bonds knitted themselves together. For the first time since I could remember, I was not in pain.

And it felt like ecstasy.

I stretched my body, easing out the kinks in my joints and tendons before striding out of my tomb.

A thousand stars greeted me from the midnight heavens, and I closed my eyes for one solitary moment of appreciation, savouring the fresh, night air of the jungle and rich soil beneath my bare feet. What a thing it was to be back.

The sea crashed in the distance, and it almost soothed the dark and empty spaces inside of me. Spaces that still screamed with the hate and anger for the events leading up to my imprisonment. But I was no stranger to such darkness. I had been born inside the eye of a storm, my cradle rocked by the crashing tide, and I always would feel that call of the great, tumultuous open. I had been weaned on chaos. I had been blooded on rage. And now I burned to make up for hundreds of years away from my kingdom.

But underneath that wild keening of the jungle was some-thing new and bright. I sucked in a breath as I felt it.

The crackling power that had awoken me.

I frowned, my eyes still closed, trying to gain purchase on it, but something shifted next to me, and my eyes flew open. Of course, my tomb was in the centre of the tombs of my brothers-in-arms and now my imprisonment was over, so was theirs.

Atax strode out of the tomb from my left, cracking his neck, his powerful form perfectly preserved and not an inch less than when I'd last seen him. He was also naked as the day he'd been born, just as I was. He saw me, and the cold expression on his face smoothed into relief. He looked up at the sky and grinned.

To our right came the thud of heavy feet stomping out the third tomb, and Raen appeared, rubbing the scruff on his face.

He nodded at us then frowned at our surroundings as if he were trying to remember what had happened *before*.

From the final tomb, to Raen's right, Kai came bounding out, pushing his unruly white hair off his face, beaming like the mad warrior he was.

Perhaps all of us were a little madder than before.

My warriors gathered around me, flexing their powerful bodies, testing their strength after so long sleeping in their own torturous positions. Atax slapped me on the shoulder. Kai grinned wolfishly, stretching his arms above his head.

Dear Goddess, I had missed them.

"My king." Raen, his blue eyes ever serious, swept down on one knee before me. "You know we live to serve you and House Boneweaver."

I frowned at him. "And you know I will not have you on your knees before me."

He stood up with a smile as the others swiftly bent on their knees, crossed a fist over their hearts and stood back up again, pledging themselves to me. To our revenge.

"Well?" Kai said, rubbing his hands together, as if ready to plan a war. "Are we going to find who woke us up?"

The centre of my chest burned, as it sometimes did, and I rubbed at it absently. All three pairs of blue eyes were drawn towards my heart.

I growled. "It's of no concern to me who released us. We're going to take my empire back." By all rights I owned two kingdoms, and that made me an emperor, did it not? Still I needed to reclaim them before deciding on titles. Leading my brothers forward, we passed the Temple of the Goddess Agnolthi. My own mother had been High Witch of the Order of Yasani, and a pang in my gut made me frown. If she was still alive, I needed to find her and rescue her from my father. But the land was different; I could feel it in the very soil beneath my bare feet. I wondered exactly how much time had passed. And if it was as long as I suspected, everyone we knew would likely be dead.

Twenty feet from Yasani Temple lay a building which had not been there in my time. Previously, it had been the abode of the witches who cared for the temple under my mother. Now there was a wooden house, built on stilts, which looked weathered with time. A dark, hateful feeling stirred in me as I climbed the back steps up to the house and banged on the door so hard it splintered beneath my fist.

Whispers sounded on the inside, and I scented three females—elderly and human. I stepped back, not wanting to frighten them into a heart attack.

Dead witches were useless witches.

The door creaked open, soft green magic lining the edges. Light spilled onto the step before me, and I cocked my head as the three tiny, elderly witches stood before me. Two of them bore the sign of Agnolthi, and it gave me as much happiness as I was physically capable of feeling. My mother had borne the black crescent moon of her order every day of her life.

The smell of their fear was sharp and enticing in the air. I inclined my head. "I am Ashzale Boneweaver. Me and my brothers are awake."

The three women stared at me for a full moment before curtseying low. "Your Majesty," they all murmured.

They might not recognise me, but they knew a Boneweaver when they saw one, I supposed. We had never really looked human, after all.

"How long have my brothers and I been asleep?" I asked.

The twins exchanged a look. "Two hundred years," said one.

I glanced at my brothers. So I had been right—everyone we knew *was* gone. I took exactly three seconds to mourn our dead and the fact that we had outlived everyone. Turning back towards the light of the house, I ordered, "Tell me all that has happened here since then. I need to know everything."

AN HOUR LATER, MY BROTHERS AND I LEFT THE WITCHES' ABODE and headed into the arms of the night jungle. But here I paused, for in the dark, something stirred.

Shadows bound in bark and palm and shell crept forward, shuffling towards me and bowing low at my feet. *My king,* they whispered. *We are here to serve.*

I reached down and picked up the smallest of them. He was made of the scraps of shells bound together by darkness with spindly arms and legs and a rounded shell for a hat. While smaller creatures scuttled around my feet, much larger, hulking shadows lurked towards the back. Big enough to wrestle a grown man to the ground.

"It seems we're not the only monsters that woke up," Raen murmured, delighted.

As I looked upon the dark creatures emerging out of the shadows of the island and bowing before me, a slow, vicious smile spread across my lips. I craved for blood on my hands and, by all the Gods, I would have it.

9

ALTARA

Just before the sun rose the next morning, a sweet chime rang out through the room. Rani let out a loud yawn followed by a long, suffering sigh from Malika. I had successfully crept back into our shared room after a long, sweaty, frantic run back from the twins' house.

I couldn't let anyone know I'd been out and about, let alone snooping on the teacher's activities in the night. But the teachers themselves had not behaved as if the tithe were a secret, hidden thing. In fact, it was more likely that everyone knew about this except me. I just had to find a way to ask about it discreetly.

Making a great show of dragging herself out of bed, Rani grumbled her way into getting dressed as the other girls quietly did the same. I followed suit, trying on my new uniform. It fitted perfectly, though was a little tight around my breasts. The pants were stretchy and cooling, and the shiny leather boots Gally had obtained for me needed to be broken in.

"We do our physical training in the coolest part of the

morning," explained Malika, as we strode out the door at the next chime of the quartz bell, which lifted up and gave itself a shake whenever the teachers bade it to. "We run to warm up our muscles and then we do combat training followed by—" her eyes darted to my white sash "—magical combat every other day."

"Very good," I said smoothly.

In truth I was excited to see all of this and take my mind off the disturbing things I'd seen last night. I was half wondering whether I should just pretend it hadn't happened.

Back in Lobrathia, while my sister and I both trained swords and grappling with our Armsmaster, we'd often then separate in our training. While she'd go off with my mother and the city midwives, I'd spend a lot of time with my father and his captains down in the palace training grounds. My mother had not always had the stomach to see me using my magic on the sick or injured, but my father had always held my hand while I practised with an unconscious patient, often saving their life. After we'd visit the army infirmary, we'd go riding, and I would practise archery on the back of Harriet, the mare I'd favoured. "Lightning never misses its mark," father would say proudly. I'd always hit every shot I'd been asked to. Moving or stationary. I think it was a part of my type of magic, but when there was a bow in my hands, I became the weapon, became the arrow, and shot myself through the air. It was exhilarating, like flying, and my father would cackle and look upon me proudly whenever the soldiers would gape at my ability.

I hoped my father was alright. And was it too much to hope that someone had accidentally pushed my stepmother down one of the many staircases in Quartz palace?

We followed the steady flow of girls surging towards the

front of the castle where we began our jog as the jungle began to wake up. Birds gave mighty calls from somewhere inside the dense foliage, and a spectacular steam floated out of the canopy, twisting and coiling into the sky. I marvelled at the view, jogging between Rani and Pia, who were glancing at me periodically as if confused. It wasn't until we were halfway around the castle's perimeter that I realised with a jolt what I'd done wrong.

I was supposed to be playing the part of sickly noble girl. Swearing inwardly, I made a show of gasping and tapped Pia on the arm, gesturing for them to go forward. I moved to the outer edge of the runners and slowed down, falling past the younger girls and right to the back of the group. Deciding it was best that I slow to a complete walk, I meandered behind everyone, a little annoyed I'd have to play weak for the entirety of my stay here. Surveying the castle grounds, I wondered if they kept messenger pigeons here like we had on the mainland. It was how all the royal houses communicated if we didn't send a messenger on horseback. But it would look very suspicious if I asked for one that knew the way to Quartz, and that was exactly the type of thing I wanted to avoid. I'd have to ask Geravie if she and the twins could organise it. I was worried about my father and Saraya, both. But Saraya was free of our stepmother now, whereas my father was not.

I sighed deeply before being startled by a deep female shout. "Ho, there, my lady!"

My hand reached for my hidden boot dagger, but I stopped myself just in time as I whirled around. A woman in her late thirties, muscular, with her hair braided back in a style that looked like it was woven to her crown was jogging over to me, one hand on the hilt of a mighty broadsword.

"Oh, hello," I said breathlessly.

"I'm Armsmistress Vari." She gave me a swift bow and cast a stern brown-eyed gaze over me. "Her highness told me you were lagging behind."

My instinct was to quip back a retort, but I'd have to suppress that urge while I was here. So instead, I nodded sombrely. "I've spent most of my life unwell, Armsmistress. I'm not so great at physical activity, although my father tells me I'm an excellent shot."

"Hm."

I shifted under her penetrating gaze as I saw her note the muscle in my arms and shoulders. I clenched my hands as if I could stop her from seeing the range of calluses I had arcing over my palms and fingers. I had been training since I was a child, and it was hard to mask that from someone like Armsmistress Vari. So I tried to clarify my story by embellishing it with the truth.

"Archery was one of the only ways my father and I spent time together," I said, holding up my hands. "I couldn't practice long before I felt unwell, of course, but I did what I could."

"And what type of illness was it?"

My mind scrambled for an answer. "Female in origin." I waved vaguely to my abdomen and coughed as if I were uncomfortable. But Vari seemed satisfied with this, at least for the moment.

"Come on then," she said, leading me into the training block at the back of the palace. "You can watch the other girls until we split up for specialised skills."

The training field was an expansive field of soft grass, well maintained, probably by magic, by the faint glittering under the dawn sun. The girls were split into age and skill groups, supervised by the other teachers, including Lady Trisana, who beamed at us as we approached. Shyly, she tucked a lock of dark hair behind her ear as Vari went up to her. Surprised, I looked between the both of them and felt, rather than saw, a faint lustful energy. Vari grinned at Trisana, and the beautiful woman in turn nodded at me.

"I see you've met my wife, Zara," she said smoothly. "I warn you she is a harsh taskmaster."

I smiled delightedly at her, and it was genuine. "I'll try my utmost, my lady."

Sitting to the side, I watched the senior girls pair off and take up their weapons. The Ellythian swords were finely made with intricate designs along the steel and quartz along the hilt. We had, of course, no such thing in Lobrathia, as quartz over there was only used for light and decoration. But *here* the quartz lit up even during the day. If I hadn't seen the pink quartz bell glinting with magic when it was being used, I might not have believed it.

Pia and Malika were paired, and with grins on both flushed faces, they engaged in a playful bout of steel against steel. Never having seen Ellythians fight before, I watched carefully, looking for the differences in our training.

Jerali Jones had taught me a straight-laced, simple style of swordplay. It was cutthroat and direct with very little pomp and embellishment, much like the Armsmaster who'd taught me.

But the Ellythians fought as if they danced. As if their thrusts and parries were a story they yearned to tell through physical movement. I drank it all in, watching as Pia smiled, spun and flicked her weapon, as if she savoured every movement. It brought back vague memories of when my mother joined us in the training ring, and Jerali Jones' sparkling gaze of appreciation as my mother fought with just as much vigour and flair.

I put my hand over my gold lotus anklet and patted it as if I could communicate with Saraya, who'd had a matching one, and smiled sadly. As a child I'd hoped that one day I could visit here with my mother, and she would finally tell me stories of her youth.

But it was not to be.

"Lady Zara!" Armsmistress Vari was jogging past me, gesturing towards the right of the field where I saw a shooting range made of rounded bales of hay, painted with target markings.

Flexing my fingers and taking out my wrist guards from my pocket, I nodded at her, leaving my seat under a palm to make my way over to the wheeled rack of weapons.

There were spears, crossbows and long and oddly shaped bows in what I think was the Ellythian style. In Lobrathia we only ever used crossbows and longbows—these asymmetrical, shorter-at-the-bottom-and-longer-at-the-top ones were very foreign to me, and I wondered at the balance of a weapon like that in my hands.

These bows were made of bamboo, as far as I could tell, rather than the Lobrathian birch I was used to.

So naturally, I took the new one and strung it with one of the coils of string set to the side. The wood was marked with traditional Ellythian symbols—birds, lotuses and decorative swirls. They were likely to mean good and swift luck. I had similar markings on my long bow at home, though they were lightning bolts in the tradition of the Lobrathian lighting kings who had loosed arrows made of lethal energy. I envied that sort of ancient power, but it mattered not. I had the skill to make up for it.

Vari set me up on the far side of the field, as some of the other girls joined us. I took an arrow from the quiver on the stand by my feet—light and fletched with grey feathers—and aimed. Choosing a spot well away from the red centre marker, I assessed my own form, quickly deciding that I wouldn't pretend I was completely hopeless. I needed *some* good reputation after all. Vari was keenly watching me and made an approving sound in the back of her throat. I suppressed a smirk and loosed the arrow, hitting my mark accurately—some inches away from the centre—as I intended. Vari whistled in sympathy.

"Try again, Zara. Your form was good."

I nodded. "I've not used this type of bow before," I admitted. "It was only longbows for us."

She nodded understandably. "These are yumara bows, made for horseback assaults. A group of archers on horseback can subdue an enemy within minutes with these bows. They have good range and are well balanced for straight shots on horseback."

I looked at the bow with renewed interest. *Enemy.* The only enemy here were the demons I'd seen last night and I imagined my target to be their wretched yellow and red-slitted eyes. I continued on to shoot for the next half an hour, making sure to miss the red inner circle a majority of the time, straying close on occasion. I tried my hand at the crossbow and longbow and found my handling of them quickly. I didn't bother with the spear because it would require too much physical performance on my supposedly sickly body.

"We practice magical warfare every second day," Vari said

to me as we prepared to leave. "You might want to sit that one out with Pia tomorrow—"she nodded to my white sash "—as the girls get quite competitive. I keep a controlled environment, but it can get…rough, eh, Malika?"

I raised my brows, glancing at Malika who looked very happy with herself. My eyes flicked down to her red sash, and I realised that likely meant her breed of magic was best at an assault. The fact that Pia sat the training out was a little odd, though perhaps they didn't want to risk of safety of the second in line to the throne. But I had been very much wanting to see this aspect of Ellythia's military style, and I doubted I'd get the opportunity anywhere else. "Is there no way I can get a peek, Armsmistress?" I pleaded. "I've never seen anything like it before."

"Absolutely not," Trisana said from behind us. "If you have no magic to protect you, Zara, I'm afraid it would be far too risky."

Frowning, I followed Rani, Pia and Malika as we trekked back to the castle. A sudden tension had come over the group of older girls, and they cast each other baleful looks.

But I was quickly distracted by Rani.

"You did well there, Zara," she said happily. "A great shot, if I do say so myself."

Pia cast me a half smile that I'm sure was meant to be encouraging, but Malika, seemingly the honest one of the group, raised her brows at me and didn't say anything. I smiled at Rani, knowing full well that this girl was possibly the nicest I'd ever met.

"What time do the suitors get here?" I asked.

"They arrive at dusk," said Malika, sighing. "Which is not far away enough if you ask me."

I chuckled, as no doubt Malika preferred a lot of time to get ready. So we had the entire rest of the day. Excitement poured through me like spiced wine, because tonight, I'd get to assess the Ellythian men.

W e returned to our dormitory to prepare for the arrival of the noble's sons.

I was a little more tired than usual as I'd spent most of the night tossing myself this way and that, unsettled about what I'd seen.

But my attention was promptly deferred to Gally, who was practically frantic about dressing me in the green and pink saree Lady Trisane had loaned to me.

It took hours to complete the various beautification processes. Our faces were threaded to remove every bit of hair except our eyebrows and eyelashes, a process that was at once fascinating and painful. We were washed and scrubbed and moisturised with creams. I watched the others get preened and dressed and made-up to be the best versions of themselves as Gally fussed over me to try and do the same.

For the most part, the girls spoke of the young men as business prospects. I learned that it was tradition that women inherited land titles in Ellythia, given it had been a matriarchy since the Priestess Ellythia had saved the land from demons when they'd first come ashore. The men the girls would marry would come to live with *them*. It was a refreshing change from the Lobrathian laws I'd grown up with but also no surprise to me, given my mother's lectures on the benefits of a matriarchy.

Pia and Malika performed as veterans do—no nonsense and directed their maids expertly. Rani, on the other hand, huffed and puffed, rolled her eyes and hunched when her saree got pinned and tucked around her.

Malika snapped at her. "You do this *every* time, Rani! This is your future we're talking about! I don't care if you marry that girl you have back at home, but you still need the seed of a male to give you children. Whomever you choose to marry will be by both your sides when you take over your family's business!"

I had been interested to know that not only was Rani already engaged to a woman back on her lands on Ellythian's central island, Tiger Island, but her family ran the biggest silk farm in all the isles. While Ellythian women readily married each other, wealthy families still needed a male coupling to bear children. Rani, therefore, would have both a wife and a husband, with her as the heir and leader to the family business. But Rani mournfully tugged at curly lock of hair. "What if I don't want to have children with one of those sea snakes! This is the worst thing. Truly, Malika, I wish you could see how awful it is for me. You might have accepted your fate to marry one of these *creatures*, but I have not. Not to mention that I always look horrendous at these things!"

Ladies and maids gasped as one, shushing her and cooing over her lovely saffron-coloured saree as Rani covered her face with her hands. I had to control myself to stop from laughing at her calling men "creatures." It was true, often enough, but one part of her tirade was nonsense.

"Now, you listen here, Rani," I demanded in a stern voice. Everyone in the room turned to stare at me, and Rani lifted her face, now wet with tears. I pulled out my floral handkerchief, stomped up towards her and grabbed her face, dabbing delicately at her cheeks. "You are a kind and lovely young woman. Any man out there should consider himself lucky that you would consider him to partner with you and your lady." She gaped at me, but it was more at my stern tone. "Now let me see about your hair because it deserves our utmost respect."

I shooed her maid away and worked with her hair, so much like my mother's and sister's that it felt familiar and easy for me and almost comforting to handle. How many years had I spent playing with Saraya's hair in our spare time, trying out different hairstyles and making our maids watch us parade about?

"Now, I don't know about what is fashionable around here," I murmured, "but it will be beautiful regardless because it's yours." And, I thought wryly, I know what men like best. Not that it mattered too much because her family's wealth would attract every manner of man available.

I went for a half-up, half-down look, taking the offered pins and carefully creating a marvel of a piece. She looked like she had a flower at the back of her head, her curls filling out the edges, making it look effortlessly stunning.

"See?" I said, once I was finished. "I barely had to do anything at all."

Rani turned her head this way and that, and Malika even wandered over to take a look. She made a surprised sound at the back of her throat. "It actually looks nice, Rani," Malika declared finally.

Rani beamed at me, lifting a hand to touch it.

"No touching, Lady Rani," I said sternly.

Her cheeks turned pink, and she nodded obediently, her gangly frame expanding and falling as she took a relived breath. "I can do this."

I placed my hands on her shoulders and smiled at her in the mirror. "I know you can."

Turning away I found that Pia had been observing me the entire time as her maid worked on arranging her hair. Her eyes shifted from me to Rani, and seeing the tall girl's bright face, nodded at me. I nodded back.

Perhaps because I could feel the giddy, excited energy now surrounding us, I practically glowed as we departed our dormitory and followed the long line of older girls, dressed in their finest, down to the entrance hall.

Rani and Malika led me to a spot in the group furthest from the door where we would get a good view of the men arriving. Rani seemed to chatter when she was nervous because she was vigorously giving out compliments to our neighbours.

"Did you make that bracelet, Yarni? My, what craftsmanship! Oh, that rouge really does suit you Hamsa, young Lord Gazzan will simply fall over!"

Malika, on the other hand, stood stone cold and silent like an iceberg in winter, glancing down her nose at the others as if assessing her competition. Except she also tapped her slippered foot over and over again on the flagstones. I felt her nervousness bubbling off her being like a hive of bees, but her face was set in determination.

Pia left us to take a seat with Lady Trisana and her Armsmistress wife to the side.

Malika caught me looking. "Pia was already betrothed from birth," she whispered. "She must play the role of imperious princess, looking down upon the other males."

Male voices sounded on the other side of the entrance hall doors, and the girls tittered where they stood. Someone giggled nervously.

But my brows flew up at this news about Pia. I whispered to her. "Will he be coming too?"

"No," she looked at me incredulously. "That's why she was exiled here like the rest of us? Because she would not leave him after he was permanently injured and is bed-bound. Despite all of it, she remains loyal to him like the honourable woman she is. She is defying the queen's royal order; that is why she is here."

Exiled. Pia had been exiled for choosing to stay with her betrothed. My heart warmed and swelled just a little with pride. I barely knew the girl, but she was family, and the thought that she held integrity and a little rebellious streak made me happy. My mother's people were good and kind. But still, a bed-bound man would not do as consort to a future queen. "I mean, she could take another husband? In the same way Rani is taking both a husband and a wife?"

Malika tossed her intricate braid studded with jasmine flowers over her shoulder. "Maybe. A king of Ellythia is only ornamental, of course. Another man might be needed to give her children."

I refrained from showing my glee. That implied the queen was allowed to have multiple lovers, and this was widely approved of? Expected, perhaps? What a dream to be queen in Ellythia!

83

The headmistress strode into the hall, wringing her hands, heeled boots clicking under her simple navy saree. I narrowed my vision upon her, that black quartz still glinting at her neck. I'd never been exposed to magic at this level, but there was nothing normal about that shadow-clad piece of jewellery, and it made me wonder at what the Ellythians thought about black magic.

Pia and the other teachers followed her to take up formal positions by the door. It vaguely reminded me of when the fae came to take my sister from our Quartz palace. We'd all waited like this, nervous and agitated, ready for the group of monsters about to enter our home.

Except we were just waiting for the sons of Ellythian nobles, not the enemy. Everyone needed to calm down.

The quartz-lights lit up around the room as dusk set in, purpling the sky I could see out of the moon-shaped glass above the entrance doors.

A resounding knock sounded on the wood, and every woman in the hall stilled. A servant hurried to the doors, the headmistress a step behind her. Pia stood regally with her hands in front of her, a purple saree clinging to her curved form, the picture of a well-trained warrior princess. Saraya would like her, I thought. They were much the same in the way they enjoyed swordplay. Perhaps one day they would get to meet, if all things went well in the Fae Realm.

The door was pulled open and a stream of young tall Ellythian noblemen strode in, pulling their hoods off their heads. Their cloaks were magical; I could tell by the way my own magic reared its head. But I wasn't interested in their magic at just this minute. I was rather excited to get my first look at any potential participants for my preferred heinous time-passing activities.

They strode in, accepting the offered wine from the maids, casting their dark eyes around the entrance hall—looking for familiar faces, I supposed.

"How does this work?" I asked Rani, who was standing there glumly. "There are less of us than there are men?"

She nodded glumly. "Slightly more men. We'll mingle for a while and then head outside for a chaperoned walk."

"At this hour?" I asked with surprise as groups of the young men began to split up and approached the ladies.

Rani looked at me and her face was covered in confusion. "It's the only time they can come to see us. And just in the palace grounds. The luminescent parts of the forest are quite lovely at night. You'll love them, Zara."

"How romantic," I said wryly, imagining quite the tableau in my head—a man and woman, their clothes in a tumble around them, making love under the full moon surrounded by glowing flowers of all colours. We didn't have any in Lobrathia, and now I was positively desperate to see it. To try it out, perhaps.

"Lady Rani, Lady Malika," came a deep voice. "You both look lovely today."

We turned to see three men had approached us from the side, and us three ladies gave swift curtsies. The men bowed in return. All three were tall, strapping young men with smooth dark skin and the crisp sloping jawline the Ellythian men seem to have in spades. The leader of the group, the handsomest, with a lovely seashell embroidered tunic, white shirt and a shark's tooth around his neck, was staring openly at me. He was tall, in his early twenties and shaped like a warrior. I realised I was already clenching my thighs.

Not wanting to give my hand away too soon, I took him in with an imperious smile. Oddly, under the quartz-light, the

85

cloaks of all three men were rather old with the shimmer of protective magic coating them like paint. Heirlooms, perhaps? They stood out against the finery of their clothes. I'd have to ask Rani about it later.

Malika, clearly wanting to impress the leader, took me by the elbow, and her voice took on a low, seductive depth. "My Lord Fangar, this is Lady Zara of Harranpul House. She joined us only yesterday. She has been ill all of her childhood."

The young lords shifted in surprise, at my advantageous house name or perhaps Malika's effort to dissuade them from me with her last sentence. They'd be looking for robust women, of course.

I graciously offered him my hand and said breezily, "I am quite well at the moment, Lord Fangar."

Fangar gave me a handsome smile I approved of and took my hand. The moment his bare skin made contact with mine, a tingle shot up my arm, and my magic surged up in surprise. I shoved it back down before it could reveal itself to those surrounding me as Fangar brushed his lips against my skin. Once he let me go, I hid my surprise, wondering why my magic was responding to him. Then again I had never touched a man with magic before. No doubt it was my lustful energy combining with his.

Nevertheless, I refrained from rubbing the sensation out of my hand and smiled prettily as Fangar licked his lips.

"Shall we, my lady?" he asked, holding out his arm.

Malika hissed so softly I thought I was the only one who'd heard it, standing so close to her. But I ignored her and stepped forward, taking his arm happily. For some reason Rani tried to grab my hand.

"Malika," she whispered when I moved out of her reach, "I don't think Zara knows about—"

But her whispers got lost in the moment as the other two lordlings offered themselves up as companions. Rani was scowling now, but Malika was ignoring the other girl and batting her eyelashes at her own Ellythian lordling.

Lady Trisana and Armsmistress Vari were now leading the couples out of the hall into the night and towards the luminescent gardens. A few discontented men remained behind while the Headmistress placated them, twirling her black quartz necklace in her fingers and asking them about their families. One of the men even angrily pushed another, but I was swept outside before I could see what the issue was.

As I walked into the warm night with Fangar, for some odd reason, I found that I was now sweating—a tiny bead of moisture slipping down my spine. Perhaps I was losing my touch, although I certainly did not feel nervous. There was an undercurrent of heaviness in the air. It could have been the humidity of the Ellythian summer or the excitement of the night.

But as the ladies giggled into their handkerchiefs and the lordlings chuckled, I could not but help notice that the sounds of jungle, usually ever present, day or night—the shuffling of creatures, the orchestra of the cicadas and other insects—were all missing, and it struck me like a song abruptly falling silent. I shivered a little, holding on more tightly to Lord Fangar, peering into the quiet of the dark jungle as we followed the teachers down the pebbled path.

It was as if jungle were waiting for something.

11

ALTARA

Fangar walked with the swagger of a warrior. He was arrogant but sharp—I knew that just by his mannerisms and the way he was constantly assessing the environment. I looked up at him, and his handsome face smiled back down at me, clear under the nearly-full moon. Perhaps if I gave the appearance of a naive country girl, he would be a good candidate to answer my questions about the demons from last night. But I didn't even have to glance behind us to hear Rani talking loudly about silkworms and their life cycles or Malika about the merits of underground irrigation systems, as if she were selling her family's land in her stead. I needed more space….more privacy.

I gave Fangar's arm a tiny squeeze and purred, "My lord?"

He looked down at me, but not before his eyes flicked down to my breasts—which I'd had Gally cleverly arrange so that while it looked demure from a front, a taller person would get an eyeful. A hungry look flashed over his face before it was gone. His voice was quiet and deep when he answered, "Yes?"

If I were being honest with myself, this Ellythian lordling was not a good candidate for any sort of dalliance in the shadows. He was high ranking, by his haughty manner and the fact that Malika wanted him, and that made it risky. I'd much prefer a village boy who I could boss around. Noblemen tended to want to take the lead on everything, which was always cumbersome when half of them didn't know what they were doing. I had trained my companions in Lobrathia well and had gotten spoiled for it.

Tonight I didn't think I had much choice. A kiss or three couldn't hurt *that* much? So, I looked around pointedly and said, "Is there not somewhere more private, my lord? I have a question I need to ask of you."

Fangar's brows shot up with interest, and that hungry look flashed over his features again. I decided then and there he was not a good match for Malika anyway. I would have to warn her against him if he was *this* easily swayed by a new woman.

I watched him look around at the other couples as we headed behind the castle, and the first of the luminescent flowers peeked through the jungle.

"Aw, how wondrous!" I gestured to the glowing pink orchids to the side of the path. I made sure to make my voice as loud as I could without being improper. "Let me have a closer look, my lord! Oh, orchids are my favourite!"

He was easily led off the path and onto the grass where I made a show of pointing and cooing at the glowing flora. The other couples passed us by as planned, allowing us to linger at the back of the group when we stepped back on the path.

Fangar ran a hand through his short, coal-black hair. "Have you seen the famous fae lagoon, my lady?" His voice had turned husky and excitement fluttered up in my belly.

"Oh, I would love to see it!" I said breathlessly.

Goddess, I loved this game. I could just about forget that I actually needed to ask him about the demons. But the thrill of the moment overtook me, and he grabbed me by my hand. We both looked left and right for anyone watching us and found the immediate area devoid of anyone at all. Grinning like children, Fangar led me at a run down a tiny, adjoining path right into the jungle.

We jogged in a frenzied, breathless hurry, my excitement bubbling over despite the darkness and the risk. Or perhaps because of the risk, I didn't know.

Fangar slowed as we veered down another path and blue light shone in the distance. I let out a delighted giggle as we rounded a corner to a clearing filled with pleasant, soft-blue light. We must have been closer to the beach than I thought because ocean waves crashed in the distance and to my utter delight, a glowing blue lagoon illuminated a spacious clearing. It was enclosed on three sides by the jungle, luminescent flowers of every colour dotting the bank.

"Here we are," Fangar said, crouching down to skim his fingers along the surface of the glowing water. He looked up and grinned at me with white, square teeth.

"What makes it a *fae* lagoon, exactly?" I asked.

The lordling proceeded to sit on the grass and gestured to the spot next to him. "You don't know?" He smiled at me, but it was more of a baring of his teeth. "What kind of Ellythian are you?"

My heart stuttered in my chest. These kinds of giveaways

were dangerous for me. So I distracted him by making unabashed eye contact and sashaying towards him. He watched me as I sat next on the grass as close to him as was possible. "I'm the best kind of Ellythian," I said coyly, shrugging a shoulder and adjusting my skirts for no good reason other than to draw his attention to my legs.

He shuffled closer to me, and I looked at him from beneath my eyelashes, the moving light from the lagoon creating pretty patterns on his face. I decided I needed to make the first move and leaned in to touch the shark's tooth necklace he wore around his throat. He hissed and grabbed my hand, ducking down to roughly crush his lips against mine. So he had the finesse of a barbarian—no matter. I tried to redirect him by sighing against his mouth and pressing myself closer. He tasted like salt and sea, and his tongue was wild and hungry inside my mouth.

Aha, my first Ellythian kiss! But my magic was coiling upwards again, demanding I pay attention. I willed it into submission, even as sweat began beading on my neck and back again. Frowning as Fangar put his large hands around my waist. I braced my own hands against his shoulders to make sure I had some control. If he got *too* excited, I had easy access to the knives in my hidden calf sheaths. I'd hastily strapped them on while Gally had her back turned, feeling as if my outfit were not complete without them.

My magic roared at me, and I pulled my face away from Fangar. My vision was blurry, and I blinked rapidly to clear my sight. Fangar's face came into view, only it was lined with navy tattoo–like patterns. I blinked, and they were gone before I could decipher them, leaving his face was clear once again.

This was clearly some sort of Ellythian male custom I was unaware of, but before I could ask, Fangar made a sound of dissatisfaction, put a large hand around the back of my neck and pulled me back towards him, crushing his lips against mine and aggressively shoving his tongue in my mouth. I allowed it, if only out of interest, because my magic was currently trying to explode outwards. Concentrating on my struggle to wrangle it down, I heard it too late.

Sticks crunched as purposeful, and solid steps burst into the clearing. Fangar jumped away from me as if he'd been bitten by something, kicking up dirt everywhere as he scrambled to his feet on the bank.

I, however, refrained from being an ass and remained where I was, turning to look at the intruders and opening my mouth, ready to give an excuse to whichever teacher had come searching for us.

I promptly shut it.

Standing there, next to the lagoon with murderous expressions, were four of the fiercest-looking warriors I'd ever seen. Magic tingled on my skin and the air around me as I registered that these people could not be human. The only clothing they all wore were dark pants, so I could see that their heavily muscled, tattooed skin was as dark a brown as the native Ellythians. The difference was that their eyes were the clear and bright blue of the fae pond they stood before. Three of them had black-as-night hair, long and loose down to their shoulders, and the fourth had hair as white as a frangipani— as if all the pigment had been stripped from it. This young man was grinning manically as if this were all very funny, but the others all had their predatory eyes trained on Fangar as if they were measuring him for his grave. Possibly the worst part of it was the fact that two of them gripped severed demon heads by their black, stringy hair. The same blue-skinned demons I recognised from last night.

The man at the centre of the group drew my eye. He was the tallest of them, with the arrogant posture and bearing of nobility. A preternaturally handsome face, all hard masculine planes—as if designed and hewn by the Goddess herself. He reminded me of the fae that had taken my sister away, only rougher, wilder, *darker*. He wore a dangling earring in the shape of a miniature sword on one ear, and the shadows around us seemed to deepen at my periphery as I unabashedly stared at him.

I had never seen a man like him before, and I could hardly blame myself for the wanton heat of desire flaring within my core. And—mother curse me—a tiny, rebellious part of me wondered what it would be like to be on top of a man like that, grinding my hips against what I knew would be a considerable-sized manhood. It would be a wild and relentless sex, the type that made you dizzy, thinking about it for weeks afterward, reliving it again and again in your mind.

A tiny movement in the angle of the leader's head brought me out of my wanton thoughts. His blue eyes threatened to dagger me to the spot, but alas, I also had daggers on my person, and I was *not* going to be intimidated. Being through what I had, nothing *truly* scared me anymore.

However, it was four against two, and the danger was as clear and obvious to me as if there were a pride of lions standing before us.

But some sort of insanity had struck Fangar because he fell to his knees and said as if he didn't quite believe it himself, "By the Reaper! Your Majesty?"

I stared at Fangar in confusion and then back at the four males.

The one standing in the centre, the leader, leaned forward, and with a very inhuman, feral look in his blue eyes, hissed with a primordial dominance that would not be denied. *"Run."*

12

ZALE

As I lunged to give chase to the Daanav scum and the human woman, Raen and Atax leapt upon me with their full body weight, wrestling me back into the dark of the jungle. Kai hooted with amusement, the demon head in his grip jangling back and forth as he picked up the one Atax had dropped.

The snarl I gave them was purely bestial, but Raen put his face right up against mine and snarled at me back.

"This is *my* land," I growled back at him, my voice taking on the feral growl that only came through when I was about to lose control. "Let me tear his fucking head off."

"You're feral, brother," Raen cautioned. "Let us think for a moment." Both my brothers had grips of steel and remained unchallenged back when we roamed freely in my father's time. Even so they sweated and strained to hold me back as I tried to wrest free of them.

The reason in his voice only served to make me angrier. "Who the fuck do they think they are? That they could soil my lands. *My fucking lands*, Raen? My fucking *women*?"

"I say we kill them," Kai called from the side, taking off two of his earrings where they lit up and enlarged to form his full-sized black skull obsidian blades. "I'll bring you their eyeballs, brother."

I grunted in approval, but I also realised then that Atax and Raen, with their fingers digging into my arms, were not going to let me go.

"Our women," Atax mused, his handsome face cracking into a smile, blue eyes glowing. "That was not one of *our* women. The witches said no Old Ones remain, remember? She was Ellythian. A half of one at that."

That realisation made me go still. Her scent had been sweet and alluring, like the night flowering jasmine, and yet a crackling lay hidden within it, like the sea before a storm, charged like clouds ready to give light that stung. This was troubling. Not for years had I scented one of the Beejli Sorcerers. What one was doing here was beyond me. But much had happened since we'd been trapped in our tomb of nightmares.

"We need a plan," Atax grumbled into the night, his skin gleaming under the moonlight. "Raen is right. There's what? fifteen of the Daanavs in that castle from their scent? We made an example of the tithe collecting demons already. That one—" he jerked his chin towards the clearing where the couple had been "—recognised you. They still see you as their leader. We can bring them into submission."

"Let us remind them who is their king," Raen said firmly. "The Daanavs will be sure to submit."

"I need a Vayashi," I grumbled, shaking myself. Only the thought of a woman to empty my power into—to take the edge off my colossal magic would serve to calm me down. I'd had a dozen such women dedicated to me back when I was prince in my father's court of beasts. Without tempering my power, I was likely to run rabid within days. Jerking off only relieved me so much.

But this woman from the fae lagoon. If I could subdue her, she would be a good contender for Vayashi for me. She might be able to handle my power. Only the strongest would do. Then I could find this Lota Princess they had here and start our campaign for recovering the Isles.

I wanted blood and slaughter. Something inside of me had always been bloodthirsty, but now I was ravenous to taste death, and it hovered over me like the Father's axe itself.

Seeing my muscles relax in the silence, my brothers let me go. I rubbed my chest the heaviness I felt there making me frown. Kai made a noise of warning as the shadows shifted around us, as if calling me to join them. The little one made of shells, scurried towards me, his long arms dragging on the floor until he leapt up and grabbed onto my pocket, where he swung happily.

"No." I commanded the others. The creatures in the dark of the jungle shuddered as if disappointed. "Not yet."

"They're thirsty," Kai said, reverently. "They want blood too."

My brothers shifted with interest, and I knew they liked these new additions to our situation. New additions that seemed attracted to me, wanted to serve me.

I sighed and rolled my shoulders. "We're done here. Let's go." I leapt into the air, and when I landed, it was four large, striped paws that hit the jungle floor. The little shell creature somehow landed on my back, gripping onto my fur with spiny, shell fingers as I stormed into the jungle.

13

ALTARA

Fangar leapt to his feet, snatched my hand and launched us into a full pelt back through the jungle.

The vision of those four men, creatures, whatever they were had been seared into my brain, and I, due to my saree skirts, managed to stumble upon my own feet on the flat path.

Fangar glanced back at me with irritation as he pulled me along, his grip like steel around my hand. "Run, you stupid human! Do you not know who that was?"

I frowned, trying to master my fear, and now anger at the lordling, but as we thudded down the dark path, the jungle felt like it was pressing in on me. I risked a look behind us as we came upon the main trail back to the school. No one appeared to be following us. I tugged on Fangar's arm to slow him down. "Who was that?" I spluttered. "Why did you call him *Your Majesty*?"

Fangar just shook his head, yanking me along in his sprint. I wrested my arm from his grip, and he finally obliged me, letting go so we could move down the path properly.

Since there was no sign of pursuit. I slowed down to a jog, already sweating in the humidity. Ahead of us were frantic voices, and my heart stuttered in my chest. How were we going to explain our absence to the teachers? Or the appearance of those warriors?

"Fangar, slow down," I called. "We can't be seen going back to the castle together."

He said nothing, sprinting ahead of me only to realise I'd lagged behind. He turned and jogged back, reaching for my arm again.

"Stop it!" I slapped his hand away. "They're not chasing us, whoever *they* are."

But he grabbed me by my shoulders, his eyes wild. *"How can you not know who that was?"* he hissed. I was alarmed to find his eyes were frenzied, his panting less from physical strain and more from fear. "We must go!" He turned away, pulling me with him again. I was about to strike my fist into his nose when he suddenly let me go and took a deep breath, running his hands through his hair.

He shook his head as if barely containing his anger. "We must get back to the castle straight away to alert everyone." His eyes were not on me but the path behind us.

The men by the lagoon were obviously predators of some sort. The headmistress had warned me of such unusual things in this jungle after all. But seeing an Ellythian warrior like Fangar under such obvious distress I relented, nodding before we hurried towards the school at a fast walk. I couldn't forget that he had also thrown himself at the feet of the leader and called him "Your Majesty."

"What were they?" I asked tentatively.

Fangar frowned at me. "You've never seen paintings of the

Boneweavers? They're legends to us." Then he muttered, "*And* supposed to be imprisoned."

A chill ran down my spine. "They're not supposed to be here?"

He cast me another frown. "No. I swear, the depiction of the king is as accurate as anything. My father had a painting of him in the palace, and I used to stare at it as a child. I'd know that face anywhere. That was Ashzale Boneweaver, Old King of Daanav Kingdom and Crown Prince of Boneweaver Island. He was heir to the throne of this very island before they imprisoned him and his three warriors for being too powerful. They're monsters and were supposed to stay in their tombs until the end of time. Something freed them. They shouldn't be here. We're all in danger."

"Heir to the throne?" I asked, thoroughly confused. "I thought Princess Rahana was heir?"

He cast me a third irritated look. "This is the basic history of your people."

When I was silent, he muttered something about stupidity and continued. "We call them the Old Ones. The beings that were here before the Ellythians arrived in their boats thousands of years ago."

All the blood drained from my body as I registered this. I knew that the Ellythians came to this island from *elsewhere* before they took it over, but I had never imaged there were people—creatures—already claiming the land. I reeled, trying to understand the politics of all this. "There were people here before the Ellythians?"

"Not people. A fae-animal hybrid was created from the island's magic over thousands of years ago. I don't have time for—" He turned to look at me, and his frown faded.

"What?" I asked alarmed.

When he spoke his voice held a deathly note of serious-ness. "Your eyes are green."

Shit.

I squeezed my eyes shut and rubbed them, absorbing the colour of the dark jungle behind me and dragging it into my irises. "Uh, no?" I said feigning confusion and opening my eyes. "They're brown, my lord."

He gave me a suspicious look and then said, "I need to leave and speak to my warriors."

Goosebumps erupted all over my skin at the anger in his voice as the path led us up to the school. We were not ten paces from the front doors when they were both yanked open with a furious Headmistress Jessine storming out.

"Headmistress," Fangar said, his tone positively commanding, "we just saw—"

"That was very improper, Lord Fangar!" the headmistress said haughtily. "And not a part of this agreement. I'm going to be writing to your superior about this. There will be conse-quences. Your marriage will be arranged as soon as possible." I gaped at her. "I will not hear another word. Inside!" She stood aside, jabbing her finger into the entrance hall.

"We saw these Boneweaver people!" I said quickly. "Headmistress—"

She gave me a dirty look. "You are not a child, Lady Zara, to be making up stories of old fae-tales. Inside immediately."

I had no real choice other than to get inside the entrance hall. Fangar gave me a furious look that made me want to stick a dagger in his face.

But I knew what we'd seen was very, very real.

The rest of our cohort of young ladies and men were mingling in the entrance hall, and whispers broke out at the sight of us. I refrained from rolling my eyes as Rani stepped out of the crowd, looking upon me with wild concern, so I waved a cheerful hand at her so she would stop worrying. Malika stepped out and crossed her arms, shaking her head disapprovingly at me.

I refrained from rolling my eyes, but I *was* a little angry with myself. I had never been caught in a near compromising situation like this before. And the headmistress genuinely believed she was getting Fangar and me married now. I needed to figure out how to talk my way out of this before Geravie gave me a lifetime's worth of tongue-lashing.

The headmistress stormed up to me, a concerned Lady Trisana following closely behind. "Are you alright, Zara?"

"Of course, she's alright!" the headmistress huffed. "Look at her. Perfectly fine."

I gave Lady Trisana a demure smile as if I were ashamed of the whole thing. The only thing I was actually ashamed of was my lack of wit. Fangar wasn't even listening; he was talking frantically with the other men, his hands waving about emphatically.

I was painfully aware of how stupid we both would sound trying to explain this to anyone. I had just come out of the bushes with a man with both of us sweating and panting. There was no way they'd take my word for anything.

The headmistress ignored Fangar as her hand lit up in a green glow, raising it high in the air. "I'm sending a missive immediately. We cannot delay when our reputation is at stake." She shot me another hateful look, but I only had eyes for her hands. I had never seen magic used out in the open and so casually. No one else batted an eyelid, so clearly this was a normal thing. I needed to talk to Pia or Rani in private. There was a chance they would believe me.

The soft flapping of wings sounded in the distance and a

grey-speckled pigeon flew into the hall. Something glinted at its neck, and as it settled down on her waiting arm, I realised it was a green quartz on a braided cord sitting around its throat.

She gestured impatiently at us. "Come, Lord Fangar!" she cast my companion an unimpressed look. "Follow me."

Fangar strode towards us, quite suddenly assuming an aura and dominant tone of command. "We must prepare the town for the return of the Boneweavers."

The headmistress scoffed. "Do not think that I will be leaving this foolishness out of my missive. You are far too old for this." She muttered under her breath about obtaining a delivery fish from somewhere although I had no idea there was such a thing or why she would need one.

My mind was racing at a way to fix this, but the men I had seen had truly shaken me...just a little. Those eyes, that clearly predatory demeanour... How *he* was supposedly the king of this island. And if so, that made him a direct threat to my grandmother, the Ellythian queen, and therefore Pia. And how these Daanav Kingdom invaders fit into this, I could barely understand.

Before we left the hall with the headmistress, I looked behind me for my cousin. I found her standing by Rani, who was frantically whispering in her ear. Pia and I locked eyes, and she immediately swept forward to my side. Bless the girl, honestly.

"I need to talk to you, Zara," she muttered before we hurried after the headmistress, now ranting about the reputation of the school.

Once we were seated in her office, she took out two sheafs of parchment and a quill.

"Please, headmistress," I pleaded. "We may be able to arrange something without contacting our parents?"

Fangar shot me an angry look. "I must contact my uncle," he said angrily, slamming his hand on the table. "I'm returning home at once."

"You bring great shame to your people on all fronts," the headmistress snapped at him. "You will wed Zara immediately. You cannot go anywhere."

I also realised that I really needed to speak to Geravie because whomever the headmistress was sending the letter to in Harranpul House would find out my ruse right away. Everything would become a mess in such a short time.

"My grandmother is still in the town," I pressed. "You must send for her. She is the matriarch of my side of the family, after all."

The headmistress's eyes lit up. "She is still here?" She clicked her fingers, and a maid appeared out of nowhere. After quick instruction, the maid bolted out of the room, and I hoped she was headed for the twins' house.

"I will write to the king, Fangar. We can arrange this within the week." Her eyes flicked down to my belly and up and again, the implications made clear. I had the sudden and intense desire to slap the woman. Wait…*king?* I thought my grandfather was dead. Perhaps my grandmother had married again.

Fangar was quiet, and I knew he was observing me closely. He'd seen my eyes in the jungle, but it had been dark. Perhaps I'd convinced him he was seeing things? On the other hand, if he believed what he saw then there would be no doubt in his mind that I was a Lota. That made me an opportunistic match on his part. I prayed, *Dear Goddess, please—*

"That is fine," Fangar said quietly, glancing me darkly, and I knew at once he'd not been fooled. "I will marry Zara. But I am sending my men back...unless you are disobeying a direct command."

Heat shot up my spine as I registered the wholly unexpected, barely concealed threat Fangar was making. Something passed between the two of them because they stared at each other with silent meaning, and I could have sworn fear flashed across the headmistress's face.

Finally, she said tightly, "Very well, my lord. Do as you wish."

Fangar stood and swiftly left the room with another backward glance at me and the tension in the room visibly relaxed.

I repressed a sigh as I was dismissed. Lady Trisana and Pia followed me out and back to our dormitory. When we were out of anyone's earshot, I turned around, and as seriously as I could said, "We are all in danger. Four...frightening men approached us in the forest. Fangar said they were Boneweavers. The so-called Old Ones."

But the two of them exchanged a look I could not read. Lady Trisana said to me in a quiet, sombre voice, as if she were explaining something to a small child, "This is not the first time this has happened, Zara. A handsome...person like Fangar can be distracting, if you've never met a lord like him before."

I could have groaned.

"I have known many men," I said in a low voice. Pia's brows shot up, and Trisana paled. "But I did see four warriors who did not look human. Fangar was truly afraid. They told us to run, and we did."

Lady Trisana peered at me closely, as if for the first time. "I think you should get some rest, Zara. You've had a long day. All will be well." She smiled kindly at me, and I could see that she genuinely thought she was being nice. I looked helplessly at Pia, who was chewing on her bottom lip.

"Is there protection at the school, at the very least?" I asked.

"There are magical protections, yes," Pia said slowly, not taking her eyes off my face.

"But not to stop the—" it was then I realised that I didn't know the Ellythian word for 'demon', so I settled for "—evil *creatures* from getting their tithe!"

Pia frowned deeply. "So you do know about the Daanavs and yet you still went out alone with one?"

"Enough," Trisana said firmly. "You are not used to this heat, Zara. I will send the maids to run you a cool bath."

She turned on her heel and swept down the corridor, and I couldn't help the sour look developing rapidly on my face. "I know you don't know me that well, Pia," I pleaded, trying to sound like a trustworthy person. "But you must believe me when I say you are in danger. You must contact your grandmother and get her to send the forces here."

She looked at me for a long moment before shaking her head. "I am sorry this has happened to you, Zara, but I'm sure this is what your family intended? Fangar is very high ranking, even if he is a Daanav. If all goes well, you have a wedding to prepare for. You should focus on that."

But I wasn't even listening to what she was saying because I had never felt more alone in that single moment. I didn't understand why the second in the line to the throne had Old One invaders in her land and she was doing nothing about it. It made the reckless darkness that sat at the corners of my being flare up. I hissed, "You're a stupid girl, and you are going to get killed."

She gaped at me, but I gave her no time to reply, yanking on the door handle and storming out. I surrounded myself in my secret magic and jogged down the corridor in a maddened fury. The maids sweeping the floor looked up in alarm as a wind passed them, but I didn't even care. I needed to see Geravie, and I needed to go home—or anywhere else, really. I had been here less than a day, and already they were treating me like a foolish girl. I would never have been treated this way at home. Never.

To think I had thought coming here would be fun.

Invisible, I fled down the corridor, through the now-empty entrance hall and back to sweating in the heat of the tropical night. I determinedly made for the twins' house.

The gathering darkness pressed on me like a stifling cloak, but I couldn't let myself get scared—even knowing that four two-hundred-year-old warriors were prowling in the darkness tonight. We needed to send word to my grandmother, Queen Cheshni. She needed to send assassins, armed forces—anything to rid the islands of these imposters. Why weren't they here already if there were demons and Daanav people invading? If it were my lands, I would chase every one of them down and execute them one by one. It couldn't be allowed, not here in Ellythia where they had *magic* and a queen at the helm of the kingdom.

Surely the twins would believe me? And Geravie definitely would. I was no tattle tale, and she knew that. No, there was only the truth about The Butcher that I kept hidden, and that was mine alone to suffer.

I was still in my saree and running was a bit more

awkward. I ended up hitching the hem of the saree up and tucking it into the belt at my waist to hold it into place. It was crass, but no one could see me, after all.

The cicadas took up their racketing chirp, and I found it rather soothing to have company of sorts. When those beings had come upon us, there had been no noise in the surrounding jungle at all. I shivered as another fevered chill swept over me.

I made it in good time to the twins' house, my anger, no doubt, spurring me on. Jerali Jones, the Quartz palace Armsmaster, would have been proud. Goddess, I missed Jerali. I missed Saraya. I even missed Sam, whose butterfly daggers were strapped to my boots right now.

Thundering up the cottage steps, I thumped my fist angrily on the door and dropped the hem of my dress to try and look decent. But it was not the twins who answered. It was Geravie, waving the headmistress's parchment in her hand.

"And *what* in the Goddess's name is this rubbish?" she asked wryly. "Not a full rotation of the earth, and you're in trouble already!"

I sighed, putting my hands on my hips. "And what dark business did you have, Geravie?" I asked sourly. "Failing to mention the farce of a marriage market that is the sole and full purpose of this place?" I gestured to the castle in the far distance.

Now it was Geravie's turn to sigh. "I should have known!" She dramatically threw her hands up in the air and headed back inside. I followed, searching for the twins and the thousand answers I needed.

Keshmi was sitting on the lounge, massaging her feet with what looked like coconut oil while Reshmi was in the kitchen, stirring a large cauldron with some type of curry in it. It smelled delicious, and my stomach growled despite everything.

"Sit! Sit!" Reshmi commanded, pointing at their wooden dining table, a freshly painted black crescent moon glistening on her head. They must have just come from the temple.

"There are dark deeds afoot, ladies," I said grimly. I then switched to Lobrathian common tongue in my anger. "Including *demons*, which everyone failed to mention!" I looked at the twins accusingly.

They both exchanged a look with Geravie, who said, "I only found out the details about it last night," Geravie murmured. "When—"

"When they came here?" I interrupted, switching back to Ellythian.

Both twins gasped in unison, and I primly smoothed my saree as I sat down. "Yes, I followed the creatures here. Once I saw them cavorting with the headmistress in the school, *then* —" I held up a finger "—I was by a jungle lagoon, just now, when four ghastly men came upon us. Fangar called one of them 'Your Majesty!'"

All three women stilled, as turned into stone. I frowned when I took in their expressions, looking at them one by one. Geravie had turned ashen, her face practically grey, and she was not a woman who turned ashen at anything. When she'd first found me in bed with Sam, she'd simply shoved Sam out the door and handed me a packet of contraceptive tea and left. Never batted an eyelid.

"Describe them," ordered Geravie. "The four men that came to you. What did they look like?"

"Well frightening, for one," I said hastily. "Muscular, like warriors, wild looking and they weren't wearing much for clothes either. And two of them were holding severed demon heads!" I looked around at them in exasperation. "Then, I realised Lord Fangar was on his knees before them! But..." I scratched my head. "He was more scared of the men than I was. And worse, no one at the school would believe us."

The room was silent and that alarmed me more than anything that had happened today, including the threat of marriage.

"We saw them too." Keshmi came over to the table and sat down opposite me. "The Old Ones. The prince and his warriors."

"Thank the Goddess!" I said, throwing myself back into my chair. "I was worried you wouldn't believe me. Hang on —" I squinted at the three ladies "—what do you mean you *saw* them? Where? Are you okay? And on top of it all, the headmistress wants me to marry this Fangar, whom I barely know—"

"You knew him well enough to go traipsing into the forest for a canoodle," Geravie said wryly. "I thought I taught you to be more careful than that."

One of the twins snorted, but I didn't know which.

"Well, if it weren't for this blasted prince, we would've been fine!" I shot back. "They made us run as if they wanted to chase us for sport. I could've daggered one of them if I had my wits about me!"

Geravie groaned and put her head in her hands. "This is a disaster."

"I know," I said darkly. "If the headmistress gets her way, I will be marrying Fangar this very week."

Geravie gave me an unimpressed look. "Your marriage is the least of our problems, *Altara!* The entirety of Ellythia is in danger!"

"Well, thanks," I crossed my arms and sat up, and Reshmi placed a plate of curry and rice in front of me. Suddenly, I didn't feel like eating at all. "How did you see these creatures before I did?"

Geravie blew a long exhale and exchanged a look with the others. "Their resting place was behind Yasani Temple. They came to see the high-witches first."

"Agnolthi is the witch-goddess," Reshmi said in response to my questioning look. "Therefore, her priestesses are witches in the oldest sense of the word. Brewing spells, researching magic, the worship of nature—these are all the things Agnolthi stands for. It was also Prince Zale's mother who was High Witch of Agnlothi's Order of Yasani in their time. It was her and the other old queens who created a key to his curse."

I shook my head, trying to digest this. "Curse?"

The twins nodded. "Prince Zale was cursed at his birth-blessing ceremony." She shook her head. "It does not matter. We know his plan. He wants a Vayashi to help control his power. I imagine he will test all the women on the island for their strength."

I shot to my feet, my heart pounding. I didn't know what a Vayashi was, but it also meant: "And all the women in the school!"

Geravie and the twins suddenly stood as well.

"I have to warn them!" I exclaimed. "Pia is in danger. If they find her there, if they see her eyes, they will know she is from the Lota family, and they are mortal enemies, right? They will do Goddess-knows-what to her...hold her for ransom? I need to get back to the school."

"No," said Geravie firmly. "You cannot go out there in the middle of the night with the four of the Old Ones, Daanavs, and Goddess-knows-what else lurking about trying to take over Ellythia. We need to get more information. We need to know more before we act."

"I've heard enough," I said, checking the straps of my hidden knives. "I can't delay. They will take them tonight. I must go now and warn Pia. You must write to the queen and have her send the Ellythian forces."

"Cheshni is allowing this," Geravie said.

I turned around and stared at my nursemaid in horror. "What? No! Why?" I looked to the twins for some answer, but their faces were so overcome with sadness that it enraged me. "I'm going right now to Pia and demanding she write to her grandmother!"

Geravie shook her head. "It is an honourable thing to do, my little star, but—"

"Can I borrow your bow and quiver?" I asked Reshmi, wanting a backup weapon. "I saw a set the other day..." I looked around and saw the unstrung bow lying against the back wall. Striding over to it, I picked up the coil of string and deftly strung the bow. It was old, but well-made and in my hands, would be enough. I slung the quiver over my shoulder. There were a bunch of white-fletched arrows in there.

"No, princess, you can't!" Reshmi ran to block my way to the front door. "I only use that bow in case a tiger comes by! You can't be killing the Old Ones with it!"

But I shook my head at the three of them, Geravie most of all. But she knew me too well. If someone in my family was in danger, even an idiot like Pia, I would defend them. I dissolved before them, blending into my surroundings, feeling their anxiety and panic as I did so. But I pushed those aside before that panic became my own.

An odd excitement had sparked to life within me. Perhaps

this is what I'd actually been waiting for when I came to my mother's homeland. Marching around and seducing noble's sons was only half as fun as predators on the prowl and a political machinations of ancient, terrifying beasts.

"I'm sorry," I said, turning on my heel and yanking open the back door. I did mean it. I didn't want to frighten the poor old ladies. "But Pia is family, Geravie, though she may not know it. I owe her my sword-arm."

Perhaps I missed my sister. Perhaps I was homesick and looking for any excuse to find a place here—I don't know. The only thing that felt *right* was that my mother's name was inscribed on the Temple in front of the tombs of these warriors, and it *had* to mean something.

And I was the last person to sit around while predators were going to launch an attack on a group of young women.

I bolted into the night, clutching my bow in a steady hand, the weight of the quiver on my back a familiar and reassuring presence to me. I'd run far tonight, but I'd been running around the Quartz military training arena daily with Jerali Jones—and perhaps the Goddess had my old Armsmaster training me for this exact reason.

But a shooting unease spun through me because neither Pia nor Lady Trisana had believed me. What would they think of my turning up to the school armed to the teeth and bellowing about an attack? No, I would have to take up a silent watch overnight and see if I could take the prince out from afar. There were four warriors, and while I *could*, in theory, shoot quick enough to take them all out, one eye at a time, it was dark, near pitch black, and I had never used this particular bow.

I sped to the school, my mind racing for some plan. I stuck

to the shadows along the dirt road, praying no predator would hear me thundering along the track.

But I needn't have worried about not having an actual plan because as I sprinted up the driveway to the school, all I could hear was screaming.

The darkness gathered around me like a cloak. My eyes had never liked to tolerate the yellows and oranges and brightness of the day, which was why I held my operations at night.

The screams that began inside the poor excuse for a palace were promptly smothered by my minions. They were creatures of the night like me and gathered the shadows around them as if they survived off the dark, revered it and loved it like a mother. The spindly creature made of shell pieces haphazardly stuck together, still clung to my pocket with tiny fingers—as if he knew that if he made the wrong move, I'd crush him to pieces. But he hadn't started annoying me yet. The bigger ones were scaled creatures made of sand and shell as well as a few appeared to made out of the husks of coconuts, their bodies furred and loping, vicious teeth gnashing, claws grasping.

They were far from demons, even the Daanav marine kind I'd ruled over for such a short time. No, these had been made of the very elements of island and shallow sea water and had grown around our tombs as in a womb, seeded no doubt, by the shadow curled around my heart like the Reaper's own claw.

They'd then blossomed into form at the same time we awoke, ready to serve and obey. And I commanded them now, as I'd once commanded my brothers in arms.

The little castle sat squat and boorish in the middle of the island, an insult to the very work the Old Ones had shed blood over thousands of years before. But I needed a Vayashi. A woman to temper the pounding in my veins, so I could think properly and take back our kingdom without slaughtering every living being while I was at it.

So I directed the dark monsters of the island to run into the castle and take all the adult females. Raen disapproved, I could tell, from the way he growled at the creatures hauling the women out. Atax was more reasonable and strode inside with me, only barking at the creatures if they got too aggressive.

And Kai...well, Kai did as he always did and rushed inside the castle nose-first to take a look at what food they had in their stores. My brothers all craved food after two hundred years worth of hunger.

As for me, I felt nothing. Not when we stormed the castle. Not when the women screamed in protest. Like my monsters, my chest was an empty shell devoid of emotion. I needed something, and I would get it. That was that. For my entire life, it was as if my emotional range started at nothing and ended with rage—there was no space for anything else.

I didn't have a problem with that. Ruthlessness meant we would achieve our task faster.

It was a sort of procession that I led out of the castle, and we trailed down the southern path where the old festival grounds used to be. Boneweaver Palace stood in crumbling ruins now, but we could rebuild later.

There had been only one male in the castle—the Daanav I had seen at the lagoon with his human woman. I reasoned that this castle was a place for their young females to get an education, judging by the various classrooms inside. Still, I would have to berate them for keeping all their fertile women together in one spot, ripe for the picking. The Daanavs had been stealing away human women for generations, and it looked like they had become tricksey about it.

The other Daanavs had no doubt fled back to their marine kingdom, frightened out of their wits, when they heard I was back. It was no matter. I'd pay them a visit soon enough.

The leader of this place came behind me, wrestled into submission by a towering palm and fern creature as she violently writhed around trying to summon her magic. The stupid woman didn't realise who we were. She was not nearly powerful enough to make a dent on one of the Old Ones, let alone four.

Kai reappeared, and had, in his enthusiasm stolen a drum from somewhere. With his moon-white hair gleaming under the stars, he played an ancient ominous beat as we walked. I couldn't hide my smirk as I looked behind me, to see the procession of women carried by the island monsters, their eyes wide with silent fear, their mouths smothered with shadowy fingers.

This wasn't the way it was supposed to be. In the old days, at the summer solstice festival, the king and his warriors stood by the ritual fire, and before them stood men and women, proudly displayed on the dais, their bodies oiled, their hair fragrant with flowers. It was an honour to be considered powerful enough to be a Vayashi for one of the royal family.

Perhaps those days were gone forever.

We strode into the jungle to the beat of Kai's drum, other creatures appearing in the dark and forming a larger group behind us, carrying quartz-lights they'd no doubt stolen from the castle.

When we arrived at the festival grounds, kept clear with ancient magic, the grass soft and spongy beneath my feet, Kai and Atax led the group into a sort of semicircle formation while Raen stood scowling next to me.

The creatures had brought us fifteen women, and I gestured to the creatures to hold them upright so they were standing in a neat row for my assessment.

"Please!" the leader shrieked. "Please, we will do as you say, just do not hurt any of the young ones!"

"If you notice, I have only taken the eldest women," I replied evenly. "I have no need to hurt them, but I do need a Vayashi."

She paled, her lower lip wobbling. "I beg of you, Old One, they will not understand. We no longer use Vayashis."

So she did know who we were. I cocked my head. "Not at all?"

She shook hers vigorously, and I found myself irritated at the response. "Are there no longer powerful queens from Ellythia's line?"

She stared at me blankly, and I frowned. Finally, I shook my head. "It matters not—I may require a few. There will be no negotiation. I am reclaiming this land under the Boneweavers once again."

As she opened her mouth to gasp, the palm-tree creature

holding her shoved a bark-roughed hand over her mouth, and I moved on to the first young woman.

I tested her power with my own, reaching into her mind, breaking past her mediocre defences and sensing the core of her magic. It was barely a tenth of what I needed. No matter —there were plenty here.

I stepped to the next, a tiny thing, barely of age, and immediately moved on to the next. But as I stepped up to each woman in the line, each only bore a scrap of the power I required. In fact all of them combined wouldn't suffice. If I tried to use a magically defunct woman as a Vayashi, she would die or be crippled, unable to contain the magic I was releasing into her. Agitated, I bristled at Raen, who looked over the women darkly as if he knew how mediocre they were. Stepping up to the last one, I saw that her eyes were closed, and she were muttering as if in prayer.

I heard the arrow before I saw it. It was coming with the right angle and force to go clean through my right eye. Snarling, I reached up and snatched it out of the air.

16
ALTARA

I stared at the self-named king for a solid three seconds in annoyance. He had caught the fucking arrow in one large, tattooed hand and was now staring at it as if it were no more than an irritating mosquito.

I had followed these vile people into the jungle and silently, climbed up into this tree to get a good look at the clearing. The eldest girls had been secured by monsters made of elements of the island. Sand, grass, palm and shell bound together by malevolent magic that made me shiver in my boots. I'd never seen such a thing in my life, but to be honest, I had expected strange and unusual things to emerge out of this jungle from the moment I had arrived.

In some bizarre, dark ritual, the king had stepped up to each girl and *tested* them. I'd felt the magic through the air like a malevolent cloud, and I used a part of my magic I didn't often call upon.

I could glean what type of emotions a person was feeling, but my mother had instilled the need to use a person's permission as such a thing was invasive. While I couldn't control my healing, I *could* control the gleaning of emotions and feelings. I used a very fleeting version of that power now, and opened myself up to the girl first in the line. When the king used his magic on her, the impressions I got was of a deft and expert observatory glance at her magical core. He was testing the size of their magic, I realised. But for what?

He'd moved to the next girl and did the same thing, then continued down the line. He didn't physically hurt them, but it was an arrogant thing to do nonetheless.

But when he'd gotten to Pia, last in the line-up, I'd known I had to do something immediately. I'd tarried too long in my fascination of these predatory, warrior males. If he'd gotten a look at her Lota House–emerald eyes, he'd know exactly who she was. Then he'd no doubt hold her for ransom or bury her body in a pit somewhere.

So I'd taken the chance and went for the kill, loosening an arrow right into one of his strange blue eyes.

I'd never seen a person catch one of my arrows. Or any arrow. It should have been impossible. But I was starting to realise that on this island, everything I'd known from before was moot.

In my shock I neither saw nor heard the white-haired warrior coming. Still balancing on a high branch, I was grabbed around the waist by strong, muscular arms and tackled right out of the tree. Panicking, I flailed, and my magic sputtered, making me visible again. But he held me tight, and when we struck the ground, he twisted me, so I ended up falling on top of him.

Stars glittered in my vision as I choked out a shocked gasp at the impact. My captor cackled madly, and I rolled myself to my feet only to see the blond warrior jumping up to angle a lethal black sword at me. I whirled around to meet a line of terrified female eyes. Pia had her hair strategically over her beautiful face, and in the dark, I couldn't see her eyes at all. Clever girl. At least *now* they'd all believe me about these creatures.

The other three warriors strode towards me, glowering. The so-called king showed me my arrow and with his tattooed hands, snapped it in two, tossing the pieces to the grass.

"You are a poor shot, witch," he snarled. The light around him seemed to fade, the shadows deepening, making him look like the devil himself in the moonlit clearing.

I crossed my arms and looked him up and down as if I were unimpressed. But I was very fucking impressed because this creature was devastating up close. Even through the gloom his presence was authoritative with a primal dominance that made me suppress a tremble. But by the Goddess, I could never let him know that. I had known terrifying creatures before; I could handle this.

So I tossed my hair over my shoulder. "Actually, I *am* a perfect shot." *Lightning never misses its mark*, and I *was* the lightning. I levelled him a glare.

"You are a Lota." The king's voice was little more than a dangerous rumble.

"Here I am indeed. My name is Pia Lota." I threw in a mocking curtsey and stared back up at him and the three warriors who were now appraising me with renewed interest. The blond one leaned forward and sniffed the air around me, and I returned him an imperious look, blinking lazily.

"She has the eyes," declared the tall warrior with his hair tied back, an expression that would make any man wilt on the spot. "Test her, Zale."

Zale. Sort of like gale. Only if he were to be named after the wind, a typhoon might have been more appropriate. I raised my brows at him as my heart pounded, wondering how it would feel. King Zale took a step toward me, and damn him, I had to crane my neck to look at his striking face —a face I'm sure, in his time, women swooned over. He could have been a fae for his beauty, with those long graceful lines, but with the pure raw savagery of his gaze, his posture, I knew he was not fae at all. Something *more*. Something rougher. His eyes, so blue they could have been birthed by the ocean itself, stared into mine, and I felt his magical presence fall upon me as if the weight of the entire castle school had collapsed, crushing me beneath it. My magic roared in my ears at the threat. Furious at the intrusion, it lashed out, striking at the monstrous man.

It struck a barrier of darkness so cold and ancient that I let out a startled yelp. Cold death surrounded me, dragging me into a pit of dire pain. A place where everything was hopeless, useless and without light. A place of death and decay. A place I had once felt deep in my heart and done everything I could to get away from. I reeled at the assault of dark emotions and forced my magic to retreat. Struggling to hide the evil I'd just felt, I glared at him.

To my satisfaction, the king flinched, and I forced my hands onto my hips. "Don't you *dare* intrude in my head."

He took an angry step forward, his eyes darkening. "I am your king. You will do as I say."

"You are nothing to me," I shot back. "And I am a princess, you will give me the respect of one."

His head cocked a fraction as if he had not considered this. "You know nothing of the Boneweavers. We are not creatures with manners."

I crossed my arms again. "Well, your kind were supposed

be lost for hundreds of years. What do you want now? State your intention. I'm sure we all have better things to do than be out here in the dark on one of your whims." My aggression was coming out as this heathen attitude I had once only reserved for my father and his advisors. It was not ideal, but adrenaline was running through my veins like a heated wind, and I couldn't help it. It was either that or striking him again. My bow lay on the grass a few steps away, but I still had the two knives in my boots. I dare not reach for them, though. If this Zale could stop a flying arrow with his bare hands, I had no doubt he'd grab my knife as soon as he saw where my hand was headed.

I shivered, the thought of those large hands brushing the skin of my calf suddenly filling my brain and taking up all its space. Hastily clearing my throat, I observed the warriors, who were staring at me with varying degrees of darkness. They either wanted to kill me or take me to bed—I had no idea which, at this point.

Zale turned his back on me, and I clenched my teeth at the insult as he waved a hand through the air, and it lit up with blue fire. It was then that a strangled noise shot to us, and I realised the blond manic warrior had been missing for the last minute. But there he was, wrestling a man-sized body into the clearing.

"Get off me!" cried the man angrily.

My heart plummeted into my chest as I recognised that voice and form right away. Zale prowled towards his warrior and Fangar—his face grey in the night. But the blond warrior had my lordling easily in a headlock, his teeth glinting in a crazed grin, and Fangar fought uselessly as he was brought to his knees. The warrior tore Fangar's cloak off his shoulders with a snarl, and all at once, Fangar's face and body changed.

Prickly horror swept down my spine as the Ellythian man I'd kissed by the lagoon was gone. In his place was a creature whose skin was a deep blue, swirling with navy markings. His now yellow and red eyes were narrowed as he surveyed me standing, stricken.

Fangar was a demon. It was a loathsome blow to the gut that had bile racing up my throat.

His Ellythian appearance had been an illusion created by the cloak—my magic had sensed it, but I'd been too occupied to listen. But it seemed that I was the only one surprised by this. When I glanced at the row of my schoolmates, though their faces were twisted in distaste, none of them were shocked. They had all known.

"You knew about the Daanavs, and you went into the jungle with one?" Pia had said to me. It struck me like a slap to the cheek. I was a complete fool! I hadn't known the Ellythian word for 'demon' but they'd been using the correct word the entire time. *Daanav.*

They'd all known the demons were wearing illusions to woo us into marriage and had assumed I did too. This was what Rani had been trying to warn me about before I'd gone off with Fangar, and being influenced by my witch of a clitoris, I'd ignored my one friend in this place.

And worse still, these girls were exiled here and trying to arrange marriages with them!

Dear Goddess, this was a mess, and I only had myself to blame for it.

Zale took one look at Fangar and gave a slight shrug before turning around and waving a hand at the dark creatures waiting patiently for their master.

"Return them to their beds," Zale commanded with the

casual ease of someone who did this all the time. "We will discuss in the light of day. I have my bride."

I had been about to bend to take back up my bow when I froze midway. Whirling around I stared at the warriors who were preparing to leave.

"Wait, what?" I cried.

But the forsaken demon Fangar answered in a strangled croak. "You cannot marry her, my king! She is my bride! I… have claimed her already."

I gaped at the blue demon, who only had eyes for the king. The blond warrior howled in amusement as Zale turned around to stare at Fangar in great irritation. The dark creatures were now in procession back the way they had come with the girls. Pia, being carried past me, gave me a wide-eyed look of great terror, Rani was next to her, shaking in the arms of her hulking, tree-like assailant. Behind me a shadow-creature made of bark and palm and earth gnashed his coconut-shard teeth, pulling me into his arms, back first. His embrace was cold and wet as multiple branches curled all around me, carrying me easily behind Pia. I fought against the solid, rough arms, but his grip was absolute as he held me in place.

But what infuriated me the most was that I was not even being included in this conversation about marriage at all.

Zale glanced back at me, his blue eyes flashing with irritation before he looked back at Fangar, still on his knees. I watched Zale's fists clench then unclench. He cracked his neck and spoke in an even, deep voice.

"Very well, Daanav. I can smell you on her, and even I cannot ignore the Old Laws." Abruptly, he turned to me and asked, "What say you, Princess? Will you marry this Daanav?"

I looked between the two of them, swearing at my rotten luck. But my mind was whirring at the options I had. If I *agreed* to marry the demon, I would be out of bounds of this Zale creature and then I could run away to avoid the marriage. I could get out of this yet.

"Yes," I said firmly.

Zale merely turned around and said to the demon in a dead voice, "Very well, Daanav. We will both wed the princess."

I could not stop my mouth from dropping open in abject horror. But Zale nodded to himself as if this were a satisfying solution and strode into the dark, the muscles of his powerful shoulders rippling along with the tattoo that spanned the centre of his back—the head of an angry, roaring tiger.

"Wait!" I cried. "You said you respected the law! It's the woman's choice! I choose no! I choose no!"

Zale turned around, and a slow terrifying grin spread across his lips. "I speak of the Old Laws, not the Ellythian law."

With that, he was gone.

I would have screamed in frustration, but my captor covered my mouth with a hand made of earth and palm leaves, smothering me. I screamed anyway, but annoyingly, the sound was absorbed by the creature, and unfazed, he ambled off behind the others.

I had come to this island, fleeing a potential marriage of convenience of my stepmother's devious concoction. Now, I'd not only managed to get myself into the clutches of demons but also *two* marriages at the same time—and one to said demon, no less.

Geravie and the twins were not going to be happy about this.

As the shadow creature of the island carried me back into the jungle, I could not help but remember the way the cold pit of darkness of the prince's core had reached out to me when I came up against his magical barrier. It had been colder than death itself. Darker than the void between stars. I frantically shoved the memory of that feeling aside. I could not let myself fall into that well of despair ever again. *Not ever.*

Curse. The twins had said the Old Ones had been cursed.

If Zale had *that* inside of him and was still functioning normally and trying to take over the island, he was a thousand times more dangerous than anyone had initially realised.

17
ALTARA

When I woke up, it was on the floor in a foreign castle room, all alone, the dawn rays of the sun streaming through the window. I groaned as I heaved my sore body to standing, surveying my surroundings.

Surely it had been a nightmare. Fangar being a demon under illusion, me shooting an arrow at the king of the Old Ones. Two proposals of marriage. It sounded like a nightmare if I'd ever heard of one.

I strode to the window and peered through the clear glass down to the ground. Sleeping in front of the castle steps was the biggest panther I had ever seen.

Granted I'd only seen them in illustrations, but I was fairly sure eight feet was far too long for any big cat. My stomach churned, and I gripped the windowsill as I watched the panther get to his feet, yawn widely and between one blink and the next, turn into a man.

My heart froze in my chest. Dear Goddess, the twins could have warned me last night!

So the Old Ones were not men after all, if they had this

power half-beast. By the light of morning sun, I could see this one lot better. This one had a face so beautiful it was bordering on feminine, with graceful planes and a long nose. He was like a deadly, dark-petaled flower, beautiful, but get too close and it would suddenly grow teeth and take a bite out of you.

Unlike the others, he had black tattoos in a line across the bridge of his nose and cheekbones. He also wore his black hair tied off his face in a ponytail. His bare muscles rippled as he stretched, and I got one brilliant look at his bare toned ass before dark pants and a shirt suddenly appeared on his body. He turned around and headed inside as if this were all a very regular for him.

Heart pounding like a stallion's hooves, I ran for the door of the tiny room I'd been put in, turned the handle and found that it would not move. Those wretched creatures had locked me in here! I pounded on the door as hard I could. "Let me out!" I cried, then put my ear to the woodgrain and listened.

All was quiet outside.

Swearing under my breath, I checked my person and swore again. My boots had been removed and placed by the door, meaning my hidden daggers had been taken. Angrily, I shoved my boots back on.

"Zara?" came a muffled female voice from behind me.

My heart leapt. "Hello?" I wildly looked around my room.

"Over here!" a soft knocking came from the wall on the right, and I recognised the voice immediately.

"Rani?" I cried, rushing to stick my ear to the wall. "Where are you? Did they lock us all up? Are you okay?"

But it was Pia's voice that came through first. "We are fine, Zara. You shouldn't have done what you did last night."

I scowled. That was possibly the worst form of thanks

ever. "None of you took me seriously, which I understand because you do not know me well. But I know for a fact that you *knew* about those disgusting creatures collecting a tithe *and* the fact that those Ellythian noblemen were actually Daanavs!" I was practically shrieking now, the backs of my eyes burning. "None of you told me about it! None of you! When they took you all, I had to do something."

There was only silence on the other side, and my shoulders heaved as I gasped for breath, remembering that Rani *had* tried to tell me, that they couldn't possibly know I wouldn't be aware of an invasion because *I* was the one lying to them.

It was clearly an obvious thing because Pia asked quietly, "Who are you really?"

I stepped away from the wall, taking a long breath. So it had come to this. The truth would be out sooner than I had anticipated. But alas, this was an emergency if there ever had been one.

"If I tell you," I said slowly. "You must swear not to tell anyone else."

"We promise!" Rani's voice called. "Just tell us!"

"I knew it all along!" Malika's angry voice sounded, followed by a slap on the wall. "I knew you were lying about being unwell! You look far too healthy!"

"We all swear," said Pia calmly, "but is it really that important you keep it a secret?"

"Yes," I said firmly. "If my...family finds out where I am, it could end badly for me." My stepmother's beautiful, cold face flashed in my mind's eye, but I shoved that image away. I needed to be calm right now—and alert. "My name," I said slowly, "is Princess Altara Yasani Voltanius of Lobrathia. My

132

mother was Yasani Lota. It's why I didn't know that Daanav meant…well, *Daanav*."

Rani gasped loudly on the other side. "Dear Goddess, what—"

Someone shushed her immediately.

"The whys of it don't matter right now," I said. "The fact is, it's better if they think I'm Pia. It keeps you safe."

"I'd never thought I'd actually ever get to meet you or your sister," Pia said softly. "We knew you'd been born, but I'd assumed it wouldn't be allowed…" there was heavy silence, and then, "I could've handled it. If he'd found out about me."

Our moment of joyful reunion came and went in a flash. "*Think*, Pia. They could do Goddess knows what to you if they knew. Use you as leverage—"

"But now *you* are in danger, and that is no better!" Pia shot back.

I groaned. "Look, let's just think about how we get out of here. My nursemaid should have sent word to the queen already."

"Which queen?" Pia asked.

Scowling at the wall, I snapped, "Our grandmother? The Queen of Ellythia?"

There was an awkward silence on the other side followed by muffled discussion I couldn't hear, try as I might to merge my ear to the wall.

"You don't know the politics of it, Zara—I mean Altara," Malika said roughly. "But Queen Cheshni no longer owns these lands. Those demons you saw yesterday? It started with skirmishes, then it was the tithe and eventually, they came to own Boneweaver Island. The queen has given it up."

Outrange spun through me, a fiery tornado of rage. "But how could she let that happen? Especially with Pia here? What about Princess Rahana, your mother?"

Silence once again.

"It does not matter now," Malika said again, and I wondered why Pia was silent. This was sensitive, and I had missed twenty years of Lota family history. I supposed I couldn't just demand to know it all now. But still...

"It *does* matter," I pointed out. "I thought she could send an army to help us."

"No army will come," Rani said quietly. "I could write to my father, I suppose, but... without any forces, I don't think he will interfere."

I squeezed my eyes shut against the irritation that was rising up in me. The Ellythians were leaving their exiled girls here for good as dead. I couldn't accept that! But every way I turned bore no help. The girls truly thought we were alone.

"So it's just us then?" I asked, clenching my fists. "We are all trained fighters. With magic too. We can beat these Old Ones."

Someone laughed, and I knew right away it was Malika. Angrily, I turned around and grabbed the chair behind me. Summoning all my rage in that moment, I held the chair up high and hurled it against the glass window with just a little push of my magic behind it.

I turned around just as the window shattered, squeezing my eyes shut as tiny shards of glass sprayed over the floor.

Someone let out a shout from outside, and I poked my head out the newly made gap. Fresh morning air met me as I bellowed, "I demand to see the usurper Zale Boneweaver!"

The Old One with the white hair ran out the castle

entrance and looked up at me, grinning excitedly. He promptly picked up my chair and ran back inside. Tapping my foot, I waited.

"Was that necessary?" Malika said angrily. "Rani, no!"

A resounding crash came from the room next to me, and I hurried to poke my head out the window again. Rani's head appeared from the window next-door, and I smiled savagely at her. "A woman after my own heart, Rani."

Her narrow face grinned sheepishly. "What are you going to do?"

I shook my head just as the door behind me slammed open. I whirled around to see the white-haired, crazy Old One rushing toward me.

"Uh uh uh!" I held up a finger, and immediately he froze. "If you touch me, I will carve out your testicles from your body and eat them. You will walk, I will follow. Understood?"

He cocked his head, considering me, and I considered him back. His brown skin was shiny with a fine sweat, the muscles of his bare torso as if carved by Goddess Luana herself. His boyish face was also handsome, but in a rough, untamed sort of way, and he had no tattoos to speak of. An unabashed smile curved my lips.

"Why, aren't you a handsome one?" I said curiously. "I'm sure they ran after you back in your day."

His head cocked the other way, and any doubt that he was more beast than human was washed from my mind.

"Will you take me to your king?" I asked again.

He blinked at me, those large, blue eyes so pale they were almost white. "Do you truly eat testicles?"

I bared my teeth. "Yes, Old One. Every other day."

He nodded as if this were very interesting. Then his face

brightened as if struck by an idea. "I will find you some so that you do not have to eat mine?"

I couldn't help the laugh that escaped me. "Oh no." I made my face serious and sauntered forward. The poor creature couldn't take his eyes off me, and his lips parted ever so slightly. "I prefer to hunt them myself."

A crooked, silly, smile fell across his lips, and he ducked his head, bowing swiftly. "Very good, Your Highness."

Goddess, I could almost forgive him for tackling me last night. Though in hindsight, with the way he'd done it and ensured my easy fall, it had been practically playful. "Now be a good boy and take me to Zale."

He looked up and frowned at me, holding a finger in the air. "King Zale," he corrected.

I sighed dramatically. "Very well, take me to his royal highness, please...what is your name?"

He smiled again, and it was so beautiful a lesser woman might have blushed. "Kaisan Bonesong, Your Highness. But I prefer Kai."

I took another step forward, and his nostrils flared as if he were scenting me like an actual predator. Wetting my lips I said, "Thank you, Kai."

The youngest Old One, in appearance at least, led me out of my gaol and into a corridor lined with many doors. This was not a part of the school I was familiar with, and I swore internally, trying to memorise the path to wherever he was taking me. Kai towered over me, and I was rather surprised to find his magical defences were almost non-existent—or at the very least, he did not feel the need to guard himself. His presence was clear for me to feel out. Kai Bonesong's energy was like the sea in storm, off-kilter, sliding, and it felt like he walked steadily on these even waters while everyone else fell over around him, feeling queasy and unsettled.

I knew that look. I'd learned it at a young age. He'd been through something horrendous in his young life. The type of trauma that led to a permanent change inside of him. Despite being probably the same age as me, his demeanour was child-like and I think, likely to remain that way.

Everything I read off him only lead to more questions.

"Can Old Ones change into all types of animals?" I asked tentatively as we trotted down a case of carpeted stairs.

He snuck a glance at me. "We do not turn into animals, Your Highness." Then he grinned, a feral look taking over his face. "We *are* animals."

"But you are not an animal *now*," I said carefully, my heart skipping a beat at the sudden change in his demeanour.

"Yes, I am, Your Highness," he said simply.

I exhaled slowly as I took this in. "And what are the other Old Ones' names?" I asked. Gleaning as much as I could before I met with the supposed king would be the wisest move.

"Ah, my brothers," Kai said with a smile that made me want to smile back at him. "Raen is the king's sorcerer, and Atax is the king's commander."

"Which is the pretty one with the tattoos on his face?"

Kai cocked his head, something he seemed to do when he was thinking hard. "Pretty? Hm. That is Raen."

That made sense, given the odd tattoos.

I observed Kai the entire way down to the entrance hall—where I stopped dead in my tracks as we emerged from the side corridor.

The other three Old Ones were standing in the hall while

the headmistress, Lady Trisana, and Armsmistress Vari were tied to wooden chairs with long lengths of rope, various expressions of distress on their faces.

"You cannot tie them up like this!" I demanded as I strode up to the group.

Zale turned around and gave me a deadpan look, and by the light of day, I was once again struck by the powerful form and sheer masculine, feral beauty that was the King of the Old Ones. His blue eyes threatened to pin me to the floor, and Goddess help me, why did I want to lift my skirts and climb into his lap? I was a wanton woman, but I had *some* discipline to my name. I immediately broke eye contact with him to glance at the others.

The beautiful one, Raen, the sorcerer with the line of runes across his nose and cheeks, gave Kai a look of great disappointment. The other had to be the Commander Atax. He was roguish, with a look of trouble about him, his features not as fine as the others although his eyes were astute and sharp. As if he were making swift calculations in his head and wondering how best to win.

Atax frowned at the two of us. "Why did you let her out?"

Another length of rope suddenly appeared in Raen's long fingered hand.

I refrained from gaping at the excellent display of magic and lifted my nose in the air. "You will not bind me, Lord Sorcerer." I looked at him evenly. "I am to be queen of your kind, am I not?"

Raen simply stared at me, anger pouring from every perfect pore of his being.

"What is the meaning of this—" and I managed to grit it out "—Your Highness?" I gestured to the three prisoners. "These are my respected teachers."

"Well your respected *headmistress*," Zale said in a dark voice, pointing at the black quartz necklace around Jessine's throat, "wears a blood contract with Daanav Kingdom to sell them her students for a bride price. Protocol demands her execution. She is a traitor to the island."

Headmistress Jessine cried out something under the cloth securing her mouth as my brows shot up. So that's what the black quartz meant. It was a blood contract and I was right about it being black magic. She was responsible for this entire business of selling the girls to the demons. No wonder she'd been so keen to marry me to Fangar. Even so, the girls consented to it willingly, and we couldn't just *execute* her.

To hide my rising panic, I said, "I see. But would it not be unlucky to execute someone so close to...our wedding?"

I wanted to cringe as I said it. Run outside and far into the jungle away from this place. Kai would catch me in a heartbeat, of course. Or I'd die of heat exhaustion. Either way I had two weddings to get out of.

"We will marry tomorrow night on the full moon," Zale said. "It does not matter if I kill her this morning."

Bloodthirsty monster. And tomorrow night! By the Goddess.

"Why?" I asked quickly, trying to buy some time. He never took his eyes off me. "What is the hurry exactly?"

He scowled at me in a way I'm sure that would terrify most men and beasts alike. And worse still, he stalked towards me, his magical signature flooding the entire room, a dark shroud that struck me like mallet. I froze, pulling my magic around me like a cloak, shielding me from that dark feeling that was inside of him. I wet my lips as he came to stand before me. "It's a simple question. I have the right to know."

"You have no right," he snarled. "You will not be queen; you will do as I say, or I will destroy this entire school, your precious teachers and students along with it. Understood?"

I narrowed my eyes upon him as the other males shifted. "You wouldn't." Those words could only be read as a challenge, and Goddess knew why I chose to do that. Arrogant male that he was, he took it in offence, his nostrils flaring, his eyes searing my skin.

"Oh, I would have no trouble doing that. *Princess*." He said it like a curse, and I gritted my teeth against a retort. But he abruptly turned on his bare-footed heel and pointed at Jessine. "How about we start with the headmistress?"

He raised an arm, and Jessine made a terrible choking sound, her shoulders heaving. Under her own cloth gag, Lady Trisana screamed.

I screamed as well. "No!" and shot forward towards Zale. To tear his eyes out, to claw at his face with my fingers. But Kai was faster. He wrapped one strong arm around my waist and wrapped his second hand around my throat, fingers gently pressing on my carotid artery. I stilled in his lethal grip.

"Stop, Your Highness," he whispered earnestly in my ear.

"Please stop!" I sobbed. My magic rose up, but I could not direct it. I only came up against the solid, terrifying, maddening darkness that was inside the Boneweaver King.

It didn't take long for a crushed trachea to kill a person—I knew that already. Headmistress Jessine turned blue, slumping forward, her head lolling. I let out a wild, animalistic cry and strained against Kai, his fingers digging into me. But my magic sparked under my skin, crackling violently, and Kai released me with a yelp. I surged forward. They thought she was dead, thought she was gone for good. But I knew better.

My vision was blurry from tears, but I did not pause to wipe them, instead flinging myself onto the floor in front of the headmistress.

Whatever she had done, whatever the contract, she did not deserve to die for it. My magic leapt up hungrily, ever ready for action, and I transferred the damage to my own body. My trachea, my windpipe, crushed under brutal force, leaving the headmistress clear. I shoved a punch of my power into her lungs, forcing her to take oxygen, and she spasmed back to life, gasping for breath as I fell to the floor, choking.

There was movement behind me, but I could only focus on my own body, my own crushed cartilage. I reconstructed my airway as well as the surrounding vessels Zale had also managed to destroy. It was wild and bloody work, but it was work I was good at, for my mother had trained me well. My focus was absolute through the pain as I built back the rigid walls of my windpipe on all sides, encouraging blood to flow there once again. I wheezed and took several gasping breaths as air flowed unencumbered into my lungs once again.

I sagged to the flagstones, my panic now fading away, though my heart still beat wildly. I breathed to calm myself, and when I opened my eyes, two male faces hovered above me: Raen and Kai. The latter reached a hand down.

"Do not touch me," I croaked through a painful throat. Grimacing, I rolled to my feet in an instant—something my mother and Jerali Jones had bade us practice many times. My shoulders still heaving, my hair askew, I looked around to find the beast king two steps away, simply staring at me, those cold blue eyes scanning my body up and down.

"You're evil," I breathed at him. "You cursed, wretched creature."

"Now you get to understand," Zale said. And there was no emotion in his voice. He flicked his fingers, and a sick crack sounded behind me. I whirled around to see the head-mistress's head rolling onto her chest, her neck clearly broken.

18

ZALE

My new bride was an interesting creature. In truth, I had known it when I'd spotted her with the Daanav that first night, but pure rage had masked any rational thinking at the time. Not only did lightning crackle beneath her skin, she bore a power that was coveted and rare.

I had not expected her to save the headmistress. Perhaps the Old Ways were still alive in Ellythia after all.

I wanted her as my Vayashi in my bed, writhing under me as I filled her with my power. Her defiance of me was a good sign. It meant she was strong, with the will to handle the amount of magic I needed her to take. But she was too defiant and that could be a problem.

By whatever means she was here, and not with the Lota family on their island, it didn't matter because I would have trouble finding another woman powerful enough. I would wed her, and she would help me temper my power. The Daanav male was a minor nuisance but I would execute him as soon as he stopped being useful.

But in order to wed her according to our most ancient rituals, I would need an object of power to bind our oaths. So after Kai had returned the girl back to her room, I stepped out of the hall with Raen, and we discarded our human bodies for our animal ones. Raen took his preferred black panther form, and I chose the fastest of my own forms—a leopard, sleek and strong.

Changing to my beast form felt good after such a long time stuck in my human one—but good in the way stretching your muscles did. I'd never felt the same exhilaration and joy that came with the crunch and release of bones as the others of my kind did. Instead there was pain, and then there wasn't. My decision to take leopard form was purely practical. It was fastest, and that was that.

By the time Raen and I reached the ruins of my family's palace, the sun was well into the sky, the heat welcome on my skin, but its warmth never got any deeper than that. With my enhanced vision and the daylight, the picture of the ruins was jarring. Crumbling rubble remained, the obsidian pillars having become an old man's decaying, toothy stubs.

I remembered the last time I'd seen my mother standing by one of those very pillars. Beautiful and terrible, her rage that last day had been something to behold. Even my father had faltered for a moment, when we all realised who my father had summoned and what he'd done to us. I'd barely had time to look upon her when the magic took me, and I was whisked away into that fucking tomb. Two hundred years ago, we'd returned from conquering Daanav Marine King-dom, just as my father had requested of me. I had made the mistake of returning with a crown on my head, given to me by the Daanav priests themselves. Unbeknownst to me, my father and uncles had taken this as direct threat to the crown and perhaps realised for the first time we had become more powerful than them.

He'd called upon his personal god, the Reaper, a cloaked, corrupted being so foul he made the air smell of burning flesh. We had been drinking kava in the Great Hall when the Reaper appeared. My father had called upon the one boon he'd been granted when he'd pledged allegiance to the living god. I'd never forget his words till the day I die: "Our sons have become rabid. They need to be put down before they ruin us all."

The Reaper looked at me, and in my head, his voice came slimy and creeping. *"There is a great war coming, Boneweaver King. Your son will still be valuable to me yet. I will rid you of him, but I will keep him until I need to call upon his particular skills."*

Me and my brothers writhed in pain as spikes had been driven through our wrists and feet and hammered into a dark place where the only thing we knew from then on was pain.

I truly think the Reaper had been trying to make us insane. But he didn't realise about the power shadow he'd given me at my birth. It protected us, I think. It made me cold and hard and unyielding to the nightmare landscape that we were sent to.

Two hundred years later, Raen and I prowled around the ruins of the once Great Hall where we'd been punished for the very thing our fathers had raised us for. We'd been born to be killers, and we'd done it too well.

Raen's dark pelt gleamed in the morning sunlight as he said to me, mind to mind, *"It was buried under magical lock, from memory. Anyone pillaging would not have been able to find it."*

Anger spiked through my blood. Anyone pillaging.

Because we both knew what we did not have the heart to

say out loud. The destruction of the savage and ancient Palace of Boneweavers could not have come about naturally. The magical fortifications upon it were thousands of years old, when my ancestors had built it brick by brick—and every king had added to it since. The magic still lingered here now in the very particles of the air and the dust on the ground. It would be easy to reconstruct, but it meant that someone had done this, and it made me want to hunt and destroy them.

It could only be one of two peoples. The Lota family or my own conquest, the Daanav Kingdom.

Growling I returned to my human form with an annoying pop of cartilage. Raen followed me as we strode up to the ruins, trying to remember the structure of our old home.

We rummaged in the stone for a while, followed by shifting back to our animal selves and digging ferociously for an hour.

Finally, I pointed to the heavy stone box set deep in the earth. Carefully, I shifted my teeth so they became tiger-long canines and brought my thumb to my mouth. I pricked my own thumb against one tooth and brought it out, already bleeding. Blood spilled onto the stone.

With an ancient groan, it opened.

I hefted out a wooden box with my mother's initials engraved by her own hand. I ran my fingers over her letters, and still, I felt nothing.

Shrugging, I prised the lid open. Inside, on a bed of black velvet was a shining needle made out of white quartz, sharpened to a near impossible point. With it was a jar of glittering black powder made from the volcanic rock that had made this island millennia ago. And finally, sitting in its own case, was a tiny pearl.

I handed our ancient instruments to Raen, who took them

reverently. We would have to walk back as humans now, but it mattered not.

"You will make her obedient to me, Raen. She's too fierce to be controlled."

He looked at me with raised brows, and I returned him a slow smile.

19

ALTARA

I trembled as Kai half carried me out of the entrance hall, one arm around my waist, the other grasping my trembling hand. I was no stranger to death, having been frequenting the quartz military infirmary since I was a child. But today? That...creature had killed the headmistress in ice-cold blood. There had been no feeling, no emotion in his eyes as he'd done it, and that shook me more even than the awful sound of the headmistress's neck being broken.

Kai, from his large puppy-dog eyes surveying me, had been startled by my sudden burst of power and subsequent healing. Maybe he even felt a little sorry for me because he didn't escort me back to my solitary gaol but instead to the room next to it.

He waved his hand about the door, and an orange glow was revealed all the way around the edges. He pushed it open and gently took me through. I don't even know why I didn't push him away, but his energy was pure in that way small animals were pure. There was no ill intent or bad thought behind those sky blue eyes, and for me that was a rare thing.

The three girls scrambled to their feet as we came in, rushing towards us and stopping short when they saw Kai supporting me. I eased myself out of his arms.

"Kai?" I said softly. "Will you bring us some food, please?"

He nodded eagerly and bolted out the door. It shut behind him, that orange glow zipping around the doorjamb, once again sealing it shut.

"What happened?" Pia asked sharply. "You look—"

"Awful? I know."

The room was a dormitory, and must have belonged to another group of girls previously. It seemed the shadow island creatures from last night had just placed the girls back into random rooms. There were four beds and an adjoining bathroom. I headed for it immediately, massaging my still-sore throat.

"I do not wish to speak right at this moment," I murmured. "I need to...I need to think."

They exchanged a look as I passed them but gave me space as I splashed water on my face—and promptly vomited into the sink.

Writhing tendrils of darkness threatened to consume me, and I pushed them away like a seasoned warrior, for I had been pushing them away since I was fourteen. If that darkness of pain and terror took hold of me, my life would be forfeit; I knew it like I knew the sun would set every day. And it had been a long time since they had been triggered to rise up.

Cool, soft hands were on me, tugging my hair off my face. Another tentative hand patted my back. I looked up in surprise to see three faces looking seriously back at me in the mirror. Rani was crying, and even Malika had lost her usual haughtiness. Pia's hands were full of my hair, her green eyes somber as she looked upon me.

I wiped my mouth on my sleeve. "The headmistress is dead. I—I tried to save her, but the self-named king was too strong. He—he said she deserved to die for selling brides to the Daanavs."

Pia's eyes darkened. Malika scowled. "We should kill them!" she said angrily. "They can't get away with this!" She stormed from the bathing room and threw something at the far wall.

"They're too powerful," I said, turning around. "We need to get out of here."

Rani shook her head as she wiped her eyes. "Running away will not fix this. The Old Ones are predators. They will have no trouble out running us and hunting us down."

We sat down on the set of beds with Malika pacing like an angry cat, muttering under her breath.

"I knew she had a deal with them," Pia admitted, clearly disturbed by my news, "but I didn't know coin was being exchanged."

"She didn't deserve to die for it," I said. "There needed to be a proper investigation. A trial. Not an execution done by a madman."

"We need to use our magic, then," Pia said. "We need to be clever about this. We can't let you marry him, Zara. Well, *them*."

"Altara," I corrected softly, giving my cousin a grim smile. "And we can't even get out of the door. How will we do anything else?"

"Hold on." Malika stretched out her neck, stomped towards the door and stopped a little way from it.

"Malika—" Pia warned

"Just let me try," Malika snapped. She raised her right hand and threw a burst of red magic at the door.

We all flinched, expecting some type of explosion. But just as my heart leapt, Malika's red-coloured power simply skittered off the door like droplets of oil on water. The angry girl huffed and plonked herself down on one of the beds.

"I'm not strong enough," she admitted, then turned to look at me. "The king tested us all last night, remember? Declared us all unworthy. But *you* could. He said you were strong enough to be his Vayashi."

"My magic doesn't work outwards like that," I pointed out. "It never has so far, anyway. But what is a Vayashi?"

Both Malika's and Rani's eyes slid to Pia. I turned to look at my cousin, who was suddenly avoiding my eye. She visibly swallowed and looked up at me, the smile on her face clearly forced. "A Vayashi is a human container for power. Very powerful beings like the Old Ones need to temper their power, or it is too explosive for them and can be dangerous. They empty themselves into another magic user to help them control their magic."

"Empty themselves?" I said, thoroughly confused.

Pia brushed off a speck of dust of her knee. "Through sex, Altara. The ritual involves sex with your Vayashi."

My brows shot up as his haste to marry me suddenly made sense. Zale…wanted to have sex with me to empty his power. I shivered despite it all, imagining that beastly king in bed with me, doing a ritual to share his magic. My thighs clenched at the thought—and I promptly shook myself out of it. Being close to that dark, malevolent power? That cold terror I'd felt from him was something I couldn't be near. I'd have to figure out something.

We spent the rest of the day brainstorming ideas, each option more dramatic and less likely to work than the last. Kai delivered us food twice from the kitchen stores, repaired the broken window with a frown and a wave of his hand and left.

By nightfall we were dozing in our borrowed beds in an unsettled silence, exhausted by our own thoughts. I couldn't move on, couldn't think, and in truth, I was more disturbed by the headmistress's death than I cared to admit to myself, and it made me fall into a disturbed sleep.

A TINY FLICKERING LIGHT SHIFTED IN FRONT OF ME, AND I RUBBED my eyes, blinking up through the now dark room.

"What is that?" I sat bolt upright.

Rani swore, and I turned to look at her. Another flickering light hovered in front of her—except Rani's body was still lying on her bed. The Rani I was looking at was *transparent*, her form a ghostly blue-green sheen. I yelped and pointed a finger at her.

"You're…you're…"

Rani frowned at me and looked down at her hand, then back at me. "You are also in astral form, Altara. Look!"

My heart pounding, I flung my hand in front of my face and found it completely see-through, that same blue glowing colour as Rani. By that time Pia and Malika were grumbling awake, the latter of whom screamed loudly. "Pixies!" she shrieked. "Why are there pixies in our dorm! Get them out! Get them out!"

I stared wide-eyed at the hovering, glowing orb in front of me. Movement flickered within it, and I could just make out the form of a tiny, winged person flitting her wings to stay in position. A faint giggle sounded like wind chimes on a faint breeze, and I couldn't help the lopsided smile that fell across my lips.

"Beautiful," I murmured, lifting a finger to touch it. The girls were muttering beside me, but I wasn't paying attention as the pixie floated toward me. She had golden skin and ivory hair that cascaded down her shoulders in rivulets. She wore a dress in the shape of a leaf in all shades of brown. She grinned prettily at me, hovered right up to my face and promptly bit me on the nose.

Before I could shout out, I was thrown. My feet lifted into the air, though I could not tell in which direction I travelled except that it felt like a greater distance than it should have been.

I careened, my stomach tumbling like a sea in storm. Darkness whizzed past me, cicadas struck up their song, humid night air rushed along my skin. I was vaguely aware of the other girls zooming along next to me, their voices a high pitched keen through the night.

When we landed it was with a thud on stone, and I recognised it right away.

Yasani Temple's circular insides stretched out all around us, but we were not the only people inside of it.

Standing in place of Agnlothi's quartz statue was a very real female form, wreathed in thousands of filaments of gold and silver that shifted as she did. The girls next to me immediately fell to their knees.

My heart threatened to beat right out of my chest as I did the same, falling with a painful thud onto the stone floor. As we stared up her, the strands of ethereal light were drawn into the woman's body in a maelstrom that made my stomach violently turn. I mastered my breathing, my eyes watering and simply gaped at what could only be a Goddess sitting in front of us.

Rani began sobbing.

The Goddess was seated side-saddle on a magnificent male lion that surveyed us with a watchful, sombre, amber gaze, its mane shining in every shade of gold. Black gauze so sheer that every part of the Goddesses' perfect form could be seen underneath it was draped across a generous bosom and hips. The material twinkled like a million stars under the night sky, making their own, sparkling light.

Her skin was a deep golden-brown that glowed with the power strumming through her. A power that pressed on me like the weight of the entire ocean. It crushed my ribs, my crown, my heart and threatened to sink me into the very floor.

But I was too struck by those eyes to care. Ancient emerald eyes surveyed us with a clarity so severe it made me want to weep. My magic, Goddess forsake it, was seizing within me, vibrating under the force of a colossal, world-shattering amount of power.

Her face was an orchestra of divine symbols of black ink brushed with pinpoint accuracy along her forehead, cheeks and down her nose.

In one long fingered, tattooed hand, she held a heavy black cauldron, and in the other, a bone-hilted dagger.

Red, full lips glittered, and when she spoke, it was the deep timbre of melodic chanting, rhythmic and severe. Like a spell within a song. *The* song, perhaps, of all women and beasts and birds. It hit me in the womb, and I did not deign to stop the tears that trickled down my face because it felt like an ode to my mother's deity.

"*There is a darkness taking over this island, and it cannot be allowed,*" she spoke within our minds.

We nodded stiffly under the weight of her attention.

But she was shaking her head so slowly, and I lapped up every beautiful movement, her long obsidian hair floating on its own wind.

"*Ashzale Boneweaver is a symptom of the darkness. He must be freed from the shadow that is coiled like the devil's own snake around his two, beating hearts.*"

Ice trickled down my spine, a sinister spider reminding me of the hopeless, empty void I'd felt within him. He had to be freed from his curse.

"*One of you bears the ancient blood of the deep infinite void that sits in the centre of all things. The breath a star takes just before it dies.*"

She shifted and smiled at me. I thought I would simply combust. "*Altara Yasani Volantius, daughter of lightning, daughter of the rabid dark that comes before the dawn. I have waited eons for you.*"

I could have fainted right there. By all rights I should have.

Somehow I made my mouth move and breathed, "You can't mean that."

She tilted her chin, her eyes dancing with amusement. "*Rare are stars that approach each other in the darkness and find an orbit just so. That they would produce a being with the perfect combination of fire and kindling. We need only a spark to begin.*"

"Begin what?" I asked, glancing at Pia and the others, who

looked just as stricken as I did. It should have been Pia, the heir to her mother's throne that should be conversing with this Goddess. It was only right—

"What is right was determined long before you were born." Her voice was a crack of thunder resounding through my being. *"If you do not fix this, child, then it will not be fixed at all."*

The darkness on the island; that was what we were here for. The dire emergency of this place. And we needed to free the Boneweaver King to save the island.

"How do we do it?" I blinked up at her.

"And thus we come to an end to my interference in this realm. My servants—" she waved her hand, and two tiny pricks of light separated from her and flew towards us on fluttering butterfly's wings *"—will teach you what they know. Then one day, perhaps, the Order of Yasani may be whole again."*

Every particle in my body stilled as if struck by lightning. But the light that was the Goddess blinked out of our reality as if it were never there, and we were plunged into darkness.

WE RETURNED BACK TO OUR ROOM THE SAME WAY WE'D LEFT IT, gasping and wheezing at the whiplash of magic and speed and whatever it was that had brought us there and back. Rani was sobbing into her hands as Malika tried to comfort her, whispering about the beauty of the Goddess we'd just seen and something about forgiveness. Pia was pale, staring into space, her hands shaking as she brushed them through her hair.

"I can't believe that just happened," Pia said, blinking

rapidly through the dark of the room. "We just saw an actual Goddess. I didn't think it would *ever* happen to me."

"She spoke to you, Altara!" Rani suddenly burst out, holding her own face so hard she left dents with her fingers. "She said...all those things."

I swallowed, trying to understand what we'd just been through. My voice was hoarse when I spoke. "Why me? I've just arrived here—I'm a foreigner."

Pia scowled at me. "My mother would have never been heir to the Ellythian throne if your mother had not abdicated to marry the Lobrathian Lightning King. I bear no ownership over anything, Altara."

My mouth dropped open as I stared at my cousin. "Abdicated?" I choked. "I thought she was the younger sister of the two! She was never heir?"

"She doesn't know about any of it," Malika said ruefully.

"My mother never spoke of Ellythia!" I cried in a full panic now. "We assumed there was a falling out between her and her mother."

"Falling out," Pia mused, shaking her head. "Your mother was coronated. She was queen for a full two weeks. She left for the fae realm to get her royal prophesy from the Mother Jacaranda tree—as all kings and queens do when they are new. When she came back, she abdicated and accepted the proposal from Lobrathia. I think...I think the Mother Jacaranda told her something about her children—you; and your sister, maybe. The Goddess Agnolthi just told us that you were created out of a pairing she had been waiting for."

I mulled this new information over. No wonder my mother had never spoken about Ellythia or her mother, or anything. And no wonder Geravie did not either. The whole thing was a mess.

A mess that had led me *here*. To speak to an actual Goddess.

"So Queen Cheshni took the throne back?" I said, confused. She would be terribly old by now.

"She went into a great rage afterwards," Pia said, a faraway look in her eyes. "It was actually terrifying. They said the Goddess Umali had come upon the earth in human form. She took the throne back and said she refused to give it up until her death. We were never to speak of Aunt Yasani again."

My stomach churned. I'd had no idea about my mother being queen. And she'd given it up because of some prophesy?

Pia put a surprisingly kind hand on my shoulder. "The Lota House never owned Boneweaver island, Altara. Thousands of years ago we were granted Lotus Island and half of Tiger Island. Abdication or not. You are descended from Ellythia just as I am. You have just as much right to be *here* as any of us."

2 0
ALTARA

All of us woke up the next morning with a start.
Something sharp was digging into my ear and I
reached for it with a yelp.

A giggle like wind chimes broke through the air, and I
scrambled off my bed, the sound familiar. Malika shot off her
own bed and thumped her own ear with a pillow, leading to
more giggles.

Rani slid off her bed to standing, staring at Malika, while
Pia rubbed her eyes awake.

On a whim I raised my own hand, palm up, and held it
still. Immediately, my little glowing orb gracefully extended
her legs and landed, her bare feet barely a tickle on my
callused palm. Her light faded, and when I could finally see
her properly, I found her crouched over, poking one of my
calluses.

"Hello," I said in what I hoped was soft voice. Were the
things spooked easily? "If you could not bite me again, that
would lovely."

She looked up at me, the round apples of her cheeks pink, raven brows raised. Standing, she pointed to herself and said proudly, "Me, Leela."

I smiled. "Nice to meet you, Leela. I'm Altara—Tara for short."

Malika was batting away her pixie like a fly, and I distinctly heard a male chortle zipping through the air. "Stop it!" she commanded. "Or I'll crush you to death, you vile creature!"

"Don't hurt him," Rani said, making a face at her. "It'll be bad luck for our mission." She turned her long face to me. "How are we supposed to go on a Goddess Quest if she didn't give us any instructions?"

"I think these are supposed to help us," Pia said, smiling at Leela, who smiled shyly back. "Remember the story of Lasha the Bold and the jungle kingdom of carnal fae? The pixies guided her on her quest through it. We rarely see them," Pia explained to me. "They usually keep to themselves."

I'd slept heavily and unmoving after the trip to Yasani Temple, but I was still somehow incredibly tired. Perhaps it was the blow about my mother being an abdicated Queen of Ellythia or maybe the fact our family were actual descendants of the Priestess Ellythia herself. I sat back down on my bed as Malika continued to wrestle with her cackling pixie.

"So here it is, Leela and...friend," I said tiredly as Pia came to sit next to me. "The Boneweaver King has some type of curse, and we need to rid him of it. Thing is we don't know how, and I also am marrying him and a Daanav tonight."

Leela's tiny head bobbed up and down.

"Make trouble!" came a squeak from Malika's pixie, who

flew up to the ceiling and shook his fist in the air. "Chaos! Destroy!"

"I mean that's one option," said Rani slowly. "But what are the other options?"

"The Goddess said you could teach us," I asked my pixie. "What did that mean?"

Leela nodded. "Look here." She raised her arm, and after a flash of light, her hand now held a jewel-hilted, pixie-sized sword.

"An astral weapon," said Pia, unimpressed. "This is an advanced technique used by sorcerer lieutenants in the Ellythian Army. But it's extremely difficult to learn. It took me years—"

"No years," retorted Leela. "Now."

"Do you think you could do it with bows and arrows?" I asked earnestly.

"Anything," Leela replied. "Astral trove. Any weapon."

We could create weapons out of thin air. The prospect was enthralling. But my magic didn't quite seem to work like the others, and I wondered what that meant for me. What could I do that others might not? And importantly, what could I do that Zale would not expect?

"But our goal is to free the king from this curse," I said. "How do weapons help us do that? No, we need information."

Rani slapped herself on the forehead. "She doesn't know the story, of course! Poor Tara."

"Oh right," Pia said smoothly.

"Well," I said haughtily, trying to hide my discomfort at being so poorly read by Ellythian standards. "Who will be the designated storyteller?"

161

"Me, of course!" said Rani eagerly. She sat on the bed opposite me, took her boots off and pulled her up her legs to sit crosslegged. "Ready?" Even Malika's pixie stopped attacking her and settled down on the quartz lamp next to me. Rani began in a sombre voice with the cadence of recitation. Clearly this was a well known story.

"THE DAY THE BONEWEAVER PRINCE WAS BORN, A TYPHOON rolled in so mighty that day turned into night. The king called it a marvellous omen for his son, but the warrior midwives watching over the queen shared unsettled looks during the labour. And it turned out that their suspicions were right, for the prince was to be as raging and volatile as the tempest storm he was born in.

"He was born safely, and as his gurgling cry rang through the entire palace, so the king assembled his people in the Great Hall of palace Boneweaver.

"As the dark of true night arrived, the queen strode with her midwives into the hall, triumphant in the pale and sweaty glory of a warrior after a long battle. Her people cheered to see her and the new babe, and the beastly Boneweaver King could not have been happier.

"So the birthing blessing began. Dignitaries came to bless the baby, and the most powerful of them were to bestow magical blessings of power.

"But just as the first blessing was to be given, the doors to the great hall slammed open, and in the dark of night, lightning flashed, illuminating a hooded and cloaked figure. He strode into the Great Hall, and the quartz-lights flickered. The queen clutched her baby to her breast, the warrior midwives drew their swords, but the king said, 'Be welcome, honoured guest. My family, do not be afraid, for we are in the presence of the Great Reaper.'

"The people relaxed for their king had never yet led them astray. The cloaked god walked forward, but never lowered his hood.

"When he spoke it was with a serpent's hiss and the smell of burning silk. 'I have come to bless the babe.'

"The queen recoiled from him, but the king urged her forward. 'Let him see our prince,' he urged. Against her better judgement, the queen showed the Reaper her new baby.

"'Make him strong,' the king said eagerly. 'Make him into the finest warrior the earth has ever seen.'

"The dark god placed a white hand over the prince's head and said, 'I bless this baby with a heart locked in shadow. He will have no emotion, bear no remorse, have no conscience. He will be the perfect warrior.'

"'That is not a blessing—that is a curse!' the queen cried, pulling her babe away.

"But as the hall erupted in shouts, the cloaked being was gone. The king remained quiet as the queen sobbed over the small bundle in her arms.

"But the Ellythian Queen stepped forward, her voice deep and melodic, said, 'Where there is a lock, there must be a key. Such is the law of the wild and void.'

"The queen hung onto every word as the Pixie Queen said, 'Three queens we have to forge one key. The power will be enough.'

"Lightning struck. Magic thrummed, and it was done. The key was forged.

"The prince grew up to be as was he cursed—a lethal warrior, undefeated in battle, and indeed, he seemed to enjoy killing and defeating more than anything else in the world. Thus he remained his father's pride and joy. But the shadow that bound his heart seemed to spread, and his cousin-brothers, raised as warriors in their own right, became like him. As a unit, they were revered among the Boneweavers and feared by their enemies, the Daanav Kingdom, who had been long terrorising the Isles for thousands of years.

"And so the king bade his undefeated son to do what no Boneweaver before had achieved. To take Daanav Kingdom down once and for all.

"Prince Ashzale and his brothers took over the Daanav Marine Kingdom beneath the Lotus Sea by themselves. Realising that he was much like them, those brutal, savage creatures came to love him and made him their king.

But the pride the Boneweaver King had for his son faded when he saw the power Zale bore as a grown adult. He saw that, quite easily, Zale and his warriors could take over the Boneweaver Kingdom if he so wished.

"So, he summoned his god, the one he called Great Reaper, and asked for the single boon he'd been granted.

'My son grows rabid. He is a danger to all. He must be put down.'

"But the dark god shook his head. 'He remains a blessed servant of mine. I will need him for the great war I must win in years to come. I will put him to rest until I need him. But he will be as good as dead to you and your people.'

"And so the prince and his three warriors were forced to lay in their tombs until such a time the Reaper needed them."

As Rani finished her story, she said with a grimace, "No doubt it made them mad, staying in there for two hundred years. If they weren't completely feral before, they are now."

21
ALTARA

"What a tragic story," I said, frowning at the words coming out of my own mouth. The girls looked at me in surprise—and rightly so. "But that doesn't excuse what he's done! He's evil through and through, *and* friendly with demons!"

"The curse gives him no conscience," Pia agreed. "He is a cold-blooded killer."

"But we're supposed to help him," Rani said. "To remove that curse."

"This Reaper gave it to him!" I exclaimed. "How are *we* supposed to get rid of it?"

"The queens created a key, remember?" Rani said excitedly. "We need to find out what it is! We need to go to the library."

"There's a library here?" I asked.

"No," said Malika, finally sitting down. "We need the headmistress's private library. In her office. That is where she kept books about dark magic. I saw them in there when I visited for my most recent misdemeanour."

"Right," I said, remembering the dark pendant she'd worn. Clearly the headmistress was versed in dark magic. "We look there first." I turned to Leela, who was still sitting on my palm. "So we need to get out of here. I can move around unseen, and I'm thinking to take one person with me."

"I'll go," Rani said, standing. "We cannot risk *two* princesses of Ellythia." She smiled at me, and I gave her a grateful smile back.

We all looked at Malika, who was now sitting quietly, and I saw why. At some stage during the story, her pixie had returned to her, and she now had him in her lap, two fingers around his neck.

"You deal with that," I said to Pia, nodding to our sour-faced friend and her errant pixie. I turned back to the pixie in my own palm. "Leela? Can you help us get out of this room?"

"You use void magic," Leela said, flying over to the door. "Be one with door. Open door."

"Huh." I'd never called it *void magic* before. I walked over the door, sitting innocently with no visible magic. But I knew it lay there, hidden beneath my sight.

"Hand on door," Leela instructed.

I obliged and instantly felt the buzz of magic under my skin. My magic reacted with enthusiasm, seeking out Kai's magic in the same way it sought out illness and disease in a human body. I felt the seeking, and the finding, then the subsequent pulling and drawing back into me. The magic of the door was literally being pulled inside of me, and I felt it like a fizzing sensation bubbling through my hand into my core. I shivered as my own magic digested it and when it stopped, realised that door was now devoid of any magic at all. I tried the handle, and it opened easily.

Leela clapped.

"I've never done that," I said excitedly. "It's like my magic has gotten stronger since arriving here." The moment I'd stepped ashore my magic had reacted and began surging and roiling inside of me. And I'd never had to control it in so much. Perhaps a part of it was that it was reacting to the familiar, the fact that there was so much magic here compared to where I grew up.

"Impressive, Tara!" Rani said cheerily. I turned to see my gangly friend grinning at me. "Shall we?"

"I'll just have to have skin contact with you the entire time," I said carefully. "We can hold hands, perhaps?"

She gave me her hand, and I took it, my magic leaping up and around us both as I let myself fall into our surroundings. Leela took her cue and came to perch on top of my head, settling down crosslegged.

It was an odd thing, melding into my surroundings. The first time I'd done it, I was afraid I would disappear into nothing and fail to exist completely. Except at that time, I actually *had* wanted to disappear into nothing. It was the whole reason that power had come about. And now, every time I fell into nothingness, a tiny, shameful part of me yearned to disappear. I think it was something I would have to fight with for the rest of my life. There were some things, some events that would never leave you. That changed the very structure of your being, and you'd have to just learn to fight it when it came calling.

But now the Goddess had come to us and told me those *things*. That she had been waiting for me. It felt almost absurd. Like something I'd made up to make myself feel better. And if the others hadn't been there to witness, I probably would have pushed it to the back of my mind, unable to accept it. I would have to try and figure out what it all meant if we were to break the curse on our evil king.

Malika made an impressed sound as we disappeared, and Rani jerked so violently she almost let go of my hand. I looked over at her, but of course, she was nowhere to be seen, only a vague ripple where her body met the air around her.

"It's a little strange," I reassured her, "but as soon as you let go, you'll come back. Don't be afraid, alright?"

Rani strode forward. "There are only two things in this world I am afraid of, Your Highness," Rani said jovially. "Intestinal worms and sharks."

"I suppose we'll have to talk about the worms later," I mused.

I opened the door, and we tentatively stepped out.

"Does your magic cover our scent?" Rani breathed next to me.

"Definitely not."

"Then we must be careful, for the Old Ones will be able to scent us. Their noses are stronger than a bloodhound, if the stories are true."

I swore under my breath as we moved down the corridor, Rani leading the way. How could I have forgotten that Kai had found me invisible on that tree branch that night? Of course, he'd sniffed me out like a predator.

"Right," I whispered. "So if we see one, we must move away from them as quickly as possible without running."

We padded our way down the corridor, with me adjusting Leela once or twice when she pulled on a strand of my hair too hard. The castle was empty, and I guessed that everyone was confined to rooms under magical lock and key.

To my surprise, our path to the headmistress's office was easy, and we were undisturbed the entire way. It made me itch, wondering where the four Old Ones were and what evil they were up to, but I needed to focus on the task at hand.

I put an ear against the headmistress's office door, and hearing nothing within, tentatively nudged it open.

We promptly stopped dead.

Fangar was sitting, roped to a chair, frowning at the door as Rani closed it behind us. There were so many ropes binding him he was almost completely covered. I guessed that it was Kai who had gone rather overboard with the rope, but as I looked at the blue demon skin and those yellow-red eyes, my skin crawled violently. I didn't think I'd ever get used it. And by the Gods, no one could find out that I'd kissed the creature. My stomach churned.

"What do we do?" Rani whispered.

I shook my head and then realised she couldn't see me, so I tugged her around Fangar towards the back of the office where the headmistress's desk and case of books were.

"Who's there?" Fangar gruffed in a loud, arrogant voice. "I can hear you."

Sighing I pulled my magic back just enough to show my head.

Fangar's eyes widened, and then he glared at me. "Untie me, Lota woman," he said through those gritted, pointed teeth.

"No," I said, promptly moving behind him and around the desk to the case of books.

"Why?" he snapped.

"Because you are lucky that I have not yet killed you. Now be quiet."

I scanned the bookcase and assumed Rani was too. On the very bottom shelf, where they could barely be seen, sat a row of books bound in black leather.

Rani let my hand go so she could pull them all out, and we began laying them on the desk. Leela whispered in my ear that she was going to keep lookout, and I nodded. The little pixie ducked under the door so fast that it was impossible for Fangar to have seen her. As we looked over the leather-bound books, I felt a little ill thinking that Headmistress Jessine would never get to use her office again. On the other hand, she had been a selfish woman, having orchestrated the illusion-demon marriage situation and profiting off it.

"Let me go, Zara," Fangar urged. "I'm telling you—"

"Do not say my name!" I snapped. "And why do you want to marry me?" I said, leafing through a book titled *Darkest Desires.* "Why did you insist upon it that night?"

The demon went quiet.

I took the chance to flip through the first text, mostly about dark objects and making deals with demons. Nothing about locks and keys.

Rani tapped her book and tucked it under her arm, nodding at me. She must have found something in that one. We put all the books back, and I took her hand again, enveloping us in my magic, but still left my head visible. I stepped us back to Fangar.

"I know you are a Lota," he said angrily, jostling his chair. "You tried to trick me, but I saw your poison-coloured eyes. Let me go, or you'll regret it."

I ignored that request. "What do you know about this Boneweaver creature?" I asked him. "About what happened to him?"

"I'll tell you nothing until you release me."

I sighed, and it was at that point that a glow under the door caught my attention. Leela's tiny hand appeared under the door, beckoning madly.

Hastily, I cloaked my head and made for the door.

"What is this sorcery?" Fangar choked out. "What are you doing? Take me with you."

I didn't feel bad at all as I opened the door, closed it shut and ducked us back down the corridor, appearing briefly so Leela could put herself back on my head.

"Patrolling the corridor," she whispered. "Big one."

That could be any of them, really. But I didn't risk speaking as Rani and I rushed down the steps into the entrance hall.

"That dung-eating mollusc!" Rani hissed angrily. "Your eyes aren't poison coloured. They are beautiful like gems."

I grinned, even though she couldn't see it. "Thanks, Rani."

The front doors were now wide open, sunlight spilling onto the flagstones like Agnolthi's light itself. Freedom. I stopped dead in my tracks, thinking. Could we make it to the twins' house? They might have a better idea of what to do than we did.

"What are we doing?" Rani breathed, squeezing my hand to make sure I was paying attention.

"I'm just wondering whether we make a run for it to the village," I whispered back.

Leela gave a frantic, painful tug of my hair, and I almost gasped out loud.

But it was too late.

"I smell a princess," drawled a voice from behind us. "Do you, my king?"

I whirled around, swinging Rani with me. Atax, the commander, casually lounged his lean, powerful body against one of the walls, a smirk on his handsome face. Next to him, Zale glowered, his blue eyes flashing with repressed anger.

He stalked right up to us, a predator assessing prey, as if

he could see us clearly, but I knew he was following my smell as his eyes searched our surroundings

"Your scent, princess," Zale said in a low, dangerous voice that hit me right between my legs—and why wasn't he wearing a shirt? "Is as distinct to me as the morning sun and just as irritating."

Rani began tugging us sideways, back the way we'd come, while Leela continued to frantically pull me by the hair as if she could make me move faster. But to my horror, Zale cocked his head, his eyes following us as we did.

Without warning, he lunged for me. Rani screamed but held onto my hand for all she was worth. But it wasn't enough, the three of us, pixie included, crashed to the floor, and I lost my grip on her.

Zale's weight on my supine body was a glorious torture, his masculine scent drawing me in like honey. If it were not for his cold, cold eyes, I would have—

But the closeness brought that shadow out of him, and my magic responded, tugging on it. That feeling was colder than death, more suffocating than terror and more soul-destroying than lost hope.

My magic stuttered as if having a seizure, and I would not, *could not* let it pull that feeling into me. My power retreated all too rapidly, and abruptly, my body was revealed. Zale Boneweaver lay atop me, his powerful, naked arms on either side of my shoulders, his pupils dilated almost all the way as he focused on my face. I could barely breathe.

He lowered his head down to mine, and just for a moment, his brilliant blue eyes flashed with heat. But it was gone in an instant, and it was more than possible, in my wanton, dazed state, that I imagined it.

"I suggest," Zale hissed, and I felt every forsaken ridge

and divot of his body against mine, "instead of attempting a pointless rebellion, you prepare for the wedding tonight." He rolled off me, springing to his feet, carved abdominals flexing. Looking down at me, his features were droll and unimpressed. "I expect full Ellythian bridal rituals."

"Why?" I asked, flabbergasted, scrambling back to my feet as Rani gaped a few steps away. "Why do you care about Ellythian rituals?"

"This wedding will be binding. There can be no doubt of its legitimacy amongst your *kind*."

Rani was suddenly next to me, Leela no doubt hiding somewhere.

"We will attend to it, Your Majesty," Rani said hastily, grabbing my elbow. "Don't you worry a thing about it." I glared at her, but she was flushed, and the hand on my elbow was trembling. "We will need time to gather the things for it. Flowers and all that. All the women will need to be put to work."

Zale turned away from us, but Atax rolled his broad shoulders as if irritated by the lack of activity—as if the only thing worth his while was a fight. But he nodded, the no-nonsense commander. "How many are needed?"

22
ALTARA

The preparation for the wedding happened with disgusting efficiency, and it was then that I learned more than a few people in our school actually accepted Zale as king of this island. There was no love left between Queen Cheshni and inhabitants of Boneweaver Island after their queen all but left them to the hands of the Daanavs. Dare I say it, but I had reason to believe there were some who were *happy* about a wedding. Perhaps they wanted something to be excited about after the headmistress's execution, and I think they felt a little betrayed by her taking profits from the enemy.

Rani and Pia managed to find and release Housekeeper Yona, who was promptly brought before Zale, who then instructed her on exactly what he wanted. Yona, being the practical woman that she was, took everything in her stride and pulled things together with the efficiency of an army general. Lady Trisana and Armismistress Vari were a little shaken but seemed to have recovered from yesterday's events. I had most of this information from the girls who'd come and gone from the room in which I was to have a bridal confinement. The wedding was to be held at midnight, the only Boneweaver requirement the king had, so we had some time.

As night fell and a definite buzz filled the air, I looked out our dormitory window, only to find the entire Taraka town milling about the garden at the front of the castle.

"Why are all these people here?" I whispered, glancing back at Malika who'd remained with me. We'd had to fake her being unwell because the male Pixie was still being an overall nuisance, flitting about and biting her. He was currently tied down with a hair ribbon, his arms bound straight against his body where Malika had placed him on a tiny makeshift bed made from handkerchiefs.

"You are a *princess*," Malika chided me, "marrying a *king*! A wedding is amongst the most sacred things to our kind. And a royal wedding needs an audience. Of course everyone is excited."

"He's not been coronated," I retorted with my arms crossed. "He's still technically a prince."

"I suppose that's true," she admitted, "but..." she gave me a pointed look, "would anyone really dispute his claim?"

"Maybe I will," I said defiantly.

"Well, you're certainly a braver woman than the rest."

I turned to face her. "Why did you and all the other girls resign yourselves to marriages to the Daanav demons? You knew who they were under those illusions, and...I was watching—you were all really hoping for a match."

Malika rubbed her eyes in uncharacteristic weariness. "It's complicated, Altara. You wouldn't understand without having lived here for the last few years but...we're alone." She shrugged. "We thought the demons were our only option.

Better for a legitimate marriage than to be sent to slavery, which is what they *would* have done to us otherwise. The headmistress organised for them to wear the illusion so it would be more palatable for us. We all thought she was helping us get through it."

I felt ill hearing that Malika thought marriage to a demon was her only path. It felt very un-Ellythian to me—very desperate. Yet again, I wondered what manner of mistake Malika and Rani had made that had landed them here in exile. I knew there was more to Pia's story as well. Refusing to break her contract to her betrothed was not enough to warrant a full-scale exile and abandonment, surely?

There was a knock on the door, and it opened to reveal Pia and Rani, except they were not alone. Geravie and the twin witch-priestesses hurried in behind them.

I cried out, running to Geravie, who opened her arms for me. I clung onto her as if my life depended on it, and perhaps, maybe it did.

"Get us out of here, Geravie!" I said, pulling away to look at her. "I'm not marrying that foul old man." Someone choked out a laugh behind me, and I knew it was Malika.

"Foul *males*," she corrected me quietly. "You are being given to a Daanav marine as well."

"He said he claimed me," I said grumpily, "which was a lie, and Zale said I had his scent on me and said 'fine, we'll be two husbands.' Can't we get out of here?" I looked around at them all, exasperated at their acceptance of this whole farce.

The twins gave me a solemn look. "Wherever you go," Reshmi said, her silver braid hanging over her shoulder, "he will find you."

"I'll leave the island then? Take a boat and escape north?

Or back to the continent? I could go by myself. No one would even see me."

"Remember the entrance hall," Rani said so patiently it made my eyes burn. "He'll find you before you could even get to a boat."

I hated that I was being outsmarted and outwitted in this. I was used to having the upper hand in any situation. Back in Lobrathia where I was a princess with privileges, the only person who'd ever gotten the better of me was my stepmother.

And now it was happening all over again. Anger tore through me like a rogue arrow, sharp and biting. I could never let that happen again. I would never. There would be some way I could outsmart him. Whether it was now or after the wedding when I could catch him unawares, I would get out of this—even get my revenge. For a forced marriage and for my rights being taken away.

I gritted my teeth and set my shoulders. Keshmi carried a length of purple fabric over her hands, smooth and glittering like moonlight over water. I recognised it immediately as an Ellythian bridal set. My mother had the same kind, and Saraya had taken it with her to the fae realm for her own wedding. How cross she'd be with me now, for getting myself into this bastard of a mess. I reached out and ran my fingers along it and found it to be silky soft.

"Three village seamstresses worked on it all day," Geravie said, pointing out the detailed gold embroidery. "They are proud for Yasani's daughter to be wearing it."

I could not stop the tears that slipped from me. "They all know?" I choked out, wiping my cheeks. This was a real disaster. If word spread that I was here, the entire point of my running away was taken from me.

"Just the head seamstress," Geravie said. "So she could embroider your parents' names, hidden, into the design as is tradition. We still must keep your name quiet."

I sniffed away my tears, running my fingers over my parents' names stitched into the leaf of one of the lotuses. *Yasani Lota. Eldon Voltanius.* I straightened, pushing back my hair. "Do you know what this key is?" I asked the twins. "To the king's shadow-locked heart? Maybe we can find it and quickly undo the curse."

Reshmi gave me a look of such pity that I wanted to claw my own eyes out. "No one knows."

I deflated like a wilting leaf. I'd actually thought the elders of the town might have an answer. "There were three queens there and these warrior midwives, and it wasn't passed down with the story?"

"I can ask if anyone else knows if there are other versions of the story in other villages," Reshmi said. "One of the other priestesses may know."

"I've been looking through this book on black magic you guys brought back," Malika said, holding up the head-mistress's black leather-bound tome. "But there's nothing specific about what it could be. Only that opposites seem to be involved in undoing curses, which we already know."

"I didn't know that," I murmured. "But my mother only taught me about my magic, which seems to have its own rules."

The room descended into quiet for a while as Geravie and Keshmi styled and pinned my hair into a complex, curled up-do.

As Geravie took me into the dressing room and wrapped a blue saree around my waist and breasts, I thought about how I'd felt when Zale had been on top of me in the entrance hall.

"He felt dark," I murmured as Geravie walked around me. "Like hopelessness, evil and terror. It was frightening. Do you think that was the shadow-lock I was feeling?"

"Possibly," she said, a crease between her brows. "This is dark magic we're dealing with. It makes sense that your magic would detect it strongly."

Once we were done, I checked myself in the mirror. I supposed I looked like a native Ellythian girl, in nothing but a perfectly wrapped saree and beautiful hair. I stepped out into the main room and for some reason, blushed as everyone else turned to look at me.

"A wedding," Rani sighed. "Who would have thought we'd be here, having one tonight?"

"You're telling me," I grumbled. "This is the exact reason why I left Lobrathia."

"The things we run from have a funny way of finding us," mused Pia. "My...*our* grandmother used to say that all the time." She handed me a silver tray with a goblet and two objects. "That's *his* ring, and Fangar's symbol. Both...er, grooms."

I nodded stiffly, picking them both up to examine. One was the shark tooth necklace I'd seen Fangar wearing when we'd first met. The second was a ring made of black volcanic glass, and in the centre was a golden, angry tiger's head.

Before I could alert everyone that I had not any rings to give to the grooms, a drum sounded outside the door. It sounded so similar to the drum from the night Zale had stolen everyone from our beds that we all jumped.

Rani hurried to the door, opening it to reveal a group of women standing in the corridor, including Lady Trisana and Armsmistress Vari, who was the one carrying the gigantic drum strapped around her neck.

"Ready?" she asked, looking me in the eye. I wasn't sure which type of ready she was asking, but I nodded anyway. She nodded back. "We've been *instructed*," Vari rolled her eyes, and I knew she appreciated Zale's arrogant commands just as much as I did, "to do everything properly, so we'll need a drummer, two candle holders and the two priestesses at the head of the group and Geravie in front of the princess."

I shuddered as the girls all hurried to volunteer for positions.

The women from the village craned their necks to get a look at me from the corridor, but Lady Trisana quickly nudged me into position far behind everyone else.

"I'm sorry your parents could not be here," she said softly to me. She, of course, did not know who my parents were, even though they'd all no doubt figured I was somehow a Lota as I'd no longer continued hiding my eyes.

Saraya and I had come to terms with the fact that our mother would not be at our respective weddings, but it hurt anew, here in Ellythia our mother's natal home with Ellythian rituals being conducted. I pressed my lips together and tried to smile at her, but Geravie looked back at me, and I was reminded I did have one family member here—two if I counted Pia.

I noted everything with wide eyes because Lobrathian custom had never meant so much pomp, especially considering we were only up to the pre-wedding bridal ritual part just now.

Rani and one of the girls from the school banged took up the big drums tied around their necks in the front. Behind them were Pia and Malika, holding unsheathed, ceremonial swords to act as guards. Behind them were two young girls with bowls glowing water they were to sprinkle to cleanse the area I would walk through.

Then came the twin witch-priestesses, the *Book of Agnolthi* in either hand. I squinted at the velvet-bound tomes and knew at once I'd have to take a look at them after this. No doubt there were valuable spells and the like in there.

Before me stood Geravie, in a saree of green and purple, with the end portion of it over her head in the proper Ellythian way—this was traditionally the position of the bride's mother.

Then came me, glowering, with the golden tray in hand.

I knew Leela and the other pixie were around here somewhere, out of sight but watching carefully.

Our two drummers began a lively beat, as if they could trick me into thinking this was a happy occasion. In other circumstances I supposed a royal wedding *was* such a thing. Our procession trailed out the door, and as we walked through the halls of the school, where all the students had excitedly gathered, they watched us pass and then followed behind us until the group became so big that when we entered the castle grounds, the place felt like a carnival with excited chatter filling my ears.

It wasn't until then that I realised what a clever strategic move this was for Zale. In basically holding a celebration, he'd smoothly reinserted himself back directly into the island community here that definitely supported his reign over the place. I hated him even more.

The entire village cleared a path to watch me go past, whispering in my wake, their eyes shifting from Pia, then to me and my Lota-emerald eyes.

They would all figure it out, I realised glumly. Everyone would come to know that there was another Ellythian girl here, and word would spread across Ellythia, and eventually, as these things go, by trading sailors, would reach to other kingdoms. I had no idea what to do about that, but I was getting married in a far-off land. This was almost exactly what my stepmother had wanted.

We walked into the humid night, the sound of the drums feeling more and more like a funeral procession with every beat.

My stepmother had won. She'd gotten rid of both of us sisters, whisked us both away for marriage, leaving her to her devices with my ailing father. Sharp pain shot up my fingers, and I realised I'd gripped onto the edges of the tray so tightly it had cut into my palms. I hissed as we walked down a dirt path, deep in my own dark thoughts until blue-speckled, moving light shone on the jungle around us.

It was the fae-lagoon Fangar had shown me, where we'd come across Zale and the other Old Ones for the first time.

How poetic. I scowled into the night.

By the rustle of the bushes, I knew a large group of women had gathered around the water. They'd separated themselves into unmarried women on my side, and on the other side the married women gathered expectantly.

Tonight I would transition from the arms of the maiden into the bosom of married life. I vaguely wondered if Saraya had adhered to Geravie's instructions and found herself a glowing pond in the fae realm to do her bridal rituals. I wondered if she, too, lamented the gaol she was about to enter.

The full moon shone ahead—Agnolthi's moon. And I wondered if the Goddesses were watching me tonight, laughing probably, at my expense.

I was supposed to enter the lagoon naked, but I wasn't

about to do that with so many people here. Even *I* had some semblance of decency. So I crouched down by the lagoon, scooped up water into the golden chalice and put it back on my tray.

When I stood, it was Pia who waited for me, a strange, sad look in her eye. She gave me an apologetic smile. "Maidenhood delivers you to the Mother. Go with the love of the Goddess at your side and fond memories of your old home." She put her hand over mine still gripping the tray and said only for me, "The lotus is patient, Altara, and strong, above all." Her eyes were earnest with hidden meaning and I couldn't help but smile sadly at her. This was the Lota House motto and her glittering eyes were telling me to wait this out. That we would get through this. I might not have Saraya here, but I did have Pia, and that, more than anything tonight, gave me heart. I *would* be patient and we would work our way out of this.

So I met her strong gaze and nodded. She stepped aside and I climbed into the lagoon with my saree and all. Rani was suddenly at my ear whispering to me.

"A fae lagoon has no bottom because it leads to the ocean!" I looked at her in alarm, but she simply pointed a finger at the pool, and something shimmered beneath its surface. She nodded to me and retreated.

Tentatively, I lowered myself into the water and found a solid metal floor beneath my feet, a slight tickle telling me it was Rani's magic. Sighing with relief, I did as I'd been told and raised my gold tray over my head and waded slowly to the other side.

Neither Geravie nor the priestesses were married, so they did not greet me on the other side. Instead Lady Trisana spread her arms out for me. "Come, bride of the King Ashzale

Boneweaver, bride of Fangar Sharksbane, the second sword of the Daanav Marine Kingdom."

Urgh.

She took the chalice from my tray, and I lowered it. As she gently tipped the water over my crown, she said, "May her husbands see that she is moon-touched and Goddess-blessed. May they worship the Goddess at the feet of their bride, at the lap of their bride and at the lips of their bride. For tonight she *is* the Goddess."

Those words only meant one thing: we'd be expected to consummate this marriage.

Trying to push away the feeling of doom in my core, I awkwardly climbed out of the pool and into the blanket Armsmistress Vari held out for me.

I didn't bother drying off because as we departed the lagoon, I needed the night air to cool my heated skin.

For the first time in a long time, I wondered if I could just fade away into nothingness and escape this fate, this wedding. I was not ready to be anyone's wife, let alone a wife to two males. My heart seemed to pound slowly in my chest, my own solemn beat. My magic flooded my skin, wanting to be used, wanting to do something to save me.

But even as the thought of disappearing into nothing came, we cleared the jungle, and my gaze found Zale's cold blue eyes fixed upon me like a hawk watching a mouse. He was completely naked, his skin wet as if he'd climbed out of water himself, standing without a care in the world for the village men and women staring at him as if he were a god walking among them. No doubt he'd returned from his own wedding rituals. Something flickered in those eyes, a flash of golden light that seemed familiar and yet foreign. He blinked as if irritated by it, and the spell he had over me was gone, his face returned to its usual cold glower.

I decided then and there that no one—not my stepmother, not any demon, and not Zale forsaken Boneweaver—would get the better of me, and I wasn't disappearing into nothingness like a coward. I might have to marry him, but I'd make sure he'd regret every second of it.

23

ZALE

I awaited my bride in the same fashion as hundreds of Boneweaver males had done before me—on the sacred Ivory Beach before the clear quartz altar at midnight under Agnolthi's pregnant moon. I guessed that this bubbling sensation responding to being in front of the wide-open sea was as close to the feeling of joy as I was capable of. The pixies were starting to arrive, pinpricks of blue, purple, green and yellow lights lingering at the edges of the jungle, as if mirroring the sheet of stars above me. They might not have seen a Boneweaver wedding on this island for the past two hundred years, but some instinct in them had them coming forth.

The second sword of Daanav Marine Kingdom stood next to me, his hands clasped before him as if protecting his manhood from me. Smart creature. No doubt he had angled himself to marry a Lota to improve his position at his own court.

It was tradition that the groom be dressed in nothing, as a Boneweaver wedding required both bride and groom to take on their animal forms for the second part of the wedding rites. But the Ellythian woman had no animal heart to speak of, weak as her species was. No doubt she'd also faint from my nakedness, and I wouldn't have that at my own wedding. Instead I compromised by wearing handwoven ceremonial trousers Kai had made and had my second groom stand naked out of spite. He needed to understand his place, and that was as far beneath my feet as possible.

The villagers were gathered on either side of the alter, dressed in what I supposed was their best Ellythian clothing while my own brothers patrolled the jungle until my Vayashi arrived. I could see Kai swinging from the branches of a tree, grinning madly. He loved weddings, though could never sit still for them.

Over the soft lapping of the waves, a steady drumbeat sounded, deep in the jungle. Raen arrived first. A few of the women in the crowd gasped at his naked form, tattooed with ancient symbols of sorcery. He walked down the aisle made of palm fronds and rose petals the young Ellythian females had prepared, much to my distaste. When he reached me, he grasped my forearm.

"My king," he said formally.

"High Priest," I returned with a nod. He couldn't help but smirk a little as he took the position his father once had behind the alter and began setting out his tools.

Next came the twin priestesses of the Order of Yasani, their hunched, elderly bodies looking like turtles under their black ceremonial robes. Both held the *Book of Agnolthi*, glittering purple, to my acute eyesight, under the weight of its own magic.

The drums began a fast-paced, cheery beat as two little girls appeared, throwing even more flower petals onto the sand, looking around nervously. By the time they approached me, they were practically shaking with fear, but their parents came and collected their pups, casting me a worried glance as I shifted impatiently. The drummer came next, one of the girls I'd assessed the other night. Tall and lean, she was built like a warrior and would have been favoured amongst Boneweaver males back in my time.

Behind her came the old Harranpul woman arm in arm with my Lota bride. The shadow around my heart twitched a little as my eyes fell upon her form, and damn me, I could not wrest my gaze off her. She was a beautiful creature—that was clear for any male with eyes to see. Her face was proud, her eyes glimmering with a steady rage as they studied me. A slow smile spread across my lips in response to her anger, the shadow in me recognising a familiar and comforting emotion. She was dressed in purple Ellythian silk, a blouse without sleeves and a high-waisted skirt that showed a slither of her waist. A purple silk veil was pinned to her head, draping around her arms and sweeping along the sand behind her. It was disappointing because a small part of me hoped she would arrive naked, in the way of my people, but I had never seen an Ellythian wedding before, so I guessed all of this was normal for them. In her palms she held an orb of magical light set into a squat lantern, and her walk down the aisle was surefooted in the way of warriors, though her wide hips moved seductively side to side. She was a woman made for kings, I had no doubt, and how I'd found her coupling with Fangar in the dark, I'd never understand.

The urge to secure her struck me like a blow to the gut. Something inside of me just knew that no one else would do for this task. But she was also troublesome, and I would need to keep my claws tight around her.

Her sweet, fiery scent waved towards me on the sea

breeze, and for some reason, my mouth watered as if it were hungry. I frowned at the sensation, unsure where to place it, and failing to, brushed it aside as she strutted up to me. The Harranpul woman curtseyed to me, and I gave her an approving nod before she took my bride's lantern and stepped aside to take her place with the other commoners.

I turned to look at the Lota woman and found her decidedly ignoring me, facing away from me and towards Raen and the two small witch-priestesses he towered over.

Fangar and I turned to look at the servants of the Gods.

A guttural roar boomed from the forest so loud it made the sand shake, and I recognised Atax's lion's voice. The crowd shifted in shock, and I grinned at Raen, as before anyone could run away, he raised his hands and boomed over crowd: "And so we begin." When they realised that no lion was charging out of the jungle, the crowd settled, and Raen continued, "We call the Gods to bear witness so that this beast and this princess and this demon be wed in sacred union." He lowered his hands and stepped back.

The twins took their cue and one of them said, "Holy Agnolthi grants us the strength to defeat our enemies, to wield the truth in our hearts and above all, to worship our mother, this island that sustains us through all joy and pain. Groom, bride and groom, join hands."

As I took my bride's hand, a tiny sting struck my skin. I hid my surprise as Fangar came around to her other side. He too, twitched when he took her hand. A constellation of callouses scraped against my own, and I looked down upon her with surprise. I'd known it was likely she was trained in fighting, but this much hardened skin suggested long years and recent prolonged use of weapons, and by the feel of her first two fingers, being her right hand, I knew immediately that the bow was her preferred weapon.

Raen allowed the priestesses to instruct us on our rites, and naturally, I went first, pricking my thumb on an elongated tooth, as was custom. She turned to look at me, her eyes glittering with anger and I smirked. I brushed my thumb against her forehead, marking her with a vertical line of my blood.

"I, Ashzale Boneweaver, claim you, woman of house Lota, as my sacred and holy wife. We are tied by words, by blood, by sea and by ink. You are mine as I am yours."

Fangar said his piece, marking her with his blood and it took all my self control not to strike him down and wipe his blood off her forehead. Raen gave me a look of warning and it was the only thing that made me dig my heels into the sand.

Then the Lota woman cleared her throat and pricked her finger on the dagger Raen offered her. "I, Pia of House Lota claim you, Ashzale Boneaweaver, as my sacred and holy husband."

I leaned down and she brushed her finger up my forehead. Her fiery presence filled my vision and her scent filled my nose—buzzing like the air before a storm and fresh like flowers. If this were a proper Boneweaver wedding, we'd consummate the marriage now and I would take her on the sand, claiming her in front of my people. In that second she was close to me, that urge filled me to bursting. But Raen knew me too well, and had scented it no doubt and growled in disapproval. I straightened, growling softly in reply, while my new wife turned and spoke to Fangar.

"And you, Fangar Sharksbane, I take you as my sacred and holy husband."

I wanted to cut the smirk off Fangar's face, but my mind was pulled by her words.

I knew she was lying through her teeth about her name because after thoroughly questioning the matron housekeeper, I found out that the green-eyed girl standing nervously at the back of the crowd, hoping not to be seen, was Pia Lota. It didn't matter to me, though, because my bride was still a Lota princess. And whatever her reason for hiding her identity, I would find out as soon as this was done.

As it hit midnight, the moon was positioned just so, and the clear quartz alter lit up with brilliant moonlight, fractals of multi-coloured glitter filling the air around us. The crowd gasped.

"A circumnavigation of the moon alter will seal your sacred vows," Raen said. "Because you are marrying two males, you need to do it twice."

Raen and twin priestesses stepped back, whispering in Old Ellythian as Raen spoke in the ancient fae dialect only Boneweaver priests knew. The power of it thrummed through the air, rumbled through my muscles and made the sand beneath my feet tremble.

Together we walked around the quartz altar once, then twice. This marriage not only bound me to the Lota royal family, but also to the Daanav kingdom. It would be the first union of its kind in history and a rather clever orchestration on my part.

Raen stood before us with his tattooing tools. My bride stiffened. "The last part of the ritual will be to bind your oaths in volcanic ink," Raen boomed so everyone could hear. "Fangar Sharksbane!"

Raen quickly tattooed the symbol of Lota House—a lotus

and sword—on the back of Fangar's left index finger. He called upon me and did the same.

"Bride, place your left hand on the altar."

She thrust her chin in the air and did so, trying not to look frightened, even though I could smell it fizzing around her.

Raen would tattoo a shark first, then a tiger and add the little spell that would make my new wife obedient to me. But as he began to tap his gold quartz needle into her finger, he frowned. My bride immediately inhaled sharply, though it was not for pain. Raen muttered under his breath and tapped again, this time a little angrily. The Lota woman went as stiff as a tree, her other hand clenching. She shook her head, and Raen looked up at me in confusion. I stepped up to them.

"The ink will not take," Raen murmured in annoyance. "Her skin heals over each time, and the ink dribbles out."

"I don't think I *can* take ink," my bride muttered.

Inwardly, I swore. Thinking fast, I mentally constructed a ring made out volcanic glass and my mother's pearl from the box we'd dug up in the ruins. It arrived into my hand with a small flame of power. Grabbing the Lota woman's hand, I slid the ring on. "There. Fangar will get you one later."

I nodded to the naked demon, and he nodded back. Together, we stepped out from behind the quartz altar.

"You are bound before the sea, before the moon and jungle," Raen boomed.

One of the twins spoke last, "You are now bound before Agnolthi and your friends and family. Goddess help you all."

Goddess help us, indeed. The villagers promptly departed after the sorcerer declared the rituals had ended. They streamed down the jungle paths as if they couldn't get home quickly enough. I didn't blame them at all, considering the malicious roar that had boomed from the jungle, like a promise of death, before the wedding commenced. In that moment I had almost leapt on top of the shirtless Zale out of fright but had looked over and seen him smirking like the insane creature he was and stayed fixed on my spot.

Geravie shuffled forward, her face intent on me as the naked Fangar attempted to take my hand and lead us back into the castle. I turned out of his reach just in time, hurrying towards my old nursemaid. But she did not embrace me, no, because such was my luck that instead, she pressed a packet of folded parchment with herbs into it.

My mouth made an "o" as I knew it to be contraceptive tea. I glanced back at the two males I'd just married. Fangar

194

had just put back on his illusionary cloak, shirt and pants and his handsome Ellythian face was now staring at me with unveiled hunger. The knot inside my stomach loosened just a little as his demon form was put away. Meanwhile, the king was talking quietly with Raen.

I was expected to consummate this marriage tonight—Geravie knew it, and everyone knew it by the way my friends were all pressing themselves close to me. Rani was wiping her cheeks, Pia was whispering to Leela in her hand and the twins were eyeing me with sympathy.

But Malika was smirking at me as she leaned in to whisper in my ear, "To be quite frank, I'm a little jealous."

I almost choked, but honestly, I knew exactly what she meant. Both men, in ordinary circumstances, I would have considered strapping and most worthy of bedding. But Geravie shushed her as Rani quite obviously suppressed a gag.

"I'd offer you advice," Geravie said, fixing me with a stern but compassionate eye. "But we both know you don't need it."

I rolled my eyes at her before sighing, "Right, let's get it over with then. I will see you tomorrow?"

Rani gave me a wet kiss on the cheek, while Pia gave me a chaste kiss on the other. Malika patted me on the shoulder, the smirk still on her face as they walked away into the night with the priestesses and Geravie, Raen leisurely tailing them.

Quite suddenly, I was alone with two males on the beach in the middle of the night.

I tilted my chin in the air and turned to look at my husbands. Fangar strode forward to rudely snatch up my hand while Zale observed from the side.

"Shall we." The way the king said it was a dark statement. Arrogant bastard.

He strode ahead of us, walking up the beach and into the dark, leaving Fangar and I to scramble behind him, me being much slower in my long and heavy silk skirt.

I was a married woman, and it sat on my shoulders like two fat gremlins sniggering in my ears, yanking on leashes tied around my neck. I looked down at the ring Zale had unceremoniously shoved on my right index finger. It was an oddly beautiful thing for a savage man to conjure. The smooth black band had tiny etchings on it and the pearl gave off an almost impossible opalescent sheen. It didn't look expensive, it looked...*rare*. I'd never seen anything like it.

The walk back to the castle school was painful, and I would much rather be stabbing my own eyes out, but alas, Geravie had forbidden me to hide any daggers on my person. I needed Leela to teach me to summon astral weapons as soon as possible because I doubted my new husbands would allow me to carry my weapons, lest I kill them in the middle of the night.

A fair thing for them to presume that I would try.

I snuck looks at Fangar as we walked as fast as we could though the dark jungle, wondering what he was like in bed. The thought of me about to have sex with a demon made my skin crawl, but I would just have to pretend he was human and attend to it like it was business.

This was an expected thing, after all, and I was not above thousand-year-old laws. Even Geravie hadn't suggested a way to get out of it. She knew me too well. Sex had been nothing but a pleasurable pasttime for me and served as a distraction from the darkness that had otherwise threatened to burst forth. I'd needed it like how some war veterans needed alcohol or how Agatha, Quartz City's head midwife, needed blue ganja to help her deal with the stressors of her work. I could do it without thinking, and that's exactly what I would do now.

We emerged out of the forest, only to find Zale impatiently waiting for us, the other Old Ones nowhere in sight.

Zale led us back into the castle where it seemed everyone had been keen to get straight into bed. We wound our way through mostly empty corridors as my heart's pounding steadily increased. Eventually, we came to a room on the topmost floor of the school, where I suspected the teachers were ordinarily housed.

As we strode in, I noticed a modification had been made just for our merry threesome.

Someone, my bet was on Kai, had knocked a gigantic hole in the adjoining wall, as big and wide as Zale was tall. Through it, was a second bedroom.

Zale said, "This is our room for the night. We are leaving in the morning for our tour of the island."

Of course, I thought glumly, as any new regnant did, he'd have to visit the rest of the villages to gain or force their allegiance to him.

"Very well," I said, haughtily. The bed sat there, broad and firm, and I wondered if I was expected to bed them both at the same time. I'd never done that before. But just as I was about to open my mouth, Zale began loosening the strings on his embroidered wedding pants.

I panicked, and the words flew out of my mouth before I realised. "I will bed *him* first."

Zale's fingers paused, and as his eyes flashed with anger, I thought he'd argue with me. But the moment passed, and he had no emotion in his eyes when he said, "Fine." And sat

197

down on the chair next to the bed and crossed his arms, refusing to lift his eyes off me.

"You can't go somewhere else?" I asked.

"No."

I gave him a droll look and turned my back on him. Fangar pushed his cloak back a little, but thankfully didn't take it off. The illusion flickered for a moment, and I repressed a shudder as blue skin came into view and disappeared.

He's not like The Butcher. Nothing like him at all. I just have to pretend he's Ellythian.

Trying not to feel like Zale's eyes were not hot pokers in my back, I strode forward and pulled Fangar by the wrist, pushing him to sit on the leather armchair. I hiked up my skirts and climbed on top of him, straddling his lap in a way that was like habit for me. Sam, back at home, was slightly shorter than Fangar with his demon height, so the angles had worked a little more differently, but it was not a trouble to put my mouth to his and press a kiss to his lips.

He's not like The Butcher. Nothing like him at all. His skin is blue, not paper white.

Fangar gripped my hips with enthusiasm, grinding himself against me. His tongue invaded my mouth, and I allowed it, my body finding a familiar rhythm that was almost habitual.

He's not like The Butcher, not at all.

My magic fizzed under my skin, curiously leaping out and exploring.

Oh, not now, I thought, trying to reel it back in. But my grasp was poor, and I was distracted in more ways than one. Fangar's fingers pressed on the bare skin of my waist, a large bulge in his pants pressing in just the right spot for a spark of pleasure to sing through my centre. I let out an involuntary gasp, but I bit it back, shocked at myself. Fangar was a demon; I was riding a *demon*. My magic spun like a tornado, reaching out, pulling and *pulling* so violently that it caught me by surprise, and I did not have my wits about me enough to rein it back in.

Pain burst from my groin, violent and burning.

Fangar let out a strangled scream just as I leapt off him, gasping and placing a hand over the apex of my thighs, right over my vulva.

Except there was no vulva there, something bulbous and soft met my hand. My insides turned into ice as I froze. I looked up to see Zale now standing up, frowning at the two of us. Fangar was in a state and ran into the corner, yanking down his pants.

A feeling of dread wound its way around my very soul as I turned around, unbuttoned my skirt and looked down between my legs.

In place of a vulva, I had a penis and two testicles.

"No," I whispered in disbelief. I put a hand down my front and touched the soft skin—before yanking my hand out. *No, no, no!* I buttoned up my skirt, my mind racing, my heart thumping like a stallion in battle. "Dear Goddess. Holy mother of all, I....I..." I blabbered, looking over at Fangar. The demon, in his Ellythian face, had gone ashen, staring at me in abject horror, his hand still down his pants.

"What did you do?" his voice was a guttural whisper.

"I don't know," I whispered.

"Undo it," he commanded, taking a threatening step toward me.

My blood was rushing in my ears. "I can't—I don't know how—"

"You—" he took another raging step toward me, but Zale was suddenly there, blocking his path. Fangar roared in anger and bolted for the door, threw it open and ran outside.

Zale merely stared at him and then back at me. Then down at the hand I'd placed on my lower belly.

"What happened?" he asked in a deep, dangerous voice.

I gathered my wits, realising that if I was going to say it out loud, I was not going to appear hysterical. I looked the Boneaweaver King dead in the eye.

"It appears," I said, tossing my head and crossing my arms. "That I have taken Fangar's penis. By accident. He is without one now. That is why he is so upset."

The corners of Zale's pink lips twitched and a slow, vicious smirk spread across his face. His eyes fell to my groin. "Show me."

"Absolutely fucking *not*."

He cocked his head, considering me, clearly unbothered by my cussing. "And you did not do it on purpose?"

I put my hand on my hips and looked out the window, taking a deep breath as I felt the thing between my legs twitch all of its own accord. *Shit. Shit. Shit.* "Of course not."

He made a sound of interest in the back of his throat as I tried to steady my breathing by focusing on the rain now pattering against the window pane. My blasted magic still simmered under my skin as if ready for more.

"You may sleep with your friends to—"

"Say no more," I interrupted, striding past him out the door as fast as I could without looking at him. Ignoring the large bulge sliding against my thigh as I walked, I swore in seven different ways and bit back a gag. Luckily, I knew enough of the castle now to navigate my way back to the girls' old dormitory, which they'd taken back up now we were free to walk about.

But I couldn't take it any longer. I burst into a sprint, one hand holding my manhood to stop it from jostling uncomfortably. Racing down the steps to our dormitory, I burst through the door.

The girls sat up from their beds with a cry, steel scraping against a scabbard.

"Lights!" Pia's voice shouted, and the quartz-lamp slammed open, flooding the room with yellow light. Rani had her sword out, angling it at the door, but when she saw me, she dropped it. Malika jumped out of bed and ran forward, hair askew. "What's wrong? Did they hurt you?"

"No!" I shouted. Then I realised I was still gripping my manhood and hastily dropped it. "It's a disaster all the same!" My throat burned, my head was buzzing, my magic was pounding against my skin, wanting *more*. I slammed it violently back down, dashing for the pitcher of water on Pia's beside table and pouring myself a glass. I gulped down two glasses to calm myself down as the girls stared at me in bleary-eyed fear. The pixies came out then, including Leela, and the two of them flitted around us like worried bees.

"Altara," Pia said slowly, as if trying to calm a spooked horse. "Tell us what happened."

"I have a penis," I said flatly. "I was...we were...with Fangar, and then I think I panicked, and my magic burst out. There was all this pain and—" I clapped my hands and gestured to my groin. "I have Fangar's real-live, actual-working cock and balls, and he doesn't have anything there, and he ran from the room. I ran here."

Malika covered her mouth to stifle a laugh. "You're joking. Please tell me this is a twisted, Lobrathian joke—"

But I was shaking my head and undoing the buttons on my skirt. "Take a look."

Leela, the daring pixie that she was, zoomed towards me, her eyes wide. She hovered above my skirt where I held it open, looking down into the gloom that was my nether regions. Her golden glow lit it up like torch, and I grimaced, screwing my eyes shut before I saw it in the bright light.

"Wow," Leela said curiously, "can I touch?"

"No!" I said, batting her away. She flew upwards, clutching her tummy and giggling before coming back to sit on my head.

The girls came forward and took a quick, polite peek each, which I was grateful for. I couldn't possibly be doing this alone.

"Urgh," Malika said. "How terrible."

"Boils and barnacles!" Rani exclaimed and lurched back to her bed and began fanning herself.

"It's a bit bigger than a boil," I grouched.

"Well!" Pia said, a hand against her chest. "It certainly is *there*, isn't it?"

"I know," I said glumly. "I can bloody well feel it. It *twitched* before."

Leela began laughing again, and I wouldn't let the other pixie look, try as he did to sneak up my skirt.

"I still have my vagina," I said, frowning as I flexed my pelvic floor and definitely felt it still there. "But it's all closed up. I think my bladder has rerouted itself." My heart hammered in my chest as I realised what this meant. My fucking magic was insane, actually *insane*.

"Have you done this type of thing before, Tara?" Rani huffed from her bed, ashen faced.

"I've never been able to do anything *close* to this before!" I exclaimed, throwing my hands up in the air. "I've actually taken one of his body parts! Previously it was just illnesses."

There was one thing I knew for certain now: My power had grown exponentially since coming to this island, and none of it meant anything good.

I left my marriage room to find my brothers sitting in the kitchen, wolfing down a massive roasted hog, and for once in their lives, they were actually using plates. The kitchen staff were nowhere in sight and I suspected Raen had scared them away for night after having them cook the entire day. In the old days, a Boneaweaver wedding was cause for week-long celebration, but seeing as we were the only ones of our kind left, this would have to do.

It should have made me sad—I knew that—but it just didn't. My heart wasn't capable of that.

Fangar was also nowhere to be seen.

My brothers were giving me curious looks. I was the first of us to get married; we always knew it would be that way, me being crown prince and all, but now it had actually happened, I supposed they were curious about the Lota woman. I'd been surprised at her first burst of magic when she'd saved the headmistress, but I'd been even more surprised at her sudden capture of Fangar's cock. I'd never met someone actually powerful enough to take organs, but if she wasn't careful, she was going to end up with a moniker she didn't like. Fangar was wondering around cockless, and I was almost sure he'd gone back to Daanav Kingdom to complain to his warden of an uncle, or perhaps he was finding a demon priest to pray over him.

That was why tonight I was to take my first hard-won kingdom back.

"Why aren't you with your Vayashi?" Kai asked. "Does she not want to bed you?"

"Take it slow, brother," Atax said, gnawing on a bone. "You scare the women sometimes, remember?"

Kai nodded seriously, delicately sampling a teaspoon of rice pudding.

"She's not scared of me," I said, leaning against the bench.

But I couldn't bed her tonight—that was for sure. And if I didn't have a Vayashi to temper and control my power, I needed something else to release this energy.

And there was nothing better than a bloody battle to do that.

I stood abruptly, jittery for a weapon in my hands once again. "Let's pay a visit to Daanav Kingdom."

Kai jumped off the bench he was perched on and rushed right out of the kitchen. Atax grinned at me as he stood, grabbing a drumstick from a roast chicken for the road like the barbarian he was. Raen on the other hand, stood up slowly, flexing his fingers. Of all of us, he would need to work the hardest tonight, even just to get us there.

"Ready, brother?" I asked.

The line of tattoos on his face shifted in their eagerness. "Brother, I've been ready for the last two hundred years."

IN OUR EAGERNESS WE MADE IT TO THE BEACH IN GOOD TIME. I could sniff Fangar on the sea breeze, though I had to say his scent had changed just slightly. Perhaps that's what losing your cock did to you. In my tiger form, I prowled right into the warm lapping waves until the water reached my chest, then leapt up and plunged straight down into the sea. I changed into my second favourite form, what I called a beast-shark. I was big and silver, fast and terrifying to look at, but most importantly, the ultimate predator of the ocean. There was also nothing in this world as good as feeling the water against my smooth skin, spearing through the deep sea like a body made into a weapon. There was little sound under the water, and as I got deep enough, I got to be alone with my thoughts. It was the only real place I could find quiet, and after two hundred years of that hellish mental torture, it was a welcome reprieve.

Within seconds the others followed. Raen was also a Boneweaver through his father, and so he too, could shift into any form he wished. But Kai and Atax, although they were also my first-cousins, their fathers were not Boneweavers and were only able to take one form. This meant that Raen had to transport them in a bubble of his power. I turned my body around and looked behind me to find Raen as a dolphin with black markings, and two man-sized bubbles glowing green through the dark next to him. Kai was spinning around in his, as he often liked to do when in water, and Atax sat on the bottom of his bubble, already bored.

I turned around again, and together, we sped down into the dark depths of the Lotus Sea, so it was now called. Before, we'd simply called it Daanav Sea, but their actual kingdom was hours into the deep.

IN THE PITCH BLACK OF THE DEEPEST PART OF THE SEA, TWO hours of travelling later, a speck of white quartz-light shone in the distance. I sped up, eager for this to begin, and before long, the glowing Kingdom of Daanav came into view, enclosed in its ancient bubble of protective magic. The place was a massive city of coral and sandstone infrastructure, easily taking hours to swim from one side to the other. Enough for an entire city of creatures to live their lives and never leave.

I wondered if it would let me in—if the city's magic would recognise me as its king. When I'd last defeated the old king and his battalion of elite Daanav warriors, the city had submitted to me willingly. That was the way of these creatures—the strongest were worshipped.

Swimming up to the main entrance where I could see two giant pillars of solid coral shaped into gaping shark heads, I nudged my shark's nose against it.

It yielded to me like an eager woman. Grinning like a madman, I pressed my body into it, taking on my human form as I passed right through the barrier and into the air pocket of the city. The magic welcomed me with a sigh, and it just so happened that we arrived during the city's peak activity. The blue-skinned Daanav guards were the same as subterranean demons, really—just a marine version with hidden gill slits and hands and feet that snapped out webs at their will. They glanced at each other as I appeared. Hastily, they bent down on one knee.

So they weren't completely stupid.

"Take me to my regent," I commanded, feeling my brothers press into the kingdom's bubble behind me.

"His majesty is—"

"Regent, you mean," Atax snapped, striding forward like he was ready to murder anyone.

The blue demon that had spoken almost toppled over where he knelt. "Oh, Reaper curse me, yes! Yes, my lords. Welcome."

I frowned at his choice of cussing but let them scramble to their feet and lead us down the street.

Things were more or less the way I remembered them with the same sandstone groundwork, and they used the same coral material to construct the tall buildings on either side of the street, although these exact buildings could have only been made in the last fifty or so years.

The street was littered with Daanav demon males, all blue-skinned with deeper-blue, swirling face markings, according to their caste and genetics. Their teeth had shrunk since the last two centuries, allowing them to speak better Ellythian and Lobrathian common tongue than they previously had. They were still breeding with the humans then, as I'd instructed them to all that time ago.

When I'd last arrived, these creatures couldn't keep their females alive. They'd died in their late twenties by some magical ailment they'd never been able to figure out. As their numbers dwindled and eventually went extinct, they'd been forced to look outside their own race for partners. They'd tried the sea creatures first—sharks and dolphins and whatever manner of sea monster they could hunt. Eventually, they found issues with the children of those pairings and sourced further, trying their hand at animals, then females from Boneweaver island. Once the Ellythians arrived, however, Queen Ellythia brought the Temari Blade, struck it into the earth and the islands were protected from demon invasion by the Goddess Umali herself.

But the protection had always been a little rough on our island, being the furthest away from the sword, so we'd often still had skirmishes with the demons. When I'd come along to take over Daanav Kingdom at my father's behest, I commanded them to leave our islands alone and instead steal their women from the bigger continent to the east. There was a language barrier with those humans, but a heavy chain around both ankles and wrists was language enough.

But according to the witches currently keeping Yasani Temple, the Temari sword disappeared twenty years ago. And with both me and the sword's protection gone, all three islands were vulnerable once again. Thus, the Daanavs began harassing the Ellythians anew, only they'd gotten clever about it and taken on the illusion of being Ellythians, aided by that traitor headmistress.

But I was back now, and my plans had changed.

We passed a familiar circular structure—a stadium intended for toughening up the human women for their harsh life here. Shouts and female screams sounded within. Some things hadn't changed. Outside, a large coral cage held a single pale-skinned human male, sitting in only a loincloth in a corner. He had a handsome face that looked a little familiar but I couldn't place him.

Some of the demons recognised me, likely from the portrait a human slave had painted at my coronation, because they whispered, "*Boneweaver*," to one another. Many of them bowed low or bent the knee as we passed. But not all of them, and I'd have to fix that.

The coral and stone palace stood tall at the centre of the city, violent spears plunging towards the shining magical dome above. That dome gave the entire place a faint-blue sheen that hurt your eyes if you weren't used it.

But as we entered the gaping shark's maw that was the entrance to the Daanav palace, two of the warden's guards drew their swords. Our guides hurried over to them, growling in their ears. But the demon guards gnashed their teeth and refused to budge.

I sighed with pleasure, stretching out my muscles, before unhooking my black sword earring. It flashed as the magic holding it together yielded to me, and in my hand now was my black-hilted blade, its obsidian tiger's mouth roaring with rage. The blade was long, made of ancient volcanic glass found deep off the western coast of Boneweaver island. I had forged it myself in the fires of that volcano when I'd turned fifteen, as was our way.

I lunged for the demon guard, Atax couldn't help himself and went for the other. Both demons fell to the floor, bleeding from their throats.

The noise brought forth more soldiers, some of whom dropped to their knees in submission, but others ran straight for me, fangs bared, yellow eyes glowing.

Atax and Kai made quick work of them while Raen filed his fingernails with a dagger.

My wife might have had a scattering of flowers to welcome her entry down the marriage aisle, but my preferred welcome was a scattering of bloody bodies dispatched by my brothers.

I weaved through the mangled mess and couldn't get rid of the smirk on my face as the song of battle chimed in my veins. The human slaves in the palace scattered when they saw us, running at full pelt down the gilded coral corridors, and I breathed in that delicious fresh scent of terror and pain.

"Bring me my regent!" I commanded the guards as we headed for the throne room. "I will wait on my throne."

They balked, sprinting down a corridor as Atax let out a cold laugh. I felt Raen's verdant magic fall about the throne room as we entered it, a battle construction designed to protect us and stop anyone from leaving once they'd entered.

I'd barely walked to the stairs to the coral throne, turned and stood expectantly, when a crowd of Daanavs charged into the hall, axes and swords at the ready.

Kai, Atax and Raen spun into action, and I couldn't let them have all the fun. I had excess energy to burn, and I wanted demon blood slippery on my hands. Our fighting styles had always been different, and perhaps that was why we always worked so well together. Kai spun like a dancer, laughing and stabbing, often toying with his enemy. Atax butchered his way through his opponents, relishing the mess of demon ichor on his face, while Raen had the most finesse, never using more energy than he had to, usually using his magic to fight multiple opponents at once. I, on the other hand, made a game of it, sometimes seeing how many different body parts I could hit in the shortest amount of time or seeing who could scream the loudest for me. I was leisurely, for this was the only joy the Gods had afforded me. Thus was my curse and my blessing.

When the throne room was a mess of dead, bloodied

Daanavs, someone stood tall on the other side of the hall. He was a menacing blue demon, as tall as my six-foot-six frame, the absence of clothes showing me every inch of his bulky mass. His face was a little pointed, making me think that his mother might have been a shark. His body was full of deep and old scars, his face pockmarked—a true, wild warrior. In one hand he held a heavy axe.

This was their king, the warrior they'd chosen, Fangar's uncle. Behind him, his court had gathered, blue demon warriors, some of them with their human slaves in tow, dressed in rags.

I smirked, angling my bloody sword at him, "So, you are my regent."

He growled at me, gesturing to his fallen. In one swift motion, Raen flicked his wrist and the fallen bodies all shifted to the side, leaving an aisle empty between us. The regent growled again. "*I* am the only king here, and we only worship the Reaper."

Beside me Kai twitched, ready to go again.

"Then come," I gloated, excitement bubbling up in me. "And let us show *my* people why you and the Reaper are the shit beneath my feet."

He roared and raising his mighty axe, charged down the aisle, his warriors a step behind.

But as my brothers charged forward, I was still laughing when my usurper came at me. I deflected his axe and sliced the tendons of his wrist. He dropped the weapon with a cry, and quicker than he knew how, I came up behind him, yanked his head back, shoved him against me and turned him around for my court to see. Deftly, I drew my sword against his throat.

Choking on his own blood, I let his body fall to the ground.

The entire court went still as I wiped my sword on my usurper's torso, relishing the buzz of violent pleasure now humming through me like spiced ale, comforting and warm. I turned and surveyed my subjects. Beckoning them in with my fingers, they came forward tentatively, perhaps trying to ignore Kai now enthusiastically beheading the regent behind me. We'd need to put it on a spike above the entrance doors, a mark of my reign.

The court stared back at me, shocked, I think, until Fangar came forward and cried. "All hail the Boneweaver King!"

Taking up the shout thrice more, they descended onto their knees.

I nodded in approval. "If any oppose my reign," I began in a bored voice. "Let it be known now."

No one said a word, though I would need someone to weed out any troublemakers. The last time I'd had to execute a handful of vagrants who'd been loyalists to the old regime. I was sure I'd have to do the same again.

"I plan to take back Boneweaver Island," I said, my voice ringing out clear in the hall. "After that I will be heading to the capital of Ellythia to reclaim what was ours before the human scum arrived."

They took a moment to process what I'd said, but once they realised how this would benefit them, the cheers began.

I beckoned to Fangar, and he strode forward, his face drawn. Briefly, I wondered if he had liked his uncle or not, then I decided that I didn't care.

"Husband of my wife," I sneered at him. "Have you fixed your little problem?" I knew he hadn't, of course. Demon priests down here were not as well read as the human ones.

Fangar said through grinding teeth, "I'm working on it."

"Good. I'm appointing you General of the Daanav forces." The boy's jaw went slack. "Can you handle it?"

He gave a stiff nod.

Thumping him on the shoulder as I moved past him, I said, "Prepare the forces. We'll need them sooner than you think."

26
ALTARA

I woke up the next morning after tossing and turning all night, trying to avoid squashing my new organs. Last night, once the girls had calmed me down and helped me out of my bridal gown, they promised they would find a solution in the morning. *Someone* would know what to do, surely?

But as I rolled out of bed, a familiar sensation in my gut made hot fear shoot through me. "Oh no!" I cried, clutching my stomach.

"Goddess! What is it now?" Rani leapt out of bed and rushed over, brown eyes scanning me head to toe.

I swallowed the lump in my throat and whispered up at her, "I need to pee."

Pia groaned from her bed, covering her face with a pillow. But Malika sat up with interest. "Can I watch?"

"I need everyone's help," I said, gingerly getting out of bed. "Come on."

"Oh wait!" Malika suddenly cried. "Trouble? Tell us how to use a penis." The raven-haired pixie emerged from Malika's side drawer where she'd apparently stuffed him. He flew out with a yawn, clearly unbothered.

"You named him Trouble?" I said with raised brows.

"It fit," Malika shrugged. "Tell us what to do, Trouble."

The pixie whizzed up to my face, stuck out his tongue and bared his teeth in a wicked grin. "Point and shoot!"

"Well, *that* I'm good at I suppose," I muttered under my breath, holding my manhood in one hand and running on tip toes to the bathroom.

They all followed me and when I raised my dressing gown. I groaned in dismay as I saw the offending *blue, marine demon blue*, organs in broad daylight, the toilet like a frame in the background.

"I don't want to touch it," I murmured, poking at my member with a finger and shivering.

"Do you want me to try?" Malika's snide voice came from my ear, and I flinched so violently she burst out laughing.

"You're far too eager about my penis, Malika!" I cried. "Suspiciously eager!"

She collapsed into a fit of giggles against the bathroom wall. "Oh, be quick before the maids arrive," she choked out.

Leela sat on one of my shoulders, her tiny legs swinging, and Trouble came and sat on the other, sniggering though his teeth. "Hold it," he commanded bossily.

Blowing out a breath, I took my first two fingers and grabbed the thing, angling it into the bowl of the toilet.

"Pull back the dongly," Trouble piped.

Malika wheezed with laughter behind me.

"That *what*?" I choked, before realising he meant the foreskin. Using the tips of my fingers I did so, exposing the glans.

"Try relax," Leela advised, a tiny thumping sensation on my shoulder as she patted me.

I took a meditative breath, relaxing my pelvis as I did and trying to imagine how I'd normally pee.

Urine began to fall, and I gave a small scream of terror. "Goddess give me strength!" I cried, jerking.

"Goddess give us all strength!" Rani turned and gagged against the wall. Pia also turned away with a hand over her mouth.

"Steady!" Trouble cried, and I hastily ensured my aim was true.

"What an odd-looking thing," Malika said, calming down enough to stand beside me again. "They really are nothing much in this state, are they?"

"My penis is not 'nothing much!'" I said, offended. "How dare you, Malika."

She covered her mouth but couldn't hide the forsaken crinkling at the edge of her eyes. "Well, it's not yours, after all?" she clarified, getting control of herself. "It's Fangar's."

It was true enough, I thought, as the stream ended.

"Shake shake," Trouble advised. I did so, my face twisting as I did. Leela giggled and flew off my shoulder now the show was done, but Trouble remained—my one true friend, apparently and, no doubt, not causing *trouble* as he was distracted by self importance. "Good job," he piped.

I let the gown fall and turned to the others. "Maybe we should chop it off? See if the village healer will do it?"

They all turned to give me horrified looks, but I shrugged the one shoulder that wasn't occupied. "What then?"

"Let's see if Lady Trisana will know," Pia said reasonably. "Her mother was a gifted healer. I'm going to go and get her."

I took a cold bath to try and freshen up after a sweaty night, Leela cackling when she saw me completely naked in the tub. It was the oddest sensation for the testicles to retreat back into my body at the drop temperature. I wondered if this meant I could try and heal male ailments now but decided against it. This organ technically wasn't mine. What if it couldn't heal itself like the rest of my body could? I shivered. It wouldn't be good form to return Fangar's penis with disease on it, demon or not. No, it was better to leave the thing alone.

I hastily got ready, choosing to wear my school-issued clothes for travelling, whilst telling the girls and pixies about how Zale planned to leave this morning.

Lady Trisana arrived to our room with Pia sneaking her in as if they were spies on a mission. I explained to her the issue, and to her credit she didn't faint.

"Are you ready?" I asked, opening up my pant laces. Leela and Trouble returned to my shoulders out of sympathy or solidarity, I wasn't sure. But Trisana nodded and I pulled down my pants, squeezing my eyes shut so I wouldn't have to see the horror on her face.

"Agnlothi's areolas!" she screamed.

My eyes flew open only to see Trisana with both her hands cupping her cheeks. Leela shrieked with laughter as Malika sunk to the floor, once again inconsolable. Trouble was the only one who didn't laugh. Bless the pixie, honestly.

"This is starting to get old," I said darkly, aggressively pulling my pants up. "I'm not showing a single other person!" I crossed my arms and glared at Lady Trisana, thoroughly unimpressed.

"I'm so very sorry," Trisana muttered. "I don't usually swear. But, Agnolthi forgive me, I've seen all manner of things in my life as a healer's daughter, but Zara, this is something else!"

"I'm well aware," I said in such a deadpan I almost sounded like Zale.

"But listen," she said, stepping toward me in earnest. "This power you have, it hasn't been seen in decades. Empathic magic of this strength is rare and—" she gave me a pointed look "—exclusive to the Lota family."

There was a hard knock at the door, and everyone jumped. That was a man's knock if I'd ever heard one. Darkness reached for me like midnight silk, and I gulped, making sure my clothes were straight around my pelvis.

Rani strode to the door and pulled it efficiently open, promptly giving a jerky bow, "Your Highness."

Zale Boneweaver stood there, looking around the room, unimpressed as usual. His hair was wet and loose, the skin of his tattooed torso shiny as if he'd just bathed. He was a living god standing before us, and it made heat swirl wildly inside of me. He found my eyes, and the coldness in them struck me like a slap. I wondered if I'd ever get used to that icy malefic power.

"We leave in one hour," he droned. "You will need ladies to attend to you. Bring your three. No more." He turned around and sauntered back the way he'd come, the large tiger's head at the centre of his back roaring at us. He raised a large, lazy hand, making the door slam shut in his wake.

We all jerked for a second time, and Lady Trisana turned her apologetic eyes back at me. "I'm afraid, my dear, that the only way this issue will be resolved is by the same manner which caused it to happen. Such is the way magic works."

I grimaced, a sudden visual of Fangar and me grinding against each other a second, awkward time. Would he even listen to me after the shock of last night? He had looked very upset when he'd stormed off, which any male would be.

We hastened to comply with Zale's instructions. The three girls all promised to come with me on Zale's mad tour around the island, even though Lady Trisana advised against them to —especially in Pia's case.

But my cousin set her jaw and said that she was sick of staying in this castle anyway, and that I'd need all the help I could get. I would be called Pia, for all intents and purposes, and she would pretend to be "Zara."

I couldn't agree more, what with Agnolthi's instructions and now *this*.

There came another knock on the door, and Rani opened it to reveal Commander Atax holding a stack of empty saddle bags. He strode in, depositing the lot on my bed with a bow. He clasped his hands behind his back and considered me. I looked at him suspiciously, wondering if Zale had told the other Old Ones about my penis problem.

"Does he want a little treat for a job well done?" Malika said as if speaking to a child, her face screwed up as if irritated by him.

I turned to try and warn her, but Malika was now smiling, her hand holding out a tiny sweet. "Here you are, Old One."

Atax cocked his head, as if assessing her in that way the Old Ones seemed to all do. Then he lunged forward, snatched up the sweet from her hand and promptly plunged his fingers into her hair where Trouble had been hiding. He yanked out the shrieking pixie by the wings, scrunching them in his hands.

"If you try anything stupid," Atax said with a gleam in his eyes. "I will take this one as my treat and eat him whole. His bones will be nice and crunchy."

We all gasped in horror.

He let Trouble go, and the pixie promptly fell through the

air. Malika caught him with a cry and cradled him to her chest.

"You monster!"

"And don't you forget it."

We all stared at the powerful Old One as he stalked back out the door without another glance. As soon as he left, we all rushed towards Trouble, as Malika blubbered over him, checking his wings.

"He's alright," Leela said, flying forward to see. "Trouble strong. Trouble wings will heal."

Trouble gave a feeble whimper from Malika's palm as we tutted over him. "I'll look after you, my precious," she said, wiping her nose with her other hand. "I won't let that nasty Old One touch you again."

We packed in silence after that, with Leela making Trouble a hammock of soft handkerchiefs that Malika could tie to her chest and carry him around in.

We all trudged down to the castle entrance, saddlebags in tow, giving each other dark looks. The four Old Ones were there, saddling four dappled mares. I looked around, but no one else was in sight.

"Where is my other husband?" I asked sourly.

"In Daanav Kingdom," Raen said. "We took it back last night so Zale is King of the Daanavs once again. Fangar is commanding the forces there for us so he won't be back for a while."

Pia exchanged a look with me and the girls. *They took it back last night*? Her look said. Raen spoke about reclaiming an entire kingdom so casually it made my skin crawl.

But if Zale had reinstated himself as their leader, I assumed that meant the island was safe from the marine demons now. I was about to ask where Daanav Kingdom was when Zale caught my eye and smirked as he adjusted his horse's bridle. I shut my mouth. He was imagining my new penis; I just knew it. But it presented a further problem if I was supposed to get rid of it by giving it back to Fangar.

The Old Ones left us to mount the horses ourselves, simply walking forward and leaving us, assuming we'd follow.

"I think you need to try and seduce him," Malika said, face screwed up in concentration as she hitched her saddle-bags to her mare. "Make him fall in love with you to loosen up his darkness a bit?"

"It'll be a little hard to seduce someone with a penis between my legs," I hissed at her.

Pia turned her snort into a cough. "Well, I sympathise. But Malika might be onto something. You're a beautiful young lady, *Pia*. A regular man would fall over his feet for you. Fangar certainly did."

"She's right," Malika said to my surprise, as I'd thought she'd considered me a rival at first. "I think you could break that Old One. And do you know what?" Her eyes glittered with evil intent. "I'm thinking that we all pick one and try."

Rani coughed, and Pia groaned because we all knew which Old One Malika had marked for breaking.

27

ZALE

W e left the women behind and leapt into the air, wearing our other bodies by the time our paws hit the soft grass. One of the women gave a yelp of fright, and next to me, Atax, in his black lion form, snorted.

We were in good spirits after our battle last night as we hurried into the shade of the jungle, expecting the women to catch up on their ponies. I'd chosen the strongest I could find in the castle stables, and they were good horses, bred for the jungle, but it wasn't the horses who had the questionable stamina for travel.

I might have been absent for two hundred years, but I still knew Boneweaver Island like the back of my hand, which meant that I knew it wasn't easy to cross even while staying on clear paths. The jungle itself could be dangerous, and then the mountain paths were perilous at the best of times. While the reclaiming of Daanav Kingdom had gone well, those marine demons were the least of my worries. Ellythians were a complicated, potentially loyal group, and I'd need to reassert my reign here in an unfortunately less brutal manner.

That was why I hoped these four women would sweeten our appearance in the villager's eyes. The old housekeeper had told me all about them. They were all beautiful, which humans approved of, and of noble birth and wealth, which also worked in our favour, and now that I was married to one of them, the other humans might soften to me.

My mother would be so proud. She'd been trying to get me married for years before we were imprisoned.

We set a solid pace through the jungle but it was annoying and time consuming to stick to the path. The sun had barely reached its peak before the humans started making blub-bering noises of annoyance behind us.

Kai lurched back into his human form first, summoning his shorts to his body as he did so. He ran back to the pack horse, probably to get more of the rice pudding he'd liked so much last night.

I didn't feel like being in my human form and neither did the others, so we prowled forward until the stream I'd heard awhile back came into view. Raen constructed a magical net in a wide dome to stop the mosquitoes. I stared at him, not understanding what had possessed him, but he shrugged his panther shoulders and lay down in the shade.

It was lucky the women had remembered that horses often needed watering. Old Ones never used horses of course, so I'd forgotten what non-apex predators needed. I watched them arrive into the clearing on foot, leading their horses in and grumbling to each other. Warily, the horses eyed me, Raen and Atax, resting in shade, but I'd given them enough space to be comfortable around us and they drank happily from the stream.

The women, on the other hand, were red-faced and sweat-ing, huffing and puffing like the pampered human girls they were. Kai even had to help one of them with her saddlebags because she didn't know how to adjust the buckles. I huffed in annoyance, and that particular woman, the one with a constant scowl on her face, had the nerve to bat her eyelashes at Kai.

"They have pixies," Atax said. *"I caught one in* that *one's hair this morning."*

"Ah, that's the shiny smell," Raen said. *"A whole family of them were at the wedding last night."*

I didn't say anything because we all knew it was a little unusual for pixies to be cavorting with humans this readily. I'd have to watch my new wife; she was full of interesting little secrets that I'd have to prise out of her. I watched my woman carefully, drinking sparingly from her skin of water as the tallest woman goggled eyes at her.

"Oh, I am jealous this once," the tall one said in what she thought was a quiet voice. "You can go easily while travelling now! It's a real advantage!"

My wife scoffed, "Hardly, Rani. I wouldn't wish this on my worst enemy. It *itches*, you know? And it also *moves* randomly. And I can't but help feel like something could damage it really easily."

I would've laughed if I was capable of it. Serves her right for not learning to use her power properly. I wondered who had taught her, if she hardly knew anything, though perhaps, I could teach her during our travels. But my new wife turned to glower at me, tossed her hair and turned her back on us. Atax huffed in a lion's laugh, glancing at me with his blue eyes. No teaching it was, then.

If she couldn't be a proper Vayashi for me, I'd need another way to temper my power. Even after the battle last night, I could feel my magic rebuilding, wanting to erupt out of me. I'd have to find another woman in the next village, or we'd all suffer for it. But even as I had that thought, my stomach churned as if it wanted to vomit.

I didn't know what it meant, but my own body was rejecting the thought of another woman in my bed.

We carried on travelling in this slow, tedious manner for the rest of the day and just as the sun began to cast long rays on the ground, Kai ran forward on his white cheetah's feet to scout a location for sleeping.

I was forced to take human form then, summoning a shirt and pants for the night as we walked into a circular patch of grass. Glancing back at my wife, a little heat flared in me at her appearance, sweat making her clothes cling to her breasts, her bronze skin flushed and glistening, strands of her dark hair loose around her face. I wanted to be alone with her, to prise out whatever it was she was hiding from me. I glanced around the clearing. In the centre, Raen was preparing a fire to heat up the food for the humans, Kai was helping the women by taking their horses and tying them to a tree branch and Atax sat preening himself, running a blade along his jaw to shave his scruff.

"The river passes by there," Atax pointed with his knife. "Take Kai with you."

My woman glanced around uncertainly, and I realised she trusted Kai more than the rest of us. I didn't realise the growl passed my throat until everyone looked at me in either alarm or surprise.

"Possessive already?" Atax jeered.

Fuck. He was right. I didn't want Kai going down to the river with my woman. The others I didn't care about, but the one who called herself—what the fuck was her real name anyway?

"Let's get one thing straight," I said, "*you*—" I pointed to the pretty, green-eyed smaller girl "—are Pia Lota. Don't bother hiding it from me. So what do I call my wife?"

My woman had been biting her lip as I spoke, but as soon as my eyes fell upon her mouth, she noticed and glowered at me, crossing her arms. "How about, *human*, hm? That's what you're usually calling us, right?"

Heat flared up in me once again, and I wasn't sure if I wanted to slap her across the ass or shut her mouth up by shoving my tongue down her throat. "How about cock-stealer? That's accurate isn't it?"

The girl with the constant angry face choked on the flask she was drinking from.

"Malika!" Rani cried, rushing over to thump her on the back. So I now knew all their names except my own witch of a wife.

"How about 'witch'?" I asked, ignoring the rest. Striding up to her, I grabbed her bicep. "Let's go to the river. The others can go with Kai."

"Let me go!" she snapped as I pulled her towards the water.

"Not until you tell me your real name."

"I don't want a bath."

"You're dirty all over. Humans catch disease if they don't bathe."

She went silent then, allowing me to lead her through the jungle and towards the swift flowing river Goshar, though it might have another name by now. I held up a branch for her to pass under, finally letting her arm go, although I was surprised that my own fingers didn't really want to.

She gave me a dark, hateful look and marched under my

arm. "Turn around and swear on your mother not to turn back until I'm dressed again."

I rubbed my temple at the headache this woman was giving me. "Fine." I obliged, turning and staring into the forest but keeping my ears alert for sounds of any disturbance. I'd never been quite so possessive over a woman. Even with the many Vayashi I used to have, I'd never craved to know their names. I couldn't think of a reason why it was different with her.

But the sound of her taking her clothes off distracted me more than anything else in the entire jungle. I listened, holding my breath as first she slid off her dress-coat, then unlaced her pants. Every muscle in my body hardened at the sound of the material of her pants sliding down her skin. I could imagine her bronzed legs around my waist, with her writhing under me—

"I don't like looking at it," she admitted in a quiet voice. "It's awful."

Well, that snapped me out of my mad dream.

"Cocks are not that bad," I said as gently as I was capable of, but it just came out as a growl. "You certainly wanted it that night I came across you and Fangar."

She made a sound of choked offence. "Take that back!"

I smirked, and I knew she could hear it in my voice. "Is it not true?"

"You're a real beast of a creature, you know that?" Water splashed, and she yelped.

I almost turned around before remembering my oath. "Are you—"

"I'm fine! Don't you dare turn around!"

I sighed and waited, listening to her wash herself as if it

were the only sound in the world. Dear Goddess, there was something wrong with me.

Far too quickly, she was done.

"Oh fuck, I don't have a towel—"

"Is it normal for Ellythian Princesses to swear like soldiers these days?" But I held out my hand and summoned a towel out of my astral repository, holding it out.

She snatched it out of my hand. "Yes. Yes, it is." Drying herself she picked up her clothes. "Oh."

"I cleaned them while you were bathing."

"Thank you."

She began to get dressed. "You can call me Tara. It's short for Altara. But you must not call me that in front of *anyone* else. It must be Pia."

I turned around when I heard her overdress settle around her body. Casting my eye toward the heavens, which thankfully, had not changed at all in these years, I pointed at a glowing point of light. "That's Altara, there. The Great Star."

She frowned, looking up at the night sky, "That big one? I didn't know that."

I raised my brows. "You did not know the star for which you were named?"

"We just call it the Great Pointer back in—" She went stiff, as if she had said something she had not meant to.

My eyes zoned in on her face, watching for every minute expression on her beautiful features, and I tried to make my voice unthreatening. "Back where?"

She shook herself. "Let's go back."

But I shot out for her arm once again, the feel of her bare skin on mine sent a prickle of static up my arm. "Where, Altara?"

She looked around with alarm. "You must not use my real

name, Zale. Do you understand? And I cannot tell you. Bad… things will happen if you do."

I stared at her incredulously. Had she forgotten who I was? "Not with me here. Nothing will touch you."

She shook her head and sighed. "Just forget I said anything."

When I did not take my hand off her, she gave me a look with her lids half lowered, and I found I could not look away. Holding me like a snake charmer holds a snake, she said in a low voice that was almost a feline purr, "Do you intend to take me on the riverbank?"

Did I? I wanted to, yes. My cock was hard, but my chest was tight like something was pressing on it. I had some sort of illness surely. With my other hand, I felt my forehead. Her eyes followed my movements with hawk-like precision, but I wasn't overly warm. I didn't have a fever.

"What are you doing?" she asked.

Not replying, I stepped closer to her, trying to gauge what in Agnolthi's name she was doing to me. "Do you *want* me to take you on the riverbank, Altara?"

Her lips parted like she was thinking about it, the smell of her skin drawing me in. Heat shot through my veins with such force my hand tightened on her arm. I wanted to know what she would say next as if my very fate lay in her hands.

But she looked me dead in the eye, her emerald eyes glittering. "If you do not take your hand off me, Zale Boneweaver, I will slit your throat."

My insides turned into blood and water—there must have been something wrong with that fowl I devoured earlier. But I removed my arm, "Oh, I have no doubt you would, *witch*."

She stomped back through to the camp, following the firelight through the gaps in the palms, and I followed her, my eyes stuck to the sway of her hips. I clenched my hands into fists to stop myself from grabbing her and taking her upon the earth. It was the Boneweaver male way, to see if you could wrestle your mate into submission. If you could not, you were not worthy of her and every instinct in my body wanted to try it out. But at this point, I didn't even know if Altara had working female parts so, I shoved my male instinct back into my own nether regions.

The other girls had not yet returned, still splashing down at the river further down.

Atax had piled two sets of three bedrolls a little apart and then another two bedrolls a little further away from the rest.

"You'll sleep next to me," I said, pointing to our pile and expecting compliance.

"I want to sleep next to my friends," she said glumly.

I pointed to my ring on her finger. "We are wed, woman, as much as either of us don't like it."

Silently, she climbed into the bedroll I pointed at, but I remembered she hadn't eaten yet.

Angrily ladling some of the stew Raen had put together into one of the coconut bowls Kai had taken from the school kitchens, I brought it to her.

"Eat," I commanded.

But she remained lying down, her face away from me and the firelight.

"Eat, woman," I commanded again.

But she did not move, and then I smelled it. Salt water. I had not smelled human tears in what felt like eons. My stomach churned again, and something like bile came up my throat. I frowned at the sensation, forcing it back down. Shrugging, I placed the bowl next to her face and went to speak with Raen.

I woke up to the sounds of a large parrot squawking and with Raen's stew all over my face, having scarfed it down as quickly as I could after Zale had left me. I was not the type of girl that went to bed without eating. Even if I was upset.

As it was, we'd travelled hard the day before, though these four Old Ones seemed to have no care in the world for how fast us humans could travel. In their animal forms they were frightening, and as I learned, for the most part, they preferred those lethal bodies over their human ones. Raen, the sleek black panther, was prowling about the camp when I got out of bed to roll up my bedding. Atax, who was the strange, black-haired lion, was honestly terrifying with that gigantic black mane haloing his savage face. Perhaps he scented my fear, or that of the other girls who were silently trying not to stare. Because in a blur of light and magic, he turned back into his human form, black hair mussed, and thankfully, with pants somehow on.

They seemed to be able to summon clothes as easily as breathing, among other things. My husband, honestly the worst of them, especially after the altercation last night, was nowhere to be seen as I stomped back towards the horses to secure my saddlebag. I was supposed to be seducing him, and for the very first time in my life, I found that difficult.

"Are you alright?" Pia asked so quietly I might have missed it. "Did you fight with him?"

I knew I looked terrible, even without the crying. The other girls, groggy eyed, pale-faced and hair askew, looked like that hadn't slept at all either.

"He said that he didn't like the fact that we were married," I grumbled. "And yet he acted possessively around me as if he did, in fact, want me. Where are the pixies?"

Malika and Rani huddled around me.

"They've gone to bathe to help stretch out Trouble's wings," Malika said. "Anyway, is he giving you trouble? Should we do something?"

I appreciated Malika's assertiveness in general, but in the case of the Old Ones, I didn't think it was working. I untied my hair and tried to put a brush through it. "I don't understand what he expects from me. To be happy about a forced marriage and spread my legs for him?"

Atax's deep voice shocked me like a cold tumble of water. "Back in the old day, Princess, females used to throw themselves at our feet."

We whirled around to find all four Old Ones, standing in a row, as if they took that position out of habit. Kai was grinning at us, holding an armful of mangoes and pawpaw. Zale was staring at me with his usual cold, menacing expression. I almost couldn't believe I'd let him nearby while I bathed completely naked. There was something during last night's interaction that had made him seem less menacing—until he'd become cruel again.

I crossed my arms, but Malika snapped first, "I can't imagine *why*, Commander Atax. You have the manners of a feral dog."

I bit my lip to stop from laughing, not failing to notice that Zale's blue eyes had dropped to my mouth as I did so. Hastily, I ignored them all and walked up to Kai, and putting on my sweetest voice, said, "Did you get those yourself, Kai?"

If seduction didn't work, perhaps jealousy would.

He nodded, white ponytail bobbing as he did. He'd braided two small sections of his hair, and they looked awfully neat tied up with his ponytail.

"How pretty," I cooed, reaching up to touch one of the braids.

The animalistic growl of warning that came from Zale hit me right in my stomach. But I ignored him as Kai's eyes shifted to glance at his king.

"May I have one?" I asked, diverting his attention back to me. "Mango is my favourite." And we were lucky to get any in Lobrathia at all. These ones were clearly ripe and juicy, their skins red and yellow, each one twice the size of my fists.

Kai nodded, and I took one, turning to hand it to the other girls. Pia came forward, taking it from me, "Thank you, Kai," she beamed at him.

The white-haired Old One practically buzzed with happiness. Rani took her cue to come forward. "Golly, Old One, these are quite something. Did you have to climb quite high to get them?"

As Malika stalked over and us girls surrounded Kai, I didn't fail to notice that Atax grumbled in his throat and turned away from us while Raen busied himself with the horses. Zale, on the other hand, had violently changed into his tiger form and charged into the jungle.

Malika discreetly elbowed me, smirking as she began to peel her mango.

THE NEXT PORTION OF OUR TRAVEL WAS SIMPLY STUNNING. WE veered towards the coast, and our path was now a winding cliff road hugging green mountains to our left with the vast open sea to our right. All the while Leela muttered in my ear, coaching me on the magic I asked her about. Astral weapons were something I was really interested in, and while Kai had returned my butterfly daggers to me, I felt uncomfortable travelling the wilds without a quiver at my back and a bow across my saddle. With Leela sitting on my shoulder, holding a thick strand of my hair over herself as concealment, she told me how to create the image of a bow in my mind and bring it into reality. It took hours for me to be able to generate anything, even though my magic was eager to be put to work. Eventually, I generated the shadow of a bow, to which Leela cheered and clapped in my ear. Pia, on the other hand, had been taught from birth how to do it and nodded and smiled at my mediocre achievement.

We were only a few hours from the seaside village of Gulaab when we entered an open area, and I could see all three Old Ones—Atax was guarding our rear—loping along the path when Zale leapt into the air, simultaneously changing forms into a massive, man-sized golden bird, his giant wings powerfully pushing him into air.

Our two front horses—mine and Pia's—reared, whinnying in fear. Thankfully, both of us were experienced riders and managed to stay on, calming the steeds down. We paused on the seaside path, murmuring to the mares and glaring at Raen and Kai who'd turned around to look at us.

The golden bird, on the other hand, did not spare us a glance as it beat its wings to gain height. He rounded a corner and was gone.

"He will let himself be known to the village first." Atax was suddenly next to us in his human form, and I twitched. But the corners of his mouth turned up as he watched Zale disappear around the mountain. He was so tall that when he patted my mare on the head, he did not have to reach up at all.

"Needs a grand entrance, does he?" Malika sneered, one protective hand on Trouble where he was cradled against her chest. Atax glanced at her, eyes dipping down to where Trouble was sleeping. Leela had managed to straighten out his wings in the water, and they were setting in tiny reed-splints now.

"Will he be alright?" Atax asked stiffly. "The pixie."

"What do you care?" Malika said darkly. "You almost killed him."

"Pixies have always been friends to the Old Ones and I didn't squeeze him nearly hard enough to kill him." With that he turned and stalked back down behind us.

"I think he likes you," Rani hissed.

Malika made a sound of deep malcontent. A savage lion's growl sounded from behind us, and the horses started forward of their own accord. Every hair on my body stood on end and I didn't think I'd ever get used to the sounds these predators made.

We heard the commotion of its people before we even saw Gulaab village itself.

Almost as big as our school's Taraka town, it seemed that every person had emerged out of their houses to gather in the open, pointing up at the gigantic golden bird circling their village in the clear blue sky.

I rolled my eyes at the girls, although they were too busy gaping at the flashes of golden light that were Zale's wings catching the sun's rays as he alternated between gliding and beating.

Raen and Kai halted us just before the first houses of the village began along the path, and it was only then that Zale, pausing just above the village, tucked those brilliant wings tight by his side and tilted forward. He plummeted towards the ground, gaining speed with every second.

The villagers screamed, but I bade my throat shut, gripping my reins tightly.

"Steady," I commanded my mare in a low voice. "We're not going to give him the satisfaction."

Pia, Rani and Malika turned their horses and led them behind Atax, who was still in his lion form. But I stayed put, gritting my teeth as Zale hit the ground with a force that made the earth tremble.

A cloud of dust exploded in all directions, and I wasn't proud enough to leave my face exposed. I flung my arm over my face and held my breath, silently cursing.

When the wind and dust settled, I blinked into the light. Zale stood in his human form, barefoot with only pants on, his dagger earrings swinging in the wind. He stalked forward, the ultimate predator of the jungle, exuding a dark and powerful aura. As usual, I could not take my eyes off the rippling muscles of his tattooed, broad back.

"Dramatic bastard," I muttered under my breath.

Pia gave me a curious look as she rode up next to me. "Where did you learn to swear like that?"

If I had been a different type of royal, I might have blushed. "As a teenager I spent most of my time in military infirmaries. And soldiers in pain come up with the most colourful language." And it wasn't hard to translate it into Ellythian while growing up with Geravie as a nursemaid.

We nudged our horses forward behind Raen and Kai, who followed Zale into the village in their human forms. Stunned, the Ellythian villagers fell to their knees.

"Old One," they whispered. "King Boneweaver."

So they knew him, I thought wryly, or at least knew the stories well enough to recognise him immediately. And even if they weren't sure, Zale had the heavy and lethal bearing of a savage king, and there was no mistake about it.

"I have returned," Zale announced in that dry, cold voice of his. "The Daanavs will trouble you no more."

An elderly gentleman, swathed in a thin white robe, hobbled forward on a cane marked with red symbols. He bowed as well as he could, arthritic knuckles turning white as he clutched onto the wood.

"We respect the Old Ways," he croaked. "Be welcome, Your Majesty."

W e were taken to the tiniest travelling inn I'd ever
seen—a squat two-story building with spare rooms
for us on the second floor and a cool tavern on the ground
floor. It seemed to be a regular meeting spot for the village as
it was stocked with food and the Ellythian's drink of choice,
kava, a muddy mixture made from a root crop and water
which had a relaxing effect like blue ganja. They drank it from
coconut bowls, and a friendly young man brought out four
bowls for the Old Ones, turning to me and registering my
eyes before bowing low.

"Would Your Highness prefer water?"

"No, I'll have the kava, thank you."

Zale turned to watch me as the young man brought my
serving. I took a healthy sip and ground my teeth as I swallowed the drink. My tongue went a little numb, and I wanted
to choke on the powerful, earthen taste, but I would die
before I showed Zale any weakness.

"She's got some balls after all," Zale muttered so only our
group could hear.

Rani choked and spluttered on her glass of water as heat rushed to my face.

"A bit of a sore point?" Zale smirked at me, and before I could reply, he clapped his hands once. "We will stay here for the remainder of the day, and I will listen to their problems and pretend to care about them as all good kings do. Then we'll leave at dawn for the next town."

I glowered and determinedly drank the rest of my bowl as Zale invited the elderly man from outside to sit with us. He looked seriously around the table and introduced himself as the chieftain of the village.

"This is my wife," Zale said solemnly, and I stilled at his first-time use of the phrase in new company. "Pia Lota." But he did grind his teeth as he said it.

The chieftain's brows rose imperceptibly as his eyes met mine. But he placed a hand over his heart and bowed in his seat. "My queen."

I smiled and nodded graciously, made easier by the light headedness I now felt due to the kava.

"Thank you for your welcome, Chieftain," I said formally, inclining my head. "Though I admit, I have not been coronated yet. We are newlywed, and I am still a princess."

He nodded, seemingly understanding that this had all come about very quickly.

I suddenly noticed Zale staring at me before he seemed to shake himself and come around to the present.

"I will hold court outside under your Tamarind tree after we eat."

"Of course, of course. The people will be happy, Your Majesty. I will have my daughter bring out the food. You must forgive us for the quantity, as our crops have not fared well this spring." He groaned to his feet, my magic jumping up and down in eager to help, but I shoved it back down for what felt like the tenth time today. The remark about the crops worried me. Boneweaver Island, with its magical climate, was tropical all year round, meaning that the land was extra fertile. Agnolthi had spoken about this, and I gave the girls an alarmed look. *"There is a darkness spreading across the land."* This must have been what the Goddess was talking about.

There were harried sounds already coming from the kitchen and what sounded like an army of women talking in hushed tones and banging pots and pans. But rather quickly, the first food came out. Taro cakes spiced with the unique local blend and pineapple cake. These, the Old Ones wolfed down with surprising speed, and I swear I saw Atax swallow his cake whole. They clasped their hands together and impatiently waited for the next course.

Half an hour later a lunch was brought out for us. An older lady dressed in a brilliant blue saree and two younger girls in cotton dresses brought out platters of food with trembling hands. I smiled up at them, trying to be reassuring in the face of the four terrifying, glowering Old Ones sitting opposite me at the square table.

"So much food!" I exclaimed, trying to make them feel better. I looked down at the plates of rice, curry, flatbread and the small amount of meat and vegetables.

"Don't worry," said Kai, reaching for the entire plate of meat. "We'll eat it all."

Pia shifted next to me, and I was just as uncomfortable. This was a small town, its income probably matching to that, and here we were devouring what must be a quarter of a year's worth of food. We needed to return the favour in kind...somehow.

I *was* starving as we'd barely packed proper food for the road, but the other girls were not reaching for the dishes, instead looking at me expectantly. With a pang of horror, I realised they were waiting for me to start eating first. As wife to Zale, I now outranked Pia. Making a face I pushed a plate towards Rani, urging, "Eat."

But she shook her head, her eyes shifting towards the two girls who were watching us carefully from where they were obediently waiting against the far wall. Sighing, I filled my plate quickly and began eating, before Pia filled hers, followed by our two friends.

I ate as much as was proper, hoping that the leftovers could be then eaten by the villagers.

ONCE THE PLATES WERE CLEARED AND OUR OLD ONES WERE rubbing their stomachs, we all went outside to the agreed spot where people were already gathering. The massive Tamarind tree had branches sprawling out so far that rather easily, dozens of adults could sit in the shade, as they were doing now, fanning themselves against the day's heat with woven paddles decorated with flowers. There were even a few cows and one buffalo loitering in under the tree. They all scrambled to their feet as we approached, and a teenager ran in with two wooden chairs. He set them side by side, and I couldn't help but feel a little ill.

They looked like thrones.

I had never thought of myself as having a future involving me be a queen. I didn't know if it was just me being hopeful that I could shirk responsibility that way, but I was also the second-born princess. Saraya was the one with the personality for leadership, and I was the one who was supposed to go have fun with a far-off duke.

So it was with great trepidation that I sat down beside Zale, though he made no reaction, merely staring imperiously at the villagers as if he were born to do it—which I supposed he was. I clasped my hands in my lap and attempted to look benevolent, though it was a little difficult when the three Old Ones took up standing places next to the Zale. They made for an intimidating sight. I was just lucky that Pia stood by my side with Rani and Malika excited to stand alongside her, mirroring the males.

"This tree was a sapling when I last travelled through these parts," Zale said to the villagers in his usual cold deadpan voice. "It pleases me to see it again in this magnificent state."

It hit me then, just how old Zale was. Though I supposed he'd spent most of that time asleep? Or inert. But as it was, he was still from another time completely. Despite his tone, they all beamed at him or simply stared as their dispositions led them. They formed a line, presenting themselves one by one to us with the chieftain on his own chair adjacent to Zale, introducing us to his people and what they did. A few of them even brought their animals—a couple of cows and even a puppy, for Zale to bless. The animals took one sniff of Zale and attempted to run away, but Zale reached out and rubbed his hand roughly along the top of their heads and they went floppy, seemingly wanting to submit to him.

Most were farming couples, and there was a healthy mixture of young and old, as well as a variety of trades. Other than the poor crop yields this year and the demons collecting their tithe, they bartered with neighbouring villages and got most of their basic needs met. It wasn't until a younger couple stepped forward, their faces worn and tired, that my magic stood to attention.

The chieftain introduced them as Rasa and Ina, and they told us of an unwell daughter.

"What ails her?" I asked curiously.

"An infection," the father, Rasa, said. "We need money to pay for the herbs that will relieve her of it, but...she grows worse day by day."

"How old is she?" I asked.

"Twelve, Your Highness."

"May I see her?" I asked politely. "I am a healer, I may be able to alleviate her pain, at the very least."

Zale glanced at me warily but nodded. "Take my wife," he commanded the couple as if it had been his idea. "See that you treat her well. In fact, I will also go with you."

I refrained from scowling at Zale's useless dominance and lack of regard for *their* suffering. I'd have to set him straight tonight when I got him alone. Shadow-lock be damned, he might not have a conscience, but I would *make* him listen to me.

When we'd seen to the last of the villagers, Raen and Atax followed the chieftain to their troublesome crops to see if the sorcerer could do anything for them. Pia and Malika followed them while I beckoned Rani to come with us as. We followed Rasa and Ina, the former now wringing his hat in his large hands. Ina looked like she hadn't slept in weeks, and when we got to their hut, I knew why.

No less than eight children ran about, and one baby was crying in the arms of a young sister. Rani immediately took to the children, taking great interest in a large carved horse they were taking in turns to ride on.

"I am not a healer," Zale warned me as we were led to a small adjoining room. "There will be little I can do to help."

"Well," I said haughtily, "it's lucky I don't need you."

The Boneweaver King exhaled through his nose but said nothing as we followed the nervous couple to the sickbed.

The room was made dark by pieces of fabric covering windows absent of glass. It was stuffy inside and a grandmother was fanning the poor child, lying in a loose nightgown on a low bed. By her side was a ceramic statue of the Mother Goddess, Lasanthi.

I smelled the infected limb before I saw it. Her shin was bound with a poultice packed with a yellow paste and crushed herbs.

I knelt down and nodded at the grandmother, who hummed a low song to the girl, lying with her eyes shut, her lips chapped and peeling.

Reaching for her hand, my heart dropped into my stomach. Her hands were ice cold. My magic charged, and I reined it in, slowing it down so I could get a clear picture before I absorbed her illness.

This was not just an infection; this was sepsis.

Her blood flow had been redirected to her internal organs in a last-ditch effort to save her life. But it was already failing. Her kidneys had shut down completely, and with her liver barely functioning, I gave her one to two days to live. My stomach twisted a little at the pain I knew would come with healing such advanced illness, as it would involve so many organs.

But it had to be done.

I glanced at the parents, standing worriedly a few steps

away. Ina's face was sallow and gaunt, and I knew that she likely understood the truth about her daughter's demise, even if the smell hadn't given it away.

"I may be able to help her a little," I said gently. "But I need you all to stay calm when I do."

"What will you do to her?" Rasa asked suspiciously.

"There is no risk to her," I said. "She will feel no pain or stress from it."

They nodded, and I looked up at Zale, assessing him for his ability and willingness to listen to my instructions. "Your Majesty," I said in a careful voice. His blue eyes bore into mine, a slight crease between his dark brows. "When it is done, I will need you to lift me from this floor and carry me outside. Take me into the shade somewhere, and I will be fine within the hour. Do you understand me?"

He took a deep breath, his eyes sliding towards the ill child, before looking back at me and curtly nodding once.

I felt Leela shift from where she was hidden in my hair. "Careful," she whispered.

Closing my eyes, I let my magic loose.

30

ALTARA

My magic surged forward like a king tide, sweeping over the child's body, seeking, taking and surging back to me. I felt my body go slack and collapse onto the floor as I took what felt like a punch to the brain, breaking out into an immediate and vicious sweat.

But this was where my greatest talent lay.

As my shin split open to take the wound, as my kidneys took on the decimation, and my liver crippled itself, I was elated. I focused on protecting my brain first, directing blood safely so I would not pass out and kill myself. Then I healed the minor damage to the lungs where excess fluid had begun to accumulate. Then I attended to the damage in my kidneys, reopening the tiniest blood vessels to allow proper filtration of my blood so urine could be made and flow freely. My blood had taken on a toxic level of acidosis from the kidneys not working, so I cleared that imbalance too.

I shunted blood flow and nutrients to the leg wound, destroying every cell of bacteria that was invading it, clearing the puss out and sending fresh blood to the area to reconstruct the muscle and layers of skin, knitting them together like a seamstress.

I revelled in this. This frantic fractal of time, where it was just me and my magic, working to reconstruct, create and redirect. I was so focused on the hundreds of little tasks I was telling my magic to do that I was only vaguely aware of Zale swearing under his breath and taking me in his arms. Only vaguely aware of the little scream Ina gave and the arms Rasa put around her to stop her from running to me.

But I did hear quite clearly when a tiny, child's voice said, "Mama?" Except the sounds of the room faded into nothing as I was carried out by strong arms.

I WOKE UP IN A DARK, COOL ROOM ON A LUMPY BED WITH someone firmly dabbing something deliciously cold onto my forehead. I blinked up to find Zale's face boring down on mine, a deep furrow between his brows as if we were disturbed by something.

"They told me to do this," he gestured to the cold face washer and bowl of water. "Is my technique correct?"

"Why didn't you let Rani or Pia do it?" I mumbled, awkwardly trying to sit up.

He didn't answer but instead got up from the bed and pointed at a tray. "Food is there." After a pause he turned to look at me. "You could have died. Why would you do that?"

"If you're worried about your political machinations," I said, using the cloth to wipe my face. "I wouldn't have died. It would take a lot more than sepsis to kill me."

"I'm not talking about the politics," he snapped. "Why would you suffer like that?"

I hoisted myself up to sitting so I could properly give him a scowl. "Because it's the right thing to do. Because I have the power to help, and so I do."

"But it causes you pain," he stated flatly, though I swore the dark aura around him flickered.

I shrugged. "Most pain is temporary; some just take longer to leave. And those that don't, you learn to live with."

He seemed disturbed even further by this, his frown deepening. "I did not like it."

That made me raise my brows. I watched him carefully, and he rubbed his chest as if something there were irritating him. The moment he saw me looking, he immediately became steel once again, promptly turning around and heading out the door. Was it possible I was affecting his shadow-locked heart? I found it hard to believe I had that much of an impact on him...but emotion had actually come across his face for that brief second.

I fell asleep again, exhausted in more ways than one. For a second time I felt the cool softness stamp across my brow, but when the bed depressed behind me, I felt no warmth.

When I awoke again it was to a rooster announcing his morning call, and I turned to find Zale's side of the bed empty behind me, the wrinkled sheets being the only sign that he'd ever lain there. A golden dawn graced the sky beyond my glassless window, the shutters open, hopeful for some semblance of a tickling breeze. But the tropical morning humidity was already building, and I was sticky from the day before. I got up and headed to the communal bathroom and finding it empty, quickly washed myself with one of the buckets of fresh water and soap some kind person had left for us. I couldn't wash my hair, however, as that was a task I could only do when I had ample time.

By the time I was done, Rani had stomped down the corridor to the bathroom with Malika and the pixies in tow. Trouble was sitting on her head, inspecting his glowing blue wings.

"Altara!" Rani cried, rushing up to me her arms, flailing in distress. "Are you alright? The old barnacle of a king would not let us see you! He is more possessive of you than I ever thought."

"It's a surprise to me too," I admitted, running a brush through my hair. "But I am recovered. That poor child was more ill than I initially guessed."

"She was on her deathbed from what I overheard the king telling Raen." Malika frowned at me. "You really can't risk yourself like that, Zara. You're a king's wife now."

"Oh, don't give me that," I said grumpily. "Not you two, of all people! I'm still the same old person I was. I'm no queen or leader or any of the things Zale might—you know what?" I straightened, frowning at them. "I don't even think *Zale* expects anything of me. He just married me for political advantage. I think if he could have had anyone else, he would have."

But Rani and Malika exchanged a look as they began stripping off to wash.

"You didn't see him yesterday," Malika said, as Trouble and Leela dived into the spare bucket. "He's not supposed to have a conscience, right? But...he wouldn't let anyone into your room. He was worried about you and wanted to take care of you himself!"

"That must be something to do with trying to make sure I wasn't dead," I said, waving a hand in dismissal. "He wants to own me, but I won't be owned by anyone, I tell you!"

"I think you should focus on seducing him," Rani pressed, and I looked at her in surprise. "I'm serious, Zara. I think it's working. Until we find the key to this curse of his, keep doing whatever it is you are doing."

What *was* I even doing?

"Being generally difficult?" I muttered. Every time I made a decision to do something, my plans all fell apart as soon as I laid eyes on him. I thought myself rather experienced around men, and yet I felt naïve around him.

"Try pressing your body close to him," Malika suggested. The pixies cackled, and she shushed them. "A brush of the breasts here, a little bump of the hip there...or give him a kiss?"

I stared at her. Once I had thought about bedding Zale, but that was before I knew who he was and what he was like. The thought of kissing him...would he even reciprocate? But that first night by the river...when he'd asked me if I wanted to bed him, his eyes had glowed, his shoulders had tensed. I couldn't help but think he *would* kiss me back.

"He might be an Old One," Malika said, "but I've been watching them. They're still males. Full-blooded males, through and through. I even caught Atax staring at me yesterday!"

Full-blooded males, indeed.

"I'll think about it," I sighed and beckoned to Leela, who

flew straight to me, fluttering her wings and shaking a mist of water in my face.

We went downstairs where I found Pia at the largest table, speaking to a couple of women as they brought out boiled taro and sweet potato for the morning meal. She smiled at me as I came down the stairs. But the Gulaab village women, when they turned around to see who it was, rushed over to me.

"My queen!" the first one whispered. "Missei is running around kicking a ball this morning. You made a miracle happen for our village."

"Oh," I said, heat rushing to my face. I wasn't used to people knowing about my healing. "I didn't really do all that much."

They looked at me incredulously, sitting me down next to Pia and filling a plate for me and putting a ceramic mug of tea in my hands. After that, women streamed into the inn, trying to give us gifts. Pia accepted a pretty woven basket, and I let a group of girls weave a bunch of flowers into my hair. They also graced me with a length of beautiful pink and gold fabric I could wrap as a saree. Except long dresses were not made for sitting on a horse, so I accepted it graciously, hoping there was enough space in my saddle bags. Rani and Malika came down, at which time the pixies were making themselves known. Leela had been fidgeting in my hair for the entire time, so I suspected she was eager to come out. Sure enough, when they emerged, the girls gasped and screamed in pleasure, which only served to make the pixies glow brighter. After that they were treated as royalty and even had new clothes quickly sewn for them.

"The Paree have not been seen since the time of the Old Ones," mused an elderly voice from behind me.

I turned to see the village chieftain, leaning on his cane next to me. Rani and I immediately stood and pulled out a chair for him, and he beamed as he sat down, adjusting his ivory robes.

"They are a sign of good luck," he continued, eyeing me closely and leaning forward to say in a whisper soft voice, "You were not born in Ellythia were you?" On the other side of him, Rani stiffened, listening closely. Everyone else was occupied with the two pixies.

I met him in the eye and said calmly, "What makes you say that, chieftain?"

He smiled, "Your accent, the way you walk, the way you *look*, as if everything is new and interesting. You hide it well, but as a young man, I sailed to Lobrathia to trade rice and tea." He smiled at me, patting my knee. "I had wondered when we would see Yasani's children returning to us."

For some blasted reason, my tears fell bright and unexpected. I cleared my throat, trying to calm the sudden mixture of emotions rising up like the head of a python.

"It's alright," he whispered, handing me a white handkerchief. "But you look too much like her for me to simply forget."

"No one can know, chieftain," I said thickly. "I escaped—"

"It is better if I do not know," he said kindly. "I will not speak of it, but you might have to work harder to remain hidden if the king is touring this island…especially if you are using ancient Lota magic."

A trickle of sweat ran down my spine as I nodded, exchanging a worried look with Rani.

It was then that a messenger ran in from outside to tell us the Old Ones were waiting for us—and by his look of fright, likely waiting impatiently.

We grabbed our saddlebags and headed outside, except our path was obscured by a small crowd who'd come to see us off. Four young boys took our bags immediately and ran off to secure them to our horses.

Us girls smiled and nodded as we said goodbye, and the pixies pranced through the air, flitting about, finally enjoying being out in the open.

Just before we reached the end of them, the crowd went silent and parted to give way to a small figure I barely recognised from yesterday. Her face was pink under her dark skin, flushed with morning play. Under her knee-length dress, I could see a long, faint white scar on her shin in the manner of wounds decades old. She smiled shyly up at me.

"I made this for you, Your Highness," she whispered.

Bending down I held out my arms for her, and she flew into them. Laughing I squeezed her gently, and we parted as she presented me with a tiny woven ring, a single tiny flower in the middle. I held out a hand, and she slid it onto my pinkie finger, where it sat bright and queen-like.

"Thank you, Missei," I whispered, and she turned and ran for her parents, who beamed at me.

I looked up to find the Old Ones standing in the jungle at the edge of the village. Zale was scowling, not at the child, but at me. I supposed he was still angry about my so-called risky healing from yesterday. But he didn't know me—couldn't possibly know that my body had taken worse, that The Butcher had given me scars on my bones that would last a lifetime. I shook those dark thoughts away and gave him an unimpressed look. I mounted my horse alongside the others and turned to wave goodbye to our hosts.

When we turned back, the Old Ones were already in their animal forms, four predators eyeing us with gazes that made the hairs on my arms stand on end. But Agnolthi had called upon us to break Zale open and find a way to unlock the curse upon him. *"Seduce him,"* Malika had said, *"break into his cold shadow-locked heart."* Malika was right, and Agnolthi had commanded me. So I pushed my own darkness aside, looked Zale right in his blue tiger's eye, and kicked my horse into a trot towards him. He bared his teeth at me, and I smiled sweetly back.

Zale was moving us around the island in an anticlockwise path, which meant our next village was the northernmost populous of Boneweaver Island. Which also meant it was the closest to Tiger Island, the land which had historically always been the cause of conflict, and thus Lota Island where the capital city was.

I'd never been closer to my mother's home city, and a strange homesickness fell over me. Even though I'd never actually been there, my heart ached to see where she had grown up. To see where she'd played as a child, how the people she had ruled over so briefly lived.

"It's said that these jungles hold the entrance to the Forests of Eternity," Rani mused, looking around us with interest.

I was always keen to hear Ellythian mythology, as I'd forgotten most of the bare-bones stories my sister and I had heard from my mother and Geravie. "Forests of Eternity?" I asked eagerly. "What is *that*?"

"I'd always been told it was a fae-tale for children," Rani

said, "but here on Boneweaver Island, the priestesses always treated it as something real. Accessible. A place full of magic and wonder that had no beginning and no end. They say there's a library there too. Full of information about old and forbidden magic."

"But these jungles already have magic and wonder," I said, indicating Leela on my shoulder and Trouble on hers.

But the pixies shook their heads. "Eternal Forest is where we born," Leela piped. "In ancient mists, under sacred lagoon of the pixie queen and her nest of strong warriors—"

"I thought pixies were born in mounds of cow dung," Rani said firmly. "That is what my mother always taught us."

The pixies shrieked in indignation, the sound of both of them crying out making my ears spasm.

"It's a joke! It's a joke, right, Rani? Just a bad one!" I cried out.

Rani was about to frown and dispute my claim, but Malika threw a rotten mango at her, and the gangly girl rolled her eyes and put her hands up in submission.

We travelled hard that day with Leela having me continue to practice summoning a bow and then daggers when I got bored of that barely working. Golden dust poofed up every so often, but not much more, so Leela and Pia had me testing out my magic to see if I could make what Pia called *constructions*, which were fancy spells built layer upon layer like a castle. My magic was keen but too unruly to put into little intricate shapes like the others could. I thought it a little bit odd, but I never saw Pia do any magic at all. It was almost as if she refused to use her power, and the other girls always made up for it. I made a mental note to discreetly ask Rani about it later.

Malika was particularly vicious with her magic and

worked it as if fighting an enemy. She zapped mosquitoes and insects with a flourish, chopped her fruits open as if she were defeating a demon and she cleaned her canteen of river water with tiny explosions. It was marvellous to watch from afar, and I knew she would be stunning in a fight.

"I didn't inherit my family's talent for silk spinning," Rani said sadly when I asked her if she had a speciality. "It's always been rather strange, but I'm quite good at black-smithing. Metal always seemed to bend to my will. Armsmistress Vari has been helping me learn the craft for the last year now."

I remembered how she'd so easily made me a metal floor inside the fae-lagoon on the night of my wedding.

"Do you think you could make me a little dagger like the Old Ones have as earrings?" Malika asked. "I'd quite like one, even just to spite Atax."

Rani promised she would try.

Unless I could rein in my rambunctious magic, it would never comply long enough for me to be able to wield it like these girls. Anyone from the outside would have thought that I needed training and discipline, but in reality, I'd *had* that from a young age. No, just like me, my magic had become rebellious with time. Perhaps in some ways, it had lost its way a little.

As night fell we stopped in a clearing next to a lake. I swatted three mosquitoes in quick succession, and Malika open her mouth to complain when Raen's magic suddenly lit up our camp in a wide green dome, and instantly, every flying insect within was exterminated. Malika abruptly closed her mouth, and Rani shrugged apologetically at her because of her missed opportunity to rile up the Old Ones. It was hard to push someone's buttons when they were being kind, and I wondered if Raen had figured that out.

The girls and I silently got our towels and headed toward the lake with the pixies—what seemed like it would be our nightly ritual when we were out in the wilds. Going to sleep sticky never helped anyone get a solid sleep, after all. We were exhausted, and it wasn't until I was dipping my bare toe in the fresh, clean water that I realised that Zale had not possessively pulled me away this time. Musing that he might still be angry about my village healing, I decided I would wear as little as possible tonight to taunt him.

The girls splashed into the water with bathing slips they'd brought with them. I'd never travelled through a tropical island before and hadn't even realised such a thing existed. The magic in the cloth protected their bodies from minor insects as they washed. Looking down at my pants, I decided that due to what was still between my legs, I couldn't do without it, so I took off my top and waded into the water bare chested with my pants still on.

The girls didn't seem to find this unusual, not batting an eyelid at my half nakedness. But they, pixies included, *did* giggle when I reached under the water to pull my pants down and wash my soft, delicate manhood of the troubles of the day's riding.

"Does it—" Malika wiggled her eyebrows "—*you know*, when you rub it?"

I cried out in indignation and splashed a good deal of

water at her. She shrieked back and slipped backwards into the lake, sending water sky high.

Pia and Rani chortled as Malika emerged spluttering, her hair plastered all over her face.

And then an arrow flew through the air and lodged itself into her shoulder.

Malika gasped in shock, her hand moving towards it, and we all just stared at her for a single moment of shock and confusion.

I reacted first, screaming in outrage, turning around to see our assailant, but my cry was cut short as sharp pain blossomed in my own side.

No less than five demons stood on the riverbank, crimson-skinned with yellow, gnashing teeth and ravenous, slitted eyes. Two of them had bows that were already knocked again with lethal black arrows.

Malika let out a blood-curdling wail, and all turned into chaos.

Without so much as a thought, one image struck my mind like a lightning bolt. I raised my hand, and the bow I'd been trying to summon for the past two days burst into reality with a frightening pop and sizzle.

I barely had the time to marvel at it. But it was the same as my bow from home—fine mahogany, inlaid with gold lightning bolts—and it was already knocked with an angry, screaming arrow, inlaid with black.

With a deftness I'd been practising since I was two, I shot the first archer demon through his Goddess-forsaken eye. The second was down before they even understood I'd summoned an astral weapon, his bow and arrow tumbling to the grass. Leela and Trouble were scratching out the eyes of a demon as he screamed and clawed at them in agony.

Then Zale was there, a vicious, curved sword in his hand, and the remaining demons scattered. But Atax was waiting for them, and with a glee that was truly frightening, he tore the head off one and punched the other in the temple, knocking him out. By the time I looked back at Zale, he was splattered in black demon blood with dead demons at his feet. Rani and Pia were splashing to the bank with Malika hanging between them, screaming and struggling to support herself. I hurried after them, trudging up the bank with a hiss of pain, my pants heavy with water.

Zale was staring at me, his blue eyes terrifying in their rage. His eyes dipped down to the arrow still lodged in my side. Without taking my eyes off him, I grasped it in my right hand. Kai let out a shout and extended his hand as if to stop me, but I ripped the arrow out, and saw among my own blood the green venom coating the arrowhead.

Malika's screams now made sense as an aggressive burn began in my side.

I fell to my knees, turning my head to see Atax crouched over a shaking Malika, his hand over the arrow in her bicep. My magic, seeing a nasty wound in my friend, leapt for Malika on reflex, yanked out the offending arrow, sucked the poison and delivered her wound right into my own bicep. Her scream made my ears ring, but she was safe. Malika was safe, and that was all that mattered.

My body began to shake uncontrollably, and I closed my eyes as I felt foreign magic, demon magic, scrape its claws through my side and my arm. This venom was not of this island, nor of the continent, I knew. This type of magic came from deep in the earth, in that dark subterranean realm no human should ever step foot in. I knew it by the vile density of it, the screaming caustic nature of it now infiltrating my bile duct, spreading through my liver and into the bones of my shoulder.

"Oh shit," I muttered, slipping into Lobrathian common tongue.

Hands were on me. My eyes flew open, and Zale's face was so close to mine. I have no idea why I did it, perhaps I thought I could glean some strength from him, but I leaned forward and pressed my lips to his. His arms came around me as if on reflex, and I put my arms around his neck, burying my face into his chest.

The animalistic scream that tore from my throat had only happened one other time. When The Butcher had pinned me down on a wooden table and cut into the bone of my thigh with a venom-spiked knife. It burned like all the fires in hell, filling my head with agony that ceased all thought.

I screamed again, and it turned into a shuddering, mournful cry. But I couldn't stop it. Not *this*. Not again. Not now. My bones raged with the heat from an erupting volcano, and it felt to me like the call of death.

Zale's black-as-night magic pressed against my mind, but just as that door opened, I shut him out. Leela was crying, pulling at my wound, her tiny magic trying to pull the edges together. Raen tried next, but I shut him out too. Shut them all out. No one could help me now.

I screamed a third time, determined to tear my own throat open if it helped me deal with this hellish nightmare of a thousand hot knives carving my body open. I would go mad if this happened again, I knew it. So I slammed down that steel and obsidian door inside my mind that would shut out the entire world.

And descended into the darkness of doom.

This was a place of infinite menace, a place worse than

hell, where nightmares were born from the wombs of the ancient monsters. Where all fears and dark thoughts were conceived for the sole purpose of torturing the mind. I was going to die, and it was going to be a slow death. But it was a death I would welcome.

To my surprise, something was there with me, and I wandered forward to take a look. Shadows pulsed and roiled with old torment, holding on with spiny fingers so old that they bled black blood. I wanted to touch it. Wanted to sink into it.

A tentative whisper in my ear: "Focus, Altara." I didn't know that voice, but it pulled my attention. I frowned, honing in on the song that carried those words—that carried my name. "Focus," it pleaded. Like the moon rising in the night sky, it was a beacon for me to follow. A light inside of me responded to the song, and my magic rose up and up and up.

The burning returned, sour and sickly and nerve wrenching, but that voice would not let me go anywhere but there, and I had no choice but to sweep the burning away, section by section. My magic fluttered through my liver, golden in comparison to the darkness I'd just emerged from. It sung through my bicep, eating up the venom, turning it into nothing, binding my bone and muscle and skin back together.

When I came to, I could only smell the sea and warm, masculine heat. Zale's muscular arms were around me, crushing me so close to him that I couldn't breathe properly. We were still on our feet, but he was taking all of my weight in his arms. All was silent except my breathing and his.

I stirred, squirming against my muscular restraints, but he would not budge.

"Zale." My voice was hoarse, barely above a whisper.

Reluctantly, oh so reluctantly, his arms eased around me a

fraction, and I realised that I was still naked from the waist up, though my pants were now dry. We were skin to skin, my breasts crushed against his naked, tattooed torso, my hands resting on his chest, clenched into fists. My nipples went shamelessly taught against his hard muscles. Heat flooded through me straight to the space between my thighs. I guess I still had a clitoris then, because, Goddess help me, I could feel it now.

I swallowed through a scratchy throat.

"I will not move my arms, Altara," he said in a low voice that rumbled through his chest.

"I am naked," I said in my broken voice.

"I know."

His heart beat against my cheek, though it was faint and echoing, as if the shadows that bound it were muffling the sound in its own evil chamber. But I did not feel the cold malice resonating from it as I usually did.

A pause, and then I said, "Why?"

He exhaled heavily through his nose and said tightly, "I don't know."

I bit my lip, my mind rapidly regaining its sharpness. But I found his heat comforting as old shame wound its way through me—that I'd screamed in front of my friends, in front of *him*, and shown them an awful weakness. Showed them all the kind of weakness that lay at my core. That part of me was supposed to stay hidden and secret, and I had never slipped up so badly.

Altara's naked torso against mine was at once sheer torture and somehow...*somehow* ultimate comfort. I did not know what she had been thinking, and I couldn't understand what had just happened.

"That's two people now, who owe you their lives," I said.

"I don't think about it that way," she said in her shredded voice. "I also killed people."

Of their own accord, my arms tightened around her again, and I consciously had to relax them. "They were not people; they were demons," I growled. "And not Daanav marines, either. Subterranean demons."

She stopped breathing, and I rubbed an urgent thumb over her soft arm, on the side that hadn't needed healing. "You must breathe, Altara," I reminded her. "All living creatures must breathe."

She was silent for a moment before she let out a whisper of a giggle. I frowned at the sound—like something sweet you might want to eat. No, that wasn't right. Like a ripened fruit? No, that couldn't be it either.

"Zale," she whispered, and my hearing stood to attention at my name on her breath. "I need to lie down."

"Oh." Without thinking I put my arms around her perfectly round ass and yanked her up. She jumped up with a yelp, putting her legs around me. And like a babe, I carried her to my bed in the shadows far away from the others. I flung up a second shield of obsidian that would keep us alone and together.

Why my insides were screaming to be *alone and together* with her was a mystery I needed to solve on another day.

She sighed as I lay down with her, never letting her skin leave mine, manoeuvring the curves of her body so they lay against me just so. Something deep in the depths of my being nodded in satisfaction.

"You let the stars show," she whispered, blinking up at the night sky through my shield.

"I need to see them," I admitted.

A calloused finger reached up to brush the line of my jaw. "Why?"

I listened to her breathing for a moment, felt it against me like an ocean tide, comforting and sure. "I don't know," I said finally.

"I know why," she whispered, touching the other side of my face now as if exploring it, checking to see how it was made. "Because it reminds you that even in the darkest of times, there is always light...somewhere."

"I just think they look nice." I shrugged, but her nipples scraped against me as I did, and I hissed.

She stilled again, stopped breathing, and I ran my hand up and down her back in slow strokes. I don't even know why I was doing it, but it felt needed. It felt as important as breathing, but for the life of me, I could not see *why*.

"Something is crawling up my leg," she whispered, trying to twist out of my grip.

"It's only my shell creature," I said quickly, lifting my head to watch the spindly-armed shell monster dragging himself towards me. I could feel the other monsters watching from the darkness from within the tree line because I'd commanded them to stay in the dark where the women would not be startled by them. This small shelled one, however, with his stupidly long, skinny arms and legs dragging on the ground from his round body, seemed exempt from my orders and was determined to stay in my pocket whenever I had pants on.

"He is made of shells?" Altara asked sleepily, squinting through the dark up at my shoulder where Shell-Creature was now sitting. "He doesn't bite, does he?"

"It has no mouth," I assured her. "They live off my magic. But don't worry; they know I will kill them if they misbehave."

Altara giggled as Shell-Creature almost fell off my shoulder but righted himself just in time. The sound of her laugh and the way it made her breasts move against me made my cock twitch.

"What's his name?" she whispered.

I cleared my throat. "Why would I give it a name?"

She grumbled under her breath then said faintly, "I will call him Wobbles because he is wobbly on those silly limbs. You should have made his body smaller...or at least his arms not so long."

I shook my head at her folly. "Leave, Wobbles, before I crush you to powder."

Altara made a noise of protest, but Wobbles slid down my back, and I heard him *wobbling* towards Altara's feet where he liked to watch her sleep every night. I was surprised he'd revealed himself at all.

"Is there a way to send word to my...Geravie?" she asked.

"That woman who came with you at the wedding?"

"Yes. I've known her since I was a baby. She will be worrying to death, I know it."

I sighed and silently beckoned to an island monster from the line of trees. He lumbered forward, a body made of a rotten palm tree and a head made of clumps of orange hibiscus. "Tell him your message. Though he can only travel at night, he is fast."

She shifted to look up at him with interest.

"Hello...friend," she breathed. "Can you tell Geravie where we are going and that I'm okay? Alive and well and... having a fine old time? Thank you."

I raised my brows but said nothing as she settled her head back down to my chest.

"You heard her," I grumbled at Hibiscus-Man. "Go, and swiftly."

The clump of hibiscuses leaned forward as if inclining his head, and the creature loped south with long strides, eating up the jungle grass. He'd would get back to Taraka town tonight.

"Go to sleep now, shiny star," I said softly.

"I'm not shiny," she complained, but it was only a sleepy mumble, and within minutes of my hand against the skin of her back, her breathing became slow and deep in the way of sleep.

I tried to interpret the strange feelings again. They spun just out of my reach, as if covered in a dense blanket. But if I concentrated just enough, I could just make out what shape they took. It was like fresh grass, a sunset that never ended, a dawn that never faded. It was blue and pink and green all at once. It was better than gliding though the water as a shark, even. "It" was likely to be the woman in my arms.

But there was some darkness in her that had allowed her to descend into that ever-dark of things. Entering that place was the only way she'd been able to brush against my own shadow-entombed heart. I'd felt her fingers of power like a whisper on a faint breeze and had pushed her straight back out. Darkness like mine should not be touched; it would drive a person mad. It had made *me* mad, after all.

But her darkness was not at all like mine, which was smooth and sharp like an obsidian blade. Altara's darkness was rough through the centre, worn with time. As if someone had taken sandpaper to her core and—

Something inside of me shuddered. And I never knew violence could be so still until I became it.

I almost didn't recognise my own voice when I spoke, for the latent threat within it was pushed so far back that actual moisture was building at the corners of my eyes in the effort it took to be calm. "What happened to you?"

Her breathing changed as she awoke, and I knew she had heard me.

"Altara, answer me right now. Who did this? What manner of monster or devil or—"

"Stop." Her voice was the heavy swing of an axe and bore its finality. "If you ask this question of me, you will never see me again. Do you understand, Zale Boneweaver?"

She only used my full name when she was deathly serious. So serious she would and could kill a person with her bare hands to see that promise through.

Spiked heat coursed through me with every heartbeat. As if glass shards had filled my veins and were scraping my insides. I needed to run, to move, to leap into the jungle and have the pure speed rid of me this fucking feeling. But something inside of me would not let me move. Something screamed at me that if I moved from her now, it would be end of me. I pulled her closer, and when she realised I wasn't asking any more questions, her taut body relaxed an inch at a time.

And I marked every moment of it. I didn't know why this was happening, why my body and my mind were clashing like demon clans in a battle over territory. Half of me wanted to roll this woman over and bury my head in her neck so I could have her scent in my nose all night, pull those legs around me and have her breasts surging under me as I thrust into her over and over until...my head began spinning, and my foul heart stuttered in its forsaken cage. I breathed deeply, trying to control myself in a way I'd never had to before.

I shifted my mind onto other matters as Altara fell asleep, turning my face towards the stars. I would not sleep, not when she was vulnerable. Not when she'd sunken into the abyss just moments ago.

When the demons had first attacked, there'd been ten more that had arrived at the camp. That was the only way they'd gotten around us to the women. We'd executed them quickly, but not before they'd fired two shots. The anger I'd felt could've had me unleashing my wrath across the entire island...until I'd seen Altara's naked, bleeding abdomen. All thoughts had been chased from my mind, and the only thing that remained was her.

I didn't understand this power she had over me. More confusing was the fact that she didn't even seem to know it. The only reason she'd fallen towards me was because I was the only one standing in front of her. It could have just as easily been Kai or Rani.

But I couldn't think about that right now, nor the little kiss she'd graced me with. Atax, in a mad fury, had gone to scout this territory to see if there were any more while Raen was currently prising open the brain of the one demon we'd left alive. Once we knew where they'd come from, we'd be able to make a plan for our revenge. I did not recognise the scorpion sigil they'd born on their armour, but by their dry, crimson skin, I knew they were subterranean demons and not from some Daanav Kingdom rebellion.

I could hear Kai softly crying by himself, sitting in a tree where he could still watch over the women. He didn't like to watch people he liked get hurt, especially women or children. I think in times like this he thought about his little sister, who'd died far too young. I listened to him climb down from his tree and crouch next to Rani, who was sitting quietly next to Malika's bed roll.

"Is she okay?" he whispered.

"She's much better. Fast asleep, I think," Rani whispered back. She paused, and I heard the shift as she leaned towards him. "Are you alright, Old One?"

"No," Kai whispered.

To my feline ears, I heard the scratch of grass and the movement of Rani's hand on Kai's. She was holding his hand, I realised in horror. I listened closely to try and make sense of it.

But they said nothing more and simply...sat still.

I looked down at Altara's small hands curled under her chin against my chest, and perhaps for the first time in my miserable life, I wondered what it would be like to hold another person's hand.

THE NEXT MORNING I GOT UP BEFORE DAWN—FOR I HADN'T slept at all while Altara was pressed against me—pulled a blanket to cover her bare skin and went over to the dying embers of the campfire. Raen sat there, placing his dagger earring into his ear.

"They were from the Scorpax Kingdom," Raen muttered, putting out the dying fire with a wave of his hand. "Directly beneath Lobrathia. The new king is Havrok Scorpax."

Beneath Lobrathia. "It was Terax Kingdom in our day, with old—what was his name?"

"Carog Terax and his reign of terror. Remember that battle they fought with the Lobrathian Lightning King? We could see the lightning from our beach."

"I remember." I glanced back at the sleeping Altara and wondered how she'd come by her power. If she knew about that old battle. "It was one of the few times our fathers actually came to sit and eat with us."

Raen's face darkened as old memories came back to him. How different our life was now that our fathers were gone—how different the entire island felt that the previous generation of Boneweavers were dead. Their betrayal had cut deep and wide, for Raen in particular. But his father was not here to hurt him anymore and nor was mine. "I wonder how many demon kings have come and gone since then?"

"No less than fifty," Raen grumbled. He would have combed through the demon's mind to get to that number. Like their marine cousins under the sea, subterranean demons were volatile and constantly fighting over leadership.

Only the strongest kept the throne, and even then, the moment he showed weakness, he got beheaded or worse.

I felt the women before I saw them. It was Pia, the real one, followed by Rani and Malika, who looked pale from lack of sleep but otherwise alive.

"Thank you, Your Majesty," Pia said softly, "for saving us last night."

Atax made a noise of surprise. I looked at the three women standing before us, so fragile as humans, and *yet* two of them had power they knew how to use. Last night I'd seen it for the first time. Malika, once Altara had quietened, went and found the demon that had shot her and screamed at him. With the power behind that scream, she tore his body to shreds. Blood had spurted everywhere and all over her, but she hadn't cared.

Rani, on the other hand, had sat extremely still, then burst into tears with an eruption that shook the ground, producing several black, lethal arrows that sprouted up straight from the earth. I had been surprised to see they were an exact replica of the ones the demons had used on them, bar the venom.

And Pia. The second in line to the Ellythian throne stood, watching her friends calmly as if she understood. No magic had sprung from her, the embers of her power lying dormant, refusing to move.

Looking at them all now, I nodded once in acknowledgement. "Prepare to leave."

ALTARA

W hen I woke, my mouth was dry, and my body felt like it had been beaten with weighted mallets. Three human faces and two sets of glowing, flitting wings hovered above me. Squinting at them I eased myself up, groaning at the stiffness in my joints. My magic was powerful, but the aftereffects of a big healing always left me feeling like I'd aged a hundred years. The girls took pity upon me and helped me get dressed. Malika even hugged me and brushed my hair.

"I felt...*you*," she said in a low voice. "It's like no healing I've ever seen. Your magic swooped in like a bird, rummaged around in my body like it was looking for something in a drawer, and when it found the injury—" she shivered "—the feeling of it being taken was like heaven."

I felt a wan smile smoothed over my pained face. "I've seen the look on soldier's faces when they've been healed. If they had known who it was, they might've very well fallen in love with me."

"I wouldn't blame them," she chuckled, "but really, Tara, I thought it was going to kill you."

"Like I told Zale back in Gulaab village, I don't think there's much that *can* kill me. It's all…whatever my mind can handle, you know?"

"Speaking of the king," Rani said, handing me a piece of the mango she was cutting for me, "it looks like it's working."

Only Kai remained in the clearing with us, but he was preoccupied with the hoof of one of the horses. The other Old Ones had disappeared into the jungle to hunt for their breakfast.

"It was all very strange," I muttered. I hadn't actually tried to seduce him like I'd planned.

"He's growing attached to you, that's what it is!" Malika said. "When we get to Levu, I'm going to ask the priestess of our temple if she knows anything about the key. I asked a little in Gulaab village, but they only knew the story we did."

Malika was from Levu village, where we were now headed, but had not been back for three years. I still didn't know the reason she'd been exiled but got the feeling that it was a bad idea to ask. Even so, she looked happy to going back.

"Good idea," I said. "We can't be relying upon me to unlock him. For all we know the key is a baboon's—"

Rani coughed loudly, covering it by drinking from a coconut Kai had given her. The Old Ones had returned into the clearing in their human forms although Atax had blood all over his mouth. Raen, who was neat in all things, was delicately dabbing at his chin with a handkerchief while Zale strode right for me, a predator hunting prey.

The girls immediately scattered, muttering excuses about

checking their bags, while I didn't move a muscle. In fact, I barely breathed as our eyes refused to leave one another. His bare skin had been against mine the *entire* night, and I could still feel his heat against my breasts, feel that hand brushing up my back, a gentle caress I might have interpreted as *caring* if I hadn't known he wasn't capable of that. But still something in him had wanted to protect me...or care for me—or something close to it.

Zale crouched his large form down and looked into my eyes one at a time, those ocean blues boring into my soul as if he were checking for my sanity. I swallowed down the heat coursing through me—the same heat that wanted me to leap on top of him and straddle him and shove his cock into...dear Goddess! I couldn't even do that. My vagina had literally closed up. Suddenly, irate with the entire world, I leaned into him so that we were barely inches apart.

"Zale?" I said softly.

A sharp intake of breath through those pink lips, followed by a soft, "Yes?"

I leaned back and said haughtily, "Are you checking for rabies? I won't catch that from you, will I?"

His face fell, and he leaned back to give me an unimpressed look. Raen chuckled from a short distance away.

But it was Kai who said, "That's not very funny, Your Highness. I once had magical rabies. That's what made my hair white."

My eyebrows shot up, as I had wondered from the start what had stripped Kai's hair of all its colour.

"Do you think I could fix it?" I asked, taking Zale's offered hand and pulling myself up. He ended up half carrying me to my feet, but I walked towards Kai immediately.

"Do not try it," Raen warned. "Kai's illness that he *calls* magical rabies will kill a human."

"How do you get it?" I asked.

Kai's blue eyes darkened, and he lowered his head, turning away from me to attend to the next horseshoe he was checking. I turned to give Raen a questioning a look.

"Another time, Princess," was all the sorcerer said. But his eyes shuttered as he glanced at Kai.

Something truly awful had happened then.

"I'm sorry, Kai," I said quietly, before turning and heading out to the latrine a few meters away. Leela flitted in front of me, protectively scouting for potential enemies, her tiny face serious. I don't think I'd ever get used to having a penis and holding it to wee, but it certainly made it easier to travel, and the girls were all envious of it, bizarre as it was. The urine took longer to travel out, and sometimes I took to making patterns in the soil.

It wasn't until I was almost finished that Zale's voice came from behind us. "Have you figured it out yet?"

I jumped so violently I almost hit Leela with my stream. We both shrieked, and I hastily shook the penis and tucked the cursed blue demon's organ back into my pants. I rounded on him and found that Raen stood right alongside him.

"Do you normally come upon a lady when she is relieving herself?" I cried. "Is it a Boneweaver thing?"

Raen had the decency to look a little disturbed, the line of tattoos across his beautiful nose twitching, but Zale's face was as unbothered as ever. "I brought Raen to see if he could help."

"Does everybody know then?" I threw my hands up in the air as Leela flitted beside me, arms crossed and shaking her head in disapproval at the males. "Told the whole island, have you?"

"Just my brothers," came the deadpan reply.

I groaned and stomped straight past them and back into the clearing. "Raen, you can't help me. I need to return it to Fangar the same way I took it from him."

Somehow Zale was in front me so fast that I didn't even see how he'd gotten here. I blinked in confusion, trying to figure out whether it was my eyes or just his speed. But his voice was a pure storm when he growled an enraged, "*No.*"

Unperturbed by his anger, I crossed my arms. "If I remember correctly, you blessed the union between Fangar and I. You *let* him marry me. He remains my husband too."

He took a step toward me, menacing and somehow even bigger than ever. Despite that, I knew his anger was not directed at me. His eyes morphed before my own, his circular human pupils elongated into slits like a cat's. He seemed to pulse with darkness that grew with every second.

"*That,*" he growled in a guttural voice that was so barely human I sucked in a breath, "was a—"

"Zale," Raen warned sharply.

But Zale's feline eyes didn't leave mine, and for what seemed like an eternity, he just stared at me, monstrous and angry. Just when I felt the dark terror of his shadow trickle out, he abruptly turned and stalked into the jungle. When he'd gone, the clearing somehow got brighter.

"Let's move out," Atax commanded in his usual arrogance. "He'll catch up." But I didn't miss the look he exchanged with Raen.

ZALE DIDN'T APPEAR FOR MOST THE DAY AS WE CUT THROUGH dense jungle paths, but I knew he was around somewhere in the jungle, always just out of sight. I could feel the shadow of him through the forest, feel his eyes burning my skin. Malika was particularly jumpy, and Rani looked upon her with concern as slowly, her eagerness to see her family dissipated, replaced by nerves.

The Old Ones now kept closer to us as we travelled. I couldn't help but notice Atax prowled beside Malika now, his lion's eyes watching Malika's every movement as if he were afraid she would fall off her mare. Raen strode in his human form beside Rani, coaching her on building a shield of metal with her powers. He instructed her on levitating it so she could move it wherever she wished with her mind alone.

Kai continuously plied us with food, rushing up trees with inhuman speed and tossing us fruits, as well as once throwing a coconut at Rani's new shield to see if he could catch her unawares. My friend deflected his attack, chortling as the coconut bounced towards Raen's head. But the sorcerer was quicker and sliced the thing clean in two, holding it out in one hand for the squealing pixies to eat from.

They were trying to cheer us up, I realised with wonder. Every action was laced with…a kindness and concern that I'd not seen from them before.

Understandably, we were *all* still shaken up by yesterday's events and were twitchy and fidgety when we lapsed into travelling silence. That led me to start talking about what we'd seen with Pia, riding alongside her at the front of our group. The fact that there were subterranean demons so close to her home city was no doubt also a worry to her.

"I never knew there were so many types of demons," I muttered. "I sort of thought there was just the one or two."

Pia nodded. "I had to memorise all the different breeds when I was being educated. There are thousands of types but a few of the more numerous sort, including the crimson-skinned subterranean type we saw yesterday. Daanav Kingdom is the only marine demon kingdom we know of. They often have blue or green skin."

I swallowed the lump in my throat. "Which type is white-skinned?"

Pia looked at me sharply. "Where did you see one of those?"

Berating myself for even asking, I shook my head. "I haven't. Just heard of them."

"They are rare—the demons of Pentarog," Pia said with a frowning. "You shouldn't be seeing one around at all. They are usually high-ranking commanders in their armies, and when they are not fighting in battles, they are sometimes used as solitary assassins."

The Butcher had not worked alone. He'd brought three smaller crimson-skinned demon apprentices with him. When my stepmother had brought me to the secluded shed, concealed by demon magic just outside Quartz City, I'd tried to run. But bony fingers had gripped me like iron and threw me onto a wooden table.

"I want you to remember one thing, Altara," my step-mother had hissed, standing over me like some righteous queen, cold and distant, "that you will *never* cross me again."

Pia's quiet voice disturbed thoughts of my dark memories. "But you did it, Tara. You summoned an astral weapon. That's quite an achievement."

A warmth spread through me at the smile on my cousin's face and I couldn't help but smile back. "I can't believe it either. I think it was the emotion of the moment that forced it out of me. I didn't really think about it, you know? And then poof!—it just slammed into my hand."

"It's tradition," Pia said softly, "when you summon your first weapon to bless it under one of the Goddesses. Usually it's Xalya, but Agnolthi's weapon is the bow."

"I'd like that," I said. "Maybe when we get back to Taraka town, the priestesses could do it?"

Pia gave me a pained look. "It might be awhile till we're back," she admitted. "I imagine Zale will want to see his family's gold mines up in the western mountains. It'll take us weeks to get back if that's where we're headed."

Weeks. I thought in horror. We were going to be travelling like this for that long? I sighed, knowing how much Geravie might be fretting over us. I hoped that hibiscus-headed creature Zale had sent got to the three old ladies alright. I peered into the dense jungle wondering where the other dark creatures were. The ones that had captured all the girls in the middle of the night so easily. There was a lot about Zale, *my husband*, that I did not know. I looked down at my pearl wedding ring, still sitting snug around my finger. It was these things that I didn't know about him that worried me the most.

Zale reappeared as we made camp that night, in a deep grove surrounded by Raen's green-tinged magic protecting us from the bugs and snakes. My husband chose to remain in his tiger's form while the others remained in their human forms and I guessed he felt more in control that way. His eyes found mine as we settled about the campfire. We wouldn't get to wash tonight, much to my chagrin, as there was no large body of water nearby. Thus us women were sticky and grumpy. Malika glared at Atax, sitting opposite her, but the arrogant Old One merely levelled her a smirk as he ate a raw piece of snake meat.

"They call it the King Cobra," Atax drawled, "Because it eats other snakes."

"And what did they call you?" Malika shot back. "The king of brutish idiots?"

Atax showed her his teeth. "No, they called me the king of snakes but for a very *different* reason."

Rani snorted into her bowl of stew, holding the new spoon she'd created with Raen's help. It was a little rough around the edges and not quite round, but I was rather proud on her behalf. That was two of us who could summon things now.

Zale huffed and came to sit by me, his side against my leg. The heat radiated off his tiger's pelt like my own personal fire and I wondered if this was his way of apologising. I knew he couldn't help himself, even if he was still grumpy about my suggesting to fondle Fangar to give him his loins back. I reached out and stroked his fur. Next to me, Pia stiffened, but Zale's powerful tiger's muscles relaxed under my hand. It was strange thing, to be so close to a predator and pet him like a domestic animal. It was then that I noticed the swinging black dagger earring they all wore was also on Zale's tiger ear.

Atax, Raen and Kai wore one on each ear, while Zale only wore the one. They were made of a shiny black glass I guessed was obsidian, which wasn't surprising since there were a few volcanoes on the western side of Boneweaver island. Rani had told me she'd seen Kai take off one of his earrings, and it had elongated into a full-size weapon.

"How do those work?" I asked Raen, pointing to Zale's earring. "And why is it on his tiger's ear?"

Raen poked the fire with a stick, adjusting the logs. "Old Ones make these weapons when we commence adult training at age fifteen. We imbue them with our blood and forge them in the fires of Agnolthi's womb—our sacred volcano. Magic weapons like that can't be summoned so we wear them like this." He gestured to his own, shorter earrings. I guessed they were daggers rather than swords, which suited Raen's more sophisticated style.

"And when you change," Rani said eagerly. "That's why stay they on?"

Raen nodded, then frowned at something near my feet.

We all looked down to the shell-creature from last night, Wobbles, walking in his dilapidated way towards me.

Leela and Trouble flew down from where they were sitting next to Pia and giggled at him. Wobbles was a little taller than the pixies—about the length of Zale's hand.

"Dark magic," Trouble sneered and lunged forward, poking Wobbles on his shelled back. Due to his large head, Wobbles fell forward immediately with plinking sound.

"Hey!" I chided, reaching down for the creature. "Wobbles is a friend!" I brought him up by the underarms like a baby as Leela and Trouble stared at me in disbelief. "You three play nice."

But Trouble wouldn't have any of it. He flew right up to my lap where I'd sat Wobbles and poked him again. "No. Refuse. He evil." He then pointed to Zale. "Evil." Then pointed at the Old Ones in turn. "Evil. Evil. Evil."

Rani gasped. "Trouble that's rude! Apologise at once!"

A rock settled in my stomach as I looked up at Kai who was staring in confusion at Trouble. Atax and Raen seemed amused by it.

But Trouble wasn't done. He tossed his dark hair and pointed at Zale. "Black heart. Spreading. Bad. Bad. Bad."

Leela came to sit on my shoulder, a look of uncertainty on her face.

"You can't say that!" Rani exclaimed. "They saved us last night, Trouble!"

But it was Malika that said darkly, "Trouble, I'm giving you *one* warning."

Trouble stuck his tongue out at her and a dark smile curved Malika's lips. She raised her finger and a whip of fiery red magic lashed out, curled itself around Trouble's wings and abdomen and pulled him back to her like a fishing reel.

Trouble let out an outraged scream as he zipped through the air, the look of horror on his face so comical, I couldn't but help let out a laugh.

Malika set Trouble down next to her, her red whip bright around Trouble, locking him in place. "You'll sit there until you learn to behave like a civilised person!"

Atax clutched his heart and blubbered in mock horror, "Did you just *defend us*, Malika?"

Malika crossed her arms. "Don't get used to it, brute."

After that we ate our dinner in a companionable, tired silence. Zale had not reacted to anything Trouble had said, remaining his usual glowering self. We went to bed, and when I lay down on my bedroll, he, still in his tiger's form, lay as close to me as possible. But I couldn't be sure if he was being kind towards me or just being possessive. Wobbles climbed up onto Zale's back and lay supine, with one leg bent and the other foot resting on it, in such a masculine pose it made me chuckle. Zale blinked at me then and there was a strange uncertainty in his eyes. As I let my own eyes flutter shut, Zale never moved an inch, remaining in a sphinx pose. As far as I could tell, he never went to sleep.

THE NEXT MORNING WE SET BACK ON THE JUNGLE PATH, AND AS the long rays of the afternoon sun stretched out before us like bars of gold, we saw the first sign we were close to Levu village.

"It's summer solstice!" Malika abruptly screeched,

pointing madly to a handwoven decoration tied to a tree. "Ellythia's Day! Oh how could we have forgotten?"

"What's Ellythia's Day?" I asked Pia quietly. In truth it was a little embarrassing that I'd never heard of this custom, being of the famed founder's line herself.

"We celebrate the day Ellythia arrived with her people and cleared the isles of the demons that haunted them," Pia said with a small smile. "It's our biggest celebration of the year, actually. There's a replica Temari Blade, a giant bonfire and the women dance around it while the men serve us food! It's brilliant. Usually, couples are encouraged to get together and dance after the adults go to sleep." Her smile became wistful, and I knew she was thinking about the betrothed she'd left behind in Lota City.

"What's his name?" I asked gently. "Your betrothed?"

"Camar," she replied softly.

"When will they let you go back?"

She shrugged slowly, as if reluctant to admit it. "The world turns as our grandmother wills. When she decides I am worthy of return, then she will summon me."

35

ALTARA

The path up to Levu town was scattered with colourful, woven and sewn decorations hanging from tree branches, tied around palm trees and bushes. There were dolls with long, flowing hair representing Ellythia, sewn broadswords stuffed with cotton wool representing the famed Sword of Temari. Quartz and flame lanterns littered our path in preparation for the night of celebration to come.

As we crested a ridge, the village of Levu lay out before us, and I glanced at Malika in delight. Beyond the decorated village proper were terraces of rice paddies, numbering in the hundreds. From this height they were lush green steps made for giants, complex, neat patterns in perfect synchronicity that made me tear up. It was a stunning display of Ellythian ingenuity, and Malika had mentioned the complex irrigation systems that made the area fertile. I felt like this was the real Ellythia, neat craftsmanship bordered on all sides with wild, untamed jungle. Mystery, magic and human skill all in one place.

"Are you crying?" Zale suddenly appeared at my elbow

out of nowhere, his human blue eyes boring into mine. "Why are you crying again?"

I wiped my eye as Malika sniffed behind me, but I knew our reasons for crying were not the same.

"Because it's beautiful," I said to him. But he searched my face so closely I had to laugh. "Have you never seen anything so beautiful it made you want to cry?"

His frown deepened, and a mildly disturbed look flashed across his face.

Abruptly, he leapt over the side of the steep hill. Pia and I let out a surprised cry, but of course, Zale transformed into his giant golden eagle form, his wings snapping out and catching the wind

Smoothly, he wheeled in big circles, gigantic and impossible for the villagers below to miss, golden wings flashing in the late afternoon sun. Leela sighed despite herself, her own golden skin glowing brighter in appreciation. Zale was beautiful, but naturally, he was also showing off. Even Trouble, still bound with crimson bands of Malika's magic, stilled his fussing to appreciate the sight.

We trudged carefully down the hill. Once again the Old Ones stopped us before the village entrance. This time, a giant arch had been erected, woven with flowers and ferns and the people of Levu, dressed in coloured sarees and silk shirts for the festivities, pointed and gasped.

Zale took a gentler route this time, descending gracefully with each turn he made, until his claws skimmed the dusty road and he beat his wings to land. In a flash he was a man again, and Atax and Raen sauntered forward, changing from black lion and panther into clothed humans.

Pia and I led the girls forward, the pixies chattering excitedly, likely expecting the same reception as in Gulaab village.

And they weren't wrong.

We were immediately swept up in a flurry of activity, where the village chieftain, an elderly woman with a red moon mark on her head and maroon robes, greeted us.

They bowed low to Zale and the Old Ones and then straightened to look at us. I turned to gesture Malika forward, but she was suddenly quartz-stiff, her fingers tight around her reins. Her lower lip trembled, and my heart broke in two at the sight. Whatever she had done to earn her exile at the school, surely her family could forgive whatever it was?

Rani whispered something to her, and Malika gave a stiff nod, dismounting her horse. The Old Ones and the entire village were staring now, and as Malika came forward, someone gave a wild cry.

It was a teenaged girl, possibly fifteen, who ran forward despite her mother's warning shout. Malika was running now, and the two met halfway, sweeping each other up in a hard embrace. I dismounted and led my horse forward as an older man and woman separated from the crowd, tentatively coming forward. The woman came forward first, tears already streaming down her face as she reached Malika, took the girl's face in her hands, let out a strangled sob and pulled her into her chest. A stony-faced man hovering at the back, whom I guessed was Malika's father, gave a stiff look to the rest of us girls before turning around and walking back through the crowd.

Meanwhile Zale and the other Old Ones were being led to the one of the two temples on either side of the village entrance—gatekeepers, of sorts. They were small, compared to Yasani Temple, but still beautiful with carved stonework of the Great Mother, Lasanthi.

To my surprise Zale went down on one knee, crossed one

first over his chest and bowed his head. Accepting a stick of incense from the village chieftain, he stuck it into a small holder on the tiled floor next to the front doors. The other Old Ones did the same before descending the steps. For some reason I had thought they would not worship the Ellythian Goddesses and perhaps have their own, but it hit me like a bucket of cold water over the head when I realised. The twin priestesses had told me that Zale's mother had been High-Witch of Agnolthi's Order of Yasani. His *own* mother. And last night, Raen had called their sacred volcano *Agnlothis's Womb*. The Boneweavers worshipped Agnolthi, and it made my head spin.

I tried to keep myself together as I came to join them, and we were introduced to the chieftain.

"My wife, Pia Lota," Zale deadpanned.

The chieftain's eyes slid around to the real Pia and then back to me. Her brow raised slightly, but she said nothing and bowed. "Princess," she murmured, "we are blessed to have two of the Lota women present here on Ellythia's Day. The festivities are about to begin at dusk. I will arrange for a room."

The villagers dispersed to prepare for the celebrations as the sun began to set. While Malika went to her own family's house, we were led to a wide, cool hut where quartz crystals provided cold air, freshening up the room. I needed to see if I could barter for one to take on the road with us. But we washed and changed clothes into the ones we'd luckily been given in Gulaab village. Pia and Rani helped me wrap and pin my saree around me, making sure my breasts were covered by the long fabric with the end of it draped over one shoulder and then rest hanging at the back. I felt like a proper Ellythian princess, bar the tiara.

I helped Rani tame her frizzy mane, while behind me, Malika returned to re-braid my hair. We made a fine team, the four of us, along with the pixies who handed us pins and held up fabric when we needed it. Trouble, for his part, seemed to relish in self importance and stayed out of mischief when he had a job to do. Seeing this, Malika continuously delegated tasks to him, putting on a haughty voice to make it seem like pinning her saree and arranging hair were matters of life and death.

When we emerged it was dark, and all the quartz-lanterns in the village had been brought out, dotting the night with a multitude of pinks, greens and yellows. The bonfire shone heartily, and young girls were already loitering around it, ready to dance.

The Old Ones were waiting for us, freshly washed and in clothes of their own summoning— actual black silk shirts this time.

As I walked up to Zale, he said flatly, "You don't look so much like a witch anymore."

I gave him a shove that did nothing to move him, and he let out a sudden laugh. Abruptly, he shut his mouth, frowning.

"What?" I asked.

"Nothing."

But the realisation struck me before I'd even asked him what was wrong. I knew what it was. He wouldn't admit it to himself, but I'd only ever seen him smirk or snigger in villainous humour. This was the first time I'd seen him have a genuine, light-hearted laugh.

It was working. *Somehow* I was wearing away at the shadow in his heart, and his recent actions towards me proved it.

36

ZALE

It was a little-known fact that the Boneweavers had been celebrating "Ellythia's Night" for the last two thousand years. Every year we'd send the reigning Lota Queen a gift of our own making. Sometimes it was weapons made of volcanic rock and gold, other times it was mysterious, magical plants from the Eternal Forest. The very first time it had been one of our own males—a goldsmith by the name of Rorax Boneweaver, who had married Ellythia as her second husband. Boneweaver Island had always been the home of the isles gold supply, high in our western mountains. Rorax had been a famed wielder of gold-magic and a worthy gift to Ellythia.

So I understood the way of these people and why it felt right to me that they danced around the bonfire until midnight, the village sword thrust into the middle of the earth before them. Pia, Rani and Malika joined the village girls and took up the dance by way of habit, as they'd no doubt been dancing Ellythia's dance since they could walk.

But Altara stood aside, a faint smile on her face, clapping

to the beat of the drums and Ellythian harp as she watched the others. As usual, I could not take my eyes off her. Wherever I went, wherever *she* went, my eyes were drawn to her and somehow, my body was drawn to her too. She was dressed tonight in a deep-pink and gold silk saree, hugging the curves of her body so perfectly she could have been the Goddess Luana herself, seducing me with her hips, those perfectly shaped lips luring me in with their smile. Her entire body was physical perfection, and it was a strange thing to see a human female like that.

I couldn't forget when she'd kissed me after the demon attack. The feeling lingered on my mouth, and for some stupid reason, I found my hand drawing to my lips, as if it were hoping that she would still be there, warm against me. Her scent was still on me too, and for all the days that I lived, I would remember it. I knew other men lusted after her. Knew that Fangar would likely come back to find her because who the fuck wouldn't? Even with that cursed mouth of hers, because her tongue was as sharp as an obsidian blade and ready at a moment's notice.

And then Altara moved.

Curse this. Curse it all.

She must have been carefully watching the movements of the other girls because she held out her hands to Pia, and the other Lota girl grabbed them. Without any hesitation Altara took up the dance, her feet moving in time with the others.

She tilted her head back and laughed, and I was struck by the sheer joy in her—by the way her body moved around the music, as if she were getting to know a new friend. Her arms caressed the air, gentle but commanding, the way her skin glowed golden bronze by the light of the bonfire; it was as if pleasure itself moved through her.

Her scent was in the air—like the moments before lightning struck, like fresh spring, like a new dawn.

But I had never seen a dawn like this. Perhaps it was the first real dawn that I *had* seen. I wondered if this was how the first Boneweavers had felt when they had seen their first sunrise after emerging from inside the earth.

This woman could seduce a blade of grass if she chose. Hell, a rabid tiger might very well take her to wife and not regret it one bit.

Well, a rabid tiger had done just that.

And then Kai was there, dragging Atax and Raen along as only he could, right up to the bonfire. Midnight had come, the elders had gone to bed and the men were allowed to approach the fire. Malika, smirking, reached for Atax, who playfully flicked her hair. She screeched at him, going in for a well-placed jab that Atax was seasoned at deflecting. He pulled her into him by the waist, making her blush and stutter furiously, his hands holding her firmly as he kept them moving in the dance cue.

Kai reached for Rani, showing his teeth in a wide smile. Rani chortled with laughter, her long frame easily following Kai's jubilant movements. Raen swept up both Pia and Altara in a good-natured spin, whirling them around until they gasped, punching and berating him. He laughed darkly, forcing them to keep moving with him. I didn't resent him for it. He knew I'd never actually dance. I never had, after all. The only dance I engaged in was that of battle.

I looked at the two of the Lota girls, clearly related. But in my observations of Altara, my suspicions had been confirmed.

She had only recently come to Ellythia from the continent.

At first I'd thought she was from another one of the

islands, maybe one of the smaller ones outlying Lota Island, and they'd taken to mating with biglanders. But I'd since concluded that there was no way she'd been born here at all. Clever as she might be to hide it and pick up on things, I saw the way her eyes moved. I saw the way she felt the Ellythian tongue as she worked her way around particular words—the way she squinted in concentration when someone used a euphemism or phrase that was unique to Ellythia. I wasn't fooled.

"*I cannot tell you,*" she'd said when I asked her where she'd come from. "*It would end badly for me.*" Then it struck me like a Voltanius lightning bolt.

Her scent, her power, her clearly royal manner...it all came together.

Fuck.

My mind racing, it was as if I'd come out of a trance.

Striding up to the bonfire, the revellers bolted out of my way when they saw my face—my rage.

I grabbed Altara by the elbow and pulled her away from the bonfire into the dark, far away from the others so that none of the villagers would hear us. She protested, stumbling over a stray chair, but I could not hear her—would not hear her in case she cast Luana's spell over me yet again, befuddling my mind.

When I was satisfied with the distance, I rounded on her, my voice no more than a guttural growl. "Once you told me that I was not to ask you about how you came to be here. That it would lead to something terrible."

She bit her full lip and nodded stiffly once. "Yes, that was true."

I narrowed my eyes. "Something terrible like a pack of Scorpax demons attacking us?"

"Scorpax..." she repeated as if she had not heard the word before. I began to doubt my line of thought when her skin visibly paled. Her voice was hoarse when she continued, "They had scorpions on their chests, didn't they? That's what you mean."

"That is the Scorpax symbol," I said, barely containing my anger. "Havrok Scorpax is the demon king closest to Lobrathia...where *you* come from. You are a Voltanius princess, aren't you?"

She blinked in shock, but I continued ruthlessly, "I can smell your lightning every time you are angry. You should have told me. You endangered us all."

"Told you what?" she shot back. "I couldn't know that they were after me. I don't even know who this demon king is! Why would he—" She stopped abruptly, her anger dissipating as if a tide had washed it away.

"What?" I snapped.

But she turned around and walked away from me. "Do not speak to me. I need...I need..." She crouched down against a tree, cradling her head in her hands.

Fury tore through me as my heart pulsed in black anger— at her dismissal of me, at...everything.

"What's going on?" Pia asked angrily, as righteous as any entitled princess, coming up behind me with the three other girls. My brothers followed them. "Why are you yelling at her?"

Cold calculation swept through my mind, and I sat down on one of the wooden chairs, leaning back, spreading my legs and crossing my arms. Raen sat a little way from me, perhaps knowing the shadow in me was pulsing like death.

"You are a princess, are you not?" I asked coldly. All three girls stiffened, but they could see there was no point denying anything.

"I am," she said, tilting her chin upwards in that arrogant mannerism all these Lota women seemed to have.

"And your mother is?" I already knew the answer, but I needed her to say it.

She clenched her jaw, and it delighted the beast in me that I had her in a corner. She said tightly, "Princess Rahana."

"Who is heir to the throne of Ellythia," I said, and she nodded. "Currently." I finished.

Pia blinked, and I could hear her heart pounding rapidly in her chest, the threat I posed clear to her. That was good. They should all know that they needed to fear me and what was inside of me.

"What are you going to do?" she asked carefully.

"Nothing, just yet," I said flatly. "But I will be paying your grandmother a visit soon."

"That was never allowed," she said slowly. "The Ellythians always stayed on our side and the Old Ones on theirs."

"And yet," I said, leaning back to observe her carefully. "You are all *here*."

Her entire body went stiff. "You promised not to harm us."

"I made no such promise."

And then Malika spoke, her voice dripping with all the venom of a king cobra. "*You*, Ashzale Boneweaver, are a *pig*."

"I've been many beasts in my life, but I've never tried a pig before, *Malika Yashra*." I studied the girl, the male pixie sitting on her shoulder, his arms crossed as he glared at me. "I know your family owes a great deal of debt to the Lota crown. That is why they ran here. That is why you slept with a married man to get a loan for your parents. Everyone found out. That is why they sent you away in shame."

Malika's nostrils flared in anger as I turned to Rani. "And Rani Umasri, whose family owns the most successful silk farm in Ellythia. No one knows that you accidentally killed a child with your power, do they? That is why *you* were also sent here to the school, to hide *your* shame." Kai looked at Rani in surprise, and I turned to Pia, wielding my voice like my own obsidian blade. "And *you*, second in line to the Ellythian throne, crippled your betrothed because he wasn't a strong enough Vayashi, and you couldn't control your power." I tutted. "Humans and their oddities. Your kind used Boneweaver Island as a place of punishment. A place of exile. That presents me with rather interesting opportunities with the people here, wouldn't you say?"

I turned to Altara still crouched against the tree behind me. But I knew she was listening to every word by the pounding of her heart. "Tell me why you came here from Lobrathia."

She ground her teeth before she said, "No."

"Well, I wedded the wrong one, didn't I? It really should have been Pia."

She flinched like I'd struck her, and in the far-flung reaches of my darkness, something told me stop. To apologise. But I couldn't. The darkness in me won. It always had.

She blinked furiously as if she was going to cry. Instead she stood, jabbed a finger at me and hissed, "Fuck you, Zale Boneweaver. Just...*fuck you*." Turning on her heel, she stormed away from me.

37
ALTARA

I found myself veering into the comfort and darkness of the palm trees. I stormed into the jungle like a charging boar, fuming with heat and shame and fear. It shouldn't have stung like someone had just peeled back the skin of my heart, but it had. The backs of my eyes burned. I wanted to punch him in both his sorry blue eyes. For his cruelty, for his kindness, for his laugh. He'd tricked me, or I'd been misled—I couldn't even tell! Malika had told me to seduce him, but instead, in a way, he'd seduced *me*. I was a complete fool to think that *I* had any impact on that black heart of his. He was just as evil and malevolent as he was from the start. He'd cruelly called out my friends' secrets, their greatest burdens. And who knew the way shame was a venom in a person's soul more than me?

I was more like my friends than I had originally thought, and I didn't love them any less for it. Instead my heart bled for them. We were a group of girls who were bound by the terrible. By unthinkable shame. We were a web of tragedy.

But were we the spiders in the web or the insects that had gotten caught in it?

I thought of Malika's fiery temper, of Rani's shield of steel, of Pia's quiet intellect. No, none of us had ever been insects.

I headed straight for a particularly large palm tree and punched its trunk in a one-two jab, and finding the pain helpful, I punched again and again. Angry tears streamed down my cheeks and I let the pain and frustration out through the burning and bleeding of my knuckles. I didn't realise that Leela had shot after me until I saw her dull, saddened glow and heard her tiny voice in my ear.

"He not mean those things," she sobbed. "Tara, Zale not—"

"He did!" I sobbed. My legs were suddenly as weak as rice pudding, and I sunk down onto my knees. "He meant every word. He's a monster. He's awful."

"The shadow-lock!" Leela sniffed, and all I could see before me was the blurry golden bubble that was her. "He means nothing when he is mean. It be the darkness. He loves you; I know it."

"You are too sweet, Leela," I sighed. "You do not know the cruelty of this world. I know it. I have seen it. I have felt it."

And I was only ever reminded of it when I was weak and hurt.

"No," Leela whispered in dismay.

I nodded sadly, understanding some of the pain that Rani, Malika and Pia had no doubt gone through when they'd made their past mistakes. Rani's constant tears, Malika's rage and Pia's refusal to use her power suddenly made sense. "Some things change you beyond repair. Some scars go bone deep." I shivered, covering my face. "Once," I whispered, "I stood at the top of the Quartz palace. Just wondering if the pain in my soul would end. But as I stood there, clouds shifted away from the city, and the stars were revealed to me, one by one." I took a shaky breath. I had never told anyone this. Not even Saraya, who had been buried under the weight of her own burdens. "And there was one particular star that shone so brightly that I thought my mother was sending me a message. I thought that it was a sign I should live."

"You *should* live, Altara," Leela urged, touching my face with tiny hands. "Please, Altara, you be loved. You must live for—"

"It does not matter if you are loved or if you are not, Leela. When one is in agony, you can't see anything else. Even if it's in front of you. That is the nature of pain. It is a great, black, suffocating claw."

"How you fix it?" Leela whispered.

"You have to find the stars, the tiny points of light, and you hold onto them with all your might."

That's why this hurt so much, I realised. "It was Zale's voice I held onto that day the demons came at the lake. It was a tiny point of light in my dark."

We sat in silence for some length of time I could only guess at, Leela's tiny cheek against mine until a distinct burning smell filled the air. It was not like scent that the town bonfire made, more like cloth burning. Turning around I squinted into the jungle and realised with a cold pang that Leela and I were completely surrounded by the dark.

I'd come so far into the jungle, I could no longer see nor hear the village. My heart hammered in my ears as sharp fear speared through me.

"Something is there," Leela whispered, hiding her light in my hair.

I felt it too, the eyes on me. The hairs on the back of my

neck raised and the feeling of threat only increased. How could I have been so stupid to run into the jungle? Perhaps it was Zale's dark creatures watching us? But I knew in my heart this burning smell had never been present when the island's monsters came calling. No, my bones knew evil, and this was another, worse type.

I called my bow, and it jumped into my hand from the ether in a satisfying flash, illuminating the trees ahead of me for a single moment. But nothing came into view—only the bare dark of the jungle awaited me. I summoned an arrow of light, and it flew into my hand, glowing golden yellow. I knocked the arrow and drew my bow, waiting, heart pounding.

A voice came from the darkness, rasping, ancient, full of venom. *"Hello."*

Oh shit.

It was clearly male, also not entirely human in its breathy, echoing lack of clarity. I said nothing, instead loosing my arrow towards the voice. The arrow flew...then halted in mid-air mere paces from me. Black fingers curled around the shaft, and then with a slight fizzing sound, the arrow was gone.

"A gift," it hissed. "Sssso kind, Princess Altara Volta-niussss."

I stiffened, my blood curdling in my arteries. Was it another demon sent by my stepmother to kill me? I summoned another arrow, this time black as night, and nocked it.

A dark figure moved towards us in the slow, meandering way of an apex predator, and my skin crawled with a thousand ants. Two burning lights came into view—no, two *eye sockets* full of burning orange flames set into a tall man in a hooded robe.

"My name is Kraasputin," he hissed calmly.

Leela buried herself deeper inside my hair, and I swallowed the lump in my throat, not moving an inch. "That's a strange name."

"Thank you. It was Reaper given. In Old High Demon it meansssss 'He who is punished.'"

Keeping my arrow drawn upon him, I thought it best to play along. "Oh. I'm sorry."

"Do not be sorry, Altara Voltaniussss. For I am here to cause you harm."

My insides turned into mush, but I maintained my position and kept calm. He couldn't do anything worse to me than had already been done. A bow in my hands helped me keep focus. This creature was no demon nor anything I'd come across before. A ghoul, perhaps? Headmistress Jessine had told me to watch out for strange things in these jungles the moment I'd gotten there. My mind raced. Keeping him talking sounded like a wise tactic. So I asked lightly, "What type of harm? Are you going to talk until my ears fall off?"

"Not your earsss, no," he said simply. "Your organsss of creation."

I almost loosed my arrow in surprise. "My organs? Sir, that is rather foul, you must admit."

"Issssss it?" he mused. "People have fought warssss over such things. But alassss, no; it is not the body organ, I desire. It is the power in them—the magic that is the essence of creation. Perhaps you, of all the people in this realm, would understand."

The information settled in me like a weight. I think it was

because I *did* understand what he meant. There was much power in taking things from people. I had taken Fangar's organs, and I would be lying to myself if I couldn't see the potential for my power there. Organs held *more* than simple flesh and blood—and mine more than anyone's. I thought back to Agnolthi's temple, where the female organ was worshipped as a wonderous and powerful thing.

I tossed my head, feigning confidence as was wise when in negotiation. "So I'm giving you something of value. What are you giving me in return?"

He laughed, though I only just made it out within the hissing. "You and your sister are much the same."

My heart sank into my nether regions, and I said with deathly calm, "Where did you meet my sister?"

"High on a mountain, in a forest at midnight. The fae tied her there."

"Those bastards! I'll—"

"She escaped."

I exhaled forcefully through my nose. Of course, she had. My older sister was nothing if not capable. But I was shaking now, concerned for my sister's welfare if the fae were tying her up in dark places in the middle of the night. What else were they doing to her?

"You possess something rather interesting, Altara Volta-niusssss."

I cringed when he used my real name. But I supposed with the appearance of the crimson demons, it didn't matter now that my stepmother clearly knew I was here. "Is that so, Kraasputin?" Tactics. Strategy. How could I get out of this?

"A man's organsssssss."

I froze. "How did you know?"

"It is in my nature to collect knowledge, secrets. I know many thingsssss."

"Then knowledge is what you'll give me in return for my...male parts. Take them, honestly. I've been trying to get rid of them."

"Sssssso I am doing you a favour?"

"No," I said quickly. "I need to give them back properly, to get my own...parts functioning normally."

"I will do you a favour, Altara Voltaniusssss, and you will give me one favour in the future."

"No, but I want this information."

He went silent, watching me with those flames licking out of his eye sockets, that burning filling my nose, making my mind fuzzy.

"I'm not giving them to you, see?" I clarified. "You are taking them from me by force." How was he going to take them anyway?

"Voltaniussss House has been born again, Altara. There are many who will value this information."

I stiffened. "You play games with me, and I do not appreciate it."

He suddenly raised his hand, black fingers curling as if grabbing, and pain sliced through my groin. I crumpled, and my bow and arrow disappeared. Leela shrieked, but all at once, the pain left. I knew immediately my penis was gone, along with the testicles. I looked back up at the Kraasputin, and his flames now burned heartily in their sockets as if, in his own way, he were digesting whatever magic had lain in them.

I cringed on Fangar's behalf, clenching my pelvic floor, and feeling that my lady parts were all back to normal.

"You could have warned me, sir," I said through gritted teeth.

He did that laughing huffing thing again, and I tried not to appear shaken. "Well, what is my information?"

"Just this," he turned and as he departed, said in a voice like midnight darkness, "*He* is coming for you."

38

ALTARA

My head was screaming with a dozen emotions. I turned and walked as fast as I could back to the village, Leela frantically flitting ahead of me to light the way, guided by the sounds of the party that seemed to have returned as soon as the Kraasputin had left. My sister, my self-sacrificing, kind sister was being mistreated by those Goddess-forsaken fae! When I got back there, I was going to—

But I wasn't going to be allowed to go back. I couldn't go back if there were demons after me on the instructions of my stepmother.

The Kraasputin had said, "*He.*" That might have meant this Scorpax demon king? He could have meant my father? How many *he*'s knew me, wanted me? A dull ache began in my bones anew. No, there was only one *he* that wanted me badly enough to cross the ocean to find me. One who would, perhaps, tear the world asunder to have at me one more time at my stepmother's behest.

I was safest with the group of Old Ones, and we were

leaving here at first light anyway. I groaned, clenching my fists in outrage at the thought that I needed to rely upon someone else to keep me safe. Perhaps if I could get back to Taraka Town, then Geravie and the twins could help me make up a plan to get away from here. They were likely already making one right now.

It was strange walking penis-free. I'd almost forgotten what it was like not to have a few somethings sitting between my legs, and having it removed felt like a sort of freedom.

When we emerged from the jungle, I found myself at the edge of the village where the two temples stood sentinel, watching over the revellers in the distance. I wondered if the other girls had re-joined the dancing or if they had felt too sick to the stomach after Zale's cruel tirade, just like me.

Leela landed on my shoulder, snuggling into my neck, her wings tickling the sensitive skin there—the best way she knew how to comfort me.

Ahead of us Lasanthi's temple glowed from within, warm lights beckoning us. Something in my heart eased a little as I looked upon the Mother's abode. If we were to leave at dawn, this might very well be my last time to look upon it.

So I walked us up to the temple, kicked off my boots and headed inside. It was warm with over a hundred quartz lights in different colours lighting up the place like some ethereal dream. Leela gasped in excitement, pointing at the central quartz-figure. Lasanthi, the All-Mother, stood, holding a baby on her hip, and in this temple, instead of coins, rice fell benevolently onto the floor from the other hand. A heavy book lay upon a short table at her feet. Looking at her visage, something in my heart broke a little. How different everything would be if my mother were still alive.

"I want to go home," I whispered to Leela.

It was a young priestess of the temple who emerged from the dark and answered in a wistful voice, "Don't we all? In the end."

I turned to see her, a bright-faced young lady in her red robes, the curved symbol of the Mother on her forehead. She smiled as if she somehow understood my pain. "Home to the eternal mother, that is."

My face heated, and my vision blurred so all I could do was nod. She made a clicking sound with her tongue and swept forward to place more flowers at the feet of the Mother.

"In the Forests of Eternity," she said softly, as if in prayer. "Only two things stand the tests of time: love and kindness. This is what the Mother teaches us."

"I don't have any of that in me just now," I said thickly. Leela sat on my shoulder, stroking my neck. How many things had gone wrong in such a short amount of time? "I...I took something from someone, and I couldn't return it to them. Now someone else has stolen it from me."

The priestess straightened, looking up at the pink quartz statue towering over us, tiny curls of incense dancing lazily through the air. "Then it wasn't intended for them."

Leela sniggered in my ear, and I shook my head forlornly. How would I explain that to Fangar when he reappeared? "May I sit here?" I asked uncertainly, looking around. "I don't want to go outside just yet."

The priestess turned, and her face held bright amusement, "Do you not know? This is the sole purpose of this temple. Solace in the tempest. It will storm soon. Sit and be welcome."

There were cushions stacked to the side aplenty, so I sat on one, Leela on another. Eventually, it began raining, and the pixie, priestess and I watched the pattering of rain in silence for long minutes.

As Zale's thunderous face swam into my vision, a thought struck me, and I asked, "What do you know about the old tale of the curse of our Boneweaver King and the key the three queens created?"

She gave me a long, assessing look. "The tremors when you arrived did not give it away? I presumed you knew it already. No? Well, you had better look at this."

She beckoned me to the front of the statue of the Mother, where she opened the huge, leather-bound tomb with an ancient creak, flipping it towards the back.

"These are handwritten by each Lasanthi priestess during their lifetimes. Any interesting occurrences during her time regarding mothers and infants. Ah, this one. The babe was born...the Reaper arrived...here—the three queens stood together..."

She shifted to the side so I could sit directly before the book and read it. Leela hovered beside me, muttering softly under her breath as she read alongside me:

"Where there is a lock, a key must also be made. Thus is law of nature," the Ellythian queen said.

"Where there is darkness there must be light," the Boneweaver Queen agreed.

"And so," said the Pixie Queen, 'the most powerful light we know comes from the stars. This key must be forged inside the light of a star—that reaches us even so far away."

"The same star," the Boneweaver Queen breathed, "that the soul of Ashzale Boneweaver was forged in."

The three queens held hands and chanted in an old forgotten tongue. The storm raged, lightning flashed, the ocean swelled. But theirs was a voice that resounded through space, through the dark. They called upon one star.

And that star heard.
"Twin flames, twin souls," chanted the queens, "tempest forged,
storm forged, lightning forged."
As the storm died down and a jdeathly calm quiet descended upon
the island, every being stopped to listen.
"His star-mate will be his key," the Ellythian Queen announced.
And about the hall, the Boneweavers cheered. In the Everlasting
Jungle, the pixies danced, and far, far away in the heavens above,
came a tiny, answering song.

I slammed the book shut, harder than I'd meant to. But the Priestess of the Mother made no remark. She merely looked upon me with brown eyes glistening with meaning. Her eyes flickered down to my buzzing hands.

They were shaking, but strands of blue-white electricity were shooting around them in orbit. I had been feeling this buzzing, fizzing sensation under my skin for a few days now, but this was the first time I'd ever seen actual lightning coming from me.

Lightning Forged.

"Did the tremors when you arrived not give it away?"

The moment Geravie had stepped ashore, the earth had shaken. The *exact* moment I'd stepped off the jetty onto the beach, I realised. And then again, when I'd been outside the twins' house, when thunder had boomed but no clouds had been in the sky.

Cold horror stripped away my insides. My very being.

"Surely not." My voice did not feel like my own. It was someone else's. Some stupid, idiotic, useless girl's voice.

My head was buzzing, my heart no more than a roaring beat in my ears. I couldn't breathe. Couldn't think. I knew what was being asked of me. I knew that I could not do it.

Descend into the all-black darkness again? Become shadow and wraith and…nothing to free Zale from this thing? This thing that had happened so long ago, that had never been my problem. What if I'd never come here? What if I'd chosen to stay in Quartz? What then? I would never have met any of the Old Ones. I'd be blissfully unaware like I'd always been.

They had it wrong. Perhaps Zale was right, and it *was* Pia? Those words in that book just meant a storm was raging at the time of the spell. They could never have known at the time it would be an actual Voltanius girl.

But even as I thought this, I knew what Agnolthi had said to me. She'd practically told us when we met with her in Yasani Temple.

"The stars aligned in just the right way. I've waited eons for you."

I turned and shot out of the temple, no more than an arrow in the dark.

Leela cried out, but I was too fast for her. "My queen!" cried the priestess, but I blocked her heinous voice out. That heinous title.

The rain beat down on me, soaking my beautiful saree instantly. But I barely noticed through the roaring in my heart, the fear that laced my insides like a vice, threatening to do much worse than end me. Death would have been a happy mercy. Anything but this—*not this*, not *me* being his solution.

Thunder boomed right above me, and it lurched me into a fevered sprint. I launched into the jungle, letting it pull me deep into its dark womb, away from everything including—

A roar pierced night through the thundering of the rain, and I knew it was *him*. Knew that he was never far from me, always watching me as if expecting something to burst forth from my skin.

As if expecting me to be someone I wasn't.

I couldn't be a queen. Couldn't be his *star-mate*. Couldn't be a saviour. I couldn't be attached to someone like that. I had always been my own person, even in marriage I had been *my own person*. But even as I thought it, my heart was tearing in two because I knew he was now behind me.

Still, I kept surging through the jungle as the rain pounded down so hard it hurt. The jungle flora was harsh against my skin and pain blossomed anew. But how could I care when my magic would take care of it? The same magic that had been called forth to save Ashzale Boneweaver.

His footsteps were behind me, and from four paws it became two. I glanced back to see a tiger leaping for me. I cried out, but just as he fell on top of me, he morphed back into his human form, and we landed on the muddy ground.

The landing should have hurt, but he cushioned me with a flash of his dark magic, and I felt no pain.

"Do *not* run from me, Altara." He was panting, voice strained as his blue eyes bore into mine, and despite the heat in his voice, when he said my name, it felt like a caress. "Never run like that from me ever again, do you understand?"

I slapped him on the chest. "I will run as I please, you insane monster!"

"Then I will always be chasing you."

"Pig!"

"Witch." But it wasn't an insult.

"I hate you."

"Why can I not stop thinking about you?"

My heart stuttered.

I couldn't even get an arm up to punch him, and it made my veins screech in outrage, and that curious expression on his face did nothing to help my anger. His body melted into mine as he calmly observed me.

"You said you should have married Pia." I meant it as a challenge, but it came out through gritted teeth.

"My brain is telling me I should have." He licked his lips, his eyes roaming my face. "But I do not want her like I want you." Heat flared through my core at the primal growl of his voice, the raw promise in it. When I was silent, he said, "Tell me that you do not want me, and I will leave you be."

"Fuck you, Zale," I said breathlessly, but all I could think of was the way his body was pressing against mine, his groin against my thighs. His large biceps on either side of my body, hovering above me without any strain. He was all feline strength and dominant masculinity. He was not a man but had the desires of one. And this time, his blue eyes were seeking and warm on me. Actually *warm*.

"You are like the dawn to me. In the dark, I see you properly."

No one had said such a thing to me. The backs of my eyes burned because I knew what he did not. That I had been called forth by three powerful queens to save him. That he had awoken from his long sleep because *I* had come to this island. That he sought me out even though he didn't understand why because we had been made in the same star.

"Why are you crying?" he whispered, kissing my left cheek and then my right. At the sensation of his lips on me, my stomach flopped upon itself, swirling pleasure rising up through my core.

He cocked his head. "Your manhood is gone." I flushed, heat spreading to every particle in my body.

But his face only came closer to mine, and it was then—that damn him—he whispered in an uncertain voice so unlike a king. "Tell me why I cannot stop thinking about you. What have you done to me, Altara?"

My blood was made of butterflies, my insides stirring with wanton desire. I hated myself for it and revelled in the sensation at the same time.

Water streamed around us, pounding on his back and sliding off him into the mud. Water from his long hair dripped onto my neck. And then his lips were on mine, soft but demanding.

Goddess damn the both of us, but it felt so good.

I groaned, spreading my legs, wanting him, needing him to be closer to me. His tongue found its way into my mouth, and I arched against him, his lips moving slowly as if savouring me.

Zale's head whipped up so fast that I flinched in surprise. Through the pattering rain, I heard what he had.

Distant, terrified screams.

My blood chilled as if struck by ice. Zale was off me in a flash, and I struggled to my feet.

Before he changed forms, Zale's eyes darkened, turning as cold and distant as the night sky, all trace of everything that had just passed between us, gone.

Zale's tiger form burst forth from his skin and the sheer force of his magic hit me like a tidal wave, sending me rocking as I scrambled to my feet. He was off into the jungle, and I followed close behind, the sound of my feet swallowed up by the dark.

I crashed through the last ferns of the jungle and halted in shock. A horrific tableau was laid out before me, and my dinner threatened to rise up and eject itself out of my throat.

A hundred armoured demons were laying waste to Levu village. Flashes of crimson skin shot through the rain, lit up with magical torches of water-retardant flames of orange and red. They set fires to the huts and houses and slashed open the homeowners.

To my right, lion-Atax leapt through the air, his jaws snapping around the neck of a demon in full plate armour. Raen was in human form, two black swords in hand, his green magic streaking towards a pack of demons surging into one of the houses. Zale was in his human form again, a sword in one hand, an axe in the other, and he fought and slashed at the stream of demons that had seen him and began an attack.

Malika, with her parents and sister by her side, shot angry red magic to blast back demons from their house, but there were too many demons and not enough people fighting.

I cried out in abject rage, summoning my bow and a full quiver of arrows. They thumped into my arms with a poof of gold smoke. Then I was running. Towards Malika's house, aiming as I went, firing by the second, never letting my fingers linger. Demons fell, and it was only a matter of minutes before I was made a target.

A growl sounded beside me, and I found Kai at my side, his white cheetah's fur sopping wet in the downpour. As three demons bolted for me, I returned my bow and arrows to my astral trove and instead summoned a sword I'd prepared. But Kai was quick, and he leapt for two of them with a snarl, taking them to the ground and ripping their throats out like he'd been waiting his whole life to do it.

The third came for me, his sword slashing through the air. I wasn't as genius with a blade like my sister, but I'd been trained in swords for just as long as I'd been working a bow. I ducked and shoved my sword in the gap between his helmet and neck. Blood spurted, and he fell to his knees.

I whirled around to face two more demons running at me, but they were heavy in plate armour that covered most of their body, and I could only see gnashing teeth through the dark of their helmets. Taking advantage of their lack of speed, I returned my sword to the ether and, summoning two daggers, threw them in quick succession.

Lightning never misses its mark.

I smiled darkly as both daggers lodged themselves into the faces of the demons, who fell to the ground, dead.

Two golden lights shot past me, and I followed their flight path.

My stomach seized into a knot as I saw Rani fending off several armoured demons, who laughed and jeered as they surrounded her.

But in an angry flash of orange light, Rani summoned six swords, which hovered in the air, their lethal points trained outwards at the demons. Rani's assailants hesitated, but only for a moment before one of them lunged for my friend.

The swords flew forward like arrows, catching three of the demons and missing the other three. One grabbed Rani by her hair and stabbed her in the arm. She fell with a cry.

I screamed, summoning my bow and angling it, only to have someone snatch me from behind. I summoned an arrow and shoved it under my armpit. It hit armour. The demon dragged me backwards by the neck, and I choked in his grip. I drew my legs up and yanked us both to the ground. Twisting my hip to make way, I daggered him in the plate-joint between his knee and thigh.

He grunted and faltered in his grip enough that I rolled myself over and stabbed him in face with a cry. I wrenched the dagger free and took both his eyes out and paused, noticing with a shooting horror that his skin was *blue*.

More demons were streaming towards me now. More *Daanav* marines.

With a rage I'd never felt before, I got to my feet, summoning another dagger. With lethal efficiency I let my daggers fly, aiming for the eye slits of each armoured Daanav coming upon me.

One of them hung back and took off his helmet. The rain slowed, leaving hot mist to hover in the air, and like a living nightmare, Fangar revealed himself. He was in his demon form, his eyes trained on me like a predator, a snarl twisting his ugly face.

He'd turned into our enemy.

How could I be surprised? He was a demon. But Zale ruled their kingdom, had taken it back. They had submitted to him.

Fangar flung out an arm, stopping another demon from launching at me. More demons gathered behind him, waiting. There was a whole company, I thought in panic. At least twenty fresh. "Leave my wife for me," he snarled in such a guttural rage that I blanched, feeling all my blood drain to my centre.

He looked upon me with deathly eyes.

I clutched a new dagger in my hand. How many could I summon and throw in quick succession? Not twenty—not even *I* was that good. They'd be on me within seconds.

"Zale is your King!" I cried angrily.

His face twisted in a hateful smirk. "We accept no king but the Reaper now."

The Reaper. The god-like being who had given Zale his curse. Fangar was going to punish me for taking his cock, and I couldn't even give it back to him. When he'd found that I didn't have it anymore, he'd kill me outright. I knew it.

A roar in the distance made my heart leap—it was Zale, coming to help me, surely. But Fangar smirked, and someone leapt upon me from behind.

An animalistic snarl came from behind us, and I just got to twist as I fell. Kai was being attacked by no less than ten demons. They were on top of him, stabbing, cutting, slicing at every inch of fur they could find. Kai ripped and bit and tore, but there too many on him now, too many blades inside his body, tearing him open. Blood spurted.

"Kai!" I screamed, but my head was pushed into the mud, and I swallowed a heap of it. My magic pushed out, seeking to help—and came against a wall of nothing.

Multiple demons were on me now, and I could see that their armour was laced with tourmaline, the one substance that repelled magic.

I gave a strangled cry as I was manhandled into submission. Thick arms, long fingernails digging into me with efficiency.

My arms were bound behind me. My legs were bound too. And then there was rope, so much rope. Over and over I was turned until I was bound and hot inside a cocoon of heavy heat.

I couldn't see Zale, but I could hear him. And his roar through the night was terrible, but terrible and choked. I knew they had him too. Knew that they'd subdued the Old Ones with sheer numbers. Four Old Ones were no match for over one hundred demons, marine and subterranean both.

"Fall back!" Fangar roared at his warriors. "We have her—fall back!" And then he looked down at me, the hate smoothing away from his face, leaving only a savage smirk behind. My very bones sunk into a black, gangrenous chill when he said, "The Krassputin gave me my cock back. And The Butcher gets to have you now."

As the demons hauled me into the jungle at a rapid pace, my mind couldn't grasp that The Butcher was here, in Ellythia, so far away from Quartz where we'd last met. My stepmother had told him that she would bring him back if I undermined her.

And she'd made good on her promise.

They'd hunted me down until they got me. The Kraasputin had been right.

I had been wrong about Fangar wanting to kill me. Oh no, I would be left alive for weeks, perhaps even months as The Butcher slowly carved me open.

The last time, my stepmother had allowed him one full day and he'd begged her for longer.

I went still as my mind froze like it were in a block of solid ice. This was not happening to me. It was happening to someone else. A stupid girl who thought she could run away from her life. From her home. I was going numb, and we had not even reached our destination.

"Is she awake?" gruffed one of the demons carrying me. "I'm going to punch her to see."

"Do not!" Fangar, *my husband*, snapped from somewhere ahead of me. "He wants her unmarked. There'll be consequences."

My demon immediately fell silent because every demon knew The Butcher. Knew what he was capable of. Even Pia had known about his particular breed: *Pentarog*.

I was bound with so much rope, that it weighed down on my body, and I couldn't even move it. It took six of them to carry me, three to a side.

As if they were pall bearers carrying a funeral casket.

I needed a way to kill myself, a part of me realised. But in order to do that, had to summon my astral daggers to cut myself out. But they'd bound my wrists against my body too tightly. With the tourmaline in their armour, I couldn't use my magic against them either.

I only knew about the tourmaline because The Butcher had told me about it.

My mind tried to think as they stomped through the night of the jungle. We travelled far, though I could not fathom in what direction. I must have fallen into a dazed sleep because the next thing I knew, there was stone around us as if we were in castle grounds. But I had never heard of one in this part of Boneweaver Island. But of course, I wouldn't have; I'd never seen a map of this place—the Old Ones had travelled us across their land on memory and a map Housekeeper Yona had given them at the school. For all I knew, that castle school was only one of many castles on the island.

"My lord," came Fangar's voice. "We have her."

My entire being turned into obsidian stone at his words.

And when *he* spoke, his voice was like a carving knife, deep and vicious. Slicing and precise.

"Altara Voltanius," The Butcher whispered. "I've missed you."

They hoisted me upright, forcing me to look upon my living nightmare for the first time in four years. I couldn't blink as I took him in.

We were in one cage of many set outside a castle in the middle of the jungle. I was surrounded by bleached ivory bars on all five sides, the night sky twinkling above me.

The Butcher stood by a solid wooden table I knew he'd nailed and hammered with his own hands. He loved using his hands.

The Butcher was huge, muscled as all demons were, and he never wore a shirt, as his kind prided raw displays of strength above all. Every muscle on his bulky body was well defined, and it was littered with scars that he'd cut into himself. His skin was bone-white and his face wide with low cheekbones and hollow cheeks that gave him a gaunt look, though the rest of him was robust. He had no hair on his body or head, and his eyes had been made by hell itself—red irises with snake-slitted pupils. He held a knife, which he stroked lovingly out of habit.

We knew each other well. He knew every inch of my body better than any lover—except my private organs. No, my stepmother had forbidden him from touching those, as she wanted to leave me "pure." Untainted.

As if slicing me open and filling me with venom could ever have ensured my *purity*. I had been tainted since that day. Ruined, on a fundamental, marrow-deep level. Literally, The Butcher cut me open to the bone marrow of my femurs and enjoyed every second of it.

"Say my name," he whispered now, those red eyes took me in almost lovingly, like an addict who'd gone without his drug for a long time.

I knew if I didn't obey, the consequences were not worth it. We had an understanding, he and I. So I licked my lips and whispered, "The Butcher."

He closed his eyes and inhaled deeply, as if he could consume my very voice—and that was not the only thing he would consume of me this night.

"I missed your pretty eyes. I missed your pretty voice too," he rasped softly, almost kindly, and it made me want to cut my eardrums in half.

His tone had changed to violence so abruptly that it made me jump in my mounds of rope. "Untie her. Lay her down."

As the demons rushed to comply, I knew it was too late to run.

The Butcher strapped me down to the table himself, by the ankles and wrists, using ropes he'd laced with tourmaline that would stop me from being able to use my magic. I knew all of this because he'd told me, as if I'd be interested to understand what was happening—or rather as if it gave him happiness to indulge his pleasures with me. His little pet.

He leaned over me, his breath surprisingly sweet. "We will start now, you understand, Princess?"

"Yes, Butcher." I closed my eyes.

Dear Goddess, dear mother, dear father, dear Saraya. Please forgive me, I chanted as he began. The sharp point of his knife pressed against the skin of my shoulder. I squeezed my eyes, clenched my fists, curled my toes. *Dear Geravie, dear Pia, Malika, Rani...please forgive me.*

"Open your eyes, Altara," he rasped. "I want to see the emeralds shine."

I let out a shaky breath as I obeyed, squinted up at his white, lined face. Corpse-white, death-white. He smiled as he returned his attention back down to my arm. I turned my eyes skyward, towards the stars. *Dear Zale, dear Kai, dear Raen, dear Atax, I'm sorry.*

They had come for me, and torn down Levu village, Malika's home, with it. That massacre was all my fault. Mine alone. Tears spilled from my eyes, and all I could do was stare aimlessly at the white bars of the cage while the Butcher hissed for his assistants to come forward. The small crimson demons, teenagers, eagerly held up a small glass phial each up to my cheeks, catching the stream of tears that fell.

The pain lanced down my arm as The Butcher first cut a long line of skin open. To stop them from healing together, he placed a series of clamps—of his own invention—along the cuts on both sides to splay them open. The burn was wildfire through my arm, but this pain, I could withstand. It was what came next that I—

The scream that tore through my throat was loud and high pitched. It always started that way—a small, distant part of me noted—as The Butcher cut through the muscle of my bicep.

"Quickly, quickly," he hissed at his assistant.

I knew what they were doing, though I kept my eyes trained upwards. I knew the process. My magic poured of out me, eager and warm. A tiny puff of gold smoke emitted from my muscle, and the assistant sucked it up with another invention—a ball and spout, where the stretchy ball created a negative pressure when depressed, so that when they allowed it to recoil, my gold magic was sucked up, and none of it wasted.

The knife clattered to the table as, so eagerly, The Butcher snatched the suction device from his assistant and put it in his mouth like a cigar, squeezing the ball and inhaling the contents. He held it inside his lungs for a surprisingly long time, his muscular shoulders and chest expanded to full capacity, his eyes closed.

It was a drug for him, I knew, but when those red eyes opened, there it was—they glowed gold with power.

He exhaled in ecstasy, tilting his head up to the heavens as if thanking some dark god—probably this Reaper being they all worshipped.

As he took up his knife, to cut yet again into my muscle, I kept my mind occupied with listing every anatomical point of the body. I started with my spine, the atlas, cervical spine had seven bones, the thoracic spine had twelve bones, the lumbar spine had five, the sacrum was fused with five, the coccyx was the tiny tail...

I knew I was bleeding heavily, but I let it happen, fighting against the instinct to heal myself. I bade my magic to recede back into my body, but it twitched under my hold, stretching out, pushing to *move*. I held tighter, gritting my teeth. But we'd gone through this before, this demon and I.

"Stop," The Butcher rasped. "Sweet princess, stop the bleeding or I will cut your pretty face open."

And he would. I knew he would do as he promised. The solid dark of defeat overcame me.

I let go.

My magic burst forward to heal the cut arteries and capillaries. As he would cut into me, my magic would seal off the bleeding, giving him neat access to my body. This was real defeat. Using my magic to *help* him do this. But that was what made it all the more pleasurable for him.

"Sweet Altara," The Butcher rasped. "Tell me how it feels."

"It hurts," I gritted out. He tutted. I knew what he wanted. "It hurts so much I could cry."

"And?" he whispered.

"It hurts like a thousand flames are burning my insides."

"And?"

"It hurts so much I want to die."

He made a noise of approval, a deep rumble in his chest. He changed tools, brought out his serrated knife, the one with thick teeth, and I knew what was coming before it began.

The scream I let out lasted as long as my breath, and when my throat tore to shreds, I began to wail.

As he sawed into my bone with the venom-coated blade, clouds of gold dust puffed up from my body.

The Butcher collected it.

The venom sunk into my core, burning anew, simmering my insides, shattering my brain, maddening my mind. More magic seeped from me.

"I forgot to tell you," The Butcher whispered, so far away, "your stepmother sends her regards."

I clung to edges of my torn mind with the bleeding stubs of hope, holding them together with the image of my sister's face. That my Saraya had torn her back open to keep me safe from our stepmother. That the least I could do in her name was suffer this for her.

But no one could survive this level of pain and shame.

Just before my mind shattered into a million rusty pieces, my stepmother's face swam into view—beautiful, cold and a smile like a bloody whip.

"You will never undermine me again."

My father had once imported a block of tourmaline to subdue a feral Boneweaver. One of my distant cousins who'd gone too far down the path of bestial blood and sex lust to let loose on the island. They chained his panther body down to the block with heavy ropes and began the process of trying to revert him back to sanity.

It was the only reason why I now recognised the tourmaline that had been used to render me immobile within seconds.

Somewhere in the two hundred years that we'd been asleep, they'd invented tourmaline weapons. It was a genius invention on the demon's part, and I had no doubt that it had come from the subterranean demon realm as the marines weren't clever enough for that. These were weapons we had never imagined, and I'd never felt more ancient or out of place on my own island.

As no less than twenty demons continued to wind the tourmaline chains around every inch of my tiger's limbs, it felt like my black heart had been torn out of my body.

Watching Fangar drag away Altara had cleaved me open with a God-powered axe, and I hadn't even realised I'd shifted into my tiger form.

Atax roared in anger somewhere to my left, but I couldn't see him.

Raen was silent, his power sputtered out by, I estimated, thirty well-placed tourmaline arrows.

And I could see Kai, lying in a bloody mess, a slashed artery in his side pulsing blood with every slow heartbeat.

As loath as I was to admit it, I don't think my brothers and I had ever been in a worse position. And as soon as my magic was shut off, my shadow-monsters faded into wisps of night air.

The women, on the other hand, had fared a little better. Pia had been able to drag a wounded Rani into Malika's house, one of the few left standing after Malika saw her father drop to the ground with a shoulder wound, and single-handedly made meat and bones of a dozen demons in one angry, screaming sweep.

But I knew if the demons hadn't all been diverted to take us Old Ones down, she wouldn't have survived. The demons simply didn't care about the humans anymore now that Fangar had ordered them to fall back and take Altara away. The rest stayed to subdue us as the humans with mastery over water—which were thankfully many because these people worked rice paddies for generations—put out fires and huddled to hide in their homes and save their injured.

The chains now burned and bound my body, so relentlessly suppressing the magic that wanted to come out of me, that they singed my fur. I gritted my teeth as the muscles there seized, making me even more frozen.

I only knew rage. I only knew slaughter. I craved for blood

on a soul-deep level. And even if this destroyed me, I would take everyone else with me. Every Reaper fucking demon, marine or subterranean. The being had taken much away from me. But he would not take this. Not her.

They were not trying to kill us, that much was obvious as I watched a group of demons trying to stem Kai's haemorrhaging chest. They wanted us alive.

"The Butcher will have our heads," one of the demons said, smacking his comrade over the head. "Fucking save him. Stitch the wound."

"I've never stitched a fucking animal before," growled the healer demon. "You! Turn back to human!" he shouted at Kai and gave him a poke into his wound.

The Butcher. I had never heard of such a person, but this was no doubt their leader. The creature that had come from the demon realm under Lobrathia. The one leading the chase for Altara.

A growl escaped my throat, and the demons dragged me onto a piece of wood. It took ten of them to drag my tiger's body onto it, but once they did, they used a wheel and pulley mechanism to get me onto a cart. They'd been well prepared by Fangar.

As soon as they took us to this Butcher, I'd have more of an understanding of what was going on. They would have Altara there, and then I could make a plan.

Four carts took a long time to haul through the Boneweaver jungles, no matter how beastly the buffalo pulling us. I didn't know how this many subterranean demons had gotten here from over the sea or under the sea, but whichever way it was, I would make it my life's mission to destroy the gateway, and the bastards who'd dared to invade my kingdom with it.

My body might be temporarily immobile, but my mind certainly wasn't. I marked each demon in this troupe and noted their injuries, which leg they favoured, their hierarchy.

I knew my brothers well enough to know what they would be doing at the moment.

Atax would be doing the same thing I was—counting, strategising, noting our surroundings, listening closely.

Raen would be working on a mental construction to work around the tourmaline in his arrows and chains. His magic might be rendered useless, but again, complex magic began in the mind first. He'd probably wheedle his way under the molecules of tourmaline and deconstruct them from the inside out. His father had made him to withstand any mental or physical torture or deficit. It had been a cruel training that started when he was just a baby, but he'd saved us countless times.

While Kai, I knew, was probably asleep, gathering his energy to heal where the demon weapons had struck his internal organs.

We were known as undefeatable, but only we knew that we'd been defeated many times; it was just that we refused to accept it and bounded back too quickly for anyone else to notice. It was in our defeats that we had been made strong.

It had started with our fathers, breaking us over and over again with fists, with weapons, with magic, in their beast forms and in their human forms that we'd had to make ourselves up over and over again. Sometimes we'd help each other, hold one another as we screamed in physical pain or sobbed in emotional pain, or other times we had to do it alone. But in those dark moments we'd faced together, we'd been bound. And bonds of blood and pain were the strongest of all.

When the demons finally slowed, I knew we were deep in the jungles on the eastern side of the island, close enough to the ocean that I could hear the distant call of the waves. I recognised it at once.

This was the Ivory castle watchtower of my mother's family.

There were many watchtowers along the coast of all the islands, built centuries ago to stave off Daanav attacks. Mostly they were magical in nature, but they'd always been attached to a trusted family of warriors. As the tower, now yellowed with age and covered in jungle vines and roots, came into view, I knew it had been abandoned long ago.

The jungle always wins—the Boneweaver family motto. And indeed, left to its own devices with the magic of the Old Ones protecting it, Castle Ivory had been taken over by the jungle.

I knew why they had brought us here immediately.

Us Old Ones had also used Ivory Castle as a prison. Outside of the castle, where all could see their shame, there were twelve beast-sized cages made of bleached bone laced with obsidian and old magic. We had never hidden our prisoners in underground dungeons; we left them out in the open, where rain and sun and heat made fools of us all. In the jungle we are reduced to the core of what we are; it strips away all lies and wears away at the masks we show the rest of the world.

This was my mother's natal home, and I felt the old magic of her family running earth deep.

As my cart was turned around, I could see that one of the cages was already occupied.

I let out an earth-shattering roar of anger that made the demons closest to me stumble away in fright. If I could have destroyed the entire world in that moment, I would have.

Lying alone, bound to a wooden table with ropes, was Altara. Her pink and gold saree, now covered in dried mud, had been hiked up to her hips, exposing what had been done to the muscle of her thigh. She'd been cut open, her muscles splayed open by instruments nailed to the table, exposing white bone.

The same had been done to both arms.

Her skin was grey, her eyes closed. But her expression... was soft. As if she were in no pain at all. The same expression had come over her face when she had been in my arms after the demon attack at the lake. Foul dread wound its way through my heart as I realised she'd gone into that dark place of nothing.

That place where she had wanted to end herself. And she would, at first opportunity.

What was worse was that her body held the acceptance of someone who was not going through something new. She'd been through this before.

My magic pulsed inside of me, wanting to work, wanting to kill and maim and destroy this entire place, and for the first time since they'd bound me, my magic spiked upwards. The chains burned around me, absorbing the heat, trembling under the pressure of holding me in.

As I was unceremoniously slid right into one of the cages, I looked over to see Raen slide into the cage next to me, lying in his human form, bundled like a caterpillar in a chrysalis of tourmaline chains, black arrows sticking out in-between. I gave him a questioning look, unable to speak into his mind as we normally could when in animal form.

Although his magical tattoos were dead and stationary on

his face, my brother's blue eyes were open, staring blankly, glazed as if they were seeing things no one else could. Or as I knew it, unravelling a complex puzzle of the structure of tourmaline. As I watched him, his lips gave a slight twitch. And I knew he was smirking.

42
ALTARA

I lay on that table for untold hours—it could have been days for all I knew, but it wasn't until The Butcher began cutting into my liver that I truly separated from my body and descended into darkness.

He'd peeled away my skin, and I sunk into the well where my magic lay.

He'd sawed away my lower ribs, removing portions of them completely, and I slammed down that steel door of death and decay.

As I dragged myself down the solitary path only tread by the truly hopeless, I knew the truth at the heart of things.

I would happily die. Welcome death, in fact, with open arms that trembled in agony. There was no choice for me, no future in this life. Time stretched out before me as a barrow downs, a place of sadness, illness and the dying. I could not save my sister from my devil of a stepmother or the fae that had enslaved her. I could not save my mother from her death, and I had walked away from my ill father—left him to rot in his own kingdom. What worth did I have? I did not deserve

335

the life of luxury I had lived. I did not deserve my sister, nor Rani, Pia or Malika, even Leela. I had caused the attack on Malika's village, murdering dozens. I was responsible. I did not deserve to walk among these people and call them friends.

There was a wallowing, hopeless, soul-destroying cloak around me, and it would weigh me down until I descended into the void of nothing. For where else did the worthless go?

Take me, I pleaded to Goddess, *Take me home to the place where there is no pain, where I might be free of this weight on my shoulders, this agony in my bones. A place where I could be—if not happy, because I do not deserve that, then at peace.*

I had descended past that point of madness where the trap door to sanity lay sealed shut behind me. Each tear was a burning flame down the sour skin of my sallow cheeks. Each breath was the strike of a whip held by my stepmother.

The flames of hell were around me, in me, burning me alive from the inside out. My brain was a tangled mess of thorns that scraped the backs of my eyes.

My magic was a carcass inside of me, its body decimated.

But The Butcher wasn't going to let me die. He wanted his demonic markings on every inch of my tired bones, wanted to take from me everything until the point of death, until which time he would make sure I recovered so he could do it again, or perhaps return me to my stepmother. She would then have me killed just to get rid of me as a final mark of her power over us.

At the end of this would come death. And that would be it.

I stayed in this state of void-sleep, floating in the dark ocean of my despair.

But all at once, something caught my attention.

A sudden warmth sunk into me like sweet nectar, and my eyes creaked open like a rusty door. Perhaps it was heaven that was coming for me. Maybe The Butcher miscalculated, and my death had come early.

Light graced the area around me, turbulent but warm. Glittering but blinding. It bounced off the bars of the cage like the flap of butterfly's wings—never in one spot, liquid gold spilling onto the ivory bars.

I knew who it was before her form entered my cage on bare, bejewelled feet, her massive golden lion at her side, snarling with his teeth bared and angry fire in his amber eyes.

The Goddess Agnolthi stormed toward me like a raging predator of the jungle. In one swift, vicious movement, she smacked me across the face so hard my vision sparkled with lights. Except so dull was I, that I barely felt the sting.

"Fight," Agnolthi hissed, her green eyes so full of a torrential volcanic fury that I came out of my dead stupor for a moment. I stared at her, but her arm moved so fast it was a blur, slapping me a second time. My head whipped to the side at the impact, but the slap had been across my forehead this time.

I gave one giant gasp as a thousand bee stings stabbed my forehead. Agnolthi leaned over me, her presence dwarfing me, filling me, making me small and big at the same time. Her gaze on me was like the weight of an erupting volcano and her power shook every cell that made up my body.

When she spoke her voice was the furious roar of a lion and I blinked at the impact of it. *"My mark is on you now, Altara daughter of Yasani daughter of Cheshni. You will no longer remain in hiding. You will claim the power that is your birthright, or so help me by all that is wild and true I will make you regret it."*

Cold terror spun through me at the pure fury in that voice.

The hairs on my peeled skin stood on end and I began to tremble.

No, *vibrate*.

A slow burn began in my capillaries, bright but lethal. I frowned at the sharpness as it ascended into my arteries, igniting into a lethal firestorm, roaring and crackling and fizzing.

Agnolthi straightened, her black gown swept as she turned away from me and leapt onto the back of her lion. When she looked at me over her shoulder, her eyes were narrowed, striking me like arrows burning with all the fire of the rising sun.

"*Wake up. Fight!*" she commanded in a voice that shook the earth beneath my table. Then she was gone, her light with her.

I gasped as my own power hit my chest, the smell of a storm now coming off me in waves.

Leela, my beautiful golden pixie friend was using her whole body weight to pull at one of the clamps holding my skin open. On my other side, Trouble was groaning as he strained to do the same.

But with a fizz the clamps popped off my skin and tumbled to the dirt. The ropes binding me to the table burned off me, sparks erupting from them.

The two assistant demons rushed into the open cage, their eyes wide, their faces panicked. But with a jolt of the force now inside of me, I leapt off the table and raised both my hands. Leela and Trouble shot behind me.

My bow flashed into reality, already knocked with a black arrow.

As the muscles, tendons and skin of my arms, legs and torso knitted themselves back together, lightning stormed down my arms and out of my fingertips, straight into the arrow. I barely registered the arrow buzzing with power before I loosed it, and a second one after that. They slammed into both demons with a vicious force, and they were thrown back by the impact, their bodies seizing under the electricity, light flashing around their bodies.

The smell of burning flesh filled the air.

Lightning never misses its mark.

I stared at my fingers and found fine tendrils of black smoke curling off my skin. Lightning danced in a fine thread around each finger.

More, it said. *Give me more.*

I felt nothing killing those demons, felt nothing now that the ancient power of Voltanius lightning charged my veins like blood made into raging fire. Light made into a weapon.

But in my chest now were the charred black remains of my soul, and my spirit remained dull, swathed in the dark of the abyss.

It was just what was needed. Three queens had called me forth. Had made it so. I had only one purpose before I let the void take me for good.

I had been born for this.

43
ALTARA

Looking around my cage, I realised there were other cages set in a row alongside mine.

But all hell had broken loose outside. Demons roared, and arrows flew and plinked against metal.

I exited my cage, confused by the noise.

And then I saw it. Emerging through the jungle was a shield of steel. As tall as a man and as wide as ten, it skimmed the grass, and through holes in it, red, blue and orange missiles shot through.

The demons ducked and shot arrows at the shield.

All at once, the steel shield flew forward and struck like a massive battering ram, sweeping up the demon guards, knocking them out cold.

Behind the shield stood Rani with Malika, her parents and Pia. Next to them was Geravie, Keshmi and Reshmi along with other villagers from Levu.

Still I felt nothing. They did not know that this girl was already gone. They had come for a ghost.

"Altara!" Rani cried, but more demons were streaming

from the castle. I took up my bow once again, and nocked a new arrow filled with lightning. I shot arrow after arrow until The Butcher strode out of the castle doors and stopped on the threshold, those red eyes staring at me.

I never missed a beat, and fired. He deflected the first, but I upped my speed and summoned two arrows at a time, filling them with lightning and shooting. Two, four, six arrows lodged in this belly. Eight, ten, twelve in his chest. I kept going, piercing his body with arrows, and he just stood there, staring at me in disbelief, not trying to defend himself. Wherever there was white space, I let arrows sprout, and because my magic in him was keeping him alive, he did not fall. He tried to summon his magic—the magic he'd taken from me—but he was shaking with the force of my lightning arrows and couldn't lift a finger. Instead he was stuck in place, his stare of disbelief morphing into pure, cold-blooded rage.

Two demons grabbed The Butcher by the arms, and only then did I stop my shower of arrows. They hauled him back into the castle, and I did not follow.

The dull dark in me no longer cared about him.

More demons surged around me, but three hunched forms shot right for me. Keshmi and Reshmi, their silver braids secured to their crowns, flew green missiles from their palms hitting a group of demons that had been making a beeline for me. They held up shields of black tourmaline, but were blasted back from the impact. More demons climbed over the bodies of their comrades, sprinting towards us, swords raised.

And then Geravie was hobbling towards me and her shout hit my ears like a war drum, "Eat shit you scumbags!" She pointed with both hands and out shot two streams of purple magic. They hit the onslaught with an explosive *boom*, fire and sparks flying upwards. Malika gave a shout of approval, fighting alongside Pia and Rani on my far right.

Dully, I registered that I had never seen Geravie use magic before. Perhaps the island had encouraged it out of her, as it had done for me.

Something dark stirred in my periphery, and my magic picked up on an oily shadow draped around a beating heart. Seeing that my rear would be covered, I picked up that string of malevolence, and followed it.

I turned to see the row of cages, each one holding a large figure lying, draped in chains on the ground.

In the final cage was the largest body, not human at all.

That way lies death, whispered a voice like the golden dawn. *That way you will be destroyed.* I nodded. I had accepted my fate long ago, truly. On the parapet of my Quartz palace home, I had known this was how my end would come.

A worthy end for me.

To sacrifice my life for another.

Before I went I wanted to look upon that face just one last time, those eyes that looked like the ocean and burned on my skin like fire.

The ground shook with an deafening boom, but as chaos erupted around me and demons and humans collapsed to the ground, I remained still.

Three of the Old Ones before me jumped to their feet as the black chains around them dissolved into nothing.

But I only had eyes for one of them. The tallest, the creature who ran to the bars of his cage, an inhumanly perfect face staring back at me. Eyes so blue they had to have been birthed by the ocean itself.

342

"You know," I whispered, "in another life I think I would've liked you."

"No." His voice had lowered an octave. "Raen, hurry the fuck up."

I gave him a sad smile and turned to the side, closing my eyes.

"What is she doing?" Kai croaked from the ground where he still lay, pale and loose. "Altara, what are you doing?"

"Altara!" Zale roared.

I took a deep breath as Atax, Zale and Kai began yelling at me, but I shut them out and descended back into myself.

They were banging against their bars, calling for me, screaming my name. But I just went deeper until I couldn't hear them anymore.

I fell into death and darkness, where the devil himself walked with the wraiths and ghouls of the world. A world I would now join.

My bow flashed into existence again, my hands heavy with the weight of it, though I could not see it with my own eyes. I was too far gone.

There was no hope for me now, but perhaps there was hope for the others.

I nocked an arrow and filled it with everything that was inside of me now. All the emptiness, all the despair and hope-lessness. But power shunted down my arms, a light that burned with the power of a thousand storms. Pure Voltanius power.

"*Voltanius House lives again*," the Kraasputin had said. Too bad it would die before it lived. Maybe Saraya could figure out how to wield lightning too.

"I'm sorry," I said to no one in particular, but really, I meant it for everyone.

"Altara," Zale's voice was a frantic echo in my ears. I barely registered the emotion. "Meet me in the place between light and dark. Do you hear me, Altara? Meet me there, and I will come. Altara!"

The entire bow buzzed in my hands, full of everything I had. I had a singular purpose now—the rest didn't matter. I loosed my arrow.

Lightning never misses its mark.

I felt Zale move away, felt my target try to evade my arrow, but nothing could stop an arrow I'd filled with myself, and I honed in on him and his shadow-cloaked heart, adjusted the trajectory and hit him directly in his left ventricle, the entire arrow disappearing inside of him.

Even as I dissolved into nothing, I heard his roar. He was still calling my name, I think, though I couldn't fathom why.

Just as my body faded into the void, I felt it.

44
ZALE

ltara was covered in darkness. Her appearance coming out of her cage, bearing Agnolthi's mark on her forehead, bloody and pale, eyes a dull green, in the midst of a bloody battle had shocked me so much that I'd roared with a foreign force. At the same time, Raen took the opportunity and spoke a word of power. Between the two of us, we shattered the tourmaline ropes into black mist.

Flashing into human form, I had jumped up and rushed to my bars as Raen began a construction to open the cages.

We could see plainly that Altara wore a shroud of darkness around her, so dense that nothing would penetrate it.

When Altara turned around, she held a bow and arrow that glowed with a black power, laced with loops of deep-blue lightning. In that single moment, two pieces of a on old puzzle clicked together, and I *knew*.

She was going to break my shadow-lock. I also knew that I couldn't allow her to do that for me. It would destroy her, as she was clearly intending.

When she loosed her arrow, I dodged, but in some magical

feat I could only guess at, the arrow followed me before striking me right in the centre of my rotten heart.

I fell to my knees at the impact, gasping at the pure jolt of light and pain that struck me.

Like a real metal lock, it clicked open with a deep, bone-weary *thunk*.

Pain exploded inside of me but I only had eyes for Altara because she began to disappear into nothing.

Even though it felt like the entire earth was pushing on my shoulders, keeping me on my knees, I clambered to my feet with the will of man going to save his mate from certain death.

"Hurry, Raen!" Atax cried.

Raen's power vibrated through the air, and with a dark groan, my cell door heaved itself open.

I rushed out of my cage, and just at that moment, Fangar emerged from the battle. Time seemed to come to a deathly standstill as we locked eyes.

I was going to have the severed bleeding arteries of his neck hanging from my teeth. I wanted to taste the tang of his blood and watch the life leave his eyes as his skin turned waxen in death.

But it would have to wait.

Because I felt a vast, bone-crushing power surround my Altara.

As the scent of old, wild magic filled my nose, realisation poured through me, and I lurched forward for my mate's hand.

As she left, out of sheer force of will, I latched onto the power that was taking her, my fingers hanging on even as they bled and sparked.

The elderly witches screamed—they were perhaps the

only ones old enough to know. To feel the eternal magic coursing through the night. Altara would not last one minute in that place of old magic and older beasts who'd taken human form like I had; I needed to protect her from them.

But as we both disappeared from the Ivory Castle grounds through the gateway into the Eternal Forest, something as strong and as ancient as the earth itself wrenched my star-born mate from my grasp.

THE END of The ARCHER PRINCESS

Things heat up in book two! Check out The Archer Princess.

If you enjoyed this novel, pretty please leave a review at the retailer of purchase, it helps me make a living out of my work.

Signing up to my mailing list means that you get first peek at everything I produce, including book covers, new releases, exclusive excerpts and bonus material that I don't post anywhere else.

Check it out at www.ektaabali.com

ACKNOWLEDGMENTS

This novel was a blast to write. Finally, I got an opportunity to represent some of my Fijian-Indian heritage in a story and, as a lot of my readers know, representation in fiction is so important to me.

Thank you to my parents, for accepting my endless questions about the fine details of what living in Fiji was like for them. My mother's village of Raralevu became "Levu" in this story and mum, I hope you enjoyed reading all the little callbacks to Fiji/island living.

Once, again, Carly has done the BEST job at this cover illustration, you've really captured her face in the most wonderful way and its definitely a cover I'll treasure forever.

Thank you to C.K. Korfo for his editing skills, professionalism and good humour even in my weirdest moments! You know I always take your advice on board.

I owe the team at Etheric Designs a million thanks for their patience with me in producing the hardcover case design as well as interior chapter designs. Such talented illustrators!

To my ARC team and proofreaders, you guys already know how much I appreciate you, but I need to say it again! Launching a book with you guys by my side is everything to me and without your support I wouldn't be bringing another series into the world.

ABOUT THE AUTHOR

Ektaa P. Bali was born in Fiji and spent most of her life in Melbourne, Australia.

After graduating Killester College in 2008, she studied nursing and midwifery at Deakin University, going on to spend eight years as a midwife in various hospitals.

She published her first novel in 2020, the beginning of a middle grade fantasy series, before going on to pursue her true passion: Young & New Adult Fantasy.

The Archer Princess is her fourth novel in the Chrysalis-verse and the first in a new trilogy.

She currently lives in Brisbane, Australia.

facebook.com/ektaabaliauthor
instagram.com/ektaabaliauthor
youtube.com/ektaabali

ALSO BY E.P. BALI

New Adult Fantasy

The Ellythian Princesses:

#1 The Warrior Midwife

#2 The Warrior Priestess

#3 The Warrior Queen

#1 The Archer Princess

#2 The Archer Witch

#3 The Archer Queen

Upper YA Dark Fantasy

The Travellers:

#1 The Chrysalis Key

#2 The Allure of Power

#3 The Wings of Darkness

Middle Grade Fantasy

The Pacific Princesses fantasy adventure series:

#1 The Unicorn Princess

#2 The Fae Princess

#3 The Mermaid Princess

#4 The Tale of the Three Princesses